QUALITY of CARE

ELIZABETH LETTS

Quality of Care

~

FICTION FOR THE WAY WE LIVE

Written by today's freshest new talents and selected by New American Library, NAL Accent novels touch on subjects close to a woman's heart, from friendship to family to finding our place in the world. The Conversation Guides included in each book are intended to enrich the individual reading experience, as well as encourage us to explore these topics together—because books, and life, are meant for sharing.

Visit us online at www.penguin.com.

NAL Accent
Published by New American Library, a division of
Penguin Group (USA) Inc., 375 Hudson Street,
New York, New York 10014, USA
Penguin Group (Canada), 10 Alcorn Avenue, Toronto,
Ontario M4V 3B2, Canada (a division of Pearson Penguin Canada Inc.)
Penguin Books Ltd., 80 Strand, London WC2R 0RL, England
Penguin Ireland, 25 St. Stephen's Green, Dublin 2,
Ireland (a division of Penguin Books Ltd.)
Penguin Group (Australia), 250 Camberwell Road, Camberwell, Victoria 3124,
Australia (a division of Pearson Australia Group Pty. Ltd.)
Penguin Books India Pvt. Ltd., 11 Community Centre, Panchsheel Park,
New Delhi - 110 017, India
Penguin Group (NZ), cnr Airborne and Rosedale Roads, Albany,
Auckland 1310, New Zealand (a division of Pearson New Zealand Ltd.)
Penguin Books (South Africa) (Pty.) Ltd., 24 Sturdee Avenue,
Rosebank, Johannesburg 2196, South Africa

Penguin Books Ltd, Registered Offices:
80 Strand, London WC2R 0RL, England

First published by NAL Accent, an imprint of New American Library,
a division of Penguin Group (USA) Inc.

First Printing, March 2005
10 9 8 7 6 5 4 3 2 1

Copyright © Elizabeth Letts, 2005
Conversation Guide copyright © Penguin Group (USA) Inc., 2005
All rights reserved

The author gratefully acknowledges permission to reprint material from *Oxorn-Foote Human Labor and Birth*, fifth edition, by Harry Oxorn, copyright © 1986. Reprinted by permission of the McGraw-Hill Companies.

FICTION FOR THE WAY WE LIVE

REGISTERED TRADEMARK—MARCA REGISTRADA

LIBRARY OF CONGRESS CATALOGING-IN-PUBLICATION DATA
Letts, Elizabeth.
Quality of care / Elizabeth Letts.
p. cm.
ISBN 0-451-21410-2 (pbk.)
1. Women physicians—Fiction. 2. Triangles (Interpersonal relations)—Fiction. 3. Female friendship—Fiction.
4. Pregnant women—Fiction. 5. Obstetricians—Fiction. 6. First loves—Fiction. 7. California—Fiction.
I. Title.

PS3612.E88Q35 2005
813'.6—dc22   2004017085

Set in Goudy
Designed by Ginger Legato

Printed in the United States of America

This book is dedicated to my mother,
Virginia Carroll Letts,
who taught me to love a good story.

ACKNOWLEDGMENTS

A special thanks to my agent, Whitney Lee, for unwavering enthusiasm, and to my editor, Leona Nevler, for believing in my book. Thanks also to Susan McCarty, who was always ready with a quick and helpful solution.

Thank you to Lori Diprete Brown, friend, reader, critic and writing buddy, and to Ginger Letts, who read every word more than once.

Thanks to Amy Goodman and John Letts, for helping me get started, and to my intrepid early readers: Judy Wurtzel, Irene Wurtzel, Betsy Wilmerding, Spencer Letts, and the group at Traveller's Joy. Thanks to Jim Letts, for technical support.

A book about obstetrics would not be complete without thanking the people who taught me what quality of care is supposed to look like: Barbara Boehler CNM, Lynn Jordan CNM, Patricia Leonard CNM, and Leon Schimmel MD.

And of course, I am grateful beyond measure to Joey, Nora, Hannah, and Ali, who made space in the middle of a noisy household for me to write my book.

For he shall give his angels charge over you, to keep you in all your ways. They shall bear you in their hands, lest you dash your foot against a stone.

—PSALM 91:10–12

With each contraction the head advances and then recedes as the uterus relaxes. Each time a little ground is gained . . . until a strong one forces the largest diameter of the head through the vulva (crowning). Once this has occurred there is no going back, and by the process of extension the head is born, as the bregma, forehead, nose, mouth, and chin appear.

—Oxorn-Foote Human Labor and Birth, 5TH ED.

Normal Mechanisms of Labor:

The mechanism of labor as we know it today was described first by William Smellie during the eighteenth century. It is the way the baby adapts itself to and passes through the maternal pelvis. There are six movements, with considerable overlapping.

1. *Descent*
2. *Flexion*
3. *Internal rotation*
4. *Extension*
5. *Restitution*
6. *External rotation*

—Oxorn-Foote Human Labor and Birth, 5TH ED.

Descent, which includes engagement, continues throughout labor as the baby passes through the birth canal.

—Oxorn-Foote

PART I

DESCENT

ONE

"Of all the gin joints in all the towns in all the world, she walks into mine."

Those were actually the first words that came out of Gordon's mouth that first night. Never mind that it was actually he who had arrived at my gin joint, or more precisely 3A East in the Ridgefield Valley Hospital. Never mind that it was he who came to me, not the other way around. Lydia, I remember, was laughing, laughing as she rolled along in the wheelchair, with a plaid wool blanket wrapped around her knees. Her laugh was like the chiming of bells, up and down the scale, always had been.

If you had asked me, in the intervening years, before they came into the hospital that rainy night, which I would have recognized first, Gordon's basso voice, or Lydia's chiming laugh, I wouldn't have known—Gordon's, no, Lydia's, no, Gordon's. But the truth was, I knew in an instant that it was both of them.

When I first saw them, Gordon wheeling Lydia down the long polished hallway of the labor and delivery floor, she was looking at him, her head turned and her chin tilted upward, her hair in that same loose blond ponytail, the one she had always worn. It was raining hard that night, though we barely noticed up inside the hospital with its double-paned glass and recirculated air. Lydia had droplets of moisture clinging to the short hairs that had pulled out of her ponytail and framed her face.

She was looking up at him, and he was pushing her, saying something, I couldn't hear what, just the low reverberation of the sound below the words. I could just imagine how he had sweet-talked the aide who walked obediently alongside. *I'll push,* he had said, smiling sweetly. *Hospital policy,* the aide had grumbled sotto voce as she stepped aside and let him grasp the plastic handles.

I was standing behind the desk at the nurses' station with a patient's chart in my hand, dressed like I usually am, in green scrubs, a lab coat, blue rubber clogs. I had just raked my fingers through my thick brown curls, so that they were sticking straight up off my forehead.

"Dr. Raymond," one of the nurses was calling to me from behind, but

I didn't turn my head for a second, long enough for Gordon to look up and see me, and that's when he said the Humphrey Bogart bit, about the gin joints. And it was true, wasn't it? For what on earth were any of us doing right then in that precise spot?

"She just come up from the ER," the wheelchair attendant said.

"The one I told you about, Dr. Raymond," said Doris, the stout unit secretary who was seated in front of me.

That was when Lydia saw me. She was smiling, but I could see the tension around the corners of her mouth, and when she saw me she slumped over a little, like she had been making an effort to hold herself rigid before. I saw what looked like relief on her face and she said in a voice that was half joy and half nervous exhaustion, "Oh, my God, Clara? Clara, is it really you?" Her expression opened up a little; her eyes looked up full of innocence, hope.

"Maybe I really do have a guardian angel," Lydia said. It would be just like Lydia to think she had a guardian angel, just like her to think that I might be one of its manifestations.

Then Gordon said, "What on earth are you doing here?" A dumb question. I was right where I was supposed to be. He was the one who was so vividly out of place.

His eyes had always been blue, and they still were—smooth cheeks, two-day-old razor stubble, black tousled hair. His smile was lopsided, irascible. There was a glint of gold at his left earlobe.

Lydia looked the same as ever, except that she was pale, and there was a small mound under the blanket. Pregnant. Of course. Otherwise what would she be doing here, on 3A at Ridgefield Valley Hospital, at 9:47 P.M. on that rainy Monday night.

"Well, a better question is, what are you doing here?"

Lydia let out a long breath, almost a sigh, and Gordon touched his fingers gently to her temple and leaned a little closer to her, like he would pick her up and carry her if it was needed. He looked exactly the same, and I remember distinctly that it seemed, right then at the beginning, that the years had rested lightly on him, barely leaving a mark at all.

Maureen, the cute little nurse, the one with the green eyes, said, "Dr. Raymond, this is a gravida one, para zero. Came up through the ER, thirty-four-week IUP, one brief episode of spotting, now resolved."

I decoded automatically, without thinking about it. First baby, about eight months along, mild complaints, maybe something, maybe nothing.

"Room three's open," Doris said, jerking her head to one of the open doorways down the pink-and-teal hall.

"Lydia, can you tell me what is going on?"

"Well, we were driving up from Philly," Lydia said.

"On our way to the Berkshires," Gordon said.

"And I started feeling a couple of cramps," Lydia said.

"Just a couple?"

"I thought it was because I had been sitting too long, so I asked Gordon to get off the turnpike so I could go to the bathroom."

"You know, the Joyce Kilmer Exit? I think that I will never see—"

"A thing as lovely as a tree?" Lydia continued.

"And so you were cramping a little," I said.

"And then, when I went to the bathroom, I felt better," Lydia said. "Except that I was bleeding."

"How much?"

"Well, not much. Just a spot or two. I think it stopped already."

"How big was the spot?"

"How big?"

"As big as a baseball? As big as a dime?"

"Oh, just, you know, pink, on the tissue, when I wiped."

I processed automatically, scant bleeding, not significant, in most cases.

"Any leaking fluid?"

She shook her head, spraying me lightly with drops of moisture from her hair.

"Cramping, pressure, lower back pain?"

She shook her head again. "Just, you know, a tiny bit crampy, um, before, but now, no."

"Are you still feeling the baby move?"

I saw the anxious look pass over Gordon with this question.

"Kicking up a storm. It's a little girl," she said.

"We saw a blue hospital sign, so I told Lydia we had to get off and get it checked out."

"I thought he was being silly."

"No, that wasn't silly," I said, practiced as ever, even under the circumstances. "Any bleeding in third trimester can be a sign of a problem. How are you feeling now?"

"I feel fine now. I mean, I feel delighted. Oh, my God, Clara, how weird is it to get off the New Jersey Turnpike and come in and find you here? I mean, maybe that's what the cramping was, like some kind of sign. . . ." She trailed off, shifted, uncomfortable in the wheelchair.

"Do you think she's okay?" he said. "I mean, don't you think we should do some tests or something?"

"Let's put her on the monitor for a while and I'll see what I think is going on."

"God, Clara. That would be great." That was the first time he said my name, and I felt it, same as I always had, the way my knees gave a little shake.

"Dr. Raymond." I saw Kathy's head peeking out from one of the labor rooms. "Angela says she has the urge to push."

I turned back to Maureen again, all business now, in a hurry. "Put Mrs. Robinson on the monitor. I'll come in and check on her later.

"I'll be back in to check you in a few minutes." I left them like that and went into room seven, where I could see that the perineum was bulging and Kathy had already set up the delivery tray.

The funny thing is that it wasn't my night to be on call. I had traded with Walter that night because he wanted to go to a Devils game. Walter has never been like that either. He never asked me to cover call lightly—he worked all the time, sick or well, holiday or not, as regular as clockwork. But his son was in town and he wanted to take him to the Devils game. Just one of those coincidences that make up a life. He would have been there, not me, and that haunts me for any number of reasons, because I still am not sure if I was meant to be there, or if I wasn't meant to be there, but the fact is that I was there, and that's how this story came about.

Of course, I wasn't there because of Lydia. I was there because I had been paged for one of our clinic patients, Angela Cochran. Room seven.

Angela was sixteen, and apparently not quite ready to be a mom. When I came into the room, I saw that she was sitting up in semi-Fowler's with her legs up on the stirrups and she was giving some wimpy little pushes, obviously not enough. Many, if not most, women look beautiful while they're in labor, but Angela was not blessed with a large number of the natural graces. Her limp brown hair stuck to her forehead, and her face was pasty and pocked with acne. A young guy was in the room when I came in, the baby's father, I guessed, but he had his back to her and was talking on a cell phone; he looked about sixteen too, a scrawny fellow who was wearing a mesh basketball jersey that was several sizes too big. He was popping his gum, loud, every couple of seconds and looking out the window at the pelting rain that was visible only in the stripes of light under the lampposts.

The anesthesiologist had her epidural cranked up so high it was a wonder that she could breathe, and her legs were like floppy fish on the bed—I don't think she could feel them at all.

"All right, Angela, bear down," I said. I looked and saw, sure enough, a wisp of black hair showing at the perineum.

"I can see the baby's head, but you're going to have to push a good bit harder than that," I said.

While talking, I glanced at the fetal monitor and saw the familiar jagged traces—everything looked fine.

"All right," I said. "Let's give it a go—big hard push with the contraction . . . one . . . two . . . three . . . *now.*"

Angela screwed up her face and bore down really hard, her whole face growing crimson/purple, the veins distended in her neck. This time I could see a good-sized bit of the caput. I was already glancing at the delivery tray wondering if it was time to gown up.

As the contraction waned, Angela threw her head back on the bed looking spent.

"All right, now, there's another one coming on," I said briskly. "Let's do just like the last time, only harder."

Angela didn't lift her head up from the pillow. She looked at me through one eye and said, "Harder? Are you outta your mind? I am *too* tired. I ain't gonna push no more. You can jus' forget it, Doc."

My urge was to sigh, to roll my eyes. I tried to do neither.

"Nonsense," I said, in a way that I hoped was both firm and encouraging. "You've got to push this baby out."

"Can't you get the sucky thing and pull it out? I don't wanna push no more. I'm too *tired* to push."

"No," I said in measured tones. "I can't. You've got to push this baby out. There is really no way around it."

Goddamn Sidney Porter, the anesthesiologist. He had her too comfy. This could take all night.

Kathy, the nurse assigned to Angela, had been a nurse for a million years, and she knew pretty much everything there was to know. She had a whiskey baritone and a chronic smoker's hack, but she knew her way around a woman in labor, no doubt about that. I didn't even have to ask her. I gave her that *Help me* look. I loved nurses. I often thought that they had been God-given all the positive attributes that I lacked. Kathy crouched down at the head of the bed, next to Angela. I could see her wince just a little as she bent with her arthritic knees. She laid one hand on Angela's forehead, smoothing the hair up off her sweaty brow, just like a mother would, and she whispered something in Angela's ear, too soft for me to know what it was. As she whispered, a contraction came on, and this time I saw Angela screw up her face with concentration and bear down hard.

Thanks, I mouthed to Kathy. God bless her. As my mother would say.

Just then Maureen came in from down the hall.

"Doc Raymond, room three's on the monitor, the tracing looks a little flat, but otherwise everything seems fine."

"Any contractions?"

"None."

"Vaginal exam?"

"Cervix is long and closed."

"Okay, just put her on her left side and give her some juice."

"I already did."

I spun around because Angela was pushing again, and now she was crowning, a round semicircle of wrinkled scalp appearing, as wide as a half-dollar.

After that, she kept pushing, steady as a rock, each time the circle of scalp getting larger.

"Dr. Raymond." It was Maureen again, Lydia's nurse. "Room three. The heart rate is in the one forties and she does have some accels, but she's having some variable decels also."

"Any contractions?"

"No."

"Start an IV," I said.

"It's all ready to go."

"And bring me a piece of the strip."

I looked at the fetal-monitor strip that Maureen was holding while I was gloving up for Angela's baby. It looked unremarkable to me—the toco line, which measured contractions, was as flat as a Kansas prairie. Clearly not labor. A normal heart rate with a pattern that looked harmless—a sleeping baby or a dehydrated mom, more than likely. Their long car trip was almost certainly the culprit.

A fetal-monitor strip is a long piece of computer-generated graph paper that shows two lines. One is the mother's contractions, and the other is the fetal heartbeat. They unspool from the omnipresent machine like a long road behind you when you are driving on a dark night. The heartbeat monitor with its glowing green flickering numbers and the rapid staccato *tat-tat-tat* that is the ultrasound echo of the tiny baby's beating heart. That's a lot of what I do for a living. I study those two squiggly lines and like a shaman or a prognosticator I say, "I see, I see. This is my prediction." We claim that it is more accurate than throwing tea leaves or reading the stars and hopefully it is, although sometimes we have our doubts. In any case, I was not thinking of shamans and prognosticators that night. I was thinking that Lydia Robinson's baby looked a little flat—nothing that lying on her left side and drinking some orange juice wouldn't fix. We called it automobile syndrome. Pregnant ladies restricted their fluids so they wouldn't have to bother their partners to stop and pee quite so often, and then they got a little dehydrated. As with almost every other wrinkle in obstetrics, I saw it all the time.

"Angela, I really need you to give it your best effort. Give it everything you've got. It's really time for this baby to be born."

I looked at the girl in front of me. Sixteen. Pregnant. No prospects. Her boyfriend had gone "to get somepin to eat." No loss. The room seemed more conducive to birthing with him gone; it was very quiet except for the gentle grunting sound that the girl made when she bore down, and the tick, tick of the monitor, the heartbeat slowing down noticeably every time she had a contraction. Moments like that, I am totally focused. There is no world outside that room, that mother, that baby, and I always feel—or I should say used to feel that my intense concentration was part of what helped to bring them safe passage.

Angela's baby was crowning now. I held a warm washcloth up to the perineum to give it a little more support. I didn't like to cut an epi-siotomy unless I had to.

"Ease up on the pushing a little," I said to Angela. "Now you can just blow."

I looked at the monitor—the heart rate was steady in the 120s. I looked at the girl's face, glanced at her blood pressure monitor and her IV. Looked back at the circle of scalp, the smooth glossy skin of the perineum stretched wide around.

"That's it, Angela. Just like that."

"Dr. Raymond." It was Maureen again, her voice sharp. Angela stopped pushing and the baby slipped back inside again.

"Room three, she's having some contractions now, says she's feeling some pressure. I've got the strip for you. Do you want to take a look at it?"

Angela was pushing again—one or two more contractions and she would be delivered.

"Just a sec, she's crowning. I'll be out as soon as she delivers." I could hear the sharp tone of my voice, even though I didn't really mean it to be that way.

"But . . ."

"Are you worried?"

"No, it's just that . . ."

"Just a sec," I said. "I'll be right there."

How long was it? Really? It's all in the hospital record. I was right. Two more contractions and Baby Boy Cochran's face appeared, first his forehead, then his eyes, nose, mouth, in rapid succession. One more push and he slid into the world, a healthy eight-pounder.

"Dr. Raymond?" Maureen again. She was young and she was new, and I knew that the new ones absolutely hated to talk to doctors. She said it in that hesitant way, with an apologetic, rising lilt.

"I'm coming." I peeled off the bloody latex gloves and dropping them on the now soiled delivery tray, littered with gauze pads and bits of suture and a little piece of the umbilical cord.

"Okay," she said, sounding anxious. "If you could come right away?"

"What is it?" Now she had my full attention.

"Um, it's room three. She says she feels like she can't catch her breath."

"Clara?" Lydia was white as a sheet and she looked scared. Pointed chin, pale face, terrified eyes. She was breathing heavily. Panting. I did a quick look at the various monitors. The fetal heart was steady, but the toco monitor, which measured contractions, looked alarming. She was having a series of contractions with almost no interval between them.

"Clara?" she said again, unable to say the word without gasping for air again.

All of a sudden, a whole scene flashed before me—it had been years since I'd even thought of it—rocky cliffs, the far-off pounding of waves, shrill heaving squeals, and Lydia's face; it had looked just like that on that other day too. I was in action by then and didn't stop for even a nanosecond to dwell on it. I lifted up the sheet that lay over her legs, and looked underneath, where a huge pool of amniotic fluid, stained greenish brown with meconium, was soaking into the blue chux pad. Obviously she was going into labor. But why the panting?

"Lydia, it looks like you're going into labor. Don't panic. Try to slow down your breathing. Maureen, get her a paper bag to blow into. I think she's having an panic attack."

It was a reasonable assumption. Sudden onset of hard labor. Painful contractions. People often started to hyperventilate. It was one of the first things we learned in medical school. When you hear hoofbeats, don't think of zebras. Already I didn't like what I was seeing.

"Call peds," I barked to Maureen. "Tell them we've got a thirty-four weeker with thick meconium." I glanced at the wall clock—it was eleven p.m. I wondered if Walter was back from the Devils game, in case I needed him. "Would somebody page Walter? I want him on standby in case I need him for backup."

I looked at the fetal monitor. The baby was in a brady—the heart rate down close to one hundred—the tick, tick of the too slow heart on the monitor filled the room.

Maureen shook her head, kind of slow and frozen looking.

"Get more people in this room now." I reached over and hammered on the call button. Heard Doris's laconic, "Yes?"

"Get me Kathy and more nurses in here *stat*. Start opening the OR—I think we're going to have to crash room three."

Kathy had already appeared at my elbow. I looked at the fetal heart monitor. It was showing a heart rate of 82, precipitously below the normal 120 to 160 beats.

"I need a second IV—I need anesthesia in here. Kathy, what's up with the monitor? Is that a maternal pulse?" I knew that sometimes the monitor picked up the mother's pulse. It could be hard to tell.

"Clara? Clara?" Lydia's voice had a breathy quality to it. "I feel all sweaty."

"What's her current BP?"

Kathy was sitting at the bedside, calm as ever, holding Lydia's hand while she looked at the fetal monitor and took Lydia's pulse. The monitor was reading in the seventies, dangerously low for a baby.

"Maternal pulse is one thirty," Kathy said evenly. I bent over Lydia and placed my stethoscope over her sternum.

"Any word from Walter? What's his ETA? Where's anesthesia? Can you call peds for me?"

I heard the gentle whir and beep as the blood pressure cuff automatically started to pump, and I watched it carefully.

Eighty over forty.

"Shall I put her in Trendelenburg?" Kathy said.

"Where the hell is Sidney?"

"I think he's in the OR," Annie, one of the new nurses who had come in, said.

"Well, get him or get somebody NOW."

"Clara, I'm scared."

"Lydia." I turned back to her. "Your baby is in distress. We need you to agree to do a crash C-section. I'm afraid the baby may be in danger if we don't do it right away."

While I was talking to her, the nurses were all doing their bit, getting ready to transfer her: One was starting a Foley; one was wheeling the gurney in, all of them murmuring in their gentle but insistent voices. *Move your leg. Get on your side. I'm just going to tape this here. Can you sign this? Don't move.*

The heart monitor continued with its ominous slow tick. The blood pressure cuff pumped up again. Seventy-eight over forty. She was holding steady, just barely. I did a vaginal exam. Two centimeters dilated.

Kathy had already discreetly changed the blue chux pads underneath her; the first one was already blackened with thick green fetal fecal matter.

This whole time, I hadn't even looked at Gordon. Hadn't thought about it. Hadn't even remembered that he was in the room. But now I looked up, looked around for him, and saw him, where I guess he had been the whole time, kneeling on the floor next to her, holding her hand, and stroking her hair, wordless, but there.

"Gordon. Lydia. We're going to move Lydia to the OR now. I want you to know that I'm going to recommend general anesthesia. I want you to stay out."

"No!" they both shouted simultaneously.

"I want to be there." "I want him to be there"—Lydia's voice much weaker than Gordon's.

But Kathy, the competent nurse, already had him in hand. She linked her arm through his, and tugged on little Maureen's hand—the nurse was still glued silently to the spot.

"Take him for coffee, Maureen," Kathy said.

By then we were already wheeling her down the hall toward the OR, jogging along, Lydia still lying balled up on her side with the head of the bed lower than the foot. I'm not sure if I had a momentary thought, rushing down that hall that night, that this was serendipity, that I had appeared in her hour of need just as she had once appeared in mine. Now, looking back, it seems that I thought that, but at the time, I really doubt it, for that was not how my mind worked. I'm sure I was methodically thinking about steps I would go through, how to get the baby out as quickly and safely as possible. And it could have been Lydia or it could have been anyone, for I have the virtue of being even more methodical when under pressure. That's what gets me through as a doctor almost all of the time.

After that, it all gets blurry. I know that anesthesia was already there when we got in the room. I remember hoping to see Walter, but he wasn't there yet.

I went out to scrub, plunging my hands under the hot water, scrubbing with the soft plastic brush up to my elbows. Holding my hands up and letting the water drip down off my elbows. Kathy had scrubbed in too. Elisa was there with my sterile gown, gloves, and cap.

They were getting Lydia ready to go under, but she was still conscious and she looked up at me with her round blue eyes, scared, but at the same time trusting. I wish they had put her under then, but anesthesia was still talking to her.

"Any allergies to medications? Any prior problems with anesthesia? Any heart conditions?"

Then Lydia all of a sudden sat bolt upright. She was gasping at the air. Turning blue. The blood pressure monitor started to blow up again. Seventy-two over thirty-five.

The room was in total motion. *One hundred percent O₂ through the mask. No, bag her. Get an EKG on her. Start a large-bore IV. Where the hell is cardiology?*

She's in sinus tach. Where the hell is cardiology?

I saw Dr. Peterson, the youngest member of the cardio team, come running into the room.

I gave him a report rapid and terse. "Thirty-eight-year-old G one, P zero. Came in through the ER. Sudden onset of tachypnea. Respiratory distress. Maybe a pulmonary embolus."

I looked up at the pulse ox the nurse had clipped into her finger. Sixty percent oxygen saturation.

"History of cardiac disease? Asthma? Any hemoptysis?"

"Doctor, we're losing her. She's in cardiac arrest."

I let the cardiologist take the lead, the paddles—then she was bleeding. First a little trickle from the corner of her mouth, then a trickle from her nose, and red tears of blood at the corner of her eyes. With each shock of the paddle her bluish body lifted up off the bed and then flopped down a little. Up and down, up and down, like a drowned dead body being washed up by the waves.

By the time we pronounced her, Walter was there. It was my case, and I was prepped and ready to slice into the still white belly. Save the mom first. Then the baby. The baby's heartbeat had been in the eighties for I don't know how long.

Walter stepped forward and made that slice through the cool pale belly. I reached in and pulled out the small limp dark blue lump and passed it to peds. Apgar of one at one minute, two at five. I thought the baby would be dead by ten minutes. If I thought about the baby at all.

That's all I really remember anymore. Except for a few blurred snatches of other moments.

Walter standing behind me with his big strong arms wrapped around me, his soft broad belly pressing into my back, his chin putting firm pressure on the top of my head. I think essentially he was holding me up.

The sight of Gordon, in his jeans, in a worn-out knitted sweater that he probably didn't remember I had knitted for him for Christmas in 1986. He was lying on the floor in the corner of the nurses' lounge, a half-empty cup of coffee spilled on the floor next to him, his head pressed hard into the corner of the two walls. He was hurling out unearthly yells and pounding one fist against the unforgiving floor. Then later, his forehead pressed hard against the incubator, tears dropping out of his eyes and rolling in sheets down the sides of the scratched-up plastic.

There was blood on the front of my green scrub shirt. Not much, just a small half-moon-shaped stain. And a single fleck of blood on my eyelid. Walter showed them to me, patiently, in the mirror while he was explaining to me why I had to go home and take a shower and get some rest. He was taking over the rest of my shift.

I can still see that image of myself, that small crescent of blood somewhere below my left breast, the brown fleck on my eyelid, traversing my eyebrow like a rakish scar. I can see him, and I can see the bloodstains, but I can't see my face.

"Don't be silly," I said. "We have a multip who just came in, in active labor. I'll stay. Don't you worry. Go on home."

"Clara," he said firmly, spinning me around. Raising his voice a little as if he were talking to a child. "You need to go home now. Get some rest. I don't want you here. It's almost change of shift anyway."

That was impossible. We didn't change shift until seven in the morning. I looked at the clock in the chart room. The hands showed six forty-five but I didn't comprehend them.

"It's not change of shift," I insisted. "You go ahead home and get some sleep. We'll change shift when we're supposed to. Walter. Really. I'm fine."

"You're not fine, Clara. You're not fine. You need to go home and get some rest." He put his big hand on my shoulder. "That was rough."

I looked down at the floor.

"Is it true that you knew her?"

"Yeah," I said. "Both of them. I knew them. Not at the same time, though. Anyway, I'm fine."

"Clara. You are going to leave now. I won't compromise on that. Go home and sleep. We can try to sort out and make sense of this later. Anyway, there's nothing whatsoever you can do now."

"How's the baby?"

"Clara, that baby's heartbeat was in the eighties for almost an hour. You know how the baby is."

"It's still alive, though?"

"Clara." Walter's voice was firm. "Go home. There is nothing you can do."

TWO

Forty-eight hours later I was sitting in Martin Hostedler's office, up on 5B. Risk Management. Martin had the demeanor of an undertaker with his thinning hair and somber pin-striped suit. I noticed that the windows of his fifth-floor office looked out over the rooftops of the neat suburban neighborhood that surrounded our little hospital. My eyes felt scratchy. I had raked my fingers through my curls in lieu of brushing them. I was wearing old green scrubs. Presentable, just barely.

"I understand that she was a friend of yours," Martin was saying.

"She was an old friend. We hadn't kept in touch recently."

"It's such a crying shame that she came up to the ER. A kind of co-incidence to bloody hell, don't you think?"

"I'm not a great fan of coincidences, Martin. Medicine doesn't think much of them either, you know."

"In any case, a maternal death is one of the hardest that we deal with, and I think it is an unfortunate coincidence that there was a"— he paused and folded his bony hands on the smooth surface of his desk—"uh, personal connection with the deceased."

"I appreciate your concern," I said, hoping to sound completely detached, the way I knew I was supposed to sound—levelheaded, objective.

"There is one fact that I'm afraid is quite pertinent here."

"Oh?" I said. I didn't think I would remember a single word he said when I stepped out of his office.

"The husband—his name is Gordon Robinson—*the* Gordon Robinson."

"Yes," I said. "I'm aware of that."

"Oh, so you already know who he is?"

"Well, yes."

"And you can see how this could have a significant impact on this case?"

For a moment I was rendered speechless. I watched silently as Martin went through a series of little adjustments: he refolded his hands, shifted in his seat, then smoothed the lapels of his jacket. All the while,

I just sat and stared at him, wondering how he could possibly know about me and Gordon. Had Gordon mentioned it to someone? It was hard to imagine. What would he have called me anyway? Former long-term relationship? Old girlfriend? *Oh, you know that doctor who failed to save my wife? By the way, she was an old girlfriend.*

"Any legal recourse at his disposal . . ."

I turned back to Martin, realizing I hadn't been listening.

"I'm sorry?"

"I actually lost a lot of money on them too, when the NASDAQ went belly-up. I guess the sorry bastard got his one hundred million out anyway."

"I'm sorry, Martin—I think you lost me somewhere."

"Clara?" He looked at me, a little puzzled. "Do you know who he is or don't you?"

"I said that I—"

"Gordon Robinson. Sol-net Technologies. One sad, sorry, but very rich son of a bitch."

"Martin. Gordon Robinson is an old friend of mine."

"What? I thought you only knew the wife."

"I know both of them. Knew them. Whatever. Only I knew them at different times."

"Oh, shit. You mean like *actual friends*? Invited-to-the-wedding kind of thing?"

"Well, yes, as a matter of fact, I was. Only I didn't go."

"Where?"

"To the wedding."

"All right. Here's the deal. Absolute minimum contact with the grieving daddy. Baby's in the NICU. If you run into him, try not to talk to him."

"Martin?"

"Come on, Clara. You know the rules. You'll end up making admissions even if you don't mean to. Don't talk to the man. Especially not him. He's rich. There's press. I'm sure he's already got personal-injury lawyers taking a number and standing in line. Do not discuss any aspect of this case with anyone, except at a closed departmental meeting. For God's sake. This baby is almost certainly going to cost the hospital a whole lot of money. Am I making myself clear?"

"You know, Martin. We did everything we could possibly do for her. Absolutely standard of care. You know me, Martin. I go by protocol, not seat-of-the-pants. It was an extremely unusual case. The odds are something like one in thirty thousand. We do, what, three, four thousand deliveries a year at Ridgefield Valley? You do the math. We got unlucky. It's like winning the lottery."

He looked at me oddly. "*Winning* the lottery?"

"I mean in reverse. Come on, Martin. You know what I mean."

"That's exactly what I'm talking about. Look how easy it is to come out saying something you didn't mean to say. Silence is golden. I mean that, Clara. Don't mess up or I will see that your privileges are suspended. I mean it. I will."

Something flickered in me when he said that. It surprised me, because right now, I wasn't feeling anything, just a kind of chalky emptiness. But when he mentioned privileges, I felt a little volcanic eruption that it took me a moment to recognize as anger.

"You can't do that. And you know you can't! That is a medical decision. The doctors make a recommendation to the board of trustees. There is absolutely no reason for them to do that to me. I was practicing in good faith."

"Clara. Look, I like you. Everyone likes you. You and Walter have the most respected practice in this whole area. I just want you to be careful. Gordon Robinson's wife comes in through the ER and two hours later she's dead and his baby is gorked for life. Not good under any circumstances. Even worse this year—when we lost the two big managed-care contracts. If the baby lives, we could be talking such a mondo settlement that both of us are looking for new jobs. I just want you to be careful."

I stood up without saying anything further, and turned to leave. I knew I had done everything possible. I knew that I always did everything possible. I was trained to respond to emergencies, and I had responded. So how could I possibly be having this conversation? I stood up. Nodded my head tersely in parting, and left Martin Hostedler's office. I had nothing further I could possibly say to him.

The departmental QA meeting was later the same day. Unlike the meeting with Risk Management, I was looking forward to this meeting, where we would go over the facts of the case, try to make sense of it.

When I came into the conference room, I sensed from the unnatu-ral hush that there had been talk in the room before I got there. The twenty-odd members of the ob-gyn department were seated around the long table. Walter looked up when I came in and gave me a reassuring smile. I was grateful to see that the chair next to him was still empty. I threaded my way around portly Dr. Washington, who still showed up for every departmental meeting, although he hadn't practiced in years.

When the room had filled, I was afraid my hands would start to shake or my eyes would fill with tears. But I was skilled at the process of detachment. It was something that my medical training had drummed into me. *The case.* That's how I thought about it. Not a per-son, not an old friend. Certainly not Lydia, the one person in the world to whom I owed a particular debt. *The case.*

So when I started talking, I found that my voice and words sounded the way they always sounded, deliberate, logical, even though I had a sense that someone else, not me, was talking and that I was sitting there listening.

"This is a very interesting case," I said. "A thirty-eight-year-old primigravida at thirty-four weeks with an uneventful prenatal course, and no significant medical history. She presents to the ER en route from Philly in a car, complaining of mild cramping now resolved and one small episode of bleeding."

I looked around the room at the circle of colleagues around me. Most were almost as familiar as family, charting elbow to elbow at four o'clock in the morning, coming in to second on C-sections, pinch-hitting for one another when we got stuck in the snow or had three rooms delivering at the same time. The Uni-Group were sitting down at the end of the table together, Dr. Praathi, Dr. Sanders, Dr. Rooney. They were the new practice in town, sent in when our community hos-pital formed the merger with the big university hospital. I really didn't know them. I noted that Dr. Praathi had a pen and a pad of yellow legal paper, ready to take notes. They were listening, intently it seemed, but with a normal degree of detachment.

I went on with the report, including all the relevant clinical details.

"She was transferred to L and D, where there was no observable bleeding or leaking fluid. The patient was placed on external monitoring, and a twenty-minute strip was obtained. On initial strip there were no measurable contractions and the fetal heart was in the one forties to one fifties with decreased variability. She was put in left-side lying position and given PO fluids for hydration."

I cast a sidelong glance at Walter. He saw me looking, and pushed his leg against mine, a silent gesture of encouragement.

"After approximately twenty minutes, overall variability was improved, but there were occasional variable decelerations to the one twenties. Approximately twenty minutes later, I was summoned to the bedside by the nurse, who told me that the patient was experiencing shortness of breath. At that time, upon exam it was noted that the membranes were grossly ruptured and stained with thick meconium, the fetal heart tones were stable in the one thirties with adequate variability, and there had been a rapid onset of almost tetanic contractions."

"Dr. Raymond. Could you clarify what you mean by almost tetanic?" It was Dr. Praathi, always a stickler for detail.

"Yes, Dr. Praathi, contractions were every minute, lasting one minute."

"Vaginal exam?"

"Two centimeters dilated. Fifty percent effaced. Initial etiology for dyspnea was hyperventilation syndrome. Patient was treated as such with no improvement. . . ."

The meeting went on like that. My dry, precise clinical presentation, the short, well-directed queries of my peers. It felt right then, so *manageable*. Not once during the clinical presentation did I actually think of the face of Lydia, the way it emerged out of the night so suddenly, her face flushed and framed with the dew that clung to her hair. Nor did I think at all of Gordon, the tangled car-skewed mass of black hair, the sinewy backs of his hands, the corny Humphrey Bogart thing he did when he first came in the door. He had a wife and a baby then, and they were both still alive, but I didn't think about that right then. *The case, the case.*

"Dr. Raymond?"

"Yes?" It was Dr. Sanders, one of the new doctors. I didn't know her well, and didn't like her much. She was one year out of her residency, nervous and cocky, characteristics that I particularly disliked, especially when paired.

"The record indicates that your initial assessment of the patient was almost forty-five minutes after the time she was brought to the floor for observation. I was wondering if you could explain why, in the presence of possible indicators of preterm labor, you didn't do a vaginal exam."

Something about the tone she was using took me aback a little. It was not a friendly question. She was looking at me, with no change in expression, her shiny cropped blond hair falling forward to cover her face as she sat with pen poised.

"Well I was . . . in with another patient." I knew that wasn't the right answer. Every clinical decision has to have a justification—"I was busy" just isn't one of them.

"What I mean is that there were no early indicators that she was in labor—she had reported one or two mild cramps prior to voiding, but this was prior to admission. Uterus was soft, no contractions on toco. Patient had not noticed leaking fluid."

Dr. Hall, the department chair, flipped a segment of heart rate monitor strip open across the long table. The doctors leaned forward to get a better look at it.

Dr. Washington shifted his bulk in his chair a little, feigning to get a better look at the strip. I was pretty sure he had no idea how to read a monitor strip. He was of the old school, when obstetrics was just a combination of luck, good hands, and bedside manner. And yet, how many thousands of babies had he brought into the world?

"Dr. Raymond." He spoke with a loud baritone undiminished by age. "Why don't you tell us what your differential was?" He was trying to deflect attention from the squiggly lines on the paper. He had no use for them, sometimes fell asleep, head on his chest, when we got too far into the minutiae of monitor strip interpretation. I was seeing the strip again for the first time since that night. As is the case in such matters, QA had whisked the chart away for "review." It was hospital policy to always give the lawyers the first look. Now that those initial fragments of strip, the ones that Maureen had carried into the room, were laid out before my peers, I could feel my hands start to sweat a little. I tried not to look at the pieces of paper—they were facing away from me, upside-down to me anyway. I forced myself to look up. I turned my head toward Hal Washington. He gave me an encouraging smile. I felt the slight pressure of Walter's leg against mine again.

"Sudden onset of tetanic contractions. Ruptured membranes indicate presence of thick meconium. Onset of dyspnea, progressing rapidly from mild to severe. Rapidly ensuing cardiac arrest nonresponsive to resuscitative measures, hematological and clinical profile consistent with disseminated intervascular coagulopathy. I feel that a pulmonary embolus, probably amniotic in origin, is certainly the most likely causative factor for this clinical picture."

There. I had said it. Rare. Lethal. Unpredictable. Unpreventable. I was the doctor on call that night. It was just one of those things, part and parcel of being in the birthday business.

The room was silent for a moment. I looked around at the circle of familiar faces. I could see it in their eyes too, memories of bad nights that all of them had had, an air of acceptance, a kind of collective shrugging of the shoulders, a there-but-for-the-grace-of-God kind of acceptance.

Except.

Down at the end of the table, where the Uni doctors sat, there was an edge of tension. Drs. Praathi and Rooney were looking down at their notes. Dr. Sanders looked up at me, challenging. She had caused quite a ripple when she had first come to the hospital, about three months earlier, among the still mostly older, mostly male obstetricians. She was a slim, smooth blonde, always with her nails done and never a hair out of place. You never saw her, even in the middle of the night, looking the slightest bit mussed. The nurses couldn't stand her.

"Dr. Raymond, if we could please get back to the strip."

Fred Hall was the department head. A good guy, in solo practice, hardworking and decent.

"Well, folks, I don't know about you, but I think maybe we ought to start wrapping this up. Dr. Raymond has made a pretty clear presentation, and I'm sure I'm not the only one here who has patients to see."

"Let her go ahead with her questions, Fred." That was from Walter. I knew what he was thinking. To give me every chance to defend myself. To leave with the air completely clear.

"Dr. Sanders?"

"Doesn't the strip show a pattern of contractions increasing steadily in intensity and duration from the time she was brought to the floor?"

"That was not my interpretation."

"Isn't it true that no one performed a vaginal exam to assess degree of cervical dilatation at the time of admission?"

"The nurse—"

"Let me finish."

"Go ahead, Doctor," Fred said equably.

"It seems to me that we have another possible interpretation of this sequence of events."

It's not like this had never happened to me before. This is what I was trained to do. How many times had I sat through meetings like this, in medical school, then in residency and beyond? Civilized disagreement. High-minded discussion in the pursuit of better science . . .

I looked down at the upside-down strip spread out on the table before me, and I could feel my palms start to sweat, my hands start to shake. What if I had been all wrong? What if somehow, some way, I had been tricked, fooled by my own eyes? Gone down the wrong path the one time that it mattered more than ever, the night that some bizarre twist of fate had brought Lydia through that door.

"Uh . . ." I could feel my voice sticking in my throat. All eyes were upon me. People who had looked ready to leave a few minutes earlier had resettled in their seats again, eyes wider. A little more interested, if only for the sake of viewing combat.

"A thirty-four-week primigravida comes into the hospital. Her initial complaint was cramping and spotting, was it not?"

"Yes, though both had resolved by the time she arrived at the hospital."

"Nonetheless. Presenting complaint leans towards a diagnosis of preterm labor, does it not?"

I didn't specifically answer, but I heard the vague murmurs of assent going around the table.

"Initial strips show a pattern of contractions progressively growing in frequency and intensity."

"That was not my interpretation." I could hear the hint of defensiveness in my tone that I was aiming to keep out.

"At twenty-two forty"—Dr. Sanders was pointing to a section of the third strip fragment, the one that had brought me into the room— "contractions become tetanic, patient complains of shortness of breath, and blood pressure drops precipitously. Am I correct?"

"Correct."

"Is it not far more plausible," Dr. Sanders said, "that we are dealing with a more obvious scenario than an embolic event?"

Dr. Praathi looked up from her notes. "When you hear hoof-beats . . ."

"Don't look for zebras," Dr. Rooney finished her colleague's sentence.

"Dr. Sanders," Walter said. His tone was typically laconic. I was probably the only one in the room who could hear the edge. "If you have a different interpretation of the data, we would very much appreciate it if you would present it as succinctly as possible." He made a show of looking at his watch very slowly. "Many of us have offices to get to."

"Fine. Let me be brief. My assessment of this data is that we have a patient presenting with a partial abruption of the placenta, hence the spotting prior to admission, and the onset of contractions. Approximately forty-five minutes after getting to the hospital, she had a full abruption. Onset of dyspnea, loss of pressure, and eventually . . ."

"Because the root cause was undiagnosed," Dr. Praathi intoned.

"And left untreated." Dr. Rooney added.

I looked down toward the end of the table, at the Greek chorus of young female heads in white lab coats.

"It eventually led to cardiac arrest." Dr. Sanders again.

It felt like someone had punched me in the stomach, and all the air was sucked out of me and the room began to spin. *Oh, Lydia. Lydia. Lydia. I was wrong. I could have saved you.* Then the vision came back again, of the sound of anguished squealing in the distance, and pounding waves, and sun in my eyes and a head aching so hard it felt broken, and the sight of Lydia's face, the face she used to have, just a silhouette with the blinding sun behind her. I could feel the pressure of Walter's leg under the table signaling me to hold my ground. But my whole body was shaking then, shaking so hard that I was making the boardroom table shake.

I jumped up from the table, but not before the tears started falling. Covering my face in my hands, feeling chairs bump hard against my hips, I ran, eyes closed in desperation, right out of the room.

The ob-gyn conference room was down the back hall on the third floor. There were two ways out: one was straight through the L&D wing, and the other was down the more secluded back hallway where the NICU was. Right then, walking through the labor wing, past the nurses and the unit secretary, felt impossible. I turned quickly down the empty back hallway, heading toward the stairs, hoping to get out quickly. I knew that Walter was still inside the conference room doing a little bit of damage control, telling everyone how upset I had been about the unexpected personal connection to the patient. The Neonatal Intensive Care Unit was built toward the center of the building, so that the hallway L was shaped around it on the outside. I kept my eyes in front of me, trying to avoid the unlikely chance that I would look up and catch a glance of Gordon through the thick glass windows of the NICU. As I spun around the corner into the second wing of the corridor, suddenly I was forced to stop.

There on the floor in the hallway, knees pulled up to his chest, arms clasped tightly around them, leaning against the wall, sat Gordon. His head was hanging down, and for a second I thought he might be sleeping, but as soon as I rounded the bend he looked up at me, blinking.

"Clara?"

As though he could hardly remember who I was or why I might be there.

"Gordon."

He climbed to his feet, unsteady looking, like a drunk, though he clearly wasn't.

"Clara, my God, where have you been?"

I couldn't answer. What could I say? That I had been warned off of him?

"I keep asking everyone, 'Where's Clara? I need her. Where is she?' And nobody will answer. They just kind of turn away. You know, like a kid on TV whose parents are dead and no one will tell him? And I started thinking that I was completely crazy and that it really wasn't you, and that I was just imagining the whole thing."

"No, Gordon. It's me, I'm afraid. It's really true."

"Clara. You have to tell me."

Gordon had always had sad-dog eyes, but now they were looking at me with an intensity of desperation I had never seen anything like before. True grief had transformed his face far more than all of the intervening years between forty-eight hours ago and our last good-bye. Two nights ago, I'd have known him in an instant. Today, his haggard look penetrated me with remorse. I had abandoned him, on purpose, in his hour of need.

"What happened to Lydia, Clara? What happened? Nobody will tell me anything. You have to tell me. Please tell me. One minute she was fine and the next minute." He stopped. I could see that he was crying.

"Oh, God, Gordon . . . I . . ." What to say? "What are you doing anyway? You shouldn't be sitting here alone. Isn't anyone with you? What about Lydia's parents? Are they coming?"

"Yeah. Yeah. They're on a cruise, in fucking Guam or something. They're coming. Of course . . ." He trailed off and I stood there looking at him. I knew that Gordon's parents wouldn't be coming. Both of them died in a plane crash his sophomore year in college—he was the most famous orphan on campus.

"Clara?" He was so diminished, his voice almost childlike. "Could you . . . would you . . . ? Could you . . . uh . . . come in and see her with me? The baby, I mean the baby. Could you come in with me to see her? Because I stayed with her all day yesterday until the nurses kicked me out and said I had to go somewhere to sleep, so I went to the Comfort Inn out near the highway and I guess I slept for a long time, and then I came back and . . ." He looked up at me imploringly. Sad-dog eyes. I had seen them before, but never ever with a hurt so deep.

"And then I came back today and I got as far as the hallway here and then I . . ." He trailed off again, looked at me beseechingly. I could tell that he was hoping that I would read his mind.

"And then?"

"I . . . I . . . I couldn't go in. It's just that here I am, and I can't make myself go in. I keep thinking about how she's this scrawny little botched-up job all hooked up to machines, and Lydia . . . Lydia . . . she's . . ." He stopped again and peered up at me with bleary red-rimmed eyes.

I had seen that look before. Seen it countless times on the faces of other people—come into the hospital to have a baby and somehow, somewhere got off on the wrong track and headed toward the land of grief. In such circumstances, it is important to be compassionate, but to maintain professional distance. But with Gordon my distancing wasn't working at all.

"Will you?"

It's not that, at that moment, I had really forgotten about Hostedler or Risk Management or any of that. It's just that I knew what the right thing to do was, under the circumstances, and I wanted to do it. The right thing was to be compassionate.

I reached out and took his hand, and pulled him toward the NICU door.

"She doesn't look good."

"I know, Gordon. I know."

Before we crossed the threshold, he put his hands on my shoulders and spun me toward him.

"I want to tell you what I named her. It was Lydia. Lydia's wish."

I pulled away from him and swung the door open.

"Come on in. You can tell me when we see her."

Gordon walked me down the aisle of incubators, some occupied, some empty, until we got to the end of the line. There I saw a small, completely flaccid baby, eyes taped shut with gauze, a respirator taped over her nose and mouth, and all manner of other tubes and wires going off in every direction. Lights flickered and flashed all over, pulse, oxygen saturation, temperature, breathing. Taped to the plastic, I saw her little Enfamil name card with the teddy bear stenciled in the corner. Her name was written in black marker.

Robinson, baby girl. Clara. Next to the name card, I could see the angular lines of my own pale face reflected back in the plastic of the incubator, the thick shock of my hair.

I felt like all the blood had drained out of me then. I fought the urge to look away, acutely conscious of how important it was not to show my distress.

I put my arms around him to embrace him. "She's beautiful," I said. I held vigil there with him for the rest of the afternoon. She was far too fragile to be touched or held. She was completely dependent on the machines for all of her basic functions. She never stirred or moved at all.

There was a hole in the side of the incubator where Gordon could put his hand inside a sleeve and rub his finger along a part of her arm that was not attached to any tubing or wires. He stood and did that for long patches at a time. I just sat and sat. Letting myself be mesmerized by the flashing lights on the monitors. Occasionally one of the monitors would alarm and the nurse would bustle over to do what she needed to stabilize her, and I would sit, watching without really watching. Finally, I started to notice faint growlings of hunger. It was hard to see outside the building from inside the NICU. It seemed like eternal day, but I could tell when I looked carefully that dusk was falling. I tried to muster the energy to move. I did not want to sit there any longer, and thought that Gordon shouldn't either. I tapped him on the arm.

"Gordon, it's time for us to go."

The hospital corridor behind the NICU was still empty. As we walked toward the stairwell exit Gordon said, "Clara. Can I? Do you think I could stay with you for a while? Just a little while. It's just too hard for me to be alone."

I knew what professional conduct called for in this situation—calling the grief counselor, or the social worker, or the chaplain. I stood without answering while I grappled with hesitation. Then without too much doubt that I was doing the right thing, I said, "Come on," took him by the elbow, and directed him toward the exit. We headed down the back stairwell toward the doctors' parking lot. Hardly anyone ever went down that way.

By the time we got to the dull red metal door that led to the doctors' parking lot, I was fairly sure I was doing the right thing.

I pushed the door open.

There stood Martin Hostedler, just coming in through the door. He took in the sight of the two of us standing together, and then pushed past us with a slight nod of his head.

I took Gordon over to my Toyota, pushed a pile of medical journals onto the floor, and gestured for him to get in. We drove in silence up the long commercial strip that led north. In five minutes, we had arrived in the parking lot of the nondescript town house complex that I called home. I parked in front of my unit. We sat in silence for a moment before opening the car doors. I glanced over at his profile, the face so familiar, the circumstances so jaggedly different.

"Come on," I said. "I'll get you something to eat."

I unlocked the door and pushed it open, so aware that I had to unlock it for him, that he didn't have a key, then saw my apartment, momentarily, through a stranger's eyes: I had two mauve sofas that my mother had picked out and that I rarely sat in, the small white table where I ate my Lean Cuisines. I wasn't there very often, and when I was there, I was usually alone, eating take-out Chinese in my bed and watching TV, or sleeping, or talking on the phone.

But of course, Gordon was looking without seeing. I ushered him inside and pointed to one of the sofas, where he dropped like a lead weight. I went to the fridge. There was not much in there, some leftover lo mein, a quart of milk.

I opened the freezer and took out two Lean Cuisines, stabbed holes in the cellophane with a fork, and stuck them into the microwave. Gordon sat, unmoving, while I did this, and stared at the wall in front of him. I stood in the kitchenette shifting from one foot to the other, thinking, What now? Started doubting again the propriety of bringing him here.

The phone rang.

It was Walter.

"Clara. Look, I . . ." I heard him hesitate. One of the things I had always admired about Walter was that he was always the master of discretion. "About the meeting . . ."

"It doesn't matter, Walter."

"Of course it matters. Look, everyone understands that this is a difficult situation for you. I went over the whole case again with Fred Hall. The clinical picture is entirely consistent with embolus. I don't know where Sanders got off talking to you like that, but you know and I know that she didn't abrupt. The placenta was still attached to the wall when we sectioned her postmortem. I mean, she could have had a partial, but that certainly wasn't cause of death."

"Right, Walter. Right. I know. I know."

"Listen, Clara?"

"Yes?"

"I had Marsha cancel your office hours and I'm taking call for you tomorrow. You need a little distance. Get some rest."

"No, I couldn't do that."

"I'm not taking no for an answer."

"I can't let you do that."

"You know you would do exactly the same for me."

"Walter, you know I . . ." I was just about to mention that Gordon was there, but then, for some reason, I hesitated.

"Nothing."

"I'll see you the day after tomorrow. Get some rest."

The microwave was beeping insistently. I walked over to get the food out, put the two plastic tins on a tray with two forks, and placed it on the coffee table in front of where Gordon sat.

"You need to eat."

"Right," he said flatly. He still sat almost catatonic, staring at the wall.

You know how people say "be careful what you wish for"? I couldn't help thinking about that right then. I had been guilty of wishing him back, of imagining him coming right through that same front door, with his lopsided grin and the terrific energy that he had always given off like a green aura around him. There had been lonely nights when I had wished him back and wanted him back, into these empty rooms, into my lonely bed, and now here he was, sitting on my sofa, staring at my wall, more impossibly distant than he had ever been before.

"Uh, maybe we should watch TV," I said, picking up the remote and flipping through the channels until I came across a Bing Crosby movie in black and white. I peeled the limp plastic off the food tray, and handed it to him, and robotically he began to put forkfuls into his mouth, now staring at the screen with the same degree of attention he had previously given to the wall.

This will work. So I sat down next to him on the sofa, not too close, with my own spaghetti marinara, and started to watch the movie. I could smell him there, that particular scent of sweat and detergent I knew so well, and I could feel the heat off the side of his body. Almost panicked by the proximity, I edged away slightly. When I had finished eating, I took my tray over to the trash can; then when I came back, I sat on the other sofa, so as to be farther away.

We sat like that all the way through one Bing Crosby movie and into a second one. It wasn't until all the way through the second movie, when Bing went to kiss Hedy Lamarr near the end, that Gordon turned to me and looked me full in the face. He looked almost himself right then. Not quite so dazed, absolutely dead serious, intent on what he was about to say.

"Clara, I need to ask you something. You have to promise to tell me the truth. Was there anything you could have done to save her? You know, any little thing you didn't think of, or forgot?"

The same question, the exact same question, I had been asking myself over and over again. Was there?

I tried to quell the sound of Dr. Praathi's voice at the meeting saying, "the root cause was undiagnosed."

"No, Gordon, there was nothing anyone could have done. It was a freak thing. A rare occurrence. A one-in-thirty-thousand chance."

He didn't say anything else for a while, just watched the scrolling credits on the little screen. Finally, he turned to me again.

"You know, I guess I could have been happy it was you, or not happy it was you. It could have gone either way, you know. But I guess I was glad it was you in a way, because I know what you are, Clara. And because I know that, I know that you must have done everything that could have been done."

I didn't know what to say, so I didn't say anything, just kept looking at the TV. We went back to our silent watching for a few minutes.

Then Gordon, unexpectedly, reached out and turned the TV off with the remote, and swiveled abruptly toward me.

"Clara? Do you think the baby has a chance of being okay? You have to be honest. Tell me. What do you think?"

Then I averted my eyes entirely and stared down at the rug, my eyes pooling with tears. I owed him the truth. I knew that.

"No," I said, shaking my head, which only made the tears run down my cheeks. "No, Gordon. I don't."

"Well," he said after a long moment. "I don't have to believe that. You're not a neonatologist. I'm sure you don't really know anything about that."

He reached over and turned the TV back on. After that, we just watched and watched until finally he fell asleep. I took off his shoes and covered him with a blanket, leaning close as I tucked the blanket up around his chin. Close in like that, the strong familiar scent of Gordon's skin filled my nostrils. With one hand, I smoothed his bristly black-brown hair off his forehead, and with a motion so quick I could almost tell myself I wasn't doing it, I brushed my lips across his warm slightly parted lips. Then, with no small amount of effort, I pulled away from him, and went to sleep alone in my cold bed.

* * *

How's this for a clichéd story? Gordon was standing behind me in line during freshman registration. This was before he had become a junior cause célèbre for losing both of his parents, suddenly, violently, in a commercial airliner that crashed into the Potomac in icy weather. After that, it seemed that everyone loved him, or loved to feel sorry for him. But I can say that for me, pity was never the first thing that came into my mind when I saw him.

He kept jostling me, by accident, for Gordon was always bursting with energy, always with his mouth and his body in motion. He was talking loud, cracking jokes a mile a minute, half to himself, half to anyone who might be listening. I didn't like the sound of his voice, and so I was staring resolutely in front of me, thinking the kinds of superior thoughts that I used to entertain myself with in those days. Like that registration was serious business, and that he should just settle down to patiently wait.

He was telling some long story about how he had bumped into "old Fry" at the Store 24 and asked him should he buy Twinkies or Ring Dings and which was more consistent with a taste for classical mythology? Why I remember that, I don't know, except that it didn't make the slightest bit of sense, for one thing, and for another, I couldn't understand how "Fry," who was apparently a professor, had already become "old Fry" to him on the very first day of the year when we were still standing in line at freshman registration. I tried not to look at him, tried to ignore his voice, hoping that by ignoring him I seemed aloof and not just pathetic. But he kept jostling me. So finally I turned around, sure I had the courage to ask him to stop, and then I saw him.

He was smiling at me, this happy, bashful, lopsided smile. His eyes were blue and his hair was shiny but kind of scruffy looking. I could feel myself blushing, but couldn't help looking straight at him, and smiling too.

He stuck out his hand in friendly greeting and grinned happily at me. I remember the feeling of his warm callused palm in mine. I didn't want to let go.

"Gordon Robinson," he said. "From outside Boston, well, and Africa, whatever . . ."

"Clara," I said. "Clara Raymond, I'm from Pennsylvania—sort of. I'm premed."

We didn't become friends then. He was just a guy I would see around campus sometimes, grin a little harder, feel my palms sweat. We weren't in the same dorm, didn't have any of the same classes. His was the kind of name you'd hear tossed around sometimes by different people. Now and then I'd look up and there he'd be. Maybe with that wacky six-foot-long blue-and-gold-striped scarf he used to wear flung over his shoulder. Maybe barefoot with a Frisbee tucked under his arm. He'd toss me one of his crooked smiles and say, "Hey, Clara sorta Pennsylvania." "Hi, Gordon," I would say, and we'd hurry off in opposite directions. And then I would think about him, now and again, at other times. There was something about his face.

I didn't know what it was then. Never figured it out until my mother met him, much later.

I remember when he presented himself to her, hand stuck out, lop-sided smile, and my poor mother had the oddest look on her face, like she'd seen a ghost.

Afterward she said, "Oh, Clara, why didn't you warn me I'd be in for such a shock? He's the spitting image of your father. My God. Could have been him at that age. Could have been his own son."

I knew that people sometimes thought Gordon and I were brother and sister with our slight, wiry builds and thick masses of brown hair.

But I could never see the resemblance to my father. My father had a side-parted pompadour, and a mustache, and wore chocolate-colored bell-bottom suits with wide flamingo pink ties. My father, whose face came to me only in static images, in the faded colors of 1970s Koda-chrome prints, didn't look the slightest thing like Gordon Robinson. I couldn't ever see it, back then. Even when my mother insisted that I hold their photos side by side.

THREE

I awoke the next morning, later than usual, to the sound of the ring-ing phone. Gordon's smell was still everywhere in the apartment, but he was gone, his blanket folded squarely on the sofa. The Yellow Pages lay open to the taxi page and next to it on the countertop there was a scribbled note.

Gone to be with Clara. Thanks for Bing. G.

The phone kept ringing. The urge not to pick it up was strong, but my sense of duty was stronger. What if it was Walter calling because he needed a first assist on a C-section? What if it was a problem at the office with one of my patients?

I let it ring one more time, wavering, then reached out to pick it up.

"Hello."

"Clara. Fred Hall here. Am I catching you at a bad time?"

I wasn't even sure what a bad time was anymore, but immediately felt wary and guarded. There was no reason for the head of obstetrics to be calling me at home.

"No, this is fine." I said. "What's on your mind?"

"Listen, Clara, I . . ." I could feel the hesitation in his voice, felt panic seize me around the middle, my blood pumping loud in my ears.

"Well, let me just shoot straight with you. The hospital is temporar-ily suspending your privileges pending an investigation of your con-duct."

"Look, Fred," I said, trying to hold my voice steady, to sound calm and reasonable, not panicked and shrill, "there's no reason to be so cau-tious about the Robinson case. Gordon Robinson is a very old friend of mine. He's not gonna sue. I'll bet my malpractice premium on it."

"Clara, I'm not in a position to hash this out with you. I can only say that there have been a number of *concerns* raised about your recent conduct."

"Concerns? About my conduct?"

"Yes, that's what I said."

"Fred, a low-risk lady came up through the ER and threw an amniotic-fluid embolus, and now suddenly that's my fault? Come on.

Which one of the members of the department of ob-gyn do you think would have done a better job? Who? Fred . . . ? Who?"

"Clara," he said, his voice steady, "I'm only the bearer of bad news, and I'm sorry about that. It wasn't just the case, Clara. It was . . ."

"It was what?" I snapped, remembering full well the sight of Hostedler's face as he saw me walking with Gordon into the parking garage.

"Well, I suppose I might as well tell you, since it'll all be on the table anyway. A couple of the NICU nurses came forward. Said you were acting strangely—one of them even thought you might have been under the influence of something."

"Oh, Jesus," I said, collapsing onto the sofa. "Oh, Jesus Christ. Come on, Fred. You don't honestly believe that, do you?"

"Clara, we all know that you are under a tremendous amount of stress."

I ended up hanging up somehow. I'm not even sure I said good-bye. The phone dropped out of my hand and I left it lying on the carpet. I lay flat out on the sofa, staring at the ceiling, for some long uncounted period of time. The phone rang twice and I let the answering machine pick up both times. The first time it was Walter.

Clara. Clara. Are you there? Pick up. I need to talk to you.

The second time it was a loud raspy voice.

Dr. Raymond. It's Dr. Washington. Hang in there, sweetheart. I may be old, but I ain't dead yet. I'm going to see what I can do.

It didn't feel right just to lie there, though. I could hear the clinical part of my brain diagnosing me: *slow motor functions, blunt affect, feelings of hopelessness—clinical depression.* I sat up.

Lying on the sofa all day just wouldn't do. On the table next to the sofa the stack of medical journals I'd been meaning to read was at least a foot high. I picked up one from the top of the pile, scanned the table of contents, and settled down to read.

The phone was ringing again. I twitched, ready to grab it—years of training ingrained into me—but then I put my hand down and listened to it ring. It was Walter's voice.

Clara. I've got to talk to you right away. As soon as you get in, call me. I'm at the office.

I stared at the small print of the abstract open in my lap, blinked several times. Realized that the words weren't sinking in and started from the beginning again.

At noon, there was a knock on the door. I recognized it in an instant. It was Walter. I sat perfectly still without moving, without getting up to answer. I didn't want to see Walter. What would I say? That's when I heard the key in the lock.

When I pushed the door open he was standing there, a pizza box in one hand, and my spare key in his other. He had fished it out from under the flowerpot.

"Clara. I was worried. You weren't answering the phone."

"You're my partner, Walter, not my father," I said, then instantly regretted it. What a dumb thing to say.

Walter looked pained, even more pained than I would have expected.

"I'm perfectly aware of that." He reached up with his hand to smooth across his receding hairline. A nervous gesture.

"Look. I'm on lunch break. This is pizza. You need to eat. Do you want me to leave? I will." Of course, I didn't want him to leave. It was only now, in his familiar bulky presence, that I realized how glad I was to see him.

"Oh, I'm sorry, Walter. I don't know what I was . . ." I felt awkward as I stepped aside to let him in. I'm sure he had been to my house before, but I couldn't think of exactly when. He paused there in the doorway as though not quite sure what to do.

"Come on in. You can put the pizza on the counter there."

"I don't want you to think I'm barging in on you."

"Don't be silly. I'm sorry, Walter. I should have called you back earlier. I was just . . ." I went over to the cupboard, pulled out a couple of plates, and put them down on my glass-top table. "Sit down, Walter."

He flipped back the paper cover on the pizza. I saw that he hadn't forgotten that I liked mushrooms with extra cheese.

"Dig in," he said.

"Thanks, I really appreciate it. Really I do."

For a few minutes we sat face-to-face occupied with our pizza and relatively silent, but then he spoke.

"I hope this isn't too personal, Clara. But why did you sit in the NICU yesterday?"

"You know, Walter, I can't really believe you're asking me that. It's not like I've never sat with a patient in the NICU before."

"I don't believe you usually sit with a patient for six hours."

"Look, Walter. Gordon Robinson is a very old friend of mine. I found him sitting alone in the hallway too scared to go in to see the baby. He didn't have anyone with him—you know they were just passing through town. He doesn't have any family and her parents are on a cruise. He was alone. I did what I thought was the compassionate thing."

"Clara, you know that baby is gorked."

"Of course I know."

"Well, you weren't, you know . . . leading him on or anything, were you?"

"Walter, I hope you know me a lot better than that."

"Because apparently he was in the NICU this morning talking about how the baby is going to get better."

"You've never heard a grieving parent talk like that before?"

"Clara, look. Fred Hall is being all cagey about this suspension thing, which is not like him at all."

"It's Hostedler. He specifically warned me to stay away from Gordon, but come on, Walter. I would have done the same thing for any of my patients. You know I would have." I pushed away the uncomfortable memory of bending over to kiss Gordon while he slept.

"How do you know him, anyway? I didn't know you consorted with multimillionaires."

"You know, he sold the company quite a while ago. He was one of those smart guys who makes a bundle almost by accident."

"You didn't answer my question."

I blushed and I could see that Walter noticed.

"I went to college with him."

"I see."

"And I . . ." What could I possibly say that would properly define what Gordon and I had been? "Lived with him, for . . . a while. On and off. In Boston."

"Old boyfriend."

"That's right."

"Married to old girlfriend."

"Exactly."

"And so are you the one who introduced them? Blind date or something?"

"You know, that's the odd thing." I set down the slice of pizza; I usually loved pizza, but now it tasted like rubber. "I had nothing to do with them meeting each other. They met out in California. She went out on a temp assignment when he was still working out of a garage."

We sat for a few minutes again in companionable silence. Walter ate pizza just like he did everything else. Unhurriedly. Like he had all the time in the world. He settled his big frame against my small kitchen chair and chewed thoughtfully.

"Clara. I don't agree with the hospital's decision, but Fred Hall assures me that this suspension is just temporary—it won't go on your permanent record once it's resolved."

"Walter. I did the best I could under tough circumstances. She didn't make it. Personally, I'm devastated about it. But as a physician, I think we did what we could for her and she was unlucky. How dare they suspend me? How dare they? We're not just going to sit here and take it."

Walter looked straight at me, with his level gaze.

"Are we?"

He didn't answer.

"Walter, for God's sake, answer me. Are we?"

"Clara, you know how much I respect you. You are the partner I always dreamed of having." Now he was coloring slightly. I couldn't believe it. Walter was a straight shooter—always the truth, always in the most direct possible way—but the way he was blushing here, obviously he was getting ready to say something he didn't want to say.

"I talked to Dick Blank over in neonatology. He said the baby is likely to hang on for a while, unless the dad decides to unplug her. Why don't you just go ahead and get the hell out of Dodge for a while? Let things settle down. You're due for a vacation anyway. When's the last time you took a break? I bet you can't even remember. Fred Hall will share call with me while you're gone."

"I really can't believe you're saying this to me."

"Clara. It's for your own good, and for mine too, because I do need you. . . ." Walter looked down at the table, then smoothed his hand across his pate.

I stood up. "I'm planning to fight this thing, Walter."

"Clara. Believe me. Let the dust settle. There's nothing to fight. Once this whole thing clears a little, you'll get your privileges back. In the meantime, take a break. You really do deserve—" He was cut off by the insistent chiming of his beeper. He clicked it rapidly, looking at the numbers on the screen.

"I've gotta go, Clara. But you know, I really mean it." He laid his big hand on my shoulder. Its steady warm pressure made me feel, for a second, like drawing toward him.

"Two, three weeks tops, and I'm predicting it will all blow over."

"I'm not going to just sit here and take this," I said. "I've worked hard for my reputation, Walter. I can't let these accusations stand. People will wonder. There will be talk."

"Nobody doubts you, Clara. Nobody. This is just some bureaucratic mumbo jumbo, and it'll pass. Really, Clara. I promise."

Walter stepped out the front door and I locked it behind him, feeling the new echo in the room that his leaving had created. After he left, I didn't even try to read the journals. I just sat on the sofa staring at the wall, much the way Gordon had done the night before.

FOUR

The next morning, I was fine. I got up early and drove to the hospital. I needed to go up to the floor to sign my birth certificates. Getting out of the car in the doctors' lot, feeling the cool morning air in my still damp hair, I felt almost back to normal. Sure, I had had a setback, but as a physician, I had been trained not to let anything get to me too much. The sun was rising; it was going to be a sunny day.

But as I climbed the stairs by twos, I felt my courage failing me. A couple of doctors were coming down the stairs toward me; they nodded hello, but I noticed how they averted their eyes. The closer I got, the less sure I was that I would be able to walk onto the floor. Then I remembered—*Oh, no, the nurses*. They would want to cluck around me with sympathy, and that was the last thing I wanted. I glanced at my watch. It was a couple minutes before seven—change of shift. The nurses would be busy giving report. I pushed open the heavy stairwell door, noticing afresh the distinct odor of a labor and delivery floor, disinfectant, hot blankets fresh from the warmer, sweat, and the indefinable earthy odor of birth.

I glanced nervously at the nurses' station. As I had hoped, the nurses were clustered there, both the ones who were just arriving for day shift and those who were coming off night shift—I saw Kathy, Maureen, some of the others who had been there Monday night. They had their backs to me and were looking up at the big white board that showed all of the patients on the floor. From force of habit, I scanned the board. It looked quiet, a couple of inductions. None of my patients, I noted with relief. I darted another quick glance in the nurses' direction, then hurried down the hall behind them. Thankfully, no one turned, or appeared to notice my presence.

The birth certificates were typed up by the registrar, and then came back to my box within a couple of days. All I had to do was sign my name on the line that said BIRTH ATTENDANT—it was usually one of the most mundane parts of my day. The bin was kept in a little room, almost a closet, down the back hall, well away from the hubbub of the nurses' station. I stepped into the closet, found my slot in the metal mailboxes, and pulled out my stack.

Right on top, I was forced to confront it again—the black-and-white facts: ROBINSON, CLARA BENSON; LYDIA ROBINSON; MATERNAL DEMISE. I stared at the document. Suddenly, it seemed like there was no air in the close little room. I couldn't lift my arm. I couldn't move at all. My knees were shaking. There was a hard ball at the back of my throat. Somehow, it seemed like as long as I didn't sign the paper, there was some chance that the whole thing had never happened. I'm not sure how long I stood there.

Then the door opened a crack, and I heard a familiar gravelly smoker's voice.

"Doc Raymond, I seen you go in, but I didn't see you come out." Kathy stepped into the closet, so close that I could smell the cigarette odor that hovered around her. Something about Kathy reminded me of my mother, the extra-large scrubs, the odor of cigarettes that clung to her between smoke breaks, the steady compassion in her eyes.

"Are you . . . doing okay?" Her voice was gentle, the one she used with patients in labor.

Nurses and that sixth sense. How had she known? With a rush of gratitude, I picked up the certificate and signed it quickly without really looking at it. I got ready to duck past her, but she put her hand on my forearm.

"Doc Raymond?"

"What is it?" I sounded abrupt.

"I just want to say that I don't agree with what they did to you. None of the nurses do."

I didn't look at her, just fiddled with the ballpoint that was chained to the countertop next to the bins. I was afraid that if I tried to say anything, I would start to sob.

"Well, it's just, um, a formality—um, I'll be back to work before long." I was so humiliated to even hear these words coming out of my mouth. I could feel myself blushing a deep crimson. I had spent a lifetime developing skills so that I would never have to say something like that.

"We do what we can, but after that it's up to God. You know that, don't you?"

Not true. The well-being of the patients was my direct responsibility. You know that song? *He's got the whole world in his hands.* Well, that's me. That's every doctor, everyone worth her salt anyway. But Kathy was trying to be kind. So I said what I would have said to my mother. "Sure," I said. "I know."

"You can't just know it up here." She pointed to her temple. Her hair was colored the stark brown that comes from a box. A generous stripe of gray showed at the roots. "You gotta know it here too." She tapped on her heart. I knew Kathy meant well, but I could feel my composure cracking. I wanted nothing more than to slip past her, but she kept hold of my arm.

"I been a nurse, how long? Thirty years? That was one of the worst cases I've ever seen, and you know me—I've seen everything." She coughed, a deep rattle in her chest.

"Yeah, a tough case. It was a tough case," I didn't want to look up to meet her eyes.

"Clara, listen to me. This is what I want you to know. If one of my own daughters, my Sally or my Rose, was in that situation, I'd be praying to the Holy Mother for you to be the one taking care of her. You're the best there is. Don't let anybody tell you any different. You did what you could."

I looked up from the floor, looked at her face. She was coming off night shift and looked exhausted; deep smoker's furrows encircled her mouth and she had dark circles under her eyes. This was a woman who had been bending down on her knees and coaxing women through labor for thirty years. Surely she could help me. I had a strong urge just to tell her—to start at the beginning, lay it all out there, the long story of my life, which I'd thought I had run away from, but hadn't. But I couldn't. I was too well trained. I knew how to hold on to my confessions.

"I know you're in pain, honey, right now. That goes with the territory. No use in pretending it doesn't hurt. You know what we always tell the pregnant ladies . . . ?"

I shook my head. What did we tell the pregnant ladies? It was always the nurses who did most of the talking.

"You try to get away from the ring of fire, you squirm this way and that way, but in the end, there's no way around it. There's no way around it but through it. You hear me? No way around it but through it. You promise me, Dr. Raymond—you just keep that in mind."

I smiled a little, even though tears were smarting at the corners of my eyes.

"Well, then can't I at least get an epidural?"

"Okay, at least you're smiling a little, and that's a start. Now get outta here and go take some vacation. Go someplace sunny. You hear me?"

Back home, Kathy's words were still ringing in my ears when I picked up the phone to call my mother.

"Mom."

"Clara, hi, honey. I'm so glad you called. I am just getting back from the sunroom. I was playing bridge with Betty Ann." My mom didn't know that I was on to her—whenever I called, which was probably not often enough, she always told me that she was "just getting back" from something, a meal, an outing. I knew my mother. She did not want me to feel guilty about her, to worry about her, to imagine that she might ever feel bored or alone, or . . . anything. I had wanted her to live with me when she became wheelchair bound, but she wouldn't hear of it. I knew the home that I was paying for was a nice place and that she would have been terribly isolated alone in my condo with me working all the time, but still, I felt guilty. I guess it just goes with the territory.

"That's great, Mom. How're you feeling?"

"Well, not too bad, just, you know my hip has been aching me a little, but I don't want to bother you with that. You have to listen to it all day anyway."

"Are you doing your exercises, Mom?" That was me, always the nag.

"Oh . . ." I could hear my mom sighing. "You know, I get so busy, I just don't have the time."

"Okay, then . . ." I hadn't yet mentioned that I was "on vacation," feeling, however irrationally, that if I did, my voice would immediately betray that something was up.

"Hey, Mom? Could you just tell me one thing?"

"Anything, honey?"

I gritted my teeth getting ready, almost didn't speak, then forged on.

"Well, it's about Dad. What was it exactly that they accused him of doing?"

I could hear the pause at the other end of the line, like the question I had thrown out there had a lead sinker attached and was sinking to the bottom of the ocean.

"Why, Clara, whatever made you think of that? Especially since I know that you already know the answer."

The subject of my father was one that we rarely ever broached. Somehow, the two of us had agreed, without ever really saying it, that when we left California, we would focus on the present. Once we got to Pennsylvania, it was as if our old life had never existed. Respectfully, we put a few pictures of us together as a family on the mantelpiece, and there they stayed, gathering dust. Closed chapter, closed book.

I waited for my mom to gather herself together.

"Malpractice, dear. You know it was malpractice."

"No, Mom. I mean, what exactly? What kind of case was it?"

I remembered asking my mother this question just one time before. I knew exactly where I had been. It was in the car—I was in the back-seat—on the way home from the funeral.

"Well, Clara," my mom had said that day, her voice oddly cold and constrained, absent of any of the passion of rage and grief that was shuddering through me. "It's really too technical for me to explain to you." I even remember how her voice lingered over the word *technical*—the word seemed so impenetrable then, so airtight, that I knew I couldn't possibly get around or through it. That was the day that I set my sights on medical school, vowing that someday no one would ever be able to say that to me again.

"What kind of a case?" my mom said now.

"Yes, I mean, what exactly did they accuse him of?"

"Oh, Clara, why do you dredge this up anyway? It was so long ago, I can barely remember."

"Well, just tell me what you remember."

"A patient died in surgery. By bad luck, it was a bigwig. So your father had to pay. That's all I remember. Do we really have to talk about this?"

"But I mean, what did they accuse him of? What did they say that he did?"

"Clara"—I could feel a hint of worry creeping into my mother's voice—"what is it? Are you in some kind of trouble?"

It was my turn to pause then, to weigh which would be the greater kindness—to tell her the truth or to shelter her from it.

"Oh, for gosh sakes, Mother. What kind of trouble would I be in? I just . . . got to wondering, that's all."

"The truth is, Clara, I don't even know, really. Your father wasn't exactly . . . forthcoming with me. He just said that people were lying about him, and that it wasn't fair."

I was dying to stop talking, but I forced the words out.

"And was it . . . unfair? I mean, what happened to him?"

There was a pause so long on the other end of the line that I thought my mother wasn't going to answer at all.

"People can always talk. Unless you know the facts of a case, there is no way to know. Your father told me he didn't do anything, and I believed him. I guess the only people who really know are your father, God rest his soul, and Eleanor Norton."

"Eleanor Norton?"

"She was chairman of the board of trustees at your father's hospital. A tough cookie, but she had a reputation for being fair."

"Eleanor Norton the dressage judge?"

"A dressage judge, was she? I know she was a horsey lady, but I don't remember that. I'm sorry, honey. I don't think I'm helping you too much, am I?"

"No, that's okay, Mom. I . . . just got to wondering, that's all."

I got ready to say good-bye, but she kept talking.

"Oh, by the way, honey, I've got some sad news for you. Do you remember Lydia Benson—your old friend Lydia? She passed away recently. I read all about it in the newspaper."

"All about it?" I asked, now feeling a cold terrible feeling that my mother not only knew the truth but also knew that I was lying to her.

"Well, I mean, it just said that she passed, complications of childbirth. Isn't that awful? It was in the *Philadelphia Inquirer*."

"Lydia . . . ," I said, for want of anything better to say.

"Oh, Clara, surely you couldn't have forgotten Lydia? Not after what she did for you. Clara! She saved your life!" I felt really shriveled up inside right then. Did my mother somehow imagine that I had ever, for one moment, forgotten that?

I didn't pay attention to much she said after that—she started pattering on about how she was going to go to Mass and light a candle for the soul of Lydia, and another extra one, the one that I should be lighting for her. My mother went back to her own Catholicism after my father died, but it was too late for me by then—the faint rubbing of church I had gotten as a child had not sunk in at all.

"It said the baby made it too. Isn't that something? Poor little motherless baby. I'm going to light two candles, one from me, one from you, for that poor little baby too."

"Please do light a candle for me, Mother. Please do." I hoped I sounded sincere; I was trying to hide my utter lack of conviction.

After we hung up, suddenly I wanted to see my father's face. On the dresser in the bedroom there were three pictures. Three pictures that I couldn't remember really looking at in a very long time. The first was of my mother, a little younger, a little thinner, smiling her familiar good-hearted smile. The second picture was of myself, sitting astride Captain, his chestnut coat brilliant with sunshine. Behind us in the background stretched the blue Pacific, and the orange of the setting sun. Next to the picture of me and my horse was a picture of my father. His hair was longish and he had sideburns. Printed at the bottom was the caption JAY THOMAS RAYMOND, MD. I picked up the picture of my father, studied his handsome face, trying to find some new nuance that I had never noticed before. But it was the same old face, frozen forever in time.

Those were my only family pictures. In the rest of my house, plastered onto the fridge, up on my dresser, and peeking out of desk drawers, were pictures of babies, babies who had once fallen gently into my waiting hands. Hands that were now tied, hands to sit on, useless for the task that I had so carefully trained them for. Kathy's words kept rattling around in my brain.

There's no way around it but through it.

I guess, if I have had one failing as an obstetrician, it's that I'm impatient with pain. I have little sympathy with natural childbirth—that's what anesthesia is for, after all. I listened to the way the nurses murmured to the patients—*Work with the pain. Sink down into it. Ride it through.* It had never made the slightest bit of sense to me. The best way to manage pain is to shut it out, to block it with a combination of bupivacaine and fentanyl administered via catheter into the epidural space.

But now, for the first time in a long time, it seemed like I was peering through that ring of fire—the world beyond the pain was blurry and indistinct and the anesthesiologist was nowhere in sight.

I guess that's what got me to do what I did, to book a morning flight to California, with no more plan than to go stare down the cliff that I thought I had forgotten, and to go on a wild-goose chase looking for an old lady who I imagined was probably already dead.

Partial flexion exists before the onset of labor, since this is the natural attitude of the fetus in utero. Resistance to descent leads to increased flexion.

—Oxorn-Foote

PART II

FLEXION

As I drove up the hills, through Jacaranda Canyon, I couldn't believe the place all over again. Gently sloping hillsides rose up all around me, some covered with soft gray chaparral. Long driveways led up from the road, and white post and rail fences surrounded carefully tended properties. Here and there were impeccable stables with shake roofs. Everything still looked exactly the same here, especially the unmistakable gleam of money.

The way I remembered it, when you reached the top of the hill there was a sudden end to the well-kept suburban landscape. There had been nothing but barren hillsides, cascading down toward the ocean—they were called the Norton Hills. The land had been unstable, a slide area, not suitable for building.

I held my breath, certain that the empty hills would now be covered with tile-roofed mansions. But then, with a rush, the old familiar vista spread before me—the hills were completely empty except for a spot down closer to the cliffs, where there was a single old house surrounded by a cluster of trees. The view of the Pacific was unobstructed in all directions.

Though the house and cliffs were straight in front of me, maybe two miles in the distance, I realized with confusion that there were no roads here, only empty hillsides crisscrossed by trails. I had followed the map to the airport hotel, where I had checked in and left my bag that morning, but I had thought that my twenty-some-year-old memories would lead me the rest of the way. I had forgotten that I had traversed these hillsides on horseback and moved away before I had learned to drive. I had not been able to find Eleanor Norton's name in the phone book, thought it was likely that I wouldn't find her, but knew that I just had to give it a try. I turned around and backtracked down the hill, consulting the map to figure out how to get to Norton Bend.

Once through the residential area of Jacaranda Canyon everything else was changed beyond recognition: a minimall, a wall of town houses, a gas station. I was thinking, hoping, that I was already past the cliff, that the coast road was so altered that I could no longer recognize the spot.

I glanced at the clock on the dashboard. Ten forty-five a.m. I thought about calling Walter to see what was going on. I hadn't talked to him since about nine a.m. the day before, right before I drove to the airport. At that time he hadn't heard anything back from the path lab about the lung cross section. He did tell me that all of the postmortem blood analyses had come back consistent with DIC—disseminated intervascular coagulopathy, a rare and brutal blood-clotting disorder that overtakes a pregnant woman, and she starts to bleed from every orifice: nares, eyes, ears, vagina. It is often part of the clinical picture in catastrophic situations—emboli, eclampsia, abruption. Lydia had had blood trickling from the corner of her mouth and from both eyes—that I remembered. Dear God, Lydia—I was glad that her mother and father, the Bensons, had not been around to see it.

Just then there was a sharp bend in the road and I saw the big yellow caution signs: ROUGH ROAD, FALLING ROCK, SLIDE AREA. To my left the craggy cutout hillside was golden red above the road. On the right, barricades, row after row of yellow painted barricades—that was new. And no more horse trail there. At turns you could see the dizzying drop-off, the hundred-foot bare walls of the cliffsides. At certain angles you could see where the waves themselves pounded up against the rocks; the road would twist again and then it was hidden.

I slowed the car almost to a crawl. My chest felt tight, my hands like ice on the steering wheel. A drop of sweat rolled down my forehead and into my eye, stinging.

Goddamn vertigo.

I took a deep breath in, looked at my hands on the steering wheel, broad and flat, unadorned. Seeing their plain blunt shapes reassured me. My hands were trained to do my bidding. I was a surgeon. I trusted my hands. I steadied them on the wheel, looked ahead of me on the road.

There was nowhere to park here, nowhere to get out of the car, nowhere to walk, to look, to glance over the edge. But now that I was actually here, I realized that I didn't want to. Resisting the urge to escape by pushing my foot hard on the accelerator, I drove on, knowing that this stretch of road was less than a mile long.

I rounded a sharp hairpin turn, where the cliffside seemed directly in front of me.

There was something in the road.

I tapped hard on the brake. *Too hard.*

The brake on the rental car seized. The car started to skid.

For just a split second, that skid kept going right across the road straight through the thick metal barricades and my car was in flight. I closed my eyes.

But that isn't what happened.

What really happened was that the car rolled obediently to a stop, far from the barricades, right in the middle of the road.

I knew I had seen something, something small and white in the middle of the road, but I could no longer see it. I looked behind me again, no cars coming, and put on my hazard lights just in case. I peered around me through all the windows, but saw nothing. For a second, I thought I had imagined it, that I had seen nothing, a white blur, *a ghost.* But I didn't believe in ghosts anyway, and I had a surgeon's fast reflexes, and very good eyes. So I opened the door to the car, trying to get a better look at whatever I had seen.

Right outside the car door sat a small shaggy white dog, no collar, bedraggled dampish feet. The dog looked up at me with its bright beady eyes and wagged its tail once or twice; then, quick as a wink it jumped right into my car, little scratchy paws on my lap, and then into the passenger seat, tail wagging, eyes looking at me expectantly.

The little dog was friendly looking, and in that mild stage of unkemptness that meant either a lost dog or a reasonably adventuresome life. The dog looked quite contented to be in my car, leaving little muddy paw prints on the front seat, but I wasn't sure what I should do. I looked around. The road behind me was still empty, the rocky hillside on one side, the precipice on the other.

Well, I'll just set him back out of the car. The shaggy dog stood up on the seat and gave an encouraging wag of the tail. He was about the size and shape of a toy poodle, but his hair was longish and very curly. I knew that I couldn't set the dog out on the road. If he didn't get run over, think how likely he would cause an accident! Hadn't I had a fright myself braking suddenly on such a treacherous part of the road?

I wasn't as far as the Norton Gatehouse yet, and I thought the Norton Estate must be just beyond. Not that I actually expected to find Eleanor Norton. She would be an elderly woman by now, in her eighties at least. Even if she was alive, she'd probably have moved on, to a retirement home or something. But I had decided I would drive by, at least to convince myself that she couldn't be found. But what would I do with a dog? I'd have to locate the pound, drop the little dog off. I looked at him again. He looked encouragingly at me, took a couple steps closer, licked my hand.

If only there was someone around to ask whom he belonged to, but this part of the road was completely deserted. But then I noticed that there was actually a driveway—just one asphalt lane leading up the hill and then curving out of sight, with a single metal mailbox at the roadside.

I glanced over at the little dog, who had now settled down onto my car seat, chin on his little paws, and was looking expectantly at me.

Oh, well, here goes. I turned up the narrow lane up the hill, away from the cliffside road. I glanced again at the dog. He had fallen asleep.

SIX

The driveway curved around a bend, up a hill, then around another. There was nothing on either side of the road, just a line of cypress trees on each side, then, beyond that, tawny hillsides. The ocean was behind me. I drove up the hill slowly, feeling like this was a questionable, even foolhardy mission. I was more than a little tempted to just open the door and let the little dog out of the car here, away from the road, where he wasn't likely to cause any trouble. But there was not a house or building in sight, just the long driveway, the trees, and the yellow grass hillsides in the sunshine.

Finally, a gateway came into view. It was made of pink stucco with red tiles along the top, and there was a Spanish-style wrought iron gate, pushed open. There were Mexican tiles inlaid into the wall, lettered in flowing script.

Villa de Vista de Santa Catalina

The little dog jumped up and put his paws up to the window and started wagging his tail harder. Promising, I guessed.

I craned forward trying to see past the gates, but could see only an overrun garden, crowded with papery red bougainvillea, birds-of-paradise, and a tangle of unkempt yellow roses. I paused for a moment, but didn't see anyone about, so I rolled past the enormous walls and gate, and into the lane that led through the garden.

The driveway went along for a few hundred more feet, past a greening pond clotted with algae and a tarnished fountain. There were paths and benches in the garden, but it looked untended, filled to bursting with flowers in hot reds and yellows.

The little dog now had his paws up on the rolled-down window and his head and snout fully out the window. I could hear the thumping pattern of his tail against the car seat next to me.

As the drive curved through the garden, all of a sudden, the house itself came into view and I realized where I was. It was a large Spanish-style villa, which appeared to be built around an open-air courtyard. Its heavy double doors were of dark Spanish wood, with stone steps leading up to them. One of the doors stood open, revealing the shadowy recesses inside the house. Beyond the house, off to the left, you could see a well-tended gravel lane flanked on both sides with cypress trees, leading back to another building, also pink stucco in the Spanish style, which I knew was a stable.

I let the car slow to a stop. I looked at the little dog. He was wagging his tail but not budging. I got out of the car and walked over to the large ornate doorway, pausing outside, since one of the doors stood wide open. I didn't see a doorbell, so I rapped on the closed door; it was so thick that my knocking barely made a sound. Through the open door, I could see a grand entryway, with dark ceramic tile on the floor. Against the wall stood a massive chest, inlaid with an intricate pattern of mother-of-pearl that glimmered faintly in the inside gloom.

I knocked on the door again.

"Hello . . . ?" I called tentatively.

Just then, I heard rapid footsteps behind me and turned to see an elderly woman, tall and rail thin, approaching down the lane from the stable. Just as quick, the little white dog leaped out through the open window of my car and jumped into the arms of the woman, who caught him gracefully without slowing her pace one bit.

"Oh, I'm terribly sorry," she said. "It looks like Oyster jumped into your car."

"Yes, you see, I found him on the road. I wasn't sure who he belonged to. I guess I found the right place."

"Well, that's one stroke in your favor. I can see that you're responsible. Half of the girls would have just left him there."

This woman had the bearing and diction of an older Katharine Hepburn. Her soft gray hair, still with some brown in it, was piled in a loose bun behind her head, and her face was deeply lined from the sun, but her eyes were bright blue and lively—it was hard to tell how old she was. I wondered, momentarily panicked, if she could possibly be . . . but no, the woman I was looking for would be much older.

"Well, yes," I said. "I'm quite responsible." It was a stupid thing to say, but I was feeling very stupid right then.

"All right, then. Do you know anything about horses?"

"Well, yes," I said, rather baffled by where this line of conversation was leading. "I do. Or I did. I mean, I used to."

"Well, then, I like your demeanor and the fact that you're not quite so young as most of the others. I don't ask for character references—I consider myself an adequate judge of character. What's your name, then?" Now I was starting to think that this was a case of mild dementia I was dealing with. She looked quite alert, but I couldn't follow her train of thought.

"Clara," I said, preparing to detach from the conversation. "I'm very pleased I was able to find the dog's owner—I'll just be . . ." I took a step backward.

"Clara," she said, sticking out her hand. "Eleanor Prescott Norton. You may call me Eleanor."

Eleanor Prescott Norton. This tall elderly attractive woman was *Eleanor Prescott Norton?* I was caught completely off guard. Though moments earlier I had been rehearsing my speech, now I couldn't figure out what to say. My hand flew up to my hair, and I pushed a curl behind my ear, an old nervous reflex from childhood. I looked at her face again—could I see the outlines in it of a younger woman? But I hadn't ever known her, had seen her only once. Her blue eyes blazed out from her leathery suntanned face. She looked at me with interest, but no trace of recognition.

"You'll be given lodging over the stables. The quarters are quite comfortable, but you'll have to share with Jazmyn, the other stable girl." She cocked her head and looked at me. "She's not your type. You'll have to make an effort to get along."

"B-b-but . . ." I didn't think anything could render me speechless, but this sequence of events did. "I'm sorry, Mrs. Norton."

"Eleanor," she said sternly.

"It's just that I think there has been a misunderstanding. You see, I just came to try to find the owner of the dog and . . . I . . ."

"I'm sorry. Speak plainly. I don't understand."

"You are looking for a stable girl?"

"My dear Clara, did I not speak to you on the phone just a half an hour ago? Did you not call me to inquire about the position as a stable girl?"

I was speechless, completely thrown off base. I stared at her like a half-wit.

"If it's the pay, I'm not budging, but the rooms are comfortable and the food is good. And of course, you get to ride."

"I am . . . I am not . . . uh . . ."

"Oh, yes, my dear. I'm sure you are a terrific rider. You've got just the build for it, slim, long legs, flat chest. Jazmyn doesn't ride, but she's good with the other duties. Run along, then. Julio!" she said, her voice shrilling up just like some matron in the movies, and she clapped her hands twice. Almost immediately a small thickset man appeared in front of her.

"Take Clara's bag and show her to her room."

"I haven't brought a bag."

"Well, of course you haven't. It is clear that you're running from something. Not to worry, the Villa de Vista is a terrific place to hide."

I like to think that at moments like this one I am a person who stops and thinks, but the evidence in this particular case is squarely against me. The small man was already hurrying down the neatly raked lane, and quite before I had made up my mind, I was already following him. Like a flash, Oyster jumped out of Eleanor's arms and followed along behind me, tail up in the air like a cheerful white flag.

SEVEN

I followed Julio down the smooth gravel lane that wound around in back of the house. The stable was laid out on a flat piece of ground, pink, and built around an open courtyard just like the house. It looked more like an old Italian villa than a horse barn. In front of the stable was a bricked-in tack-up area with crossties that stood empty, a washrack, and a longeing ring. Out behind the barn you could see a riding arena. Though the garden had looked wild and untidy, the stable was neat as a pin, even the gravel in the courtyard raked into even rows. The stalls opened onto the inner courtyard, so that the horses were looking out toward the center over double stall doors.

I was struck immediately by the particular combination of sounds and smells, viscerally familiar even after so many years—fresh sawdust, the tang of manure, dust, and alfalfa hay, the slightly antiseptic odor of fly spray. I could hear the quiet *thump, thump*ing as one of the horses stamped in his stall. But the general feeling was one of stillness. Julio stopped and pointed at a doorway of a wing of the stable that led off the courtyard.

"That's the door. You go in there, then upstairs. Jazmyn, she's there. She'll show you what you're supposed to do." He turned, then walked with short rapid steps back out of the courtyard, leaving me standing in the central area, no one watching except the soft eyes of several horses that were looking out at me, flicking one ear or the other back to switch a fly, but otherwise totally uninterested.

"Thank you, Julio," I said. I looked at the open doorway.

The Lord works in mysterious ways. That's what my mother would have said. I myself didn't believe that, of course. It was just dumb peculiar luck.

Eleanor Prescott Norton was the matron of the Norton family, whose forebears had bought a two-hundred-thousand-acre ranch along California's gold coast for forty-nine dollars in the days of the California Republic. She was also, by sheer coincidence, by the fact that their money put a Norton finger in every pie in these parts, intimately connected with the downfall of my father. I had met her briefly once before, if *met* was even the right word for it. She would have no reason to have the slightest recollection of that meeting.

I looked at the open doorway in front of me. It was as though I had tried to walk away from my past in a long straight line and ended up walking in a circle. I had found Eleanor Norton. All I had to do was turn around, walk back down the lane, and ask her my question. I took a few deep breaths of the alfalfa-scented air, hesitating. The air smelled like fresh hay, and the mineral odor of hard-packed dry earth sprinkled with water to keep down the dust. The dappled sunlight in the stable courtyard was warm on my cheeks.

Oh, and then there was the other thing she had said, that the Villa de Vista was a great place to hide. Not that I was hiding or anything. I had kept my cell phone turned on in case Walter or the office needed to reach me, but right at the moment, as I stood on the raked gravel and looked around at the closed contours of the stable yard, staying there for just a little while didn't seem like such a bad idea.

I walked through the open doorway that Julio had pointed to and found myself in a tack room. The room itself was a little dusty, with cobwebs strung across the one silty window, but the saddles lined up neatly on saddletrees were all dark and soft with saddle soap, and the snaffle bits in the bridles shone with polish. I smelled Murphy's oil soap, neat's-foot oil, boot polish, and fly spray that had rubbed off the horses onto the saddle pads.

Alongside the tack room there was a stairway leading up, with another dusty window letting in a pane of light.

I walked up the stairs, rather slowly, hearing them creak under my feet. When I got to the landing, I saw another open doorway, through which I could see a long narrow bunk room with dormer windows on both sides. There were four single beds in the room, each covered with a clean turquoise bedspread. In one lay a chunky teenage girl, her thick brown hair fanned out behind her. Her cheeks were flushed and one had a red imprint where one of her oversized earrings had pressed into her cheek. Her hands were curled up next to her; her mouth was slightly open. I didn't want to wake her, so I went back out of the room and crept down the stairs again, planning now determinedly to find Mrs. Norton, confess my identity, confront her with my question, and leave.

Only problem was that when I got down to the courtyard, there was a seventeen-hand chestnut standing in the middle of the courtyard. I blinked and stared in confusion—

Captain.

But no, of course that was impossible. And this horse, however similar, was heavier boned, a little bigger, but still . . .

Looking at the big chestnut, the empty saddle, the ground telescoped up around me, a loud clanging sound in my ears, the feeling that I was about to fall. My heart was thudding like hoofbeats at the base of my neck.

I shot my hand out to steady myself, leaning against a half stall door, which was ajar, and swung shut when I leaned on it, leaving me to trip after it like a fool, barely staying upright. *Vertigo.* I had thought I was over it, hadn't felt the sensation in years, and now twice already this morning. I tried to right myself, stared at the carefully raked gravel in the courtyard, sandy and solid beneath my feet.

While I was righting myself, a lean fellow wearing tight Harry Hall breeches and carrying a thin black dressage whip strode out of the tack room, and took the reins from Julio. He fussily adjusted the keepers on the bridle, and tightened the string girth. Then in a fluid motion, he slipped his toe into the stirrup and swung up on the horse. Such a beautiful horse, and then also such a strong resemblance . . . certainly it wouldn't hurt to watch him just a little bit, just for a few minutes, before I left.

Eleanor stood at the gate of the riding ring, attired as before in blue jeans, a blue turtleneck, and a down vest. She had a riding crop in her hands and was standing with one foot on the bottom rail of a post and rail fence, looking out to where the big chestnut was executing small circles at a collected trot. The wiry rider had him on a very short rein. The horse was under control, but just barely—he was chafing at the double bridle and sweating profusely, the sides of his neck foaming up under the reins.

Marking for marking, from the four white stockings to the white star and snip, to the burnished chestnut coat, now sleek and dark from sweat, he was remarkably similar to Captain, similar enough it made something ache deep inside me—a feeling, more like a memory of a feeling, of what it felt like to ride. The rider shortened the reins even further, collected the trot even more—an arduous movement for a big horse, almost dancing in place, but not quite, like moving in slow motion. In my mind, without even meaning to, I started to make corrections: *loosen up on the reins; use softer hands; don't drive so much with the seat.* Lost knowledge, bubbling up from some forgotten part of me . . . I hadn't actually forgotten, even after all these years.

Just then, the cell phone in my pocket vibrated again, so I took the phone out of my pocket and looked at it.

Six missed calls. I checked the number. *Walter.* I put the phone back in my pocket and headed back toward the stable and upstairs to the long narrow room. The girl, Jazmyn, was nowhere in sight. I sat down on one of the unused bunks and dialed.

I heard Walter's familiar voice, like a ghost, out of the distance.

"Clara. Sorry to bother you. Really. You're on vacation."

"Walter—"

"I just wanted to tell you that we got the path sections back."

"And?"

"They were inconclusive."

"Inconclusive." For a moment, I felt like I didn't even quite remember what the word meant.

"Come on, Clara. You know that they are usually inconclusive. Sometimes you stumble upon a glob of vernix, but most of the time you don't. By the way, where the hell are you? Do you know you never told us where you were planning to go?"

"I'm . . . at a dude ranch," I said.

"Really?" said Walter. I could hear that he was trying not to sound unconvinced.

"Did you know that I know how to ride horses?" I asked him. One of those inane Clara comments. Now he would really think I was nuts.

"Actually, no, I can't say that I did."

Walter's voice was so familiar, so much like home, reassuring, that I didn't really want to say good-bye. At the same time, I didn't feel like I could talk to him right now. It made me too aware that I was not anywhere I was supposed to be.

"Oh, and Clara."

"Yes?"

"The baby."

"Yes?" I said. He didn't have to tell me which baby. The mention of the frail baby in the NICU made my stomach heave.

"It's still hanging in there. On an oscillator."

"Hanging in there?"

"You know, questionable brain function, but otherwise pretty stable."

"Oh," I said.

"I'll keep you posted."

"Sure," I said. When the phone clicked off, I pushed the off button and slipped it back into my pocket. I heard footsteps coming up the stairs.

EIGHT

The young woman whom I presumed to be Jazmyn came into the room carrying a wastepaper basket, into which, every few seconds, she was retching. She didn't even look up at me, but proceeded directly to the bed she had been sleeping on before, which was still unmade, and she sat there, peering into the insides of the black rubber wastepaper basket and making occasional vomiting sounds. I had just hung up the phone with Walter and so was still sitting on the bed with nothing to do except stare at the girl, who was so nonchalantly barfing. Finally after a couple of more halfhearted heaves, she looked up out of the recesses of the trash can and said, "It was the pine tar that did it. I was picking Blackie's hooves and packing them and I got one whiff of that shit and I just started puking all over—and I'm thinking any minute now ol' Norton's gonna come in and see me pukin' and throw a hissy. And then I'm cooked."

"Are you ill?" She was wearing a loose baggy sweatshirt, but the situation looked pretty obvious.

"In a way of sayin' it," she said.

"Pregnant?"

"What are you, some kinda spy or something?"

I was just about to say what I would have normally said, which is, "Well, you see, I'm a doctor," but I decided to hold my cards.

"I'm the new stable hand," I said. "Clara. You Jazmyn?"

"You got that right."

By now, I had a better look at her, and I could see that under her loose gray sweatshirt was a late-term pregnancy. I decided to risk it.

"How far along are you?"

"Eight months, but Norton don't know. And if you do one thing I don't like, I'll let the horses out and say you did it. So you can just forget telling her."

"She really doesn't know?" It seemed unlikely that the matron hadn't noticed.

"If she did know, she'd kick my butt outta here so fast you wouldn't even see my shadow. That's what she did to the last girl. So don't breathe a word of it."

"Mum's the word."

She looked at me curiously. "Who the heck are you anyway? You talk funny."

"I'm from New Jersey," I said.

"Oh," she said, seeming satisfied, at least for the moment. Just then, she gagged a couple of times. "Shit, they call this morning sickness, and I get it all day, and they say it goes away, and I still got it."

I wasn't surprised—this constant gagging was pretty typical with pregnant teens. She probably wasn't drinking enough.

"You need to increase your fluids," I said to her.

"Yeah, I know." She eyed me suspiciously. "That's just what my doctor said."

Figures she'd be pregnant. I guess that, in the end, there is really no escaping.

I slept fitfully that night. Jazmyn was restless in the other bed and, as it turned out, was afraid of the dark and had to keep a table lamp burning all night. As an obstetrician, I had long ago trained myself to be able to sleep anytime and anywhere, whenever the opportunity presented itself, a survival mechanism, but that night, sleep, it seemed, wouldn't come, and so finally, I got back out of bed and walked down the steps into the stable courtyard.

It was a bright night—the moon was almost full and it shone down into the courtyard. The air was cooler, but still relatively warm and quite damp, with the briny odor of coastal air. A couple of the horses were looking out of their half stalls peacefully. Other than that, the stable was still. I walked beyond the stable gates, out onto the lane. The big villa was completely dark except for a small light over the door. I could smell the moist air rising up in the garden and the mingled scents of rose, mint, alfalfa, and horse manure.

It was quiet, but not perfectly still. I could hear the sounds of cars driving by on the coast highway and a few ragged peacock calls in the distance. The ocean was dotted with the lights of boats and barges, and the air was lit up both by the blinking lights of airplanes and by the distant gleam of stars. I walked softly, but that didn't stop Oyster from finding me, and soon he followed along, the tags on his collar, which I guess Eleanor had put back on him, jingling softly. I sat down on a bare hillside, looking out at the dark ocean, with my knees hugged to my chest and I let myself think about Lydia.

It was Lydia who rode horses first. She had a large pony named Shackles, a plump dun with a flaxen mane and tail. She used to ride Shackles around bareback. He was as soft as a pillow, and you had to clap your legs hard onto his broad barrel just to nudge him into a reluctant trot. Lydia liked playing with Shackles, I think, more than riding him. He would stand peaceably no matter what she did: combing checkerboards onto his rump with a wet pulling comb, painting his hoofs with Hooflex, braiding pom-poms into his mane, and wrapping ribbons round his neck. "I want a pony," I begged my father from almost the moment we moved in two houses down from Lydia. "I want a pony like Lydia's."

But it wouldn't have been like my father to just go down to the stables and buy me a pony—not just *any* pony. He plunked down lots of money and got me a horse of show caliber—a beautiful chestnut with four white stockings, Captain. Pretty soon the excavators were out plowing out a riding ring behind our house, and a trainer was there almost every afternoon for private lessons. And it turned out that I had a flair for it. I used to be convinced that I could guide Captain with my thoughts. I would think *flying change,* and the opposite foreleg would flash out in perfect cadence. Lydia, who had joined in the lessons, of course, was still bumping along on Shackles, who really preferred to walk. So pretty soon, I started to gallop around the ring, taking fences, while she was still struggling with the posting trot. Not long after, Lydia's parents bought Lydia her own show quality mount, a twelve-year-old gelding named Greystoke. He was a seasoned event horse, a real packer, but he was big and strong, and Lydia was afraid of him. The pony was sold and Lydia struggled with her new horse, all the joy gone out of riding for her.

Now my butt was starting to feel stiff from sitting on the hard, ridged ground, and it was getting chilly. I wasn't sure what time it was, but was certain it was well after midnight. I was supposed to be up to groom and muck in the morning. I was looking forward to having a job to do.

I walked back through the now familiar courtyard and creaked up the dusty stairway. Jazmyn was sleeping soundly and so I decided to turn out the light. Now the warmth of the cot felt appealing, and I fell asleep before I had a chance to ponder anymore.

The next morning I awoke to the first pale rays of light, and when I rolled to sit up, I saw that Jazmyn was already gone. On the foot of the bed were clean folded clothes, a toothbrush, a hairbrush, a bar of soap. Discomfited, I realized that Eleanor had taken me for a charity case. I reminded myself that she knew nothing about me, that it was a kindness on her part. My stomach was growling. I hadn't eaten since I'd been there. . . . Julio had called me for dinner the night before, but my stomach had felt like a lump of lead. The air was slightly chilly, and out through the window, I could see that a bank of fog had rolled in and that the air outside was white with mist.

Down in the stable courtyard, two of the horses were out in the crossties: the bay was being groomed by Julio, and the chestnut was lipping alfalfa out of a red nylon hay net.

"Good morning," Julio called out when he saw me. "Do you know where breakfast is?"

I realized I was ravenous.

"You go around the back of the big house. Maria will give you some breakfast and coffee."

I walked out of the stable courtyard. Today, the coastline was completely hidden in fog, and the purple blossoms on the jacaranda trees stood out like daubs of finger paint against the white sky. The fog was so thick I could barely see as far as the big pink house. If I turned left, the lane led around to the back of the house, where the smell of strong coffee was wafting out of an open window.

A small middle-aged woman with a crisp white apron tied over her dress was standing in front of the window.

When I walked through the door, she turned and smiled warmly at me. "You must be Clara. Did you find everything you needed?"

I nodded, coloring as I remembered that I was wearing someone else's cast-off clothes, then reminding myself that I was a grown woman with a good job, and by no means the object of anyone's pity. But wearing hand-me-downs brought back memories. I could never forget how for a year or two after we left California, Lydia's mother, Mrs. Benson, used to send me boxes of Lydia's cast-off clothes. Maybe Maria sensed my embarrassment, because she smiled encouragingly at me, obviously trying to make me feel at home.

"Coffee?"

"Yes, please."

She handed me a thick brown mug filled with steamy coffee mixed with hot milk, and a rolled corn tortilla with the creamy white Mexican cheese that I remembered from my childhood. I ate the tortilla in two bites, washing it down with the thick sweet coffee. Then I rinsed out my mug and set it on the spotless sideboard.

"Thank you."

"Clara," Maria said, giving me another warm smile. She put her hand on my arm, gave it a squeeze. "Sometimes it's a little tough when you get started here. Eleanor can be intimidating, but she is fair."

I noticed that she used her employer's first name. It was clear that Maria spoke of Eleanor with true affection.

I hurried back to the stable, surprisingly eager to get started on the hard physical work that awaited me. By the time I got there, I saw Eleanor Norton standing next to the bay in the crossties, going over the fitting of his bridle.

"So you're not an early riser, I see," Eleanor said sharply.

I glanced at my watch. It was five forty-five.

"Stable breakfast is at five fifteen sharp. If you oversleep, I expect you to skip it. Of course, I don't expect you to oversleep."

"There is certainly no chance that I will oversleep, Mrs. Norton. But *you* need to give me *clear* directions about my responsibilities." Eleanor's eyes widened slightly in surprise, but I thought I could see a hint of amusement in them.

"Well, then, at least you're feisty. I hate the passive ones. And please, call me Eleanor. Come along, and I'll show you your duties."

Feeding, grooming, tacking and untacking, cleaning stalls, cleaning tack. Eleanor took me around the stable and showed me what I was supposed to do. There were only five horses in the barn—she said several others had gone out for training. The stable itself had twelve stalls.

"This is Blackmore, twelve-year-old gelding. He is very well schooled, and he is my primary mount. Alfalfa hay, and flaxseed, that's it. No grain. He doesn't need it."

I nodded my head. The big chestnut I had admired the previous day was peering over the stall door disinterestedly. I was hoping that he would be assigned to me. But she pointed to two others—both mares.

"Why don't you let me take care of the chestnut?" I was trying to sound more nonchalant than I felt.

"Benedetto? He is beautiful, isn't he?" I could hear the pride in her voice. "He's my very best horse. I imported him from Germany two years ago—he's a Hanoverian. I'm paying that Hans an arm and a leg to ride him. I'm quite certain that he is a Grand Prix prospect."

"I'll take good care of him," I said.

She appeared to be thinking about it. "No, I don't think so. Jazmyn is quite trustworthy, though she's lazy and complains a lot—you so often see that in young women of her class."

I cringed but thought it was better not to argue with her.

"She needs to learn responsibility, and she's doing fairly well so far. Better than I might have imagined *under the circumstances*. You, though—you haven't proven anything yet."

"Then let me prove it."

She studied me for a moment, and for that moment, I felt like I had regressed about twenty years, to when I was just starting out and had to prove myself at every turn.

"Well, I like plucky," she said. "But I'll be watching you. You haven't earned my trust yet, and there's something about you that I can't quite put my finger on. But all right. I'll allow you to do it, on a trial basis only."

I learned that Eleanor always went for a ride first thing in the morning. I had to groom and tack up Blackmore, Eleanor's horse. She stood not three feet away, watching everything I did, but I found that the old habits of taking care of horses, once deeply ingrained, came quickly back to me. Though she was scrutinizing me, she didn't say anything or tell me what to do, just watched.

When I handed her the reins, I was surprised to see that she was able to mount from the ground rather than needing a mounting block. That was a neat trick for such an old woman, to pivot gracefully onto the horse's back by tucking her toe into the stirrup. Unable to resist, I followed her out to the ring to watch her ride. She was circling the ring at a controlled canter. From this distance, with her straight posture and relaxed control of the big horse, you would take her for a young girl out riding. For a second, I felt an intense admiration. She was exactly the kind of eighty-year-old woman that I would want to be myself.

That thought was swiftly followed by a stab of remorse. I thought of my own mother's pale white face, of the tired slump of her shoulders, the heaving overweight way that she moved. My mother, who had worked hard for years while she helped send me to college and then to medical school. And those years of wear and tear had gotten to her too. She had been a hardworking nurse who had cared for everyone except for herself. Now she was in a wheelchair, from complications of diabetes—preventable complications.

When I was finished with my barn work, there was a pleasant ache in my shoulders from wielding the big heavy pitchfork, and I had a couple of blisters that were forming on the palms of my hands. My final duty of the morning was to tack up the big chestnut, Benedetto. Hans was coming to ride him, and I groomed him until his coat shone in the late-morning sun. The dust that came out of his coat stuck to the fine sheen of sweat on my arms and forehead. I hadn't been this sweaty and dirty in a long time—I didn't quite want to admit to myself how much I was enjoying it.

Hans rode the big horse out to the ring, where Eleanor stood with one foot resting on the bottom rung of the post and rail fence. Done with all my barn chores, I had followed along to watch. The early-morning fog had burned off, and there was a slight breeze, though the sun was warm. Again I was struck by the scene—the ocean was a deep blue, and from this distance looked calm. You couldn't see the cliffs from where we were, just the gently sloping hillsides—the turbulence of the ocean when it crashed up against the rocks was hidden from view.

Again, Hans was working on collection, working toward a very challenging movement called piaffe. In this movement, a horse essentially trots in place, appearing to dance in slow motion. It is exceedingly difficult—a horse's impulse is to move forward, not to move in place.

Hans was on the horse, and as he got ready to piaffe, he collected the horse's gait more and more until the horse was barely moving forward. Then Eleanor moved in with a longeing whip and she flicked it behind Benedetto's buttocks to try to get him to continue to move his legs while he was no longer moving forward.

It was not working. Each time they would attempt to slow him into the piaffe, he would bolt forward. Hans had the reins very short and was riding with what looked like a very heavy hand. Eleanor was patient, but it seemed to me that she was moving in just a moment too soon before the horse was ready. Typical Clara—I hadn't been on the back of a horse in years, but still I felt like I could do it better.

Finally, without really meaning to, I blurted out, "Soft hands."

Eleanor turned around and frowned at me, but said, "She's right, Hans. You need to use softer hands."

"Oh, so now we take advice from a stable girl, do we?" Hans grudgingly let the reins out just a little bit.

It's funny, but *soft hands* was a term used in obstetrics too. I had just never thought of it that way. You need soft hands to deliver a baby, just the right combination of movements, nothing too forceful. You're just going along with what nature has in mind—not unlike riding a horse. It suddenly occurred to me that I might not be leaving tomorrow. Somehow, I was getting sucked in here.

I watched as Hans, now using a lighter hand, started to get better results, and the horse actually started to take a step or two in the slow-motion prance. But I could see that the horse was tiring.

"Quit now when you're ahead," I called out, feeling like I was part of the team.

"What?" Hans called over to me. "So now *you* are the Olympic medalist and I'm the girl with the pitchfork in her hand?"

I saw him tighten the reins a notch, draw the horse in tighter. I realized that I should have kept my mouth shut.

"All right. We try it again. Get the girl. She can stand in front. Hey, you. Come stand over here."

Hey, you? I opened my mouth to protest, but remembered that I was keeping a low profile.

This time, Hans wanted me to stand a few feet in front of the spot where he would try to slow Benedetto into the piaffe to discourage him from moving forward.

I stood with my arms out to my sides and watched the drill. The horse came toward me; he slowed to a jog; Eleanor prodded him gently with the whip—not inflicting pain, just as a reminder.

It was working. I could see the pleasure in Eleanor's face. Hans was rock steady. I watched the powerful horse, now dark with sweat, harness all his power into a few controlled slow-motion dance steps.

He did it once, twice. He was getting tired. At that point I would have quit, put the horse out on a long rein, patted him for a job well-done. But Hans wanted to try it one more time. I looked at Eleanor to see if she would intervene, but she was all for it.

He rode toward me, collecting the trot. I could see the lather working up on the horse's neck, the foaming around the bit. He was working so hard; it was clear that this was a horse with a big heart.

He trotted toward me, slower, slower. Hans reined him in more and more while continuing to urge him forward with his legs. He was just a few feet in front of me, but this time the horse slowed almost to a stop, instead of continuing with the trotting prance.

"Whip, please," Hans called out.

"The horse is tired," I said.

Hans was goosing the horse hard with his legs. Eleanor raised the whip, preparing to flick it behind the horse—

"I didn't know who to call, so I didn't call anyone. I thought you were going to come around."

Eleanor was standing across from me. I was lying on some kind of a dark maroon divan. The room I was in was filled with heavy dark furnishings, and the walls were covered floor-to-ceiling with bookshelves lined with old leather- and clothbound books. The light was slanting through the windows at a late-afternoon angle, and motes of dust floated lazily in the panel of light.

Late afternoon? How could it be late afternoon?

"I don't really remember. . . ."

"Oh, dear, then you may need medical attention. Do you remember what happened? Benedetto bolted out of the piaffe—poor horse, he didn't try to hit you. . . . It was an accident."

Now I remembered—he had bumped me on the shoulder, knocked me off my feet. My hand flew up to my head, which was throbbing.

"I cracked my head?" It was a question. I remembered hitting something hard.

"I'm afraid so. When he knocked you off-balance you hit your head on a jump standard. Don't you remember?"

Well, actually I did remember. I remembered now icing my head, walking over to the big house, and lying down on the couch. I must've fallen into a deep sleep.

"You need to see a doctor."

I rubbed the sore spot. "That won't be necessary," I said. A mild concussion. Self-diagnosis. Case closed. I quickly did my own little mini mental-status exam. Did I know who I was? Yes, Dr. Raymond—*and Clara the stable girl*. Okay. Did I know where I was? In the pink house. So far so good. Did I know what day it was? How long had I been here anyway? Today was only the second day.

I had a bump on my head. Nothing that Advil and ice wouldn't cure. I could ask Walter to take a look at it—*Walter*. Then a pain worse than a headache overtook me. The case. Lydia. My privileges. Somehow momentarily I had forgotten why I was here.

I groped in my pocket for my cell phone, thinking it was high time for me to switch it back on.

Eleanor obviously knew what I was looking for.

"I'm afraid I answered it once, hoping for an emergency contact," Eleanor said, producing the phone, which was no longer in my pocket, from an oriental lacquered table. "But it was a man's voice, so I hung up. I do not wish to compromise your privacy."

I picked up the phone and flipped through the digital messages, Walter, Walter, Walter, my mother—damn, I had forgotten to call her. Walter again. I sat up quickly and felt my head throb and a wave of nausea ball up in my throat. For a second I thought I was going to pass out. I must have hit my head a lot harder than I'd thought.

"Maria is holding dinner for you. I'll show you the staircase to the back kitchen."

As I stood up, I saw that on one of the bookshelves there were several old color pictures, probably from the seventies, of a young woman with straight sun-bleached hair whipping around her face. In one she was holding a surfboard and wearing Hawaiian swim trunks. In another she was standing next to the garden fountain, clowning in Levi's and a suede fringe jacket. The resemblance was unmistakable.

"Your daughter?" I asked Eleanor.

She pulled herself even straighter—she was at least five eight, taller than I am.

"Did I ask you who Walter was?"

"That would be none of your business," I said.

"Precisely," Eleanor said.

That would have been a good moment, right then, to stand up and pull my shoulders back and confront her. My question, after all, was simple enough. I wanted to know why she had chosen to do what she did to my father. But somehow, the question kept sticking in my throat. The words just wouldn't come—my head was aching. Maybe it would be better to take some Advil and start to feel better before we had the confrontation.

"Run along now. Dinner is waiting." I had been dismissed and I knew it. I turned toward the stairs. *Tomorrow. I'll ask her tomorrow.*

I walked down the narrow back stairway to the kitchen, where Maria laid a plate of steaming food on the cloth-covered table and I sat down to eat. The kitchen looked out over the overgrown garden. The sun was starting to set—through the tangled branches of a bougainvillea, I could see the ocean, now turning dark purple, and then above it bands of orange and pink. It was puzzling that the garden was so unkempt when the rest of the house and grounds was so tidy. Obviously Eleanor could have paid someone to keep it in better condition. From where I was sitting, you could just see the green head of the marble cupid that graced the old fountain.

"That garden must've been beautiful," I said. "It's a shame it's not kept up better."

"Yes," Maria said, following my gaze out the window. "It's a real tragedy."

"It doesn't seem like Eleanor," I said. "To let it grow wild like that."

"Well, that's just because you don't know her as well as I do," she said. It was a puzzling comment, and I didn't know what to make of it, so I didn't pursue the subject any further.

Even though I felt hungry, I was exhausted and my head was still aching, so I left most of the food untouched, said good night to Maria, and walked out through the darkening garden. The path was choked with overgrown rosebushes that scratched my arms as I walked by; then, emerging from the garden out onto the well-kept gravel drive, I turned down the lane toward the stable.

NINE

I was lying on my back on my bed, head propped on a stiff pillow that felt like it was stuffed with straw. I had gone out behind the stable and taken a shower in the makeshift shower stall: it was enclosed by a rough fence with faded plastic shower curtains tacked to it with thumbtacks, and was open above to the great blue sky. My head was feeling better, just a sore bump on one side, but no more ache. I had just dialed Walter's number.

"Clara?"

"Hi, Walter." It was amazing how his voice was like balm to me.

"I've been trying to get ahold of you all day. I started thinking you'd had a run-in with a horse or something." I could hear the low rumble of his chuckle. I loved Walter's laugh.

"As a matter of fact I did."

"Mmm-hmm," he teased. He didn't believe me!

"I did, Walter. I swear I did. Landed right on my head."

"Are you all right?" He sounded genuinely concerned. "Are you sure you're okay?"

"Minor contusion," I said. "I'm still in possession of my senses."

"Thank God," he said, with such warmth that I was surprised to feel my face flushing a little and tears coming to my eyes.

"Look, I've got some more stuff to talk about with you. Is this a good time?"

"Shoot."

"We got the placental analyses back from path lab. There were numerous microcalcifications and a number of areas that looked like previous small abruptions."

"Had she been hypertensive?"

"We've gotten her prenatal records. Husband gave the okay. Apparently her baseline blood pressure had risen very slightly but not to the PIH threshold. Other than that, an uneventful prenatal course—history of infertility treatment—that's about it."

"Hmm," I said, mulling over these new pieces of information, and where they fitted in the puzzle.

"Clara? There's one other thing."

"What's that?"

"You remember that our contract with the clinic is coming up?"

I hadn't thought about it. Walter and I handled the hospital "clinic," the patients without private insurance. We lost money on it every single year and paid higher premiums on our malpractice because those patients, who were often disadvantaged, were considered "high risk." Walter and I did it out of a sense of duty. Besides, no one else wanted to touch it with a ten-foot pole.

"What about it?"

"Uni-Group is going to bid against us for it."

"What?" This was totally baffling. "Why would they even want it?"

"The usual reason."

"What usual reason? A lack of instinct for self-preservation?"

"Money."

"There's no money in the clinic, Walter. You don't need me to tell you that."

"Well, here's the deal. St. Mary of Mercy is closing its obstetric wing because of malpractice premiums. Everyone is anticipating that the bulk of those patients will come into our caseload. With the way that HMOs have been reimbursing, I guess the Medicaid payments don't look that bad anymore for a huge group like Uni—that's how they work. Economies of scale."

"Yeah, right, I know. The Wal-Mart model."

"It's their modus operandi. They come in and eat up everything in sight. The only reason they didn't bid for the clinic before was that it was too small potatoes."

"Well, we were there when nobody wanted it. I don't think we should give up that easy."

"When do you expect to be back, Clara?" Now he sounded wistful. God, I was so selfish, I hadn't even thought about what covering the practice alone this whole time had been like.

"When do I get my privileges back?" I asked, suddenly feeling eager to get back to work.

"Clara, I'm sure it's all going to work out. They're just letting the dust settle. I'd say another week tops."

Then, not wanting to know the answer, but still needing to know, I asked.

"The baby?"

"Slightly better, I guess."

"You guess?"

"I ran into the dad in the hallway. He says they're weaning it from the respirator."

"Oh." Then a pause. "Did he seem okay?"

"Who, the dad?"

"Yeah."

"Well, you know, under the circumstances . . ."

My heart felt pierced, as though there were a huge hole in the middle of it. "Well, see you, Walter."

TEN

I lay back on the bunk then, staring out the dormer windows, which were stained with streaks of red light from the sunset. I was hollow and shaky inside, and my head was pounding again. I wasn't honestly sure that I was really okay. This running-away thing wasn't working at all. My practice, my patients, my partner, my mother, the flickering candle of a frail baby, and the ghost of a person who everybody assumed I had forgotten had once saved my life. They had all come along with me here, my ghostly entourage.

But thinking about ghosts wasn't a good idea, not a good idea at all, because the wind was coming up outside. I could hear it whistling around the courtyard, rattling the barn doors, and there was a draft in the room now. Nothing was really sealed up tight here. Maybe it was just the bump on my head, but I had a dizzy, almost vertiginous feeling.

The cliff. It was only a mile away, just down the hill. The wind that was sweeping around the stable now might just sweep me up and hurl me over the cliff once and for all. But this time Lydia would not be there to come along and find me just before I plunged. I shook my head, but that just made it hurt more, and then I shook it more because I wanted it to hurt. I closed my eyes and listened to the wind and thought about my father. I was thirty-eight, and he had been dead since I was fifteen. But here, maybe in a way I was close to him. My head was throbbing, throbbing, throbbing. *Oh, Daddy, Daddy*, I mumbled to myself. I tried to sink into the oblivion of sleep.

That was when I heard the slight sound of crackling paper. I sat up a little too quickly and had to press my hand against my head to calm the throbbing. I heard the crackling again, so I looked around the room, which appeared to be empty.

The crackling was coming from the far side of the room, back where there was a dusty-looking wardrobe of sorts. Mice maybe.

"Hello?" I said tentatively. The door of the wardrobe pushed open and Jazmyn climbed out, a pink candy package in one hand, and a Big Gulp mug from 7-Eleven in the other. She was grinning like she thought the whole thing was terribly funny.

"Gotcha," she said. " 'Oh, Daddy, Daddy!' You can just forget your big daddy 'cause he sure ain't here." She flicked a small square of something neon pink into her mouth.

Not even sure where to begin with her sudden appearance, I started with the obvious.

"What are you eating?"

"Now and Laters," she said. "You want one?"

"What's a Now and Later?" I asked.

"Jesus, which planet were you born on anyway? Now and Later—watermelon flavor. They're good. I have to eat them 'cause I'm craving them. That and freezer frost. I just can't get enough freezer frost."

"Pica," I said. One thing about medicine, there is a name for absolutely everything.

"Is that what they call freezer frost?"

"That's what they call craving something that isn't food—you know, like laundry starch, or dirt."

"Or freezer frost. My doctor told me it gots iron in it."

"I kind of doubt that's exactly what she said."

"You're a social worker, aren't you? I don't know what you are doing here, but you're the weirdest stable hand I ever saw. If you're from CFSD, you can just forget it 'cause I'm seventeen and I don't want to hear nothin' from nobody." She sucked thoughtfully on the pink candy. "Then again, I never heard of a social worker who is handy with a pitchfork. Are you like one of those people who ol' Norton hired to poison the horses so she can get her insurance money? Or something like that?"

I looked at Jazmyn, a husky girl with bushy brown hair, olive skin, and thick eyebrows. She was pretty, in a plus-sized kind of a way. She was wearing baggy green sweatpants and a huge T-shirt that really did hide her pregnancy pretty well—she had one of those figures that was mostly boobs and belly anyway. She had a clunky gold necklace with her name in gold script across the collarbone, and thick gold hoops that hung almost to her shoulders. Her nails were elaborately painted, in two-tone silver and gunmetal gray across a diagonal, with a tiny sparkle set in the center of each one.

"How do you do stable work with nails like those?"

"What, is this, like, another social work question?"

"I'm just wondering," I said. "Look at mine." I stretched out my hands to let her inspect them, then was startled for the first time to see how unfamiliar they looked. Usually they looked like surgeon's hands, thick and blunt with spotless nails and neatly trimmed cuticles, but now they looked like a horsewoman's hands, with ragged cuticles and a faint ring of dirt under each half-moon of nail.

Jazmyn looked at the proffered hands with lively interest. "Wow, you're old! How old *are* you, girl? You got hands like the ladies in the Palmolive commercial. You better use some Oil of Olay."

"Thanks," I said. My feelings were actually a tiny bit hurt, though I struggled to hide it. I didn't think my hands looked old. I was not old, was I?

"Here, take a Now and Later," she said. "It'll sweeten you up."

Jazmyn tore off a curlicue of paper and handed me a small square of candy wrapped in white wax paper. I tore the paper off and looked skeptically at the hot pink candy in the palm of my hand. But I was in need of a friend, so I popped it into my mouth. It was sweet and tangy, and when I tried to chew, it felt like a filling was pulling loose from my molar.

"You know, it's okay to eat this kind of stuff once in a while. But your baby needs food."

"Yeah, but I can't stand the stuff they serve up at the big house. It's all vegetables. I hate that shit. I usually go out when I get time off and get chicken nuggets and a Coke or something. Maria's real nice. She lets me get to the freezer frost whenever I want."

"That stuff is not good for you," I said again. I couldn't help it. I was a nag by nature—my mother, my patients, basically anyone in sight.

She cocked her head, studying me intently. "You know what I think? I think you're one of those rich ladies from up the hill who drives around in a big SUV and then your rich husband dumped you—maybe like he wanted you to get a boob job or something, and you refused."

I tried but failed to resist the temptation to look down at my modest chest.

"And so he cut up all your credit cards and moved a bimbo into the house, and the only thing you know how to do is ride horses, and that's why you ended up here."

"Why is it so important to you to know why I'm here?" I asked, aware that I sounded more like a social worker than ever.

"Well, let's put it this way. I know why I'm here. It's because I'm pregnant and the baby's father wants to beat the crap out of me, and I ain't gonna go into no shelter, and besides, I got a knack with the horses—not to ride them, but like to take care of them—old Norton says so herself. And I know why the girl before you was here, for more or less the same reason as me, until she started to show and old Norton kicked her out. And Maria and Julio, well they're not really what you'd call hired people. They're like ol' Norton's family more or less—she ain't really got nobody but them. And Hans is just a regular faggy riding guy who walks around in those gay-looking tight riding britches. And so that pretty much just leaves you, who I can't explain—you, who don't clean a stall like a social worker, but you don't talk like a stable girl—and you've got me feeling suspicious, and even downright uncomfortable."

I was also uncomfortable. I was not used to hedging about my identity. I decided the safest course was to change the subject.

"Doesn't Eleanor have any family at all? There was a picture in the library that must be her daughter. She'd be grown by now. Grandkids and such."

"I never heard nobody talk about a daughter. They say old Mr. Norton died, like, a real long time ago. But I ain't never heard nothing about a daughter. You know what they say?" Now Jazmyn was leaning forward. She had her arm draped across the top of her belly in a classic pregnant posture.

"What?"

She leaned forward, hand still draped across her belly, eyebrows working up and down dramatically. "They say old man Norton killed himself. They say sometimes you can see a light sweeping across the cliffs below the house when the night is dark. They say it's his ghost." She lowered her voice for effect. "And sometimes"—she was almost whispering now—"you can hear the sound, mixed up with the waves on the rocks 'n' all, of a screaming horse!"

The hair on the back of my neck was standing up by now, even though I certainly didn't believe in ghosts, but still, that story, that particular rocky cliffside . . .

"Don't you want to know what happened to him?"

"The horse?"

"No, old man Norton. Don't you want to know what happened?"

I nodded.

"Yeah, they say he got in a fight with the lady and said he was going for a walk and a smoke and he never came back, and they found him the next morning, at the bottom of the cliff, all pounded by the rocks."

"He jumped?" I asked.

"Some say he jumped. Others say she followed along behind him and when he got to the edge she pushed him."

She sat reflective for a minute, hand draped over her big belly, probably feeling the baby kick.

"What about the crying horse?" I asked, overcome by curiosity, but still afraid to hear the story.

"Some say a horse went over one time. Some say the rider went with him. You used to be able to see skeleton bones of a horse down there, or that's what people say, but now they're gone anyway. I don't know too much about the horse."

I didn't say anything for a while. Trying to find a normal speaking voice to use.

"Any . . . people?" I finally said, hoping I sounded nonchalant.

"Oh, yeah, people, well, sure. Tons of people. Those poor sorry bastards go over all the time. Not anybody, though. Not anybody, you know, famous, or anything like that. They say John Belushi's cousin went over, but that's probably just made-up."

I lay back on the cot then, and stared out the window in silence, for a while, for a long while. Until I heard Jazmyn get up and scuffle out of the room, leaving me in increasing darkness and silence. I felt small then, tiny, smaller than the tiniest pinprick of a star that had appeared in the night sky through the window.

What had I really expected, after all? That my sad story would be inscribed on these hillsides like crop markings? That twenty-three years later my story would still not be forgotten?

Bones of a horse on the rocks, washed away, whitened down by the rain and the sun.

It wasn't true of course.

There hadn't been any bones. They had winched his poor battered carcass up with a tow truck. You can't just let an animal rot—there are public beaches just past the cliff after all.

We think our own stories are so big, so big as to never be forgotten.

I must've fallen asleep like that, because the next thing I heard was Jazmyn whispering to me, *Get up. You gotta eat. Come on, let's go,* then gagging three or four times as she pulled her dirty green sweatshirt over her head.

ELEVEN

Jay Thomas Raymond and Annie O'Neill were high school sweethearts. They lived in Garden City, Long Island, and both of them had moved out to the Island from Flatbush when they were old enough to remember where they came from. My mother, Annie, I've seen pictures of her, and she was adorable—she's just over five feet and though her hair is gray and spiky now, then it was thick and a rich auburn curling about her shoulders. I've seen pictures of her, like the one at her high school graduation from St. Anne's, holding a bouquet of flowers, her small feet crossed at the ankles, her eyes so lively—at least to me much livelier than the other girls'. My mother tells me that she wanted to go to Adelphi—that's where the smarter girls at her school were going, some taking secretarial courses, others studying to be teachers—but it wasn't going to happen for Annie. Of six children, she was the oldest girl. Her brother, Thomas, was away flying helicopters in the Korean War.

My father, handsome Jay Raymond, was the essence of up-and-coming. He knew what he wanted and was headed there in a hurry. There were two things on his list: medical school and my mother. The way my mother tells it, she was determined to do something other than marry my father right out of high school, because she was afraid that being saddled with a wife would slow him down. So she did what seemed like the smart thing to do at the time—she enrolled in the hospital diploma program at St. Mary's. Three years later, when she got out with her nursing pin and white peaked cap, she did marry my father. He was a junior at Adelphi by then, and she worked to pay tuition for him. Then when he went to medical school, she kept on working to pay tuition—they were careful too. I wasn't born until my father was a resident and was pulling a salary, and as soon as he did, she "quit my job and put my feet up," as she described it. I can't imagine that she ever put her feet up, though. She managed his tight budget, baked bread, kept their apartment and later my baby self spotless, while my father worked, worked, worked, residents' hours, eighty, ninety, one hundred hours a week. The way my mother tells it, he was home so rarely that when he did show up, she would have to remind me, over again, who he was.

I like to think of my mother and father as I imagine that they were then, my mom dressed in pressed button-down A-line dresses with aprons over them, stirring things like custard in her little Formica kitchen with the red and chrome dinette set. My father, the young doctor, ambitious and hardworking, and me, Clara, the beloved little daughter wearing hand-knit sweater sets with pom-pom ties. I like that image of them. The only problem with it is that I don't remember it, at all. I was too young then. Who knows if it was ever really like that or not?

There was a family story about why we moved to California. Of course they weren't from there. As far as I know, neither one of them had ever been there. They were New Yorkers, through and through, both from Flatbush and then later from a short respectable hop farther down the Long Island Rail Road. So why California? My mother tells it that once, in a bitter snowstorm, she was carrying me in one arm and a bag of groceries in the other, and she slipped on the ice and fell. She managed to hold on to me, but I still bumped my head and got a goose egg. The groceries rolled all over the icy sidewalk—even the two oranges that she had bought as a special treat rolled under the car and got into the gutter where she couldn't reach them. My mother says my father came home that night and found her crying about the lost oranges and he said, "I'll take you somewhere you can pick oranges off a tree. And you'll never cry again."

We did have an orange tree, as it happened, in our backyard in Jacaranda Canyon, but it is not true that she never cried again. In any case, knowing what I know about my father, I believe that story to be apocryphal. Jay Thomas Raymond, from Flatbush and Garden City, was going to make a mark in the world, and what better place for a man like him to make a mark than one far away from the place where he came from. I distinctly remember, or at least I think I remember, occasions where people would say to my father, "You're a New Yorker, aren't you? What part?" And he would say to them, cool as a cucumber, "Manhattan."

Lydia and I got off the bus from middle school at the corner of Jacaranda Canyon Road and then walked toward our houses down the horse trail covered with eucalyptus mulch. We lived two houses down from one another, on a street lined with big sprawling California ranch houses that spread out along the street in a friendly way: the lots were large, but not so big as not to be neighborly. It was hot. I remember that we were both wearing shorts and that I had pulled my pale blue sweatshirt off and tied it around my waist.

"You wanna come to my house?" Lydia asked.

She hardly needed to ask, since I stopped at her house almost every day. We came in her back door, and found Marvin there, the Bensons' shaggy golden retriever, who gave our hands a bath with his tongue.

"Hello, girls," Mrs. Benson said. She was a medium-sized woman with graying hair and blue eyes. She loved to bake and there was usually something good to eat on the counter. Mrs. Benson didn't talk to us too much, just "How was your day?" but I liked the way she kept busy around us—wiping down the kitchen counters, sweeping the floor, sorting the mail, nearby in case we needed her. That day would have been like any other: we would have done our homework lying on our bellies on Lydia's white shag carpet, maybe called a couple of friends up on her pink Princess phone; then we would have gone and saddled up our horses to go riding—she would have come to my house for that, so she could ride in my ring.

Only that day, I remember, before we had even finished doing our algebra, my mother pulled into the driveway. She drove a forest green Jaguar in those days, with a tan leather interior, and I saw the hood of the car with the crouching feline on it as it pulled into the Bensons' circular driveway. It struck me as odd that she would come for me like that. She got out of the car. I remember the way my mother dressed in those days, in the oranges and browns of seventies California, only she always looked—I don't know—stiff, to me, like everything was just a little too lacquered in place. Hair spray, lipstick, nylons—my mother, at that point in her life, always looked "done." I used to wish she looked softer around the edges, and then later, she did.

My mother got out of the car, rat-a-tat-tat across the driveway on her stiletto heels. See, I can hardly believe that this was my mother at all, because later she was nothing like that—almost aggressively not like that—she was soft and fat and kind of lumbering. But I'm sure I remember right, because I've seen pictures of her in California, and she looks just the way I remembered her.

That day, she came up on the porch and Mrs. Benson met her at the door.

"Why, Anne, what a pleasure to see you. Of course, she's right here."

I heard my mother standing and chatting at the door, pleasantly, about something—I think it was the book drive at school. I could hear an extra note of tension in my mother's voice, more than what was usually there anyway, and so I remember that I stopped doing my math for a minute and started listening to her voice.

A moment later, she came into the room; she was wearing an orange-and-brown silk dress from Robinsons that wrapped around tightly at her waist. She was wearing dark glasses, so that I couldn't see her eyes.

"Come along, Clara," she said. "I'm going to need you home for a while."

This must have been very unusual because I remember that her request struck me as odd. I remember the way my stomach felt tense and fluttery against the white shag rug. My first thought was that something had happened to Captain.

I shrugged at Lydia, who smiled. She of course noticed nothing out of the ordinary. Her mother often wanted her home for various things. I don't really think Mrs. Benson felt too comfortable letting Lydia hang out at our house, where my mother was rarely home and we had a Mexican "live-in" who was probably barely seventeen and used to sneak her boyfriend in the back way when my mom wasn't home. But my mom rarely came to get me. She liked the Bensons and was perfectly happy to let me stay there. Later I asked her what she was doing all that time. Why she was never home. She didn't have a job after all. And she said, "Volunteer work, with the other doctors' wives. To help your father's career."

My mom gestured to the car, and I climbed in, thinking that she was going to take me somewhere other than home, but she didn't. She just pulled down the street into our driveway and then switched off the ignition, but she didn't move. I still remember that feeling of that car—the soft calfskin seats. It was gone—the car—not that long after, and after that, my mother always drove nondescript cars, little Toyotas and Fords. She paused for a minute, hands gripping the steering wheel. She always kept her nails polished back then, bright red. I could see that there was something she wanted to say, and I was apprehensive because my mother didn't normally mince words.

It was all I could do to sit there. I wanted to burst out of the car and run down the back steps to the barn to see if Captain was okay, but I knew that I needed to wait until my mom spoke, and finally she did.

"Clara," my mother said. "I think there is a good chance that you may hear some unpleasant things said about your father. I want you to know that they are all untrue."

I didn't realize right away that this was the main point of the conversation. I was still thinking about my horse.

"What's the matter with Captain?" I blurted as though I hadn't even heard her, and I remember my mother just looked at me, through her dark glasses, inscrutable. I didn't have the slightest idea what she was thinking.

"May the Lord have mercy," she burst out. "I have raised a spoiled brat."

"I'm not spoiled," I huffed. "I just care about my horse. He is an Olympic prospect."

My mother took her sunglasses off, and I noticed that her eyes were puffy, although not red as if from crying. She didn't say anything, just stared at me, and I stared down at my lap and out the window. I remember that I was feeling petulant, and terribly misused.

I knew my mother was getting mad, could feel the suppressed anger buzzing around the car like heat waves, but still she just sat there. I waited, making it a point to stare out the window. Finally she spoke.

"Clara Raymond. You are not the subject of this conversation."

"What is the subject?" I said, not looking at her, mad and self-righteous, running my fingers along the cross-stitched seam of the leather seat.

"Just remember what I said, Clara Raymond. Don't listen to anybody's lies."

Let's put it this way: I was fifteen, when the urge to know was in direct conflict with the desire to appear to not care. So I just shrugged my shoulders and swung the car door open. But in truth I was puzzled and felt sick to my stomach. That was the beginning of an almost constant ache that lasted—well, now it is more of a memory than a feeling, but it is still there.

*   *   *

My mother was right. Remember, this was Jacaranda Canyon, California, where everybody's dad was either a doctor or a lawyer and I guess
people were talking about it around the kitchen table. Josh Kerlin, the
big sports agent who represented NBA players and lived in the huge
house up on Crestline Road, had died during routine knee surgery. All
of the rumors were saying that it was my father's fault.

TWELVE

By the fourth day, my muscles had grown accustomed to the ache; the pitchfork rested familiarly in the grooves of my hands. I had had to resort to taping my palms with adhesive tape to cover the raw blisters on both palms, and now the tape was frayed and browning at the edges, which gave my hands an unkempt and savage look. I was banking the sawdust around the worn stall boards in Benedetto's stall. I could hear the sounds of his measured footsteps out in the ring, along with the voice of Eleanor, from time to time, and the sharp accented replies from Hans. I used the wide tines of the steel pitchfork to pick out the balls of manure, turning them into the red wheelbarrow, then raked away the lighter sawdust on top to expose the urine-soaked sawdust underneath. The harsh ammoniac scent of the wet sawdust stung the insides of my nostrils. I worked until the bare dirt floor of the stall was exposed. I sprinkled a handful of lime on the wet spots, then started pulling down the dry sawdust from the banked edges of the stall. I evenly distributed the fresh sawdust until the stall was filled with a fresh and inviting blanket of the sweet-smelling shavings. I attempted to pull the bandage over the palm of my hand where one of the blisters was now exposed and was starting to get rubbed raw. I looked at the clean well-organized stall with pleasure. Surveying the smooth bed of sawdust and inhaling the dusty fragrant air. The ache in my muscles was pleasant; my brain, mercifully, was on hold.

I was so focused on the task at hand that when my cell phone started vibrating in my pocket, at first I wasn't sure what it was. I thought it might be a fly buzzing; then I realized it was coming from my pocket, and only then did I realize it was my phone. I took a quick furtive look around before I answered it, but seeing only the empty courtyard, with a couple of horses looking lazily over the half doors, I stepped back into Benedetto's stall and answered.

It was Walter.

"Clara, glad I caught you. Look. The baby's father."

"Gordon."

"Yes, Gordon."

"He caught me in the hall yesterday. Told me he wanted to talk to you and did I know how to reach you? What do you want me to do?"

I leaned against the rough boards of the stall, feeling a dull headache flare up at my temples. Just a second ago, I had felt a little distance, but now I was plunged right back into the terrible complications of my actual present, aware again that I had no business being where I was, that I was hiding.

"What did you tell him?"

"I told him I couldn't give out personal information without checking with you, but that I would call you and let you know that he wanted to speak with you."

"What do you think I should do?"

"I don't know, Clara. You do whatever you think is right. Just . . ."

"Just what?"

"Just be careful about what you say. You know you handled that case appropriately. Don't . . . you know . . . don't . . . say something you might later regret."

"Look, Walter, just give him my number. Tell him he can call me anytime. It's the only decent thing to do."

"Whatever you say. By the way, how's the dude ranch?"

"Oh, yeah. Great. It's great."

"There must be a side of you I never knew."

I looked around the neat stall that I had so carefully tended. "There is, Walter, there is."

The rest of the day, I couldn't fall back into the spell I had been in before. I was acutely aware of the silent phone in my pocket and kept thinking I felt it was starting to vibrate. I had my routine pretty well down by then. First thing in the morning I would do my stalls and feeding. Then down to the kitchen of the big house for breakfast. After that, I would hot-walk the horses when Hans had finished riding. My favorite horse was Benedetto, who was always ridden last. I was amazed at how fit I was getting after only a few days on the ranch. At first I had walked them around the stable area to dry them, but now I had ventured out on the trails, leading the horses on a loose rope, and letting them stop to lip tender leaves of grass from time to time. From every spot on the trail, the entire panorama of the ocean was laid out in front of me, and on either side there were fields of tall grass, already scorched to a golden color by the early-summer sun.

Benedetto walked eagerly forward, so that I had to step quickly to keep up. I could see why Eleanor thought he might be Olympic material—as many had once thought about Captain—not just the fine confirmation and springy gaits, but also something about the keen expression in his eyes. We had reached the highest point of the looping trail. Benedetto's sleek coat was already dry, and his dapples were starting to shine up on his rump. I had a thin sheen of sweat on my forehead from the effort of walking up the hill. It was breezy and pleasant; the sun was shining and it was probably about seventy-five degrees. I looked up at Benedetto's broad back, and imagined for a moment that I was astride. Maybe I should ask Eleanor if she would let me ride—just out on the trail, like this. For a second, it actually seemed possible. Wouldn't I still know how to ride? Wasn't it like riding a bicycle? You couldn't actually forget something like that, could you?

They say that after a fall you are supposed to get back in the saddle, but how could I have? My horse was dead. And so soon after, we moved away to Pennsylvania. After that—it was true—my fear had grown and grown, so that I could never disassociate my memories of riding from a feeling of vertigo. I had never gotten on the back of a horse again.

My phone was ringing. I picked it up, looking around to see if anyone was nearby, but the field was empty.

"Clara speaking."

"It's Gordon."

My knees went weak. I stopped walking, tugged on Benedetto's lead shank to get him to stop.

"Gordon."

I was acutely aware that I didn't know what was going to come next—a tirade, a fit of accusations, a heartbroken abundance of grief.

"I want to invite you to Lydia's memorial service. I don't know if you can make it. It's going to be out in California. On Friday. It would mean a lot to Lydia's parents if you could be there."

"Friday," I said stupidly, realizing I didn't know what day of the week it was. "In California."

"I'm sorry it's such short notice. It's going to be at Ambler's Chapel."

Sarah Benson said you would know where it is. Two p.m. on Friday. You don't need to tell me now. Just come if you can."

"Well, I . . ." I didn't know what to say. Of course I knew where Ambler's Chapel was. It was a southern California landmark, a chapel made of glass, perched on a hillside overlooking the Pacific Ocean and the cliffs below. You could practically see it from where I was now standing. It was built just on the edge of the Norton Hills.

"Good-bye, Clara."

Right at that moment, there were so many things I wanted to say. *I'm sorry. How is the baby? How are you holding up? Do you hate me for not saving your wife?* But I didn't say any of them. Lack of guts, I suppose. I couldn't get over Gordon's voice, had never been able to. That's why, over and over, he had been able to melt me with just one phone call. Now I was at a total loss for words.

"Good-bye. Thanks. Take care. Good-bye." That's all I said.

Benedetto was eager to get back to the barn, so I followed him, walking blindly, stumbling down the hill. Going to Lydia's memorial service was something that I couldn't do. And yet, I could never forget my father's memorial service—the way that the Bensons sat in the front row, right near us, how Mrs. Benson kindly offered to hold the reception at their house since my mother was obviously in no condition.

THIRTEEN

This time, Jazmyn wasn't barfing—though when, halfway up the stairs to our room, I heard her, I thought she was. I heard a muffled barking sound, and felt resentment and impatience surge through me. I needed some time alone to think, and yet it seemed like she was always in the room. She tended to finish her tasks faster than I did—more practiced no doubt, and also less of a perfectionist. Didn't she have anything better to do than lie around our room? Come to think of it, I had seen her drive out this morning, in the old barn Volvo, before I had taken Benedetto on his walk. She had headed down the tree-lined lane. I hadn't asked where she was going. I had no desire to hear her intimacies.

Now I had no choice. She was lying flat on her back, legs splayed out, hair in disarray behind her, a pillow over her face, which she pulled off at the sound of my footsteps, revealing a blotchy tearstained face.

As soon as she saw me, she sat up and swung around. Her nose was red and puffy looking. In one hand she held a wad of shredded pink Kleenex; in the other was a small shiny square of paper. She held it up and looked at it, then dissolved into tears again.

I realized that the paper she was holding was a small printout from an ultrasound machine—a picture of her baby in utero. The first thing I thought of was that the sono must have picked up an anomaly. The ultrasound was usually a happy event—unless there was something wrong.

I still felt impatient, but tried to muster a feeling of concern. I sat on the edge of her cot and put one hand on her arm.

"Jazmyn," I said. "What is it? Do you want to talk about it? Can I see?"

I slipped the little printout out of her hands, a series of two sonographic images of a fetus. With rapid practiced eyes I scanned the particulars—the measurements printed out in the corner—this was about a thirty-four-week pregnancy. I looked at the images—there was no obvious anomaly that I could quickly pick out, but that meant nothing. I wanted to know what they had told her.

"It's . . . it's . . ." Jazmyn was sobbing so hard she couldn't even talk.

"Is there," I said, trying to be gentle, "something wrong with the baby?"

That stopped her crying right on a dime. She sat up looking very indignant, her mouth wide open, her thick black eyebrows arched up. Her blotchy red nose started to run, so she dabbed at it furiously with her Kleenex.

"What are you, sick or something? Why do you think there's something wrong with my baby? There's nothing wrong with my baby. I can't even believe you said that to me!"

This was not what I was expecting her to say.

"Well." Now I felt like an idiot. "I just saw you crying and holding that sonogram and I thought there was something wrong."

"Well, I don't know what planet your brain is on, because there *is* something wrong, but that don't mean something's wrong with the baby."

She rubbed her nose again. "You wanna see him?"

"Well, thanks, I saw him."

"Pretty cute, huh?" she sniffed.

"Yes, cute," I said, but using the brisk voice I had found better to elicit confessions. "So what is wrong?"

"Well, there's two things wrong."

"And what are those two things?"

"The one who's the baby's father and the one who's not."

It took Jazmyn a while to backtrack through the whole story.

"My ex-boyfriend, he was a jerk," she started. "That's Frank. He was a jerk. He was verbally abusing me. Like, if he didn't like what I was wearing, he wouldn't let me go out. He used to work down at Hollywood Park, as horse boy. He's the one brought me into taking care of horses. Then he got pissed off at me because I was better at it than him. I was real quiet around the horses, so I got along with them. He would jerk them around a little, acting big, when the boss wasn't looking."

"So you left him?"

"I wanted to get away from him, but I was scared of him. We were living in this ratty trailer, right there next to the racetrack, but I didn't have nowhere to go. I kept asking my mom if I could come home, but she kept saying no, she didn't have no room for me—she's like that."

When I did my first rotation in women's health, I used to be surprised by these stories. Wise as I thought I was, I didn't know that there were mothers in the world who wouldn't give shelter to their own children. It was one of the things that had actually helped me put my own life story in perspective.

Jaz shifted her bulk, rubbed her tummy reflectively.

"Finally one day, he kicked me real hard, right on the butt, left a big ol' boot print on me, so I went to my mom's and I tole her, 'You gotta let me come here just for a little while, to get away from him,' and she said, 'Okay, just for a little while.' "

"So you went back to stay with your mom?"

"Yeah, and she was actually being okay for a change. She was working as a cleaning lady for one of those rich ladies up on the hill, so she was keeping her act together pretty good. And that's when I met Angelo—he was cleaning the pool, up at the house where my mom worked. He's a really sweet guy, really nice—nothing like Frank."

I knew where this story was headed already.

"Then somebody told me Frank got fired from the track, and so I took a chance, and I went back there to try to get my job back. Damned if he wasn't practically the first person I saw there, and he asks me what've I been doin', and I tell him I'm stayin' someplace, and I don't want to see him no more. But the SOB followed me home, he pulls up a few minutes after I do, and my mom, she was already laying back the vodka and she let him in . . . and they started drinking—they got along real good, Frank and my mom—and then once he's good and drunk, he just comes to the back, where I was, and he starts pounding on the door yelling, *Come out, you pussy.* Then my mom, she starts yelling, *If he breaks down that door, I'm gonna kick you outta my house. I don't want nothing to get broken. If he breaks the door, it's gonna be your own goddamn fault.* So I mean, what was I supposed to do anyway? So I opened the door."

Jazmyn stopped talking here, breaking off into sobs again, folding and refolding the bit of Kleenex, mopping her eyes and nose, holding up the little sonogram picture to look at it, then flopping back on the bed so hard that the springs shuddered underneath me. This whole time I had been sitting on the bed, doing the "mm-hmm, mm-hmm" thing. I wish I could say I had never heard a story like this before, but of course, in my line of work, they're a dime a dozen.

"So that's what happened. I ain't never done it with Frank but that one time, and after that I was only with Angelo, and Angelo, he loves me and he says he's gonna look out for me, and the baby too after the baby comes, so long as it's his. But then every time I get the ultrasound they keep telling me it could only be Frank, that low-down son of a bitch."

I knew from hard-earned experience that the Franks of the world could be dangerous.

"Does Frank know where you are right now?"

"You know, the only weird piece of luck I had this whole time was that old lady Norton put the ad to come here up at the track, and I tore it down just a couple minutes before I saw Frank that day and stuck it in my pocket. So after he left that day, after, you know, he done what he did, I took out that little piece of paper and called. Ain't nobody knows I'm here, except for you-all, and . . ."

She started sobbing again. "I was just waiting to get this ultrasound done so I could call Angelo and tell him it's his. . . ." She smiled rue-fully. "Or that's what I was going to do."

"Where's Angelo? Does he come around here?"

"Yeah, well he would, but . . ." Jazmyn looked up at me, eyebrow cocked, like a little girl trying to act bigger.

"But?"

"Well, right now currently he's . . ."

"He's . . . ?"

"Incarcerated."

I took a deep breath and sighed it out slowly. I leaned forward, put my hand on her forearm, gave her a pat. I couldn't help it—against my better judgment I was starting to feel responsible for her. It's an occu-pational hazard, I guess.

"You know what, Jaz, why don't you just lay low for a while. Don't talk to either of them. You know a thirty-four-week ultrasound is only accurate for dating purposes within about three weeks. If you had one in the first trimester, that would be more accurate." This popped out of my mouth way too easy, before I had a chance to remember that I was posing as a stable hand. I bit my tongue, but too late.

Jazmyn's thick eyebrows shot up and she gave me a skeptical look.

"I got it," she said. My stomach quivered at the thought of being found out. "You're a doctor's wife? That's it. You are. Aren't you?"

We didn't have much time to ruminate on that statement, though, because we heard Eleanor's sharp voice echoing through the stable courtyard.

"Jazmyn, Clara, we need you! Benedetto's been hurt."

FOURTEEN

Somehow, the big chestnut stallion had put a foot through the stall board, just like that. The stalls on both sides of him were empty—he was probably just kicking at a fly.

He stood still for now, coat wet with sweat. He had been thrashing to try to get his leg out, but it was caught. I could see bright spurts of crimson—he must have sliced an artery on his gaskin. Eleanor had tight hold of him, a lead chain cinched around his nose. Eleanor was tall, and surprisingly strong for a woman her age, but if the big horse started thrashing again, she would be no match.

As though the horse had read my mind, he reared up a little, lifting Eleanor all the way off the ground, and started kicking frantically with his hind leg, trying to kick clear of where he was caught. I could see that the jagged edges of the wooden stall boards were cutting his leg up even more, and there was a lot of blood everywhere. If he kept bleeding like that much longer, he would start to get shocky.

Without thinking, I started barking orders.

"Jaz, take the lead shank from Eleanor. Brace your feet on the ground."

Jaz grabbed the lead shank and got control of the horse's head. Then with a deft rapid motion, she slipped the chain up around the horse's upper lip, so that the loop of chain was holding the upper lip in a tight circle.

"Twitched him," she said. Now obviously, she had firm control over the horse. It was a technique that, though it looked cruel, was useful in situations like this, where the horse could be in danger. I could see that Jazmyn was good under pressure. So much the better.

"Eleanor," I barked. "Get the tool kit. We need to pry those boards away. And bring a cotton polo bandage—the horse will need a tourniquet."

"You sure you got him?" I asked Jaz.

"I'm okay," she said. She was stroking along the horse's neck and saying soothing low words. He was standing still again, at least. I could see the thick stream of blood pulsing over the jagged edges of the board.

The horse was starting to shake a little. I ran out of the stall, and across the courtyard to where the thick woolen coolers hung on blanket racks.

Back in the stall I covered him with the two oversized woolen blankets to try to keep him from going into shock.

Then I bent down to try to see if there was any way to extricate his leg. There were scrapes all along the front of his cannon bone, skin and hair peeled away to expose raw skin, but the big cut was up higher, just above the hock.

Just then, Eleanor came running in with a crowbar and a saw. I took the crowbar and started prying away at the board that was entrapping the horse's foot. I had trouble getting good purchase on it—it was slippery with hot blood. I tried twice.

Damn. It slipped just before it felt like it was going to give. I braced my foot against the wall of the stable and threw more weight into it.

The board started to give with a satisfying *crack,* but then I could feel the cold iron slipping through my fingers. The wedge lost its grip on the splintered board, and my arm with the crowbar in it jerked backward, prodding Benedetto hard in the ribs.

Then he just exploded, in fear and pain, and I could see his hooves flashing toward me—one rammed me hard in the shoulder. Then I was rolling in the sawdust, hooves flying above me in all directions—I hid my head and rolled out of the way. None too soon. With one enormous shudder the big plank that had been trapping the horse's foot flew free, taking with it the one below it. It conked me on the back of the neck. I cried out and saw stars. Jaz had kept hold of Benedetto's twitch the whole time and she moved him forward, away from me, and got him subdued again.

For a minute I didn't move, afraid to try. I winced and felt the sore area on my neck gingerly. It seemed to be intact. Slowly, I stood up. Now that the board was loose, I could get a better look at the good-sized gash on Benedetto's near hind leg—spurting out bright red blood in rapid little gusts.

"Get me the bandage," I said to Eleanor. I saw her standing in the corner with the bandage in her hands.

She tossed it to me, and I wrapped it as tight as I could up above the area of the wound, but the cut was in an awkward place, and it seemed like I couldn't get the tourniquet tight enough to control the bleeding.

I took the bandage and tore it into a thinner strip. Then tried again, wrapping it tightly above the hock. Benedetto didn't want to put his weight on that foot—he kept raising the leg, then putting it down just resting lightly on the toe, which made it hard for me to work on him. Finally, the tourniquet was secured and the blood flow subsided to a slow trickle.

I looked over at Eleanor.

"Well, well. I see that someone is competent in a crisis. I have to be honest. I expected less." This was certainly a backhanded compliment if it was one at all.

I looked at the laceration on the horse's leg. It was a little irregular, and relatively deep, but I thought I could quickly suture it up. The quicker it was done, the better, the less scarring there would be.

"I saw that there are some sutures in the vet box," I said. "I can sew him right up for you. The quicker those skin edges are pulled together, the better."

"Absolutely not. No amateur fiddling. I'm sure your intentions are good, but this horse is an Olympic prospect. I've called the vet."

"I know what I'm doing," I said. But I was aware that my protest felt weak. I had nothing to justify my words.

"I appreciate your offer, Clara. I'm sure it is well-meaning. But Franny Baker is on her way over right now."

"Franny Baker?" I was startled to hear a familiar name. Though I hadn't known her well, she had ridden with me on the eventing circuit.

"She's the only vet I use. Thank you for your help. Clara, you can run along. Jazmyn, I want you to keep holding Benedetto until she gets here."

Apparently, Eleanor hadn't noticed the line of perspiration on Jazmyn's lip. It was hard work holding a twitch on a seventeen-hand horse. Jazmyn had both hands gripped firmly on the lead shank, and her hands were up over her head.

Now that the situation was calmed down, I could feel the ache in my occipital bone where the stable board had banged me, the sore shoulder that had been slammed by Benedetto's hoof. But it didn't feel right letting Jazmyn stand there like that, her pregnancy hidden under her big gray sweatshirt. At least here was something I could do.

"Let me hold him for you for a little while," I said, closing my hands around the lead shank.

Jazmyn shot me a grateful look and whispered, "Thanks."

Now that I was standing there, though, I had to think about a different problem. What would happen when Franny Baker showed up?

Would it be possible that she would recognize me after all these years? I stroked Benedetto's neck. The sweat was drying and leaving a sticky white cast to the coat. He seemed calm enough, so I slipped the twitch off his nose and put the chain just under his chin. In repayment, Benedetto relaxed his neck a little and dropped his head lower, brushing the side of my arm with his velvety muzzle.

I looked at the hind leg where the tourniquet was tightly strapped. Leaving a tourniquet on too long could compromise circulation. I could have easily stitched him up, or even put in some holding sutures to control the bleeding while waiting for the vet to come. But here I was nobody, just a hired hand, a stable girl. Of course, nothing was keeping me here, except my inability to screw up the courage to ask Eleanor my question.

I stroked my hand along Benedetto's muscled crest, looking out into the quiet stable yard. Then I forced myself to think again outside of the small stall, the enclosed stable courtyard, and the beautiful solitude of the Norton Hills.

Friday. *Friday.*

Lydia's memorial service. I thought about seeing Mr. and Mrs. Benson, about seeing Gordon. I really did not want to go.

FIFTEEN

Franny Baker drove up in her red truck, all in a hurry because she had a case of colic on the other side of the hill that she needed to get to quickly. She gave no sign of recognizing me, and I am sure I wouldn't have known her either, had I not had the benefit of hearing her name. I had known her as a lithe jumper champion with fiery red hair; now her red hair was cropped short and flecked with gray, and her well-muscled biceps and sunburned face demonstrated the physically demanding nature of her job. She drove the same kind of red truck that horse vets had always driven. It had a camper top fully fitted out with a million little cubbies and drawers. I admired its simplicity, a kind of roving hospital. I had often thought that if I hadn't become a doctor, I would have liked to be a vet, driving around free in my little truck, taking care of big hulking patients that couldn't talk.

Franny set to work stitching up Benedetto and was finished in about five minutes. Watching her work reminded me freshly of the pleasure of doing something that you know how to do well. I enjoyed watching her deft fingers as she skillfully handled the jagged laceration. It would have been a challenge to close well even in the comfort of a well-equipped medical office, but here she was, just squatting in the dusty stable yard in her boots, picking up her equipment off a sterile field she had created on the back of an upturned bucket. That left me standing there, holding the lead rope, thinking about work, where I had always felt I could depend on my skills, where I was competent. But now it was hard for me to think about work without an immediate sinking feeling.

"Clara!" Eleanor was stomping around inside Benedetto's stall. I could hear her administering sharp kicks to the stall boards with the pointed toe of her paddock boot.

"Clara!" The imperious undertone grated on me, but I reminded myself that if you sign on as a stable hand, you might expect to be treated as one.

"Yes?"

She came to the stall door and looked out at me, her blue eyes sharp in her weathered face.

"You are the one who cleaned Benedetto's stall this morning. Part of your responsibility is to examine the stall for safety. The safety of the animal is always primary. I hold you responsible for failing to notice that anything was amiss."

I hadn't noticed anything unusual about the stall this morning. Certainly I was sure that there had been no broken boards or anything like that. I had carefully banked the sawdust up around the wall and had seen nothing.

"I didn't see anything this morning," I said.

"Well, then I presume you weren't looking," she said.

My face grew hot and I started to protest, "No, if something was wrong I would have noticed. It was just a fluke, a freak accident—he was probably just stamping away a fly or something."

"Oh, then you neglected his fly spray this morning."

"No!" I protested. "I put the fly spray on him, first thing. But if something had been wrong with the stall, I would have noticed. It must have just been a freak accident, a fluke. . . ." Even I could hear the hot, defensive tone in my voice. I did not like the sound of those words in my mouth, *a fluke, a freak accident.*

"You know," Franny, who had clearly been listening to this interchange, drawled, "from a vet's point of view, most 'accidents' happen to horses who belong to careless owners"—she looked up at Eleanor and winked—"or the ones with careless stable hands."

"I don't know," Eleanor said. "I think I'm going to need to put you on probation. You said you knew how to take care of horses, and my prize horse gets injured on your watch. Being a stable hand is no laughing matter. I'm going to need to see if you're really up to the task."

By now my cheeks were feverish, and I could feel suppressed tears burning on the backs of my eyelids. *This was incredible. It was so unfair!* It was not my fault that Benedetto had gotten injured. I had seen nothing out of the ordinary. He had kicked his way through a stall board. . . . Maybe it would be better if I just revealed myself and blurted out my accusations now! Confronted her about what she had done to my father, and then went home, went back to work, where at least I knew what I was doing—but then the sinking feeling again as I remembered that I had no work right now, my privileges were suspended. I had no choice—I couldn't even walk away because Franny was still suturing.

So I stood there, head hanging, racking my brain. Had there been anything unusual in the stall this morning? Had I forgotten the fly spray? Finally, Franny finished, and Eleanor told me to go prepare an empty stall for Benedetto until his stall could be repaired.

"And this time," she snapped, "please do a thorough safety inspection before you put him in the stall. Look for loose boards, protruding nails. Check to see that the hay net is hung high enough that he can't get caught in it. Make sure the waterer is working."

Eleanor started to walk out, but I could hear her mumbling. "Call themselves stable hands and don't know the first thing about horses. Impossible. Impossible to find decent help these days."

The rest of the afternoon passed quickly. I spent a couple of hours combing over the new stall, sanding down barely perceptible rough edges with sandpaper, hammering nails that were already flush with the wall. I retightened the screw eyes that held the rubber stall guard. By the time the stall was ready it was as spanking clean as an operating room. Benedetto needed to be walked around the stable yard for fifteen minutes every hour, and then have his gaskin iced where there was swelling from my hasty tourniquet. Eleanor hovered about the whole time, watching me like a hawk, her blue eyes icy. I knew that I was trying to prove myself to her, like I was an intern again, trying to be busier and better than anyone so as to catch the favorable eye of the chief.

It was futile, though, because I was not the person who I seemed to be. But still I tried, frantically, to prove that I was dependable. The best stable girl in the world.

SIXTEEN

There is a principle in medicine that you try to get to the root cause of things. If a person is ill, you want to know what caused it, and what caused the condition that caused it, and so on. Maybe I am temperamentally suited to the practice of medicine because I always think of life that way too. I used to think that everyone was like me, and perhaps many people are, but not everyone is. That is something I learned from Gordon.

I may have mentioned that his parents died in a plane crash, sophomore year. They were foreign-aid workers, both of them, and quite a bit older than average—Gordon was an only child. I know that everyone loves his or her parents, but I sense that Gordon admired them, rather than felt close to them—his parents worked so far out in the bush that most of the time Gordon had to attend schools in other towns. But still, they were his parents, and they were *dead*, and not in some glamorous African accident, but right into the Potomac forty-seven seconds after takeoff. Gone.

Part of why I gravitated to Gordon, hung around, tried to make him my friend, was because of that steep plunge that the airplane took, a rude seventy-five-degree angle into icy water. I thought I could connect to him about it, that I knew something about the way that felt.

After I got to know Gordon, though, I realized that not everyone thought it was that necessary to look for root causes. He said it didn't matter whether the engine blew out or they forgot to deice the wings. It didn't matter if it was pilot error or poor visibility.

"In the end, it's all the same." That was one of Gordon's favorite sayings. But I couldn't accept that. I thought that somehow there was a lack in the quality of his filial love.

I, unlike Gordon, kept up in my quest for root causes. Was it the moment that my father died? Or was it the moment he was barred from practice? Maybe it was five minutes before the surgery, when some piece of preparation was left undone? And what about Captain? What had led me to be down the Norton trail that day? That brought me back to the day before the accident, the day that I was riding in the final qualifying event for the Olympic equestrian trials, the day that I would have come in first place if the judge in the dressage event hadn't said she saw Captain's hindquarters leave the ring for just one step—a disqualifying moment.

Eleanor Prescott Norton scored my dressage test that day and just by adding the columns of numbers, it was clear that I would have had the winning score, but as I came into the final turn, as I rounded past A at the far end from the judge's stand to trot up the centerline for the final halt and salute, Eleanor Prescott Norton said that Captain and I completely left the arena (there is an opening down at that end of the arena, so it is only an imaginary line that we crossed).

Though I was eliminated, I was allowed to complete the event *hors concours*, which means that I was no longer officially part of the competition. I had a clear round in cross-country and stadium jumping, and my test would have put me in first place.

And I did what I would have never normally done; I went to the judge and begged her. I told her that I was in line to qualify for the Olympic trials, and that she was mistaken, that I was certain we had not crossed out of the ring. My father was at the sidelines with a V8 camera and he swore the film proved that I had stayed within the lines. But the truth is, he was standing at an angle that made it impossible to tell, and besides, he had panned the camera at that moment—since my test was almost over, and so clearly flawless—to the felt-covered table in the awards tent, and zoomed in on the trophy and medal that he had been so sure would soon be mine.

But when I begged Ms. Norton, she was implacable.

"Young lady. You are an impressive rider on a beautiful mount. But the rules are the rules, and you stepped out-of-bounds." Eleanor Prescott Norton was a California Dressage Society class-A judge, she sat on the board of the United States Equestrian Team, and she had owned several Olympic medal–winning horses.

I remember exactly the moment that I stood there, rubbing my nose with my white string gloves, elated because I had received a compliment from a woman who was not known to praise lightly, but also crushed, because I could already see the look on my father's face. He had been bragging for six months that his daughter, at the age of fifteen, was certain to ride in the Olympic trials at Pebble Beach.

I knew how it had felt as I came around that last turn at a collected trot and felt Captain's hindquarters swing out a little too far. The very first thing I did was glance up at the judge, and hope against hope that she hadn't seen. In later years, I often wondered if that quick glance, that instinct to bluff my way through or hide, that first gut response, might have revealed a flaw in my character too deep to overcome. I pledged eternal vigilance against this trait, but knew too that deep within me it lay there coiled like a snake.

Did I mention who came in first that day, after I was eliminated? Did I say that it was Lydia, who, surprisingly, had a pretty good run? Of course, her overall record wasn't nearly good enough to get her to the Olympic trials. I believe that was the only event she ever won.

Looking back, I would like to be able to say that it softened the blow of my loss to see her pleasure. I would like that to be true, but I only remember the brown sun-scorched seed of my anger, a little burning ember at the pit of my stomach, and how it stayed with me until the following day. That day, Lydia and I were going to walk the horses in the Norton Hills. That day, I took Captain on a ride and he never came back.

When I finally finished walking Benedetto, and put him in his stall, I headed up for the stable loft, my legs aching from fatigue. When I got up the stairs, I saw Jazmyn, flopped on her back on her cot. The light wasn't turned on and the light in the room was fuzzy with blue twilight. I tried to enter the room softly, but as soon as she heard my footsteps, she swung her legs around and sat up, grimacing and grunting as she did, to accommodate her large belly.

"Did I wake you up? I'm sorry. I thought you were asleep."

"No, I'm not. There's no way I can sleep. I feel like crap. My belly has been aching and I feel all this pressure down there. I was trying to rest, but it keeps waking me up."

Now I was really listening. Aching belly. Pressure. These were classic symptoms of preterm labor.

"How long have you been feeling this way?" I asked. Trying to sound casual, not overly intrusive.

"Well, my back started aching this morning. That bitch Norton made me work my butt off today. All that time you were fussing over her damn 'Olympic prospect' she had me doing everything else! I did all my stalls and all of yours and then I had to rake the courtyard to boot! Rake it! Who the hell ever sees it anyway? Nobody looks at the damn thing except us and the horses, like they care."

All the time I had been so carefully tending to Benedetto, I hadn't even thought about my other duties. Now it turned out it had all been heaped on Jazmyn.

"You should have come and gotten me."

"No way, I could see Norton was hell-bent on punishing you—as if you made him kick the stall board out. . . . I figured I could manage, but now I'm paying for it."

Jazmyn stopped talking and started to breathe heavily. I could see a sheen of perspiration across her forehead.

"Jazmyn," I said. "What are you feeling?"

"Like a stomachache."

"Like labor pains?"

"Like how the hell should I know? I'm not a doctor."

"Have you felt anything like this before?"

She looked at me like she was going to say "none of your business," but thought better of it.

"Well, yeah, I felt something like this, but not this bad."

"Did you talk to your doctor about it?"

"Yeah, she told me to rest more and avoid heavy lifting, and to call if it started again and wouldn't quit."

"Well, then, don't you think you better call her?"

"No way. She tole me that if it keeps going like this I might need to go on bed rest—but I can't go on bed rest because then old Norton would fire me and I wouldn't have anywhere to go."

"Well, that's beside the point. You have symptoms of preterm labor and you need to be evaluated."

"No, that ain't beside the point. That *is* the point. That's how I know that you're rich, even though you ain't saying so. I don't have anywhere to go! I don't suppose you are planning to go back to that rich husband of yours and give me a room out back, now, then, would you?"

"Get up. I'll drive you to the hospital. You need to get checked out."

Jazmyn rolled over and looked at me, head propped on her elbow, other hand running a thoughtful circle over her round belly spidered with purplish striae.

"You're not that bad. But you're a busybody. I got a doctor's appointment tomorrow. Tonight I'm not going anywhere. I'm staying right here on this bed—except I'm gonna go out and get me some Burger King."

"Jazmyn, you really don't have a choice. You have to go. Come on. Get up. I'm taking you."

"No. *You* don't get it. I'm not going. Just save your fucking breath."

I looked at her pretty face with the double chin, her big belly, and her swollen breasts. She didn't really look uncomfortable, didn't seem to be in labor, but then, as a physician, I knew that you couldn't tell just by looking at someone—you had to do an exam, to check. At home, this would be a routine occurrence—rule out preterm labor—a trip to the hospital, a quick evaluation. Most of the time it wasn't labor at all, just fatigue, a sore back, a fed up pregnant body. Some of the time, it was labor and then you tried to stop it, which didn't always work anyway. I looked at her and I weighed my options. First, I wanted to say, "I'm not who you think I am, I am a doctor, and you have to do what I say." Then I thought about threatening to tell Eleanor—but where would that get me? I needed to convince her, somehow, but had a sinking feeling that without my white coat, I wasn't going to get her to do what I wanted. Let's face it—even with the white coat, people do what they want. I've always found that hard to accept, but it is a fact.

Jazmyn heaved herself up out of bed and jammed her feet, without socks, into the worn manurey boots that were lined up next to her bed.

"I'm gonna go get me some fries. You want something?"

Barely shaking my head, I turned my back to her and walked over to the low dormer window. The sun was setting over the ocean, and the sky had turned a brilliant shade of orange. Barely discernible among a grove of pines, just a dark outline against the sky, was the slim spire of Ambler's Chapel.

Lydia's memorial service was tomorrow.

SEVENTEEN

The drive up to Ambler's Chapel snakes in tight switchbacks all the way up the steep hillside right off Peninsula Drive East. I drove down the long driveway, then past the barricaded cliffs. My window was rolled down. I was wearing the slim linen skirt that I had arrived in. My legs were bare, and nicked in a couple of places. All morning my mind had been bouncing around from one sore spot to another—unable to find a comfortable place to rest.

The entrance to Ambler's Chapel was not more than a quarter mile down the road. As I had expected, the parking lot was already jammed with cars. The chapel, which was made of rough-hewn redwood beams and large clear panes of glass, was surrounded by pines. It sat on a narrow ledge of ground, with an unobstructed view of the cliffs. From up here, you could see the actual precipices, their steep white sides cascading downward to the rocky shores several hundred feet below. The parking lot was small and in no time I had joined a crowd of people who were thronging toward the doors of the little chapel. Through the clear panes of the church I could see the Norton Hills and the grove of Italian cypress trees that surrounded Eleanor's house.

All of the pews were already full, so I shuffled into a corner in the back, pressed up against a wall, a potted palm half in front of me. Before I was even aware that I had seen him, I knew Gordon was in the room by the feeling of prickly heat across my forehead. He was seated in the front pew—all I could see was the back of his head. Next to him, two bowed silver heads. The Bensons. There was soft organ music playing, the whispering sounds of paper and shuffling feet. Reassuring church sounds, comforting, the closest to believing in God that I was likely to get.

I looked around at the backs of heads again, looked through the glass walls of the chapel, up at the waving fields of yellow mustard covering the bare hills, down at the rocky cliffs and the blue ocean. It was right that I had come. Walter was the one who always told me that these kinds of things mattered. Formal ceremonies for rites of passage, even for stillbirths and miscarriages. I had always had mixed feelings about this, couldn't see what difference it could possibly make. I allowed myself a glance at the back of Gordon's head, felt that familiar pining *want-it-so-bad-I-can-scream* feeling, followed swiftly by the sickening remembering of why everything was now even more impossible. He turned his head slightly and I craned forward in spite of myself, tickling my nose on the potted palm. I wanted to see his face, but it was hidden from me.

A few more people were pushing their way into the tiny church. The spot next to me, behind the palm, was practically the only standing room left. I looked at the few remaining people coming through the door; an older man, a woman with cropped red hair—with a start, I recognized Franny Baker, looking ill at ease in a cream linen pantsuit. I cringed back behind the palm trying to disappear. Franny was looking around for somewhere to stand, and her eyes grazed across my face momentarily, but she didn't seem to see me. Then I saw her push into a space on the other side of the church, and then lost sight of her.

The minister was a tall thin man of middle age, soft-spoken and uneffusive. The Bensons had stuck to a traditional service, somehow soothing in its predictable rhythm. I let myself slip into the moment, listening more to the tone of the words than their content.

For none of us liveth to himself, and no man dieth to himself . . .

The service didn't seem to be about Lydia, so I was lulled into a feeling of not-thereness as I stood, shifting my weight in the uncomfortable pumps I was wearing, brushing the scratchy palm fronds out of my face, staring at the ropy neck of the minister, which rose above his surplice.

The glass walls of the chapel were so clean that the division between inside and outside was blurred; the rocky cliff faces and the crashing waves seemed so close I could reach out and touch them. Now the minister and congregation were doing a responsive reading, back and forth from his low tones to the louder, deeper, hesitant mumbling of the assembled crowd.

But now it was as though I couldn't see the people assembled around me, it was as though I weren't there at all, as though I were part of the scene outside and no longer inhabited my body.

Blessed are the dead who die in the Lord.

My heart was hammering hard at my collarbone, and my hands were ice. The minister's voice intoned onward.

I will lift up mine eyes unto the hills; from whence cometh my help?

For a moment, I was overwhelmed with certainty. *It wasn't Lydia. It was me!* I had come to my own funeral. There was that same cliff, and the same blowing wheatgrass on the hillsides. Lydia hadn't saved me. I had died, and here I was at my funeral.

I scanned the room certain I would see my mother, feeling a little flicker of hope—the one I thought had finally died away—that I would see my father.

But no. There was Gordon, head bent, wad of Kleenex clutched in his hand. His head was turned slightly so that I could see his profile.

And I was still here, mind, body, and spirit. Ever the survivor. The last man standing. Again.

I steadied myself against the redwood beam behind me, worried that I would faint, or do something histrionic. Maybe I had been standing still for too long; the blood was pooling in my feet, leading to irrational thinking. I looked down at my feet, grown unused to being constrained in thin leather pumps. I tried to let myself be lulled into a feeling of something like peace or closure, but now the feeling was wrecked. Lydia was dead; I was responsible.

Through Jesus Christ our Savior, amen.

The minster stood aside and I saw a middle-aged, balding man wearing a light blue oxford shirt stand up, heavily, holding a paper in his hand. At first he didn't look familiar to me, but then I recognized him—it was Benjamin, Lydia's older brother. I hadn't known him well—he was already away at college when I knew Lydia.

He walked to the front of the small nave and placed a couple of wrinkled sheets on the simple wooden lectern. The sound had changed in the interior of the church, more hushed, expectant.

Benjamin looked down at his paper, then out over the assembled group, then back at his paper, the pause long enough for those of us in the audience to wonder if his courage was failing him.

My sister, Lydia, Benjamin said, clearing his throat, starting softly but then gaining volume, *told me she had already lived long enough when she was only fifteen.*

For the second time that day, sweat stood clammy on my skin and I had a strong feeling that I might pass out. I knew already what Benjamin was going to say, because Lydia herself had already told me the same thing.

Lydia, my sister, is . . . was an extraordinary woman, grown ever smarter and more beautiful from an extraordinary girl. Those of you who have known my sister more recently have probably never heard this story, because she was nothing if not modest. But those of you in this room who knew Lydia for a long time certainly know this story, and I think it is one that illustrates what my sister is . . . was like quite well.

I heard the collective shuffling in the room, of those eager to hear a new story and those eager to hear the story again. Sweat was collecting between my breasts, under my armpits, and between my legs. I wished that I could find a way to slip out unseen, but it would have been impossible. Standing where I was standing, wedged behind the potted palm, I would have drawn so much attention to myself just at the time I didn't want to. So I stood, and tried not to listen, but listened in spite of myself. Benjamin droned on and on, it seemed, the long-ago day, the forgotten ride, the dearest friend, the daring rescue.

But what I'll never forget, Benjamin said, *is what she told me afterwards. A beautiful fresh-faced fifteen-year-old, and she told me, "I've lived as long as I needed to—I lived long enough to save a life. Everything from here on in is just extra. I did what God put me here to do, and so now I can just relax and enjoy whatever's left."*

I heard the crowd stir—admiration, and a shiver of gothic horror about the way things ultimately turned out.

I remember her saying that to me too, at the time. She said, "It doesn't matter if I die now. If I get run over by a truck or something tomorrow, because I've already done what I was put on the earth to do."

I didn't get that sentiment at all. Didn't have the slightest idea what she was talking about. It was morbid, seemed like a death wish, and made me supremely uncomfortable. I remember we were sitting on two alfalfa bales up in the hayloft of her barn, just chitchatting about this and that, watching the dusty bits of hay floating in the shaft of light that came through the open barn window, and then she said, "It doesn't matter if I die now, because I was there when I was supposed to be there to save you."

She was beaming and looked all relaxed and nonchalant about it, picking little alfalfa leaves out of where they had fallen in her hair.

I remember that it seemed really wrong to me, but I couldn't quite put my finger on where the flaw was in her logic. I felt certain that

Lydia wasn't put on this earth to save me, but I couldn't think of a convincing way to contradict her, just knew that when she said it, it made me feel all hot and squirmy inside.

"Just shut up. Shut up. Just shut up, will you?" I said. I remember stopping then for a minute, staring at her—she had a beautiful face, just like an Ivory soap commercial. I was trying to think of the way that I could hurt her the most. I looked at her—she was smiling at me, the late-afternoon sun casting a shine on her hair.

"What's the big deal anyway?" I said. I stared at her wide-open face, full of trust. "You should have just let go."

She didn't answer when I said that to her. She just stared at me, blue eyes reddening and filling, lower lip quivering. I sat there looking at Lydia—she was pale as a seraph, and the sun through the window haloed her head in a bright burst of light. That is the first moment I ever remember looking inside myself and seeing what an abyss might look like. Something dark, and not nice at all. Maybe the cliff was inside me after all and I was doomed, like Sisyphus's rock, to perpetual falling.

Our friendship was effectively over then. She didn't know it then, or ever, I guess. We kept in touch—she called occasionally, sent notes, and birthday cards. But I decided right then and there to cut her out. Grabbing my wrist and snatching me from over the precipice was not going to give her the right to be my savior.

Make you perfect in every good work to do his will, working in you that which is well pleasing in his sight . . .

It was over.

Suddenly the minister was walking briskly toward the back of the church, and people were standing and gathering up purses and jackets, and I was standing behind the potted palm trying to decide if I should bolt for the door and try to leave first or hang around and try to slip out unnoticed near the end. Then just as suddenly, I realized that I wouldn't have a choice. The Bensons and Gordon stood and filed out. I waited for Gordon to spot me, knowing that he had never been in a room for more than five seconds without finding me and catching my eye, but this time he just kept walking, eyes fixed far out into the distance, out toward the horizon over the ocean, and Mr. and Mrs. Benson walked out together, both looking like they would crumple if they weren't holding each other up. I waited behind my palm tree until the group was thinning out. I had been looking for Franny but hadn't seen her, so was taken aback when I entered the flow of people leaving the church and I found myself elbow to elbow with Franny Baker. I studiously looked at my feet, and tried not to glance at her—even if she had seen me, how likely was it that she would recognize me? I was dressed differently, and again, she wouldn't have expected to see the stable hand here. I tried to hold back and let a few people pass in front of me.

I got in the receiving line, rehearsing in my mind what words I could say, but all I could think of was "I'm sorry for your loss." I couldn't imagine what the Bensons might say to me, but I steeled myself, thinking whatever it was I would just take it.

As I approached Mr. and Mrs. Benson, I realized how small they seemed, and how old.

I could tell my hand was shaking. I put it out in front of me.

"Clara Raymond," I said. Waiting. Afraid of her response.

Sarah Benson put her small cool hand in mind, her expression like a fish swimming in an aquarium.

"Clara Raymond," she said in a flat voice, the same voice she had used with the group in front of me. "So good of you to come."

I started to feel clammy again, hesitated, tongue-tied, staring into her face.

"I just, I just wanted to say . . ." No words came. How do you say to someone's mother, *I'm sorry I didn't save her.*

But Mrs. Benson was already looking past me, toward the group behind me. With a start I realized that she wasn't thinking about me at all.

Then I heard my mother's words drumming in my brain—

Clara Raymond, you are not the subject of this conversation.

Except my mother was wrong. This time it *was* about me. This time I lost my privileges. This time I was hiding, ashamed to be seen.

But no, the memorial service was about closure—wasn't that what Walter was always trying to tell me? I saw Gordon, just beyond me, surrounded by several people. Without forethought, I ducked out of line and headed out into the sunshine through the side door. I had run out of courage, felt like I couldn't see him right here right now.

Closure, closure. I repeated it as I walked through the parking lot, thinking that saying it might make it true. Maybe for starters, I could be done with the cliff. Resolutely, I kept my eyes trained on the pavement in front of me as I walked down the hill, determinedly blind to the waves on the rocks in front of me—so close now that I could feel a faint spray of salt water dampening my face.

I had almost reached my car when Gordon's hand encircled my arm, or I think I felt the heat of his hand approach me first, and then felt his palm grasp my biceps. At that exact moment, I stumbled, tripping over my shoe or some speck of gravel in the road, and without missing a beat, he righted me and simultaneously drew me close.

"Clara. No, don't . . . don't go. You're running away again."

I looked into his eyes and then wished I hadn't. Too many things reflected there—the red rims and fat lids of sleepless crying nights. The familiar deep blue flecked with gold like little fingernails, the new dark shadows of pain in their depths. The pleading look—*Stop, I need you. I need you. Don't go.*

"I . . ." Words failed me. "I . . . I'm glad I could make it to the service. It . . . was beautiful. A beautiful service. I'm glad I could be there." Falling back on platitudes because I had no idea what else to say.

"Clara," he said, then stopped again, gripping my arm just a little tighter. Without thinking, I stepped in close toward him, then just as soon stepped back, remembering where we were, at his wife's funeral, and suddenly the small distance between us seemed to widen to a gulf, a canyon. I tried to loosen my arm from his grip. I looked away from his face, looked somewhere around the knob of his collarbone. I needed to say something, but what?

"How's the baby?" I said.

"Clara," he said. I had forgotten that the baby was also Clara.

"Yes, how's she doing? I heard they were weaning her to room air."

A shadow crossed his face. "No," he said. "They said they might try to wean her from the oscillator to a regular vent, but then they decided not to. Doc Blank says she can't breathe on her own, but I don't think so. They're just not giving her a chance."

Now I put my own hand on his arm and said, "Gordon. She is a very sick baby. I know that. Maybe . . ." I said this as gently as I could. "Maybe . . . we should talk about that sometime."

None of the emotions that I could see on Gordon's face looked anything like Gordon. It was like some person who didn't know him had inhabited his body, but was playing the role all wrong.

He looked at me with a kind of desperation I had never seen in him before. I was trying hard not to want him, but I didn't know how. I wanted him desperately, now more than ever—wanted him so hard that the small distance between us seemed to cause physical pain.

"Clara, I need you. You're my oldest friend, but you're holding out on me. Please don't hold out on me." Probably in spite of himself, he reached out and stroked his hand against my cheek for just a second, like a feather drifting past as it falls from a bird in flight. In spite of myself, I put my hand over the spot he had touched and held it there pressing on it.

"Clara, won't you come? I need to see you before I go."

"I just . . . I just . . ." Time to blurt. "Oh, God, Gordon. I just can't do the reception. I'm sorry."

"No. I mean, of course. I didn't mean that. I mean after. I'm not leaving until after midnight—catching the red-eye. I'm staying at the gatehouse until then. Do you know where that is?"

Incomprehension swept over me like a cloud passing over the sun.

"The Norton Gatehouse?"

"Well, yeah, I think that's what they called it. The big pink gatehouse, just down the road. You can't miss it. Just for a little while."

I nodded my assent still without fully looking at him, then ripped myself away from him like a Band-Aid from hair. The car parked right next to us started to back up. I recognized Franny Baker's red head, as she backed out of the spot and pulled away.

EIGHTEEN

When I got back to the stables, the courtyard was neatly raked and the stable hung in the stupor of midafternoon, silent except for stomping hooves, whisking tails, and the loud buzzing of a single horsefly. The church, out on its cliffside precipice, had caught a bit of breeze, but up here, the air was surprisingly hot and sullen. Benedetto's head hung over the Dutch door, one eye closing lazily, but he lifted his head and pricked his ears forward at the sound of my footsteps. I walked over to him, reaching up to stroke his satiny crest. The afternoon sun was catching his stable door, and his coat reflected bright reddish gold in the sun. He was the same color as Captain had been, bright chestnut with white markings on his face and legs. Flashy, they had called Captain, and so was Benedetto. Although he was heavier boned—Benedetto was a Hanoverian. Captain had been a Thoroughbred—bought green from the track as a three-year-old. Rescued from the track, we used to say, since the horses that didn't get sold for riding went straight to the knackers to be made into dog food and glue. Thinking of the track made me think of Jazmyn—the courtyard's neat raking could mean only one thing—that Eleanor had come and asked her to redo it after I had left.

The frustration from the night before rose up in me again. I knew that Jazmyn could go into preterm labor. This was something I was trained to know how to try to prevent. But here, outside the hospital walls, I was a powerless bystander, and it only reinforced my feeling that hiding here was unethical, and I chastised myself, once again, for stalling about confronting Eleanor. I unlatched Benedetto's stall door and went in, shoving on his shoulder to make him move out of the way; then I did a thorough check of the stall—waterer working, hay net tied up out of harm's way, no loose boards, nails, or screws. I checked his halter, and the screw eyes that the rubber stall guard hooked on to. Benedetto looked at me incuriously, swishing his tail occasionally, although the flies weren't bothering him, since I had coated him with fly spray in the morning. I stepped back out into the sunlight, relatching his stall, double-checking it to see if it was latched, finding the routine soothing, like setting up a tray table for a delivery, checking it, then rechecking it to see if I have everything I need.

Up in our shared room it was hot and close, and Jazmyn was flung out on her rumpled unmade bed, flat on her back, snoring. I sat down on my bunk. It was still another hour until mucking and feeding time. I went to the windows, trying to force them open. It was quite hot now outside and there was a Santa Ana wind. Fire weather, my mother used to call this. I looked at the Italian cypresses and saw that the leaves were dusty and dry looking.

I lay back down on my bunk, thinking that maybe I could close my eyes and rest a little, but sleep wouldn't come. I was trying to think about work—the clinic contract coming up, the news from Walter about the lab results—but I couldn't concentrate on work. It seemed fuzzy and distant, almost not real. The longer I was here, the more impossible it seemed that I would be able to go back and start up again as Dr. Raymond. I felt like someone who had gone into the witness protection program, and gotten a whole new set of identity cards.

It was a familiar feeling.

We left California almost immediately after my father's funeral, went to stay with my mother's sister, who lived back east. By the time my mother and I had driven all the way across the country, from Los Angeles to Avondale, Pennsylvania (in the used Ford Pinto without air-conditioning that she had gotten when the Jaguar disappeared), I was transformed. I was no longer Clara Raymond, the doctor's daughter from Jacaranda Canyon. I had turned into another Clara Raymond—the one wearing her old friend Lydia's cast-off hand-me-downs.

The funny thing is, I didn't miss the old Clara that much. Just as I didn't miss my old mother, the one with the silk dresses and Jackie O. glasses. I never tried to tell people, like some old White Russian empress, all about how privileged I used to be. The old Clara was like a neighbor who had moved away. I missed her a little when I thought about her, which wasn't often . . . but at other times, I thought that I was happy enough to be rid of her.

My mom worked the evening shift at the hospital. She came home tired, smelling of latex and antiseptic, and full of stories about all of the people she had cared for that day. My father had never talked about his patients at all—he had come home from the hospital often late, or sometimes not at all, still smelling like himself, and sometimes with a story about one of the doctors, but I never really thought about what he actually did while he was there. With him, it was being a *doctor* that had seemed important. Not what he actually did.

My mom, though, it was pretty obvious what she was doing was hard work—she cut her hair shorter and stopped dying the gray out and put on some weight. But somehow she seemed more real to me, and so by extension, I felt more real to myself. Sometimes I used to try to imagine the roads that connected Pennsylvania to California. I knew that there were roads that unspooled and unspooled without stopping until the one place was connected to the other in hard and unambiguous real space. But to me, it always seemed that there was a total disconnect between the two places. Here and there. Then and now. Who I am now and who I used to be.

I stared up at the ceiling, noting the water cracks, thinking about how wrong it seemed to connect Gordon to Lydia, and then to connect Gordon to this place and then to me. Like a kid's dot-to-dot that doesn't follow the numbers in the correct order and so fails to make a picture.

Should I go to him? Just the thought and I had to grip the side of the mattress to steady myself. Hadn't he asked me? So shouldn't I go out of a sense of duty? Weren't we, above all else, old friends? In the back of my mind, I could hear that thrumming sound I get when I know that my logic is off, but I tried not to listen to it. Guiltily, I also realized that I had not checked my phone since I had gotten back from the funeral.

I could feel that someone was looking at my back, so I rolled over to see Jazmyn's round face, flushed from sleep and from the stifling heat in the room, staring at me, her chin propped on her hand.

"Hey, Jaz," I said, rolling over and reaching for my phone.

"Some guy named Walter has been trying to get ahold of you."

"And how exactly would you know that?"

"Well, duh. I answered your phone."

I flipped over and stared at her, mad. "You had no right to answer my personal phone."

"Oh, for chrissakes, keep your socks on, girl. I was trying to sleep and it kept ringing and ringing. You're the one who told me I needed to rest. For the baby, you know."

I stared at her round sleepy face. She was just an overgrown kid really, with a soft hint of a double chin and sleep-flattened hair.

"Jazmyn. Please do not touch my phone, even if I'm not here. You don't need to answer it. It will pick up messages for me."

"That's *him*? Right?"

"Walter?"

"Yeah, that's *him*, isn't it? I could just tell from talking to him that he's your man."

"You *talked* to him?"

She shrugged.

I sighed. "Look, Jazmyn, can you just tell me what he said."

She giggled. "I think he thought I was you."

"What did he say, Jaz?"

"Alls he said was, 'Clara, I have some stuff I really need to talk to you about.'"

My stomach dropped. Anything urgent was not likely to be good. "And what did you tell him?" *That I was posing as a stable hand?*

"I told your sweetie that you had went somewhere and that you'd be coming back soon. And he said, 'Well, can you just tell her to call me?'"

"He's not my sweetie," I said, irritable that I had to discuss this with her at all.

"Well, then you're breaking his heart, 'cause you sure as hell are his."

Stupidly then my face turned bright red, making it even more useless to deny it. Walter held me in high regard—or at least he always had until now. I also admired him. He was sixteen years my senior. Divorced after twenty-four years. A grown son. A bald head. My business partner. I tried to change the subject.

"You shouldn't have been out there raking that courtyard, Jazmyn. Have you felt any more contractions?"

"Oh, they were getting really bad while I was raking. I had to do it all hurry-up before Franny Baker got here."

"Franny Baker?"

"Then after I all rushed, it turned out she was running late. Had to go to a funeral—I mean for a person, you know, not for a horse."

The window that I had shoved open had starting banging with the hot dry wind, and it wasn't helping to cool the room anyway, so I stood up to close it. Down in the courtyard, I could see Franny, now back in her normal vet garb—blue jeans, a white polo shirt, and hiking boots. She was leaning up against a wall in the shade of a bottlebrush tree, talking to Eleanor. I leaned forward to grab the errant casement window before it banged again, and heard a couple of scattered words float up to me. I could have sworn that one of the words was *Clara*, and one was *Captain*, then just as soon was sure that my ears were playing tricks on me.

I fastened the window back up tight, trapping more hot air in the arid room. I felt as trapped as the air in the room. I wanted to talk to Walter, but I could see from the way that Jazmyn was settled there that she was not going to give me any privacy.

"Make sure you're drinking enough water," I called over my shoulder.

I headed out into the hallway, and into the small, not too clean water-stained bathroom in the hall. It was just a cubicle: a toilet, a small rusted sink, an eroded rubber stopper on a chain. I pulled down my jeans, sat down on the toilet, which rocked slightly beneath me, and emptied my bladder. Then still sitting there, pants around my ankles, I called Walter, heard his warm and familiar voice, and then practically whispered into the phone.

This is what had become of me in the just over a week since I lost Lydia. Hiding out in a bathroom stall whispering into a phone. It was even hotter and more airless in the toilet cubby and there was a vague rank odor in the air, probably from Jazmyn's incessant vomiting.

"It's Clara," I said, as softly as I could say it, and even across that distance, and to where I was sitting, I heard his voice like two big hands steadying me on my shoulders.

"Clara, it's good to hear your voice." Solid, everyday, always the same Walter. "Are you ever coming home?" he said. "Or do I have to come and get you myself?" I didn't answer, so he kept talking.

"Listen, I talked to Dick Blank over in the NICU today. Apparently that baby hasn't improved at all—she's still totally dependent on a respirator. She may have some residual brain stem activity, but that's it. She keeps spiking temps—they've amped and gented the hell out of her, but there's nothing happening. . . ."

"Bottom line?" I whispered, feeling like even the full sound of my voice might cause me to cleave in two.

"Bottom line? The dad's been pushing for every possible intervention. Save the baby. That kind of thing. But he's been out of town for twenty-four hours—*wife's funeral, Clara, just so you know*. Dick's hoping that he will have gotten some distance. He'd really like the dad to let him stop all the heroics and just try and let things happen the way they're going to happen."

"She's going to die," I said. It wasn't a question. It never had been.

"I'm not God, Clara, but you know, the prognosis at this point . . ."

"I know," I whispered.

"Listen, Clara. I don't mean to get too personal, but are you all right? Do you want me to . . . come or something? Do I need . . ." There was a silence on the phone, dead air, static. The rest of the sentence he just blurted, words falling on top of one another. "Do you want me to come out there, wherever you are, *and bring you home?*"

There had been many times, and this was one of them, when I had wondered how Walter's ex-wife had ever let him get away.

"No, really, that's okay, Walter," I said, finding my voice again. "I'm getting ready to come home again now. Just tying up some loose ends. Getting ready to leave. Thank you, though, really, thank you."

"Well, I figured you could find your way, Clara. It's just that . . ." I heard emotion clutter up his throat, almost cutting off his words.

"What is it?"

"It's just that I have been a little worried about you. Thought maybe you needed . . . some moral support."

"No," I said quickly. "I'm fine. It's time for me to get out of here. I want to come home."

"Clara . . ."

"Yes?"

"I really miss you."

My heart thudded too hard, then missed a beat.

"I miss you too," I said. I forced lightness into my voice, but still felt embarrassed that I had revealed more emotion than I meant to. "I miss everyone. Please tell all the girls in the office I said hello."

I punched the off button on my phone and stared at the little orange-stained sink, at my bare knees, at the toilet paper roll that was hanging askew, and I wondered how much lower I could go.

NINETEEN

After I talked to Walter, I lay down on my bunk again, and I must have fallen asleep, because all of a sudden the light, now hazy and yellow, was slanting into the room at a different angle. If anything, it was even hotter now. I could smell the tang of horse manure rising up through the floorboards. I glanced at Jazmyn's bed. She was asleep again, curled on her side now, the hair along her hairline clinging to her face in damp tendrils. I looked at my watch, four fifteen. Both of us should have already been down at the stable fifteen minutes ago.

I jumped up, smoothed down my hair. I needed to wake Jazmyn but hated to do so. She obviously needed the rest, after spending the hot midday raking the courtyard. Could I start late and still do all of my chores and all of Jazmyn's without attracting notice? I didn't want to get her in trouble. Momentarily indecisive, I took a step toward her, then stepped back again.

I turned and bounded down the steps, determined to do all the work in double time. Once in the courtyard, I saw Benedetto, ears pricked forward, eyes looking at me. He knew my footsteps now. Then I just set to work, stall by stall, banking the sawdust, wheeling out the soiled bedding and dumping it out on the manure pile, then liming the stall floors, the fine powdery lime getting into my nostrils and making my eyes water.

Thrumming on the back of my eyelids, like a dull headache, were my awareness of Gordon's invitation, and the memory of my resolve to confront Eleanor about my father. I tried to focus on the positive part of what I was doing, looking after Jazmyn, since obviously no one else was going to do so. I was doing her work for her so she could rest. The talk with Eleanor could wait until later—and Gordon—I just let it buzz dully around my head while I steadied myself in pure motion—lift the shovel, wheel the wheelbarrow, unlatch and then carefully relatch the stall. It was just a few minutes after five when I finished. Then I started with the feeding, carefully measuring the oats and flaxseed, and tossing flakes of hay down from the loft into the steel feeders. There was still a hot wind whipping around the courtyard.

I was measuring out the last scoop of rolled oats when Eleanor came striding into the courtyard.

"Jazmyn?" she called out, her voice rising with an imperious lilt.

I could see her through the open window of the hayloft, but I don't think she could see me. I wanted to try to find a way to cover for Jazmyn, but I knew that Eleanor was a persistent woman who was not easily distracted.

"Jazmyn," she repeated louder, this time letting a hint of disapproval enter her voice. She ran a tight ship. No doubt about that. I did admire her for it too. She was absolutely diligent about every aspect of the way those horses were cared for. The barn was in tip-top shape. Well, as long as the work got done, what difference did it make who did it? I stepped out of the shadows and peered through the open window.

"She's not feeling well," I said. "But don't worry. I'm just finishing the last feed now. The stalls are already done."

"I should expect so," she said. "It's five minutes past five. I demand very little of you girls, you know. Feeding and cleaning twice a day. It's not much. You're finished at ten in the morning and don't start again until four in the afternoon. I give you three meals a day and a roof over your head and the chance to live in a wholesome environment. I expect you to do what I say. If you are not feeling well, please limit that to the hours between ten and four—you are free to be as sick as you want at that time."

She stopped looking at me and looked up at the window of our room—the one that had been banging and that I had fastened shut.

"Jazmyn?" she said again impatiently. With the window shut and the wind rattling the roof of the barn it was likely that Jazmyn didn't hear her.

She turned back to me.

"When you're finished, I want to see you up at the house, Clara. Come up from the kitchen. Come right up the back stairs."

As she left, I was surprised at how angry I felt. Angry at the way she felt free to boss us around—the resentment of the underling, a feeling that as a doctor I was almost never obliged to feel. I remember seeing it in my mother sometimes. When she came home and slammed her purse down on the counter, obviously bone tired, and told me they were making her work Christmas, *again*. Or when she told me about some doctor screaming at her for awakening him in the middle of the night for orders, then screaming at her again that she should have awoken him sooner.

Clearly Eleanor Norton had not the slightest regard for this poor girl's welfare. Jazmyn was upstairs, asleep, at risk of preterm labor. I knew that the Jazmyns of the world, single working girls with bad jobs, had four times the risk of middle-class married women of going into preterm labor. I knew that there was something painfully and sublimely unfair about the fact that fresh-skinned young women of means had the fewest problems in pregnancy, and that girls like Jazmyn, who lived on Burger King and earned minimum wage, would face more than their fair share of problems. I jabbed the metal scoop into the rolled oats angrily, stirring up the fine dust that got into my nostrils and made me sneeze.

Here was a woman who had absolutely everything—a grand oceanfront estate, a stable full of horses, and a bevy of poor working people at her beck and call. She didn't even have the milk of human kindness running through her veins at all. It was plain as the nose on my face that the girl was pregnant—Eleanor must've known, and yet was pretending not to know. According to Jazmyn, the last girl, the one whom I had replaced, had been pregnant too, and Eleanor had tossed her out into the street! That's the kind of thing we were up against, Walter and I, when we took care of the clinic patients—

What was going on with the clinic anyway? I hadn't even asked. It had always been a labor of love for us, to care for the needier pregnant patients, the ones who didn't have private insurance to pay for private doctors. We had assumed this burden at significant expense to ourselves—of course, Walter had been hit even harder than me, after that one case. . . .

The memory of that case, and its aftermath, shuddered through me. Walter and I had already weathered something pretty terrible together, and the way that he handled it, rock solid, made me only that much more aware of my own inadequacy in a similar situation.

The sound of Benedetto stomping and pacing in his stall below the hayloft brought me back to the present. He was waiting for his food, and I was daydreaming. I poured the last scoop of rolled oats into the rubber bucket and headed down the stairs to his stall, where as I poured the grain into the bottom of his metal feeder, I lingered for a moment in the quiet of the stall, my hand resting companionably on the big horse's muscular shoulder. It was a feeling, a posture, a set of sounds and smells, that had once been so familiar as to seem completely natural, almost inborn. I could feel myself falling under the spell of this big horse, taking unexpected pleasure in the simple rituals of caring for him. I had long ago stopped remembering the pain, the shattering loss I had felt, when I lost Captain. But now, it had come back to me exactly how it had been. But that pain had stood alone, distinct, for only a brief time before it was subsumed in the whirlwind of losing my father.

I took a last careful look around Benedetto's stall. Nothing amiss, everything safe. For a moment, I felt content, but that contentment was quickly replaced by a rush of longing. It took me a moment to realize what I was pining for, and then it came to me, like a lost love remembered—I wanted to ride again.

It was time for me to go up to meet Eleanor in the big house. I steeled myself for the idea of confronting her, and then felt myself waffling—maybe just one more day. . . .

Maybe tomorrow I would have the courage to get on the horse and ride him. *Maybe tonight I would go see Gordon.* I carefully latched the horse's stall behind me and headed out of the stable courtyard down the path to the big house, patting my hair down and wiping my sweaty, dusty forehead in an effort to look presentable. Inside the thick stucco walls of the stable it had been slightly cooler, but out here on the lane, the sun was beating down hard, and the hot wind came in fits and spurts, kicking up dust that stung my eyes.

I had made up my mind. It was not because of Gordon, nor for the horse. I was going to stay here for a few more days to take the load off Jazmyn. It seemed like one small positive thing I could do. If, skirting around the edges of my mind, I was wondering if this was a rationalization, I didn't see it at the time.

I was simply doing what I did best. I was the little boy with his finger in the dike—holding back catastrophe by using the scientific method, telling myself that I was making decisions that were methodical, logical, and precise.

TWENTY

The last really clear images I have of my father are from the morning before the accident, Captain's accident. That, of course, was the day after the debacle at the Norton Bend Horse Trials.

My father was sitting on our brown corduroy couch in the family room. The rattan shades were pulled down over the big sliding glass doors to cut down on the glare from the pool. He was watching the super-8 of my dressage test over and over again, screening it up against the white wall of the room. The *tick-tick-tick*ing of the movie projector was driving me crazy.

My father hadn't shaved that morning. He was wearing a blue nylon tracksuit and had a vaguely rank beery smell, as though he had tossed and turned all night, sour at the thought of injustice.

In the clip that he kept screening over and over again, Captain was gleaming like burnished gold in the morning sun. His mane was braided and then fixed with white adhesive tape; his white stockings were whitened with cornstarch; his tail floated silkily behind him. And I looked no less perfect, clad in my black hunt coat, canary britches, and custom-made boots.

"You got robbed!" my father kept saying, over and over, from his position on the sofa. Each time it ended, he would stand up and rewind the film, and get it ready to screen the clip again. Every time, I would see him leaning forward, just as I came around the bend past the K marker, toward A. We looked in perfect control at the sitting trot: Captain was alert, composed, on the bit, and I sat tall in the saddle, with a supple seat—and I can hear the voice of my father repeating triumphantly on the film, "She's got it! She's got it!"

Then, just as Captain and I were getting ready to turn up the centerline, my father made a fatal mistake, and he panned triumphantly over to the judge's booth, where just fleetingly, you could see Eleanor Prescott Norton sitting in a straight-backed chair, a clipboard on her lap, then on to the trophy tent, where the Norton Bend Horse Trials cup was on display, names of the horse and rider winners engraved into its sides, dating back to 1956. Then just as quickly it was back to me in the center of the arena, Captain poised in a perfectly square halt, and I was saluting the judge, head bowed, reins clasped in my left hand, right hand—dazzling white in the string glove—resting on my canary thigh, and you could hear my father's voice crowing triumphantly on the film again, "We've got it!! We've got it!! We're going all the way."

Each time I passed by the family room my father called out to me, "Clara, you got robbed!"

I knew what he wanted from me. He wanted me to go into that darkened room and sit on the couch and run that film over and over dissecting all the different ways that I had been gypped, had, and otherwise thwarted by our newfound nemesis—Eleanor Prescott Norton. But I felt hot and guilty inside—I remembered that moment when I had felt his hindquarters swing out, when I had had a moment's doubt and looked up at the judge's booth to see if she was looking. I wished to God that my father had held a steady hand for just another moment, so that I could have seen Captain go around that corner and then known for sure if he had left the arena or not. Because as it was, I was left wondering, at the most fundamental level, about myself.

Had Ms. Norton not judged that I stepped out of the ring, I would have won the competition hands down. The eventual winner, Lydia, hadn't even been close. The cross-country course had been challenging, and there had been very few clear rounds. As my father was fond of saying, Lydia's horse was "a packer." She was scared to death over the big outdoor jumping courses, but if she could just manage to hang on for dear life, she usually made it around. But in the dressage test, where the horse and rider performed a delicate dance, her scores were always mediocre. Lydia was a tense rider with little feel, and she always seemed slightly nervous when she rode. So Lydia, with a mediocre dressage score, down in the middle of the pack somewhere, had managed to go clean on cross-country and stadium jumping, and had surprisingly come out on top.

I had watched the awards ceremony. Because it was the Norton Horse Trials, there was a lot of pomp and ceremony. The winners dismounted and stood up on blocks as they received their medals, and Lydia was grinning delightedly as she held the large silver cup above her head. Then they remounted their horses and took a victory gallop, the large medals, on blue, red, and yellow satin ribbons, thumping wildly against the riders' chests as they circled the ring. As I remembered this scene, I was startled to remember who had come in second that day, a blood bay Connemara pony with a feisty redheaded rider—Franny Baker won the silver medal. I have no idea who won the bronze.

I couldn't stand being in the house with my father's movie show going, so I went down to the barn to take care of Captain. He stood placidly watching me with a steady eye, seeming at that moment to me a lot more loving than my father. Outside, in the warm morning air, the events of the day before didn't seem so important.

"Oh, there you are, Clara." Lydia had come around the corner of the barn. "I figured you'd be here. Are you gonna ride Captain today? Or are you just going to let him rest?"

"Yeah, I'm gonna ride. I don't want him to stiffen up." I was feeling self-righteous. I would do the right thing—she would no doubt prefer to slack off.

"Gonna ride with me?"

"I guess," she said. "I guess I should."

"Great. I'm going down the Norton trail."

I knew Lydia didn't like to ride out on the trails. Her horse was a little spooky and she preferred the security of the ring. "Why don't you come with me?"

Lydia looked at me, doubt screwing up her forehead. She liked to be agreeable, but she hated the trail.

"It'll be fun," I said.

"Well . . . Suuure. But let's only go as far as Peacock Flats."

"Right," I said to her. "Only as far as the flats."

It was a long ride from where we lived—down Jacaranda Canyon trail, then down behind the fire station toward Peacock Flats. It was late spring then. The fields were still green, not disked up and brown as they would be later on into the summer. Lydia and I rode along side by side. I had hopped on Captain bareback and was riding with no safety helmet, so my long thick hair was whipping around my face. Lydia was fully tacked up and had her safety helmet on. Her body posture was stiff and tentative, and she kept tight hold on the reins. Her horse would occasionally spook on the trail, taking an unexpected leap or hop in an awkward direction

As we headed down toward Peacock Flats, there was a slight breeze and the air was pleasant and mild. In front of us in all directions was the Pacific, the gray indistinct lines of Catalina Island visible in the distance. The hillsides were variegated, some fields of tall grass scattered profusely with goldenrod, others a harmonious blend of dense low-lying chaparral, bluish green to gray, like a natural patchwork.

All this, to my fifteen-year-old eyes, was just as natural as breathing. I was not thinking about the beauty of the day—I was thinking about my dressage ride, about that moment when Captain did or didn't swing out of the arena for a stride or two. How could it be that Lydia had happened to win? She didn't need to win; she didn't expect to win.

We were quiet until we got to Peacock Flats—so-called because there were peacocks, released from someone's estate, that had established themselves in the wild. It was nothing more than a flat outcropping on the terraced hills leading down toward the ocean, with four or five lone pine trees incongruously sticking out on the otherwise treeless horizon. We rode up under their spreading branches and slid off the horses, taking a moment's respite from the hot sun. From this vista, you could see the pink house, down in the distance. It looked like something out of a fairy tale, perched out alone on the bluff, completely surrounded by spiky evergreens. Next to it, there was a perfect stable with private rings around it, everything painted spick-and-span like something from a movie set.

Lydia and I used to ride out to the flats all the time to hunt for peacock feathers, before she got the new horse and didn't want to go out on the trails anymore. Out of habit, I guess, we got off the horses and starting shuffling around under the pines looking for peacock feathers. There didn't seem to be any, though, just dusty pine needles and bits of broken branches.

I wasn't really aware of our silence, but I guess Lydia was, because she seemed nervous when she broke it.

"Um, Clara, I just wanted to say . . ."

"If it's about yesterday, just drop it," I said. I didn't trust my voice not to come out all funny-sounding.

"Well," she said hesitantly, "I know it really sucks that you won't get to go to the trials this time, but I'm sure you'll get a shot at it next time, Clara, and when you're older you'll have a chance to actually make it."

I knew she was right. At fifteen, I was too young to be picked for the Olympic team—the Olympic riders were much older and had several horses and did nothing but ride full-time. I had just been vying for the chance to ride in the trials—no one had expected that I would be a real contender. I hadn't thought it was that important—until I saw my father's face. When they announced that I was eliminated, his face crushed in, making his chin look wrong-shaped, and his eyes looked at me like I don't know what. That's when I realized that it was a lot more important than I had thought, and the moment too when not winning became unbearable.

"A lot of people think that you never did leave the arena. That you shouldn't have been eliminated at all, and the judge just didn't see it right. But you did . . . step out . . . didn't you?" It was a question. Her face was in shadows under the pine boughs, and the blue ocean that lit up behind it was so bright that it made me blink. "Because I'll be happier about winning if I know it was fair and square."

Suppressed rage flipped over in my stomach like a sleeping cat. I stared out toward the ocean, aware that my face felt frozen.

"Let's ride out to the cliffs."

"No!" said Lydia. "I don't want to go down there. Greystoke will get all spooky out there."

"I'm sick of it here. I want to ride to the cliffs." I felt like a cannonball down in the chute, could hear the wick crackling in my ears.

"I don't like that trail. It scares me. It's too close to the cliff."

"Well, then stay here," I said. "But when we get back, I'll tell your mom that we split up out here."

"Oh, Clara, you can't. I'll get in trouble. You know we're not allowed to ride out here alone. What if one of us falls? No one would know."

"Well, then come with me, Lydia," I said. "Just to keep me company, we only have to do the low loop once." I kept my voice light and even now, friendly persuasion.

She looked torn. Both of our families had a hard and fast rule about trail riding alone, especially out here, where the trails were almost always empty and there were no houses around for miles. I tried to push my advantage.

"Well, I'm going," I said, vaulting back up onto Captain's back, tossing her a look of challenge. "Do what you want."

Lydia gathered up her reins, and pointed her toe into the stirrup and swung up then, holding the reins just a hair too tight, so that Greystoke jigged nervously in place as she adjusted herself into the saddle.

"Can't we just head back towards home?" she pleaded.

I looked back up the trail: it led in gradual switchbacks up the side of the barren hillsides until you could see the edges of the landscaped suburban yards that abutted the Norton Hills. I looked down the trail to where it looped gracefully past the big pink house. You couldn't see from where we were, but the path crossed the road and ran along the edge of the cliffs at Norton Bend for about a quarter mile, then crossed the road again, and wound its way back around the pink house and up the hill to return to where we were now standing.

Just then, a big awkward peacock flew into the branches above us with a loud *ray-ah*. Both Captain and Greystoke started at the sudden sound above them. I remained seated, but Lydia, who as always was holding her body too tense to handle any sudden movement, went flying off, landing with a hard thump and a sharp cry of pain.

"Are you all right?"

She had fallen on her arm. After rubbing her elbow and then inspecting it, she stood back up.

"I'm okay," she said. "I just scraped it a little." She tested it tentatively, flexing and extending it.

"Ow. It's okay," she said. "Just a little scrape. Come on, Clara, let's head back, okay?"

That was the moment when I was supposed to come to my senses, and I could feel that I almost shifted my weight to head Captain back toward home. Didn't I? Didn't I almost choose something different then?

"Right," I remember myself saying. "Right, let's go, then." I squeezed my calves around Captain's broad sides.

I headed out fast on the trail at a gallop, down, down, down toward the cliffs at Norton Bend.

TWENTY-ONE

It was warm in the kitchen, and filled with the smoky odor of roasting chili peppers, cilantro, and cumin. Maria was there, cooking, and she gave me a pleasant smile. Jazmyn told me that Maria and Julio had lived on the estate for thirty-some years, and that they took care of Eleanor and were loyal to her entirely. I couldn't imagine putting up with someone like Eleanor for that long.

"Eleanor is waiting for you in the library," she said. "You can go on up."

I went up the long kitchen stairway, letting my fingers trace along the rough white stucco wall. It was surprisingly cool in the house, no doubt from its thick-walled Spanish-style construction, and after the racket of wind outside, the air seemed hushed. The stairway was dark Cordovan tile, covered with a worn, faded Persian runner. I walked up to the top of the stairs and found myself in the large room where I had convalesced from my unfortunate encounter with the fence post. I looked around the room, catching sight of the two photographs I had seen before. I took in, once again, the heavy dark mission furniture, the gorgeous thick Persians over Mexican tile, the casement windows that framed their breathtaking views.

"Over here."

I heard Eleanor's voice from the hallway facing me. I knew that I had been called here to be confronted; I could feel blood racing at my wrists. The only reason I had stayed here at all was because I thought Eleanor Norton could shed some light on my father's story.

But then I had dawdled and meddled and posed and pretended, until now I was going to be in the position I least wanted to be in—with Eleanor Prescott Norton having the tactical advantage. Obviously she had found me out. Franny Baker must have recognized me and ratted. But in reality, I felt nothing but relief. I was going to be forced into the confrontation I had been avoiding. The tension I had been living with since the moment I stepped onto her property started to drain out of me. At least I would know what there was to know; then I could move on.

I moved toward the sound of her voice, and saw that she was sitting in a small office that adjoined the main room. It had the same tiled floor and heavy mission furniture, but the room had no windows on the ocean side.

Eleanor looked at me, glanced at her watch, and looked up again.

"Have a seat," she said, nodding to a heavy oak chair with a worn leather seat. "There is something I need to discuss with you."

"Yes," I said, relieved that my voice sounded steady.

"Pregnancy is not a disability."

The first time she spoke I wasn't sure if I had heard her correctly.

"I beg your pardon?"

"I know what you've been doing. And it isn't necessary. I think you need to know a bit more of the story."

"Mrs. Norton."

"Eleanor."

"Eleanor. I don't have the slightest idea what you are talking about."

"You have been doing Jazmyn's chores for her, encouraging her to rest, mollycoddling her in every possible way. You are not doing the girl any favors."

"But Mrs. Norton . . ." I was dumbfounded, both by her hard-heartedness and by the fact that I didn't want to betray any confidence of Jazmyn, who at least believed that Eleanor did not know she was pregnant.

"You are a grown woman, and it makes me feel positively ancient to be called Mrs. Norton. So please call me Eleanor. Now listen. I don't know exactly what Jazmyn may have told you to generate pity, but let me set the record straight." I wished that the office had windows, because I would have liked to look out them, to look anywhere except at Eleanor's bright blue eyes peering steadily out of her wrinkled face.

"Jazmyn Thompson is eight months pregnant. She was working down at the track and ran into some problems with a violent boyfriend."

I nodded my head. This so far matched up.

"There are a lot of girls without much going for them down at the track—they're usually good with the horses, since the Thoroughbreds are so high-strung. I've made it a habit over the years to hire girls from down there if word gets back to me that there is someone who really needs a safe place to go."

"But I thought . . ."

"That she saw a notice?"

I nodded.

"Yes, Marisol works in the stable office. She has a wonderful way of tacking it up at exactly the right moment. I don't want the girls to know they're beholden to me. Anyway, just like the others, Jazmyn is going to be a mother soon. She doesn't have much in the way of skills except for looking after horses, but I don't believe that that is such an unimportant skill. Horses need to be cared for with both diligence and precision—you can slap a bun on a Big Mac any which way, not so with horses. Jazmyn has pleased me with the quality of her work, and she gets on very well with the horses. Until you started in, that is. Make no mistake. You are not doing the girl any favors."

"But—b-b-b-but." I realized a little too late that I didn't have anything to say.

"She needs to do her work. She has less than another month here, and then she'll be on her own, with another life to look after, and a duty to keep looking over her shoulder to keep the both of them safe."

"B-b-but, she's been contracting," I said. "Preterm labor," I said.

"Clara," she said slowly like she was talking to the village idiot. "She has a doctor, you know. She's allowed to keep working normally right up until she delivers. She's not exactly lifting hay bales after all."

"What did her doctor say?"

"I believe that's called doctor-patient confidentiality."

I was so astonished by the totally unexpected tenor of this conversation that I could hardly think of what to say next.

"But Jazmyn told me that you didn't know she was pregnant, and when you found out about the last girl you booted her out."

"I'm afraid she's not being very up-front with you. Either she's trying to manipulate you, or she doesn't trust you. Probably a little of both."

"Well, are you going to boot her out?"

"I most certainly am. A stable is no place for a baby after all. I've provided a safe haven, and have saved out enough of her wages to provide her with enough to rent an apartment."

"Then what will she do?"

"That certainly is none of my affair!"

"But certainly a young girl with a baby—no income, no support system. A violent boyfriend in the background . . ."

Eleanor waved her hand dismissively. "No, no. None of your bleeding-heart stuff. It doesn't do the slightest bit of good. It's actively harmful, if you want to know my opinion."

She studied me pensively for a moment. "You've been a tough nut to crack, Clara. Much more difficult than most. Every girl comes to Villa de Vista with a heartbreak story. But yours, I haven't gotten a handle on it yet. I don't even know your surname, you know. How's that for trust? I never even asked you."

"Robinson," I said, blurting out the first name that came into my mind.

I guess it was a mistake to say it, though, because I saw Eleanor's eyes flicker when I said it, just a little. But why? What on earth would the name Robinson mean to her anyway?

"Right, then," she said, standing up abruptly and waving toward the door, a clear sign of dismissal. "Run along, then. I hope I have made myself perfectly clear."

I stood up and hurried away from her, through the large dark living room and down toward the kitchen for dinner.

Clara Robinson. Of all the names in all the world, why had I chosen that one?

TWENTY-TWO

The first night I ever spent with Gordon, I was doodling on a napkin in the campus dining hall. I was drawing a trajectory. It was a funny kind of bad habit. The trajectory, over and over again, an arrow pointing down. I tried different angles—forty-five degrees didn't seem steep enough—eighty was a little too much. Plunging over and over again, down, down, down. Gordon was there, and I knew it—I didn't know him then, just saw him around sometimes, but always noticed when he was around.

The first time he came up behind me, I felt his hand on my back—hot as a cattle brand. He leaned over me, and his breath tickled my ear.

"What'cha drawing, not from Pennsylvania?" he asked me. Then said, without a beat of hesitation, "Looks like you're drawing a crash." I don't think he meant to say that really. It was just black arrows pointing downward—no pictures. It just popped out. Right away I could see the embarrassment wrinkle up on his face—like he'd been caught out in only his underpants.

"What I mean is . . ."

I had never seen him embarrassed before. Never seen him looking anything other than cocky.

I looked at the black lines on the paper, and wondered if I was so transparent. The only other possibility was that somehow he understood.

He leaned in closer, and a heat field sprang up on the cheek and arm that were near him.

"Yeah, that's right," I said. My voice sounded funny to me. Like it wasn't my voice. "Crashes. How'd you guess?"

He leaned over and looked me deep in the eye then. Deep enough that I got a good look for the first time, at the crescent-shaped gold flecks in his eyes. He was looking at me to see if I was laughing at him. But of course I wasn't.

Then wordlessly, he sank down in the empty chair next to me that I had pushed toward him with my foot.

He didn't say anything for a couple of minutes. Just picked up a glass of milk and stared at me, trying to pretend like he wasn't.

Finally, he said, "Everybody in this whole goddamn place, and in the whole fucking country, knows my story. Flight two oh nine. Ice on the airplane's wings. Forty-seven seconds after takeoff. I'm sick to death of my story." He stopped for a second, looked at me, half challenging, half pleading. "Why don't you tell me yours?"

I guess I told him. I don't remember anything else about that night, only the startling urgency with which I wanted to get out of there with him.

Up until Gordon, I had always seen men as a sum of their parts—I connected their faces with their words and their clothes and whatever else I happened to know about them. I totted up the numbers and got some kind of a rough total that represented how much I did or didn't like them.

Not so with Gordon—it was all of him, at once, pure and unmediated. Nothing in the world had ever felt like that.

I don't know where we were headed. The night was cold. It was raining, and a cold drizzle was falling on the slick wet flagstones outside the dining hall. The door to the courtyard outside was half open, but it looked too inhospitable out there, or too far away, so we backed into the coatroom, thick with the smell of wet wool and old rubber boots. I remember the rough stubble of his two-day-old beard scratching hard on my cheek, and the cold brass coat hook that was stabbing me just over my left ear, but besides that, I was drowning in him, plunging somewhere deep and fast—on that same speedy trajectory that a car would take when the land beneath it disappeared, or an icy airplane that decided to drop from the sky. He was nuzzling up along my hairline, his body pressed hard into me, pinning me against the wall so hard that my feet were barely touching the floor.

"Gordon," I whispered. "It's just that I always feel like I'm falling."

"Well, then go with it, Clara," he breathed into my ear. "Just go ahead and ride the plunge."

That was the beginning of Gordon. It began with a ferocity that both terrified and ignited me. I no longer had to doodle a steep precipice on a napkin because I was living it. My days were lived in the soft hair of his groin, the smoky odor of his armpits, the hard expanse of his thighs, the thin soft skin behind his ears, the rough centipede surface of his tongue.

I came up for air only in the library. I didn't stop studying. I never stopped studying, because I knew I had to become a doctor. So that I would understand things that were technical, and never, never make a mistake.

I couldn't tell if Gordon was grieving, but deep down, I suspected that he was not. I didn't know how he managed it, and I admired it as a special genius that I tried to emulate. It was part of the swirling vortex of things that drew me down into him like a wind tunnel. I understood that he hadn't really even lived with his parents—he had gotten shuffled around to different schools, been sent to stay with distant relatives—but I still couldn't believe that it didn't hurt to have them fall from the sky.

"They were older," he said. "We were not close."

"Yeah, but your mom, your dad. Come on, Gordon."

"It's not like I'm hard-hearted. I'm really sad about it." I looked into his eyes, counting the gold flecks and then recounting them. The pain I saw there looked so finite and manageable. Grief, yes, but a grief with limits. That was one of the things I admired Gordon for—for the way he could sustain grief without letting it penetrate him. It had been four years, yes, but I hadn't found a way to do that yet. I had found Gordon, whom I could fall into and fall and fall but then land in the flesh and blood of him. Before that, I had had no recourse against the feeling of vertigo—nothing but the far-off image of Lydia's impossibly slim white wrist.

I remember that he seemed to be a grown-up then, not in need of parents, or of anyone. There was something completely self-sufficient about him. He was nineteen—so was I. I had found him and sewn myself to his side, slipped my hand inside his pocket, and started thinking that he was almost just an extension of my own body. It didn't occur to me that it wouldn't stay that way indefinitely, the way my hair, every morning, was still brown and curly, my hands were large and blunt, and my feet were size eight and a half. And my neat stacks of books and notes on my desk. They were as much a part of me as my hair and hands and feet and Gordon. They were sewn onto me too.

We do not know accurately why the fetal head, which entered the pelvis in the transverse or oblique diameter, rotates so that the occiput turns anteriorly in the great majority of cases and posteriorly in so few.

—Oxorn-Foote

PART III

INTERNAL ROTATION

I was fifteen when Atlas momentarily lost his grip on the ball, fumbling just long enough for the floor of my world to collapse. Ever since then, I had been carefully reconstructing it, block by block, with the careful precision of an engineer. One of those stones was the premise that my father had been done a grievous injustice. Recently, that injustice had gotten a face and a name—Eleanor Prescott Norton. Every imperious word, every thoughtless deed, had in some small way made me feel better. *This,* I kept thinking, *this is the kind of woman who passed judgment on my father.* So this new information didn't fit into my picture very well. Eleanor Prescott Norton the rescuer of wayward girls? The Villa de Vista a safe haven from the storm?

When I got out of the outdoor shower, the wind was blowing so hard that a sheer coat of dust stuck to my damp skin as I walked around from the back of the barn toward the stairway up to our loft room.

Jazmyn had gone to Burger King, which was just as well. I was in no mood to talk to her. The fine grit that stuck to my skin and the hot puffs of wind that were rattling the barn doors and cypress trees seemed to fit my mood exactly. Rage. Nature was pissed off—hell was breathing down our necks letting us know that even here in paradise all was not well. The desire to see Gordon had grown into a driving urgency, a rushed, sickening feeling that I was being pulled along, carried on an ill wind.

My mind was filled with a relentless loop of chatter. *Why shouldn't I see him?* After all, Lydia was dead now, and I was his old friend. We both needed a friend more than ever right now. It was the most natural thing in the world.

I rubbed at my bare legs with the damp towel, trying to rub off the thin layer of grime that clung to them. I raked my fingers hastily through my hair, pulled on a pair of jeans that were tight and stiff from the wash, jammed my feet into tennis shoes that were now greenish around the edges from barn muck. I rushed down the stairs, feet thumping on the wooden planks. Looked up to see that Benedetto was watching expectantly over the Dutch door at the sound of my feet, felt for an instant the calming influence of his liquid eyes, then ran through the courtyard and out to the car, the eastern wind at my back, my hair whipping around my face and stinging my eyes. I gunned down the driveway, and took the turn around onto the cliffside road so fast that I had to swerve away from the red-and-orange barricades. The gate-house was just beyond the stretch of cliff road, in the opposite direction from Ambler's Chapel. I drove toward it like it was magnetized, any memory of the day I had walked away from Gordon just erased. I was in free fall, again, nothing to cling to, nothing whatsoever to stop me.

The gatehouse, the Norton Gatehouse, unlike the Villa de Vista, which was hidden from view, was a local landmark. I guess it had originally been the gatehouse to the Norton estate, but the county had put the coast road between it and the big house—so now the gatehouse was right out on the road. Like the Villa de Vista, it was a Spanish-style structure made of pink stucco with a tile roof. It was three stories tall with elaborate turrets—like a castle in a children's illustration. It was the only structure on the cliff side of the road—apparently it had been built on a shelf of solid rock that was more stable than the rest of the surrounding road. It always looked like the last outpost on the very ends of the earth.

As I approached the gatehouse, something was troubling me, like an almost forgotten headache. Why was Gordon staying at the Norton Gatehouse? I had always assumed that the gatehouse was part of Eleanor's estate. It made no sense that he was staying there. But I pushed aside my concerns. The gatehouse was probably some kind of pricey guesthouse now. It always slipped my mind how much money Gordon had now—he had probably rented it, like a hotel room. It made perfect sense.

I pulled off the road. The driveway led into an interior courtyard. I sat inside the car for just a minute, trying to pull myself together. I was so taut I could feel my individual hair follicles, my pores, my toenails. I got out of the car, greeted again by a hot blast of wind, followed swiftly by a cool breeze coming in from the ocean side. I took my eyes off the steering wheel and looked up at the doorway, where I already knew Gordon was waiting for me.

*   *   *

Life is not always made up of second chances. There are some elements of fortune that cannot be undone. As a doctor, I have had to deal with many people who are being forced to learn that lesson for the very first time: pregnant ladies whose amniocentesis has just shown a fetus with Down syndrome, flawless full-term babies who are born dead because there is a perfect knot in their umbilical cord. Things that are so supremely unfair that fortunate people simply cannot accept the absoluteness of it—so they rail against it, as though their protests might make a difference.

Bad things cannot always be undone. I had learned that lesson the hard way one spring at age fifteen. That's when I stopped believing that with enough glue you could put Humpty Dumpty back together again—when my belief in a world of endless solutions was dashed hard against the rocks.

"Clara," Gordon said, as he held the door open for me. "It's so good of you to come. I knew you would understand."

Understand. There was a level at which Gordon and I would always understand each other—it was at the level of mouth to mouth, thighbone to thighbone, skin to skin.

He led me through the shadowy interior of the room we had entered, and I noticed that the furnishings were quite similar to those in Eleanor's house: dark mission-style antiques, tile floors, thick Persian rugs. The room we were passing through was very gloomy. There was a two-story ceiling with dark beams high above, and all of the windows were at the second-floor level, so that you couldn't see outside at all and the light that filtered down had a sepulchral feel. At the back of the room there was a hallway, with heavy oak French doors lined up in a row. They were cloudy and so speckled with sea breeze that they were almost totally opaque.

Gordon pushed one of the doors open onto a flagstone courtyard and gestured me through the door, but I felt a surge of vertigo, and leaned back, to steady myself onto the firm surface of his chest. The flagstone patio was sheltered on three sides by the high walls of the gatehouse, but across the front, the view was unobstructed. The flagstones went right up to the cliff's edge, bordered only by a bed of unkempt perennials. Before I could think, Gordon spun me around, kissing me hard, his hot tongue jamming into my mouth, and I let myself go then, let myself into that familiar falling feeling, stayed like that, deep inside the dark tunnel of him for what seemed like a very long time.

Finally, we pulled apart from each other, and stepped out onto the patio. The sound of the waves crashing on the rocks below was almost deafening. With a start, I saw that the flagstone patio had a completely unobstructed view of the face of the cliff—*my cliff.*

I had always thought that day that there wasn't a single place anywhere that anyone could have seen me. I actually remember that I could just see the blank sides of the pink gatehouse from where I had fallen—there were no windows that faced in my direction. But here, from the secluded patio on the small promontory, you could see directly across to the cliff edge that abutted the orange barricades. Anyone on the patio that day could have seen exactly what happened.

There was a glass-topped table with chairs around it, and I sank wearily into one.

Here I am. No going back now.

The conversation skittered forward in awkward fits and starts, like a heart in code blue that comes back to life in irregular tentative bursts.

"I really miss Lydia," he said.

Gordon's face looked uncanny—deeply familiar, and yet strange. There were new planes and hollows carved into it. Both of us were mired in grief over Lydia, but what different landscapes.

He had pictures of the baby, Clara. My trained eyes saw not a baby but a collection of other things, an enterostomal feeding tube, an oscillating ventilator, an IV drip of Pavulon. Gordon couldn't have known it, but to me the pictures were accompanied by an explicit text—critical baby, gorked baby, bad outcome. . . . I racked my brains for something to say.

"She's beautiful." I hoped that he couldn't hear the bleak note in my voice.

"Oh, Clara, she is, she is. She looks just like Lydia." He leaned forward and clasped my hand, but I withdrew it. I could not touch Gordon without it being erotic, without wanting to dispense with words entirely and move to another level.

"She's . . ." I hesitated, then plunged forward. "Quite ill."

"I know, I know," he said distractedly, as though that were completely beside the point. "Did you know we did in vitro? No, of course not. How could you know?"

I remembered now that Walter had mentioned infertility. Gordon ran his fingers through his thick black hair.

"Lydia couldn't get pregnant. . . . Of course I knew that I could—" He stopped and looked at me. We both remembered the college pregnancy, the hasty abortion. "And then it was such a miracle for her. For us. After trying for four years."

I couldn't decide how I was feeling. I could feel the bright hard ring of pain around me, so encompassing that I couldn't quite tell where it was coming from—was it the pain of Gordon and Lydia's story? Was it the little botched baby? Was it nothing more than the white cliff face in front of me?

"I'm going to save her, Clara. I'm not going to let her go. I'm going to use all my goddamn money to buy her whatever there is. . . ."

"Sometimes there isn't anything."

"That's impossible. There is always something. Always a solution for every problem. There has to be. I've hired a team from Children's Hospital to go in and evaluate her, and then as soon as she is stable enough they will transfer her. They're there right now. That's why I'm going back tonight. I want them to do every single thing that can be done."

I looked at the wan lump in the pictures, remembered for a moment how the baby had looked when I had pulled her out of Lydia's still white body.

"I can help her. I can help her somehow. . . ." He stared past me, into the wall of the gatehouse. Then in a smaller, less certain voice, "Can't I . . . ?"

I knew, even in my current state of agitation, that I needed to choose my words carefully now. And it wasn't my best skill—my best skill was not letting them get to this point, by practicing the very best goddamn medicine I knew how to do, so that the moms and the babies came through safely, so we never, ever had to talk about things like this. What would my mother say at a time like this? My mother, who had gone from working on a cancer floor to working in hospice, my good-hearted, God-fearing mother would have found just the words to say. Or what about Walter? Walter could come through in a pinch like this too. Words were failing me. I resisted, once again, the urge to stop talking and fold him in my arms, touch so much simpler, after all, than speech.

He was asking me a question. I tried again to find a way to answer.

"Gordon, I'm not familiar with the details of what is going on with the baby."

"With Clara."

"With Clara. She's your baby, and I know how much you love her, and especially under the circumstances, it's so much more difficult." Now I could see he was starting to suppress sobs—he was rubbing his eyes, and his chest was shaking.

I wished again for my mother, for Walter, for any of a dozen nurses I could think of who would be doing this so much better than I was, but feeling a sense of duty, I stumbled on.

"I'm not a pediatrician, and I can't advise you what to do with her, or her care, but . . ."

Gordon looked up at me with wounded incomprehension, like a child who has just been slapped for something he didn't do. "You're going to say she's terminal, right? And that I should just accept it, right?"

I looked at him. I didn't answer. He knew me far too well not to be able to read me. "I'm sure you're very angry."

"Clara," he said wearily. "I am too tired to feel angry at anyone, least of all you. I don't blame you for what happened. I stood right next to you and saw that you did every single goddamn thing that you could, and I saw that your partner did the same, and that is something that I'm grateful for every day, because if I had to worry that it was somebody's fault, like if some goddamn pilot should have remembered to tell some runway guy to deice the wings, then I know I would lose my mind once and forever. So I don't even go there. I thank God that you were quick enough and clever enough to save the baby, and now I will do everything in my power to keep on saving her."

"Gordon." Now even here in the sheltered patio I could feel some of the hot wind swirling around my feet. The sun was starting to set, and it was going to be spectacular from where we were sitting, bloodstained clouds radiating out across the sky.

"Clara, I know she's gonna be handicapped. I know she's not going to grow up to be normal and have a normal life, but I just can't help believing that she's alive for a reason. I can't help thinking that you were there for a reason too. . . ."

"Gordon, I . . ." How could this be Gordon, the one who tried so hard to teach me to accept the fact that there doesn't have to be a reason, that sometimes bad things just happen. I could feel that words were failing me. I was leaning in, closer and closer to him, looking into the deep recesses of his eyes, wanting just to let go and plunge. I could feel that I was gripping too tight to the metal edges of the patio chair, the rubber straps cutting into my hands.

I forced myself to look away from him. I stared over at the white cliff face, now almost orange from catching the rays of the dying sun. I tried to make myself remember just for an instant what it actually felt like when I was falling, the actual physical moment, not the metaphorical moment of a life spinning out of control. What did I really remember? Just a few sparse details, a white blur, a loud thud, dirt thick in my mouth, mixing with blood from where I had bitten my tongue. The deafening sound of crashing waves and squealing below me—the place where my elbow was abraded and stung.

Gordon reached out and placed his hands on my cheeks, turned my face back toward his. Now his face too was an eerie orange, the light from the sunset reflecting back from and heightened by the glare of the pink stucco walls.

Then just as abruptly, he took his hands away again. I could still feel the spots where they had rested an instant earlier, like ghostly imprints.

"Clara, do you know how I made my money?" It was such an abrupt change of subject that it caught me totally by surprise.

"Well, yeah, sure. Sol Net Technologies. Everybody knows."

"Well, weren't you surprised that I made money that way? I was a geology grad student. All of a sudden I'm a computer gazillionaire?"

"Is that a question?"

"Yes, it is."

"It did surprise me a little bit that you got rich so fast, but then it seemed like a bunch of other people were doing the same thing you were doing. The nineties, you know. I always thought you were smart, Gordon. I always thought you could do anything you wanted to do."

"Well, let me tell you exactly how it happened. Remember Ben Sollus?"

"Of course." He had been a classmate of ours, real smart, kind of nerdy kid.

"Well, Ben was the one who came up with the idea—it's a trafficking system for SSL encryption. He had the whole thing done. I didn't even understand what it was. He was trolling around for investors—wasn't getting anywhere because he didn't have a lot of business savvy. So he comes to me, asking if I want to get in on it. Well, guess what I had, burning a hole in my pocket?"

"Money?" It didn't seem likely. Knowing the old Gordon, the Boston, bum-around grad student, the one whose parents' will had only paid off part of his college tuition.

"There was a class action lawsuit—you know, good old flight number two oh nine. I didn't even want to go in on it at all. One of my father's brothers was an attorney, and he almost forced me to be a party to it. He kept telling me I needed the money to pay off my college debts. Somehow, it didn't feel right to me. I didn't feel like I needed to blame anyone for what happened—I didn't see how money would help set anything right. But I agreed to go along. When they settled, I got the money—I paid off my college debts, and the rest was just sitting there, waiting for Ben Sollus and me to go out for beer and spuds and for me to decide that what the hell, I might as well be an investor."

I still didn't see what he was getting at, or how this connected to anything that had gone before.

"Don't you see it, Clara? Don't you see it? Somebody somewhere on the runway has a bad day, fight with his wife, you know, or a bad case of gas, or maybe a hangover, and he doesn't put enough deicer on the plane. Then boom-boom-boom like so many dominoes, there I am and now I'm a millionaire."

"I don't see anything wrong about it, or immoral, if that's what you mean."

"Listen," he said, shaking his head, forging on impatiently. Obviously there was some point that he absolutely wanted to make clear to me. Now the light was fading, the orange dwindled to streaks, and a purple twilight was falling, casting his face into shadows. "Do you know how I met Lydia?"

I nodded. "I do. Yes, I do. At least I know her version of the story."

He looked a little surprised at this. "Tell me."

"You were working out of your garage in LA, just you and Ben. Lydia came out on a temp assignment, right?"

"That's right. She knocked on the roll-up garage door just as polite as you please, as though she had just driven up to an office on Century Park East, and not a dumpy garage of a stucco twin in Palms. She was wearing one of those little pink suits, like Tipper Gore, and these spike heels."

"She told me about it," I said. "She said she was holding the trigger on the pepper gun in her purse and ready to run until she saw you."

"She was?"

"She thought you were cute." In spite of himself, in spite of everything, he smiled.

"Do you know how long it took us to figure out that we both knew you?"

"How long?"

"Not even twenty minutes. Not even ten. I was going through the whole formal interview thing, trying to act like I thought that it was to-tally normal that we were sitting on metal folding chairs on Astroturf in the garage. She was gorgeous." He stopped, looked a little embarrassed.

"Don't worry. I had noticed that before."

"So I was trying to ask her lots of questions just so she wouldn't leave. So I got to the question—you know that standard interview question—the one that says, 'What is the most unusual thing about you?' and she says, 'I saved someone's life once,' and she starts telling me all about it, the riding accident and the cliff and the horse, and pretty soon I started going, *Whoa there, whoa there*, and then she blurts it right out loud. *Clara Raymond*."

Gordon stopped talking and looked right at me.

"You know, Clara, it still hurt then. Still hurt a whole lot then, and here is this gorgeous chick and pretty much the first thing out of her mouth is 'Clara Raymond,' and I thought to myself, *Lord have mercy, I'm damned*."

"She called me," I said. "She called me, and told me that she had met you and that she really liked you, and was I sure it was really over between us?"

"And what did you say?" I could hear the clotted choked-up quality that had come into his voice, and it surprised me.

We sat there in the gloom for a moment. I remember the intense jealousy I had felt when Lydia had called, the rainy afternoon I had spent balled up in an afghan in my apartment knowing that this was it—this was the point at which you knew you wouldn't get a second chance.

"I told her that we weren't right for each other and had had a permanent parting of the ways."

He leaned in closer now, his face still lost in shadows, and slipped his hand around mine. The callused palm was as familiar as blind sight, but for the hard edge of the wedding ring that cut into my hand as he squeezed tight.

"I couldn't have loved Lydia any more than I did." He was leaning in so close now that I could smell the slightly sour fruity smell of his breath, the smell of his armpits. I could feel myself weakening the closer we got to each other.

"I know," I murmured. "I know." It felt somehow right that he was telling me this. It seemed okay. I knew he had loved Lydia, and she was so right for him, so happy-go-lucky, so unintense, so much the opposite of everything that I, intense, perfectionist, weight-of-the-world-on-my-shoulders Clara, was.

"But you know, Clara"—now his hands were cupping my face again, and he was whispering to me, almost lip to lip—"I never stopped loving you. I couldn't stop loving you. She's gone, Clara. And you and me. We're left behind again. Alone again, and I just can't be alone. I can't be alone and shoulder the responsibility of raising that poor left-behind motherless baby. . . ." He was talking so softly now that his lips were brushing my lips as he spoke, and I was giving in to him—I could feel it. Whatever that core substance was that was Clara was melting into him and being subsumed into him, again.

"We can face this together, Clara," he was whispering. I had to strain to hear him over the loud crashing of the surf below us. "We can try it again together. You don't have to save the whole world, Clara," he whispered, the words blowing into my mouth, right down into my body. "You can just save one little child."

Now there were no more words, only the silent language of touch. I stood up and tugged on his hand. There was a stone bench at the edge of the patio, right at the very edge, with virtually nothing between it and the precipice below. I pulled him toward its flat expanse. It glowed palely in the now completely dark courtyard. I pulled off my T-shirt and stepped out of my jeans, standing perfectly still for a moment, the cold wind coming off the ocean raising goose bumps on my naked flesh. At the same time, I could feel the undertone of the hot Santa Ana wind that was coming in gusts over the gatehouse walls behind me. I swept my hands up under his sweatshirt, my fingers lingering to read the familiar lines of his chest. Then I pulled him down on top of me and we cleaved together. With each thrust he pushed me backward on the bench until my head was hanging over the edge of the bench and over the edge of the precipice and I could see the white face of the opposite cliff upside down, with the dark sky like the ocean above it. Gordon and I climbed up and up together, and when we came, we shuddered down together, down, down through infinite unending space.

We might have stayed like that for a long time, but after a while his watch beeped and he jumped up and said, "My airplane. I've gotta take a shower. I've gotta go." I followed him, naked, into the house. The central room was now completely dark, and when he flicked a light switch, it illuminated only some candle-shaped sconces that led up the stairs. Upstairs, there was a bedroom, where Gordon had obviously slept the night before. I noticed that on the nightstand there were photographs—of Lydia, and of Lydia and Gordon together. Odd that there were would be framed photos on the nightstand, but then I realized that Gordon must have brought them in his suitcase. I stood next to the bed, cold and stiff, holding my jeans and T-shirt in front of me. When he came out, I got into the shower and washed quickly, eager now to get as far away from there as possible, aware that my brain wouldn't start to function properly until I got away from him.

By the time I came out of the shower room, he was standing by the door with his suitcase in his hand. I noticed that the framed pictures were still on the bedside, and knew that there was something wrong that I had been trying not to notice. Why was Gordon staying in Eleanor's house?

"Gordon," I said. "You forgot your pictures."

"Those stay here," he said.

"You mean," I said, hesitating, confused, "those pictures belong to Eleanor?"

"Who's Eleanor?" He looked genuinely puzzled.

"Eleanor Norton, the Norton Gatehouse? It's her house. Why are you staying here?"

"Clara, this gatehouse belongs to me."

"To you?" Relief flooded through me. Of course, he was rich. There must be lots of things that belonged to him.

"Well, I mean, it was Lydia's." He looked at his watch, "Listen, Clara, I really have to go." He came back toward me again, opened his mouth, and kissed me. "You'll think about it? Won't you? Promise me that you'll think about it?" I wanted to tell him no right then and there, but wasn't strong enough to overcome the simultaneous feeling of desire.

"But Gordon . . . ," I said, still not satisfied. "Why did Lydia own this place?"

"Oh, didn't you ever hear that story? Some old lady gave it to her, as a reward for an act of bravery."

"An act of bravery?"

He frowned.

"You, Clara. You. Lydia saved your life. So the old lady gave her the house."

"But why?"

"Right out of the blue, you know, without any explanation. Just said she didn't need it and wanted it to go to someone worthy. It took her a while to convince the Bensons, but she was so persistent eventually they just gave in. It's worth a bloody fortune. . . ." He looked sad again. "Just like everything else I end up with for all the wrong reasons."

He looked down at his watch again, and then pulled me with him out into the courtyard. "I'm sorry, Clara. I can't miss my flight. The baby—I feel awful already to have stayed away this long."

My car was blocking his, so I had no choice but to back out into the street. I knew he was rushing because he wanted to get back to his baby, and I was rushing too, though I had no idea where I was going, or what direction I was headed in.

TWENTY-FOUR

If I was confused before, I was only more so now. It was like I had been to another country and crossed through time zones at warp speed. I backed carefully out of the driveway, but the cliffside road was silent and still. I pulled into the road and paused for a moment—funny I had never noticed that the road curved here so much that the cliff face would have been visible from behind the gatehouse, but now I noticed more clearly the sharp bend in the road.

Why would Eleanor have given Lydia the gatehouse? I felt sure that Lydia had not known Eleanor. I remembered the times that Lydia had sat up on Peacock Flats looking down at the Villa de Vista—everyone knew it was the Norton Estate, but Lydia had never once mentioned that she knew her. Of course, the whole story of the rescue was in the paper and everything, so she might very well have heard about it, but still, there was something about it that seemed very odd. I made a laborious three-point turn, but just as I was headed back in the right direction, the phone, forgotten in my pocket, started to vibrate. I fished it out and turned on the interior car light—four missed calls, Walter.

He must have called when—I felt an unexpected pang of disloy-alty—I had my pants off.

It seemed like it would be infinitely easier not to call him back, to keep the doors between my two worlds shut tight. But then I remembered that Gordon had said a team of neonatal specialists had been planning to visit that day to assess the baby. Maybe Walter would have heard something about that. . . .

Punching Walter's number eagerly into the keypad, I was startled to realize that my allegiances had shifted. I had always thought of the baby as a lost cause, felt that it was part of my difficult duty to help Gordon to realize that. But now, I was hoping against slim hope that Walter would have good news about the baby. I glanced at myself in the rearview mirror, caught just the top of my part, where there were just a couple of thin threads of gray among the brown curls. I was alone, I was single, and apparently I wasn't good at the one thing I'd thought I was good at, which was helping mothers have babies. Maybe Gordon was right—maybe there was something I could do to help.

The phone was ringing, with no answer. One more ring and I knew Walter's voice mail would pick up.

"Walter."

"Clara. It's you! That's great! I've been trying to reach you. They've reinstated your privileges."

"What?" The news I had been waiting for . . . but somehow now I felt completely flat. Like I didn't care at all. "What happened?"

"Apparently somehow the baby's father, Gordon Robinson, got wind of what they did to you. He went and talked to Hostedler himself. Took a lawyer with him. Said he was confident that you had cared for his wife with the utmost of skill—somehow convinced Hostedler that he had no intention of suing you."

Gordon hadn't even mentioned anything. Hadn't even let on that he knew that I was in hot water.

"Anyway, the OB Risk Management Committee had completed the whole review of the case and the consensus was that you were right in the first place. Pulmonary embolus—probably amniotic in origin, complicated by onset of DIC." I held on to the phone tight in that empty car, tight as though it were a rope someone had tossed to me off a lifeboat.

"Clara, are you there? I can't hear you. Isn't this great news?"

"Yeah, it's great, it's just that . . ."

"It's just that what?"

"Nothing, Walter. This isn't a good time for me to talk. Can I call you back tomorrow?"

"Yeah, but Clara, I really need to talk to you. This thing with the clinic contract is pending, and I really need to know what you're thinking on it. Uni-Group has got this whole big proposal going—they're trying to build on their network. I'm sure they can handle it, from a manpower point of view, but . . ."

"Walter, why don't you just let it go? They've got the big staffs, and the telephone triage, and all that. Why don't you just let them have it?"

Walter paused, then spoke with a weariness that he seldom let creep into his voice.

"I thought," he started, then stopped. "I thought the reasons we took it on in the first place were still valid, and I thought that we've done a pretty good job of it, and there haven't been any more incidents like the one that brought us into it in the first place. Not that, you know, there are any guarantees about that kind of thing, but at least we'll know that we've given it our best shot."

He was right, he was right. Of course he was right. Until the past few surreal days I had always seen eye to eye with Walter on almost everything, and that was why we were so good together. But now, my whole connection to that way of thinking seemed more tenuous than the fragile wireless phone conversation we were having from opposite coasts.

I no longer felt up to it. I didn't want to take on the clinic patients, stumbling their ways toward motherhood in an indifferent and sometimes hostile world.

"Walter, I'm sorry. I'm going to have to call you back. This isn't a good time."

"Of course," he said, but I could sense guardedness in him, like he had smelled another man's scent upon me, marking out the territory, and was no longer sure where he stood.

I sat there in the car a minute longer, then put my foot down and gunned it, hearing my tires screech as I went around the corner in front of the barricades.

TWENTY-FIVE

It was only a couple of days into our working together. Walter was still orienting me to Ridgefield Valley Hospital, so we were up on the floor together. Ridgefield Valley is a small community hospital situated right in the middle of an affluent suburb. The labor and delivery wing was considered state-of-the-art. We had a level-one Neonatal Intensive Care Unit, staffed with full-time neonatologists, that was comparable to any big city hospital. Maybe better than a big city hospital because we were well staffed and our resources were not stretched so thin. We got the triplets and the quads coming to deliver at our hospital because of the high level of service. The bread and butter of labor and delivery were suburban women with private insurance, a group of women who in general had very high expectations. They wanted things like birthing suites and Jacuzzis and well-equipped nurseries, but more often than not they were on the good end of the bell curve, and they tended to be healthy, well fed, and low risk. As the hospital was situated in an affluent suburban area, it did not draw a large indigent clientele. However, every hospital has some patients who do not have private insurance, and Ridgefield Valley was no exception. "The clinic," as it was known, tended to have eight to ten deliveries a month. Not a lot. Not enough to keep a full-time obstetrician in business doing only that.

So when I started working with Walter, all the ob-gyns on staff at the hospital used to rotate through the clinic, each taking his turn, two weeks on, and then passing off to the next group. Obviously, this left something to be desired for continuity of care.

On one of those first days, I was up on the floor with Walter when we got a call that a clinic patient was coming up in labor. The clinic charts were supposed to be sent over from the office at thirty-six weeks so the doctor on the floor had some idea what had been going on with the patient during prenatal care. The patient's name was Agnushe Cerba—she was a stout thirty-nine-year-old Albanian woman. The records were not on file, which was not that unusual for a clinic patient. With the shuffling around of patients from doctor to doctor, sometimes the follow-through just wasn't there.

I followed Walter while he went in to assess her. She was obviously in active labor, huffing and puffing and moaning words in another language, presumably Albanian. She was accompanied only by a man who said that he was her brother-in-law. He spoke a little English, but refused to come in the room with her, saying that he could not look at his brother's wife. Walter stood in the hall with the man, trying to elicit some kind of a history. He said that this was her eleventh child, that the others were all born healthy in Albania, that she had been to the clinic once and that the doctor had told her "everything fine."

The woman was in active labor; the tracing looked fine. Though we had no prenatal records and knew nothing about her, my best guess was that the case would be straightforward.

Agnushe Cerba progressed rapidly to fully dilated and was ready to push. We hung around for a few minutes when she started to push, and then went back to the doctors' lounge for a cup of coffee. The nurses would call us when it was time to come back for the delivery.

I hadn't known Walter for long, but already my feeling that he would be great to work with was panning out. He was smart, capable, and principled. He held himself to the very highest standard of care, no "emergency" C-sections so that he could get out to the golf course. He had stayed in solo practice far longer than most doctors because he wanted to provide that personal level of care—to remember his patients' names and their kids' names and what their last delivery was like. He had sacrificed personal income to do that. Volume was where the money was nowadays—enormous behemoths like the Uni-Group that practiced on economies of scale (might as well locate their offices in Wal-Mart was what Walter had to say about that). He did tell me, right up front, that one of the things his ex-wife had held against him was a less than slavish devotion to earning the highest possible amount of money. It was one of the things that had convinced me to join forces with him. I wasn't in it for the money either—I had seen what the pursuit of money had done to my father. I was in it for the quality of care and that was what I sensed about Walter—that was what he was in it for too.

I guess we'd been chitchatting for about five minutes or so when the nurse buzzed Walter and said that the patient was not cooperating, and could we come take a look? When we got over to the room, we could hear loud wailing from the bed, so loud that it was echoing down the hall, and she was saying something, but we couldn't understand what, since it was in Albanian.

We went into the room together, and we saw that there were two stressed-out-looking nurses there, each holding up one of the woman's stout, varicose-vein-riddled legs. One nurse was watching the toco monitor, and whenever she could see a contraction starting, she would say to the woman (even though it was obviously futile since the woman didn't speak any English), "One, two, three, okay now PUSH!" and the other nurse was doing an elaborate pantomime of bearing down, complete with bulging eyes and red face and little grunting sounds. God bless the nurses—they were obviously giving 150 percent, but the woman was just thrashing and kicking with her enormous legs and hollering something that we couldn't understand.

"Where's her husband?" Walter said.

"It's her brother-in-law."

"Right. Sorry. Where is he? Can you get him to come in here for a sec? I'll take one of these legs off your hands." Walter was always the perfect gentleman—he never seemed harried or flustered, never ordered the nurses around, always took the time to be respectful of them and what they were doing.

The older nurse, Debbie, passed the heavy leg over to Walter and stepped outside the room. A moment later, she stepped back in.

"He says he can't come in because it would not be appropriate to see his brother's wife."

"All right, all right," Walter said calmly. "Well, Debbie, if you could just ask him what it is that she is saying . . ."

Another contraction had started and the woman was hollering like crazy and thrashing her legs around wildly, but obviously was not trying to bear down to push the baby out.

Debbie popped her head back in the room.

He says she's saying, "It's too big. Can't you just cut it out?"

You would be surprised how many women, in the moment of truth, say the exact same thing.

Walter said calm as ever, "Well, do you think you could get him to tell her that if she will just bear down, the baby will come out and she'll feel a lot better?"

Debbie's head disappeared around the corner again, and another contraction started, and the woman took up her moaning again—no, it was more just flat-out screaming—and kicking and bucking her big legs up and down. Brenda, the other nurse, was still holding the leg, and I could see her wincing, trying to spare her back. I knew that all the nurses had bad backs just like my mother did. I took hold of the big leg myself.

Debbie's head disappeared again, and then I heard the man's voice saying something in Albanian. Then the woman, who looked all wide-eyed, seemed to calm down again and she yelled something to the man out in the hallway.

He answered something to her, and then said something to Debbie, and Debbie peered through the doorway again and said, "She wants to know if she pushes, will the baby come out?"

I was rolling my eyes by then. If this was her tenth baby, then certainly she knew that if she pushed, the baby would come out! But Walter just smiled reassuringly and said, "Yes, tell her the baby will come out if she pushes."

God bless him, as my mother would say. He was the soul of patience and I knew right then that I had picked the right partner.

After that, things seemed to proceed pretty normally. Her contractions were every two minutes or so, and she was giving a good pushing effort. Usually the pushing stage is quite short for a woman who has delivered several babies already, and hers was proceeding a little more gradually, but you could see that the baby was moving down the birth canal. Many doctors would have left the room at that point, entrusting the nurses to manage the pushing and waiting to call them when the baby was ready to deliver, but Walter just settled down at the end of the bed and watched and waited. Something about his big presence seemed calming to the woman, and I think he sensed that.

Before long she was crowning, and Walter stood up to get gloved and gowned in preparation for the delivery.

When a baby's head is fully crowning, usually it is just one more push to deliver the head, and then the shoulders come through right away.

The big woman gave an enormous push, and slowly half of the head slid into view. Then it stopped. The perineum was just at the baby's eye level. The wrinkled purple top of the head and the forehead were out, the rest of the baby's face still inside. The woman had stopped pushing and starting screaming. This was not good. You wanted the entire head to emerge.

"Push," Walter said to the woman. "Come on now. Keep pushing."

Obviously futile, because she didn't understand, and she was lying there with her eyes closed, looking like most women look—exhausted.

"Debbie, get the boyfriend in here, or whatever. She needs to push. *Now!*"

Walter's voice was calm, but with an unmistakable air of authority.

He picked up a pair of scissors from the delivery tray and carefully pulled the perineum away from the head. He snipped straight through, the two sides peeled out of the way like orange peels, but the baby's head didn't budge.

Right then, I felt that tick up of anxiety, and I saw the quality of Walter's movements change too. I swung around and grabbed a leg, jerking it back as far as I could. Brenda, on the other side, followed my motions exactly.

"Fundal pressure?" I asked Walter. He nodded.

"Get that fellow in the room *now* and tell this lady she has to push."

I heaved down hard on her fundus as another contraction started. Slowly the face slid into view, slowly, too slowly.

The head was out.

Walter saw it. I saw it. The nurses saw it.

No sooner had the head emerged than it sucked back against the pelvis. *Positive turtle sign.*

The big woman started screaming and trying to thrash her legs. I made sure I held on tight. Another nurse had come into the room, and she stood next to the side of the woman's head and stroked her hair, trying to keep her calm.

"Okay, we've got a positive turtle sign. I'm going to try to deliver with McRoberts position and fundal pressure. On the count of three . . . one . . . two . . . three."

I watched Walter. Big hands. Completely steady. I saw him cup his hands around each side of the baby's head, I pushed down from the top of the uterus, and he put gentle traction on the head. Too hard and he would damage the complex nerves on the brachial plexus and the baby would be born palsied. Not firm enough—that wasn't an option. As long as the head was out and the body wasn't, the baby was not getting any oxygen.

We tried once, then tried again.

Now the cards were on the table.

The shoulders were too big and the baby was stuck. Shoulder dystocia. Seconds were crucial now.

Walter was in charge. The rest of us were silent, listening for his commands.

"Okay, listen up, everybody. I am going to attempt a Woods maneuver. Dr. Raymond, I want you to glove up in case I need you. Debbie and Brenda, you each take a leg, and be ready to do fundal when I tell you."

The brother-in-law had come in the room at this point, and was standing with his back to the woman, looking pale and shaky. There was now a fourth nurse there, holding him steady.

"Tell him to tell her to push."

The brother-in-law said something in Albanian.

Steady as a rock, Walter tried to do one of the most difficult moves in obstetrics—where you slip your hands inside and attempt to rotate the baby to free the shoulder that is stuck behind the pubic symphysis. Walter was well over six feet and he had big hands to match—I saw him trying to work his hands in, but there was not enough space.

He looked over at me. I was already gloved up. I stepped forward and tried to slip my hands in, but even my hands were too big.

The baby's big head with fat cheeks was rapidly turning a dark purple. The woman was bellowing nonstop and though the only word we could understand was "Allah," it was clear that she was begging God to take her out of her misery.

"Widen the epis," I said to Walter.

He picked up the scissors and snipped again, this time cutting clear through the anal sphincter, which bloomed apart like a small pink rose. The woman was bucking and thrashing on the table, trying to get away and yelling. More nurses came running into the room—there were now several people attempting to hold her down.

I tried again to slip my hands in far enough to rotate the shoulders, but it was impossible. I could feel the anterior edge of the shoulder, but couldn't even wiggle a finger inside.

Walter could see it wasn't working.

"All fours?" I asked. Sometimes flipping the woman would unjam the shoulder, but she wasn't likely to comply and precious seconds would be lost.

"What about the posterior arm?" I tried again—this time slipping just one hand inside, I was able to get in with about three-fourths of my fingers. I could feel the baby's fingertips—obviously the arm was bent in some way.

Carefully I slid my fingers up along the posterior aspect of the arm. I managed to crook my index finger around the baby's arm, but I couldn't get a purchase on it. I tried once, twice, three times, but each time it slipped from my grasp. I was sweating profusely. I could already tell that the baby's body was going limp. This baby needed to come out now.

"I can't get it," I said. "Shall we try a Zavanelli?" A Zavanelli, a doomed last resort—where you try to push the baby back inside and do an emergency C-section. This baby was still alive—at least for a few more seconds. With a Zavanelli it would certainly die.

"Snap the clavicle if you can," Walter said.

The clavicle. Sometimes, you could break the baby's collarbone and that would allow the baby through.

I slipped my hand in again and felt along the top of the shoulder for the clavicle, finding the thin ridge of bone. I pushed firmly—nothing. At the angle I was at, I couldn't generate much force. I squatted down, twisted my shoulder around, and tried again. I felt the little bone give way with a sickening snap.

"Done," I said.

"Okay. Legs. Fundal pressure." Walter reached in, and once again tried to deliver the body with downward traction. Nothing doing.

"Feels a little looser but . . ."

"Come on, Walter. It's time to move to Zavanelli. Let's go."

"No," he said. "Try Woods one more time."

The woman's screaming and thrashing were bloodcurdling and relentless. The baby's head was a sickening dark blue, the lips almost black.

Hold it together, Clara, I said to myself. Now was not the time to panic.

"Okay," I said. "Here goes."

I wormed my hands in again. It was true—the baby had shifted position just slightly and there was more maneuvering room. I slipped my hands in, millimeter by millimeter, until I could get ahold of the baby. It seemed like it took hours, although it was almost certainly at most a few seconds. And then, somehow, I got purchase on the baby and millimeter by millimeter, I rotated that baby stuck so tight like a sausage in a casing, until by some miracle, it finally slipped free.

The baby died. It lived for about six hours on a vent, but the mother made it clear that she wanted no heroic interventions—her brother-in-law kept saying that she wanted to respect God's will. The mother had a severe postpartum hemorrhage, and so before Walter and I had any chance to cool down from the harrowing delivery, we were back in the OR doing an emergency hysterectomy. The niece, who was a college student and spoke perfect English, arrived from the Bronx the next day and explained that all of the woman's nine babies born in Albania had been healthy, but the one born the year before at North Central Bronx Hospital had been born dead—too big to fit through the pelvis. Shoulder dystocia. It was like someone had punched me in the stomach when I heard that. This woman should have been a scheduled C-section. She should never have been allowed to attempt a vaginal delivery.

There was an internal investigation. It turned out that there was a notation in her chart—? *macr.*—possible macrosomia, or oversized baby. She had been given a prescription to go for an ultrasound, but she had shown up at the doctor's office, not understanding she needed to go to the hospital for the ultrasound, and the receptionist, not understanding why she was there, had said, "You don't have an appointment today," and sent her home. So she had never had the ultrasound, which would have certainly indicated the problem—the baby weighed eleven pounds.

The bottom line—preventable. Preventable. Preventable. Preventable. All our heroics at the time of delivery didn't amount to a hill of beans.

The Quality of Care Oversight Committee decided that the lack of continuity of care had been a significant cause of the problem. The committee decided that the clinic needed to be in the hands of one practice, and put up the clinic for bids. But nobody bid except me and Walter. We had looked at each other and not even had to discuss it. We both already knew. Then the malpractice carriers doubled our insurance rates, and the bean counters at the hospital refused to absorb any of the cost for us, and we saw our profit margin shrink even more than before.

As for Agnushe Cerba—as Hostedler said at the time—she was a poor immigrant woman and we were "lucky" that she didn't know a good lawsuit when she saw one. It turned out that she was the mother of nine boys. The last one, the one that I delivered, too late, had been a baby girl.

The night after all that had happened, Walter invited me to come over to his house for dinner. He was still living in the furnished one-bedroom he had rented when he and his wife had split up earlier that year. I'm not even sure he knew how to cook. His wife had never held a job. I guess she had pretty much stayed home and raised their son and spent his money. But he had gone to the deli section at Kings and gotten some prepared stuff—I don't even remember what it was, only that I didn't really feel like eating, and that neither of us could drink because we were both on call.

We sat around the little table together, awkward, because we still barely knew each other, and yet now intimate too in the way that you feel with people with whom you have been through something difficult.

"Thirty-six hours into life in private practice and we have shoulders," I said.

It wasn't that I had never seen this before. Four years of residency: one-hundred-hour weeks in a big city hospital. I had seen pretty much everything at least once, had delivered thousands of babies, had stepped in to help in countless emergencies, had had to make hard decisions on the spur of the moment, not always certain I was making the right one. But still, in a suburban hospital, something like this wouldn't happen often at all. It was not what I had expected right off the bat, and in any case, something like this was never easy.

"You did very well, Clara," Walter said. "I like what I saw. I know now that it was a smart decision to hire you."

"Maybe we should have snapped the clavicle sooner. Maybe we shouldn't have let her push so long."

"She pushed for ten minutes—and the first five she wasn't cooperating. You know full well there was nothing to tip us off."

"Maybe we should have scanned the baby to see how big it was."

"Clara, you know that's not the standard of care for a woman in active labor."

We picked at the stale eggplant parmigiana and the soft too-buttery garlic bread.

"There's always something. Something we could have or should have done that might have changed the outcome."

I remember Walter looking at me then. He had this bemused half smile on his face most of the time, and this was no exception.

"You know, Clara," he said. "I've been in practice for sixteen years. Every day, I show up to work and I try to do the best I can. Just one foot in front of the other. Sometimes, you do what you can and it doesn't turn out to be enough. I feel quite sure in the end that the balance is in my favor."

"The balance?" I said.

"The balance of harm to good. If you show up every day with your game clothes on, you may win some and you may lose some, but I'm pretty sure you're right with yourself and with the patients—right enough with God, the way I reckon it."

I was a little surprised by the God reference. I tended to cringe when people brought that stuff up—thought they were getting all born-again on me. I looked at Walter and I didn't see any trace of irony there.

"You win some, you lose some, Clara. Your biggest job is to just keep putting your shoes on in the morning, and going out with the same degree of bravery to face the day."

"God, huh?" I was trying to be flip, trying to inject a little more of the ironic skepticism I was used to into the conversation. But at some much deeper level his words resonated with me. Like me, Walter had a credo. He was doing what he did because he really believed it mattered.

It wasn't quite my credo, though. Mine was vigilance, eternal vigilance—it was the promise to try hard enough not ever to make a mistake.

"Oh, don't worry, Clara. It's just my age, and the fact that I'm from

Iowa. That's how we corn-fed farm boys talk." Now he looked embarrassed, and I think both of us were suddenly aware of the age difference between us. He was sixteen years my senior, the father of a son who was already in college. Old enough to be my father. Well, almost old enough, but not quite.

I did feel better, though, after his little pep talk, felt the keyed-up hypervigilant state starting to slip away, being replaced by intense fatigue.

When I stood up, he did too, and he stood there facing me for a moment that held a little too long. He was a big man, well over six feet, strong and heavily built—nothing like Gordon (the comparison was automatic, almost unthinking), who was slight and wiry and not much taller than me.

Right then, I wanted nothing more than to step forward and lay my head on his chest. Walter must have felt the pull too because he took both of my hands into his two hands. Then for just a moment, just a brief moment, I did step forward and lay my cheek against his broad chest, hearing the gentle thumping of his heart. One of his hands came up and smoothed away the hair from my forehead.

I could feel that this was a moment of choosing. All I had to do was look up and I knew he would kiss me, and I wanted nothing more than to fold myself into his comfortable bulk. But I held myself off, thinking, *No, this man, this skilled and compassionate man, is the person I have chosen to be my partner*—so I took a step back, and when I looked up at his face, the moment was broken. I don't think we have ever touched each other like that again.

TWENTY-SIX

As I drove up the driveway to the Villa de Vista, I was aware that something seemed amiss. The place was lit up like a Christmas tree. All of the floodlights around the barn, and the ring lights, and the lights in the big house were turned on. I didn't have to wonder long, because as soon as I got close to the house Eleanor came running out into the driveway yelling.

"There you are! There you are! Ten more minutes and I would have called the police. Get out of the car and give me some kind of explanation!"

I was confused and also self-conscious—self-conscious because I was so fresh from sex with Gordon that I was afraid it would be obvious in some way. I also had no idea what she was talking about. Obviously she wanted me to park right there in the driveway, so I switched the car off and got out.

"All right, Clara. I need some kind of explanation immediately!"

"Explanation?" I asked. "For what?"

"Where is he?"

"Where is who?" I thought of Gordon. Almost answered, "The gate-house," but caught myself.

"What do you mean, where is who? The horse has been missing for over an hour."

"The horse?" I said. "Which horse?"

"You mean you don't know where Benedetto is?"

"No," I said. "I've been gone for a couple of hours. The last time I saw him, he was in his stall."

"Well, the stall was unlatched, and the rubber stall guard was attached crooked, just snapped once, so he may have gotten under it. It must have just been your carelessness. He must have just gotten out."

Eleanor was speaking with steely precision. I could hear the anger in her voice.

"I left the stall unlatched and the stall guard buckled wrong?" It was a question. It seemed impossible that I would do such a thing. I tried to remember the moment I had latched the gate, tried to remember the click of metal on metal. All I could really remember was the feverish crotch-driven feeling I had had as I was getting ready to leave to see Gordon.

"Are you sure?" I asked again. It seemed impossible. Would I have left the stall unlatched? It just didn't seem like something I would do.

"Clara. Shut your mouth. This is perfectly in keeping with the pattern of carelessness I've seen from you all along. . . ."

Just at that exact moment, we could hear the loud sound of tires screaming as they negotiated the turn on the road below. We all looked at each other, and I could feel my heart start to hammer. The property was adjacent to the road for a full quarter mile. Wherever the horse was, we needed to find him before he got out into the road.

"I'll take the Jeep and go up the high loop. Clara, you and Jazmyn need to go down along the road, start at opposite ends, and work your way toward the middle. I'll get Julio to take the pickup on the other loop trail that goes up toward Jacaranda Canyon."

"I'm not feeling that well," Jazmyn whined. "My back hurts."

"I'll not hear that right now. There is a horse in danger and he is our responsibility." Eleanor strode over toward the kitchen back door, presumably to get Julio, or her keys.

I looked over at Jazmyn, remembering everything that Eleanor had told me, felt doubt flutter up in me, wondered if I should trust her.

"Clara, I'm serious," she whispered, giving me a pleading look. "I don't feel that good." I remembered what Eleanor had said.

You're not doing that girl any favors.

"Look, Jazmyn, you go up to our room," I said. I couldn't, I just couldn't, disbelieve her. She was thirty-four weeks pregnant after all. "I'll take the road by myself. I'll cover for you with Eleanor."

I took off down the driveway on foot, determined to be out of sight by the time Eleanor got back. It was at least a quarter mile back down the driveway to the road. It was a very dark night. The hot wind was still whipping around in fits and starts, but there was heavy cloud cover now—there was neither moon nor stars. In the distance you could see the even darker blackness of the ocean, spotted occasionally with red and white lights. The fields alongside the driveway disappeared immediately into obscurity. The thin beam from my flashlight barely seemed to penetrate the darkness.

I scanned the surroundings wondering how I would see a loose horse, and wondering how likely it was that Benedetto would have headed toward the road. I had just come from the road, and it had been so quiet. . . . Not too many cars came this way—most took the bypass—but then, they wouldn't be looking for a loose horse either.

Eleanor's words were still ringing in my ears. A *pattern of carelessness* . . . Could I really have left the stall unlatched? It seemed so unlikely. But then, I had done the feeding and mucking, so who else would have needed to go into the stall? And now the horse was loose at night, near a road, and it was my fault.

I was getting down to the end of the driveway now, and as I approached the road, I stopped to listen for any telltale sounds. The sound of hoofbeats on pavement should have been obvious, but as I got closer to the cliffs, the sound of the surf got louder—and the hot wind had picked up again and was swirling around. Just then a car emerged, or it looked like a small truck or camper—its lights tracking around the bend, illuminating the barricades for a moment—and then went on. Over the roar of wind and surf I hadn't even been able to hear the car coming—obviously I would not be able to hear Benedetto's hoofbeats.

I walked along the far edge of the road, away from the cliffs, picking my way carefully among the rocks, dirt clods, and clumps of brush that lined the road. If Benedetto was down here, he would have to be on the road—there was no shoulder. If he was walking along the road *and a car came along and spooked him* . . .

No! He probably wasn't even down here. Why would he come this way? The trail where he got hot-walked was up above. A horse is much more likely to follow familiar paths than to strike out in a new direction.

I stumbled along, the thin beam of my flashlight growing ever weaker, wind whipping around my face, surf roaring in my ears, the familiar trio of sickening sensations: the sweaty hands, the constricted feeling in my throat, the telescoping dizziness. First thought: *Vertigo*. Next thought: *Get a grip on yourself. Now is not the time.*

Now I had walked almost to the end of the roadside loop. I could see the gatehouse in the distance around the bend—it was completely dark, just a black silhouette against the sky. My flashlight was almost dead anyway—I switched it off.

Switching it off was a big mistake. The flashlight had helped a little. Now, enveloped in wind, surf sounds, and all-encompassing darkness, it was as though a veil fell away and I realized where I was—on the cliff road, at night, missing a horse.

If a car had come by and he had spooked . . . ?

I forced my wooden legs to cross the road, feeling the cascading waves of dizziness worsen as I got closer to the cliff. I kept pushing forward, toward the cliffside trail. There wasn't much trail there now—most of it had eroded. It was only a few feet wide, with crumbly edges that I could barely see in the dark. The sound of the surf pounded as though inside my head—maybe it was inside my head. I could no longer sort out waves from wind from the agonizing pounding in my cranium.

I stumbled, hard, over a chunk of asphalt that had broken off the road, felt the dropping sensation in my stomach, then righted myself.

I tried to switch the flashlight back on, but its beam was so thin that the light did not make a perceptible difference in the darkness. *Push on, push on.* I needed to know what had happened. I needed to follow the cliff trail. I no longer felt there was any room for doubt—I knew that Benedetto had gone over.

That quarter mile, along the cliffside, was the longest distance I had ever walked. I crept along slowly, picking each foothold carefully, every step a battle just to keep myself upright. At one point, I had to stop to vomit. Then I couldn't stand anymore, so I just crawled, the weed-choked ground cutting into my hands until I could feel that my palms were bleeding. Like a blind man, my hearing got more acute. Now I could separate the different sounds, the dry rattle of the wind, the wet pounding of the waves on the rocks, my own hands and legs as I dragged them along the rough ground.

Through the din, I was listening for a particular sound, a sound that I had heard only once before, but that I knew I would never forget. The sound of a horse that has fallen hundreds of feet and is dying, the sound of unmitigated terror.

I listened until it seemed as though I could hear the individual sound of waves hitting particular rocks, but through that sound I heard nothing.

Maybe this time there was mercy. Maybe he's already dead.

I had gotten as far as the barricades. Gotten so close without seeing them that I bumped my head into the first one as I was crawling. The trail ended here—now the distance between the cliff and the barricades was only a couple of feet wide. I pulled myself up to a standing position, wincing as I realized how cut up my hands were.

I put my arms around that barricade and held on tight, wrapped my arms as tightly as I could, terrified that I would lose my grip and plummet. I squeezed my eyes shut, held on tight, and cast around in my mind for something to hold on to. *Please, God.*

Something like a prayer.

I screwed one eye open and then the other, willing myself to open my eyes and look—and then I saw it. Two of the barricade posts had been knocked over—flattened down by something.

I let go of the post and ran.

TWENTY-SEVEN

My legs pounded so fast up the long driveway that when I finally reached the big house I was completely winded. I could see that the Jeep was back, parked out in the circular driveway. Back because they hadn't found him. Obviously they hadn't found him.

My lungs felt like they would burst, and as soon as I was in earshot, I started hollering.

"Benedetto." Huff, huff. "Gone." Huff, huff. "Over the cliff."

Eleanor appeared out of the shadows and waved impatiently at me. She couldn't hear, or didn't understand.

I got closer, slowed up.

"Benedetto."

"Well, there you are finally. We thought you skipped town."

"No, you don't understand! Benedetto."

"Found munching on old hay just behind the dressage arena. We'll have to keep a good eye on him to see he doesn't colic."

"He's . . . okay?"

"Well, for the time being, yes, but I'm not sure how long he was out—a belly full of moldy hay for a barn-fed horse."

"But Eleanor, I was down on the road. Two of the barricades were knocked over. . . . I thought . . ."

Maybe she turned pale and looked discomfited or maybe I just imagined it.

"You thought . . . you thought what? I already know about the barricades. Franny Baker told me that she saw a car come around the corner too fast earlier this evening and knock them over. She called the county with her cell phone."

"But . . ." *But I could see the barricades from the patio at the gatehouse. They were clearly all still standing upright.*

Then I remembered, with a thud of an imprecise emotion, how it had gotten dark, and what Gordon and I had been doing, and how I likely wouldn't have noticed if they had been knocked down somewhere near the end.

"Franny Baker was here?"

"Yes, doing some worming."

"What time was she here?" I wondered what time the barricade had been knocked down—obviously after it had gotten dark.

"Oh, no, you don't. I know your kind. You are looking for someone to blame for your own incompetence. Franny Baker did not go near Benedetto, and besides, she is a professional. She would never be so careless as to leave a horse's stall unlatched."

It hadn't even occurred to me to blame Franny Baker. I had racked my brain to try to remember leaving Benedetto's stall. I couldn't remember the actual moment that I had fastened it.

"I'm going to go over and help Jazmyn take care of Benedetto."

"No, you'll do no such thing. I've had quite enough of your incompetence. You are terminated. Go up to your room and pack up your things. Stay away from the horses. You may stay the night, but I don't want to see you here in the morning."

With that, Eleanor whirled around, her back to me, and strode off at a brisk clip toward the house.

I was dismissed. There could be no mistake about that.

Inside the stable courtyard, the floodlights were on, and I saw Jazmyn, sitting on an overturned bucket, her big belly protruding and obvious now. In the crossties stood Benedetto. His ears pricked up and he whickered when he saw me, and in spite of Eleanor's admonition, I was so glad to see him there, fit as a fiddle, that I walked over and threw my arms around his big neck.

I stroked his soft nose, readjusted his halter, and pressed my face into his broad neck. Like seeing a ghost. But there was the big horse, standing placidly, unharmed. The first small blessing that had come along in a very long while.

"Jayzuz! For all the fuss you'd a thought there was a murderer excaped from jail or something. And there he was all along, eating old hay, just behind the barn. He wasn't going anywhere. I don't see why old Norton had to make such a federal case out of the whole thing." She groaned a little and resettled her bulk on the upturned bucket.

Suddenly guilty again, I remembered that she was supposed to be resting, that I had told her I would cover for her. Obviously I hadn't covered for her—I had come running up that hill screaming like a banshee, no thought about Jazmyn and her backache at all.

"I'm sorry, Jaz. I totally forgot to cover for you. I thought the horse had gone over the cliff. I got all panicked."

"Over the cliff? Jeez, girl, you gotta think like a horse. Remember that the feed truck was here yesterday? There's all this hay on the ground right behind the feed ramp. That was the first place I looked— I just strolled over there, and there he was, happy as can be, munching on the hay."

"But I thought . . ." Surely Eleanor had checked around the barn before she had sent me off on that wild-goose chase.

"You really gotta be morbid to think a horse would go over a cliff. Why would he do a thing like that?" She groaned a little again, and shifted her weight.

"How are you feeling, anyway? How is that backache?"

"Oh, it ain't too bad. As long as I stay seated. It kinda comes and goes."

I opened my mouth to say, "No bleeding, no leaking fluid," then shut it again. I was not her doctor. I was not anyone's doctor. My little busman's holiday had come abruptly to an end, and I had some hard choices to make.

"I'm going up," I said. "But if you need me, just give me a holler."

I walked up the stairs to the loft bedroom. I heard Oyster's friendly footsteps following behind me. I had come to deliver a dog. I stayed, at least I had told myself, to ask Eleanor what she knew about my father, but I had never asked her. The questions I wanted to ask rattled around in my head like loose marbles in a box.

I had come all the way out here, to California, because I wanted to try to understand what had caused my father's downfall—but now I was realizing that maybe I had never wanted to know. Maybe that's why I had never asked.

I thought about the short list of things that I was certain about—a malpractice suit that was "too technical," finances that were in such disarray that my mother and I were left penniless, our house foreclosed on, our car sold, our possessions sold off, so that we when we left for Pennsylvania we left behind all traces of our previous life. And of course, the final known and incontrovertible fact—that my father, in his white Cadillac Eldorado convertible, with the retractable roof and built-in car phone, had taken flight. Sometime after midnight, at Norton Bend, on a slick foggy night after a day of June gloom, he had sailed off the edge of California, and landed on the rocks—the rocks that had greeted Captain when he fell, the rocks that I had been headed toward when, for some reason that I had yet to fathom, Lydia's arm descended from heaven and bore me up out of harm's way.

TWENTY-EIGHT

I don't remember exactly if my mother told me that we had no money, or only that we were moving away. I do remember that after my father died, the change in my mother seemed instantaneous. Before, she was always wearing dark glasses—in the time after, I can see her eyes. Looking back, I can see my mother's achievement more clearly: she got me out of there, took me to Pennsylvania where two of her sisters had settled, got a job, went back to work after more than a fifteen-year absence, found us a decent place to live, and started constructing a whole new life. It was only after my father was gone that I got to see who she really was—hardworking, caring, and kind. According to my mother, the sad state of our finances would have become clear shortly anyway—my father's death just accelerated the process.

After my accident, my mother didn't let me out of bed for three days, as though I were ill, although I had essentially escaped injury. My tongue was a little swollen where I had bitten it in falling, I had a few scrapes and bruises, and I had twisted my ankle, but I was not really hurt. My mother and father and all visitors were tiptoeing around the house and talking to me in hushed voices, and I couldn't stand the presence of anyone—I felt like I had huge hole cut out of me and that for all the sympathy I was getting, no one really understood how I felt inside.

A couple days after the accident, Lydia came. It must have been after school, because she had her backpack with her, and her hair was falling out of a disheveled ponytail. She looked so ordinary, so everyday school day, that it brought a lump to my throat. I remember the way that my mother came to the door and told me that she was there, like it was a special occasion, like I was about to receive a prize. That was when I first realized that something was now irrevocably changed between Lydia and me, that nothing would ever be quite the same.

She held out her arm and showed me the bruises on it. Like five purple petals, there they were, the imprints of each of my fingers around her forearm. After she left, I looked at my own hand and wondered how it could be that it had no marks on it, that it looked so perfectly ordinary.

But then, a few days after that, all hell broke loose. I don't remember the exact moment, but only that I was no longer the center of attention, because I could see that my parents' world had become radically unsettled. Though the death of my father's patient had occurred sometime before my accident, the repercussions did not begin until a few days after. Now my mother and father were always immersed in these heated private conversations behind closed doors. . . .

I wasn't ever told directly what was going on, but I managed to piece it together. There had been an investigation into the case of the recent death of my father's patient during surgery. In those days, medicine was a far simpler world, and I know that back then, the chairman of the board of trustees, especially in the case of a privately endowed hospital, could have absolute say about the staff. The hospital my father worked for, the Norton Community Hospital, had been privately endowed by William Simon Norton, who had served as chairman of the board of trustees until his death, at which point, his widow, Eleanor Prescott Norton, took over his role.

In this case, the chairman of the board, Eleanor Prescott Norton, had ruled that there was clear evidence of misconduct and had permanently revoked my father's staff privileges at the hospital—she had forwarded a complaint to the state board for possible disciplinary action.

I went back to school, and was treated with a touch of awe, as the fragile survivor, which suited me fine, as people tended to be intimidated and leave me slightly alone. I remember that life at home was constantly punctuated by urgent phone calls to and from lawyers.

Then one morning the whole thing ended.

When I stumbled out of bed, and out to the kitchen for cereal, I saw Mr. and Mrs. Benson sitting nervously on our blue floral sofa, hands clasped in their laps, looking at me with a kind of eyes I had never seen before.

Terror set in before they had said anything—I stumbled toward them, crying, "Where is my mother?"

Mrs. Benson stood up, and wrapped her arms around me tight, crushing my face up against her soft bosom, which smelled of perfume.

"Oh, Clara, honey . . . ," she said. "Your mother is okay, but I'm afraid there's been an accident."

I pulled away and looked up at her face, not comprehending.

"An accident?" I looked down at my bare legs, where the bruises were fading, turning yellow. "But I already know. . . ."

There was this one moment, when the room seemed to flood with light, and I actually believed she was going to tell me it was all a big mistake, and that Captain was still alive.

Then just as swiftly, the room dimmed to blackness and I fell down on the hardwood floor, my ear grazing the edge of the glass coffee table. I lay there with my cheek pressed hard against the solid surface of the floor. Knowing that I already knew.

I would swear that my vertigo set in right after that—before I even knew exactly how it had happened. From then on, if I didn't grip on to something, I was always falling, falling, falling.

But I never landed. Never felt the sharp impact on the rocks, the splintering, the salt water filling my eyes and lungs. Never had to be brought back up swinging from a mechanical winch, swaying ever so gently like a pendulum just beyond the ends of the earth.

TWENTY-NINE

I was the one who left Gordon. It was the hardest thing, besides bury-ing my father, that I had ever done. I kept going back over it, taking the history, doing the physical exam, listening intently to the four chambers of the heart, trying to hear the ailment that caused us finally to come asunder.

The first symptom, without a doubt, was that first summer after our junior year. I was still a Californian, only a thin veneer of Easternness over my Western core. Spring still came as something of a shock to me. Born and raised on eucalyptus and evergreen trees, I couldn't get used to the blowsy pink blossoms on the trees. It was as though they wrote everything you were thinking across the sky in a way that I found em-barrassing and obvious, like the crinkling sound of plastic when you're changing a tampon in a public stall. So with the trees. In the spring, it was worse than ever—it seemed that my blood positively boiled and in between the marathon study sessions and the late nights at the library, it seemed that all I wanted to do was have sex.

I could always find Gordon—all I had to do was stroll out to the quadrangle and there he would be, or I would find him in the wan strip of grass behind the dormitories that somehow had cheerfully been dubbed "the beach club," as though wishing would make it so. Gordon, it seemed, magically, was always there—worn flip-flops, frayed khaki shorts, Frisbee in his hand. Then he would look up and see me, smile that lopsided smile of his, and follow me—back to my room, a spartan single that I kept woefully clean: a bed, a desk, and a stack of books that was always a mile high. I would take his hand and hurry with him down the uneven flagstone walkway, past the pink and white trees in bloom, through the thick humid air that still felt foreign to me, and into my room, where we would pass the afternoon, spent in each other's heat. Then I would get up and take a shower and get my neat stacks of books and carefully sharpened pencils, preparing to study, and Gordon—he always seemed to have a rolled-up paperback in his hand, a tattered Søren Kierkegaard or a well-worn *The Great Gatsby*—and then who knows what he did? I had never seen him study. It used to puzzle me that he seemed to have so much time to play, when I had none. All I know is that he was always there when I looked for him, Frisbee, sun-sweaty body, happy-go-lucky smile.

I was happy enough to have things the way they were. Unlike many of the other kids, whose summers were filled with all kinds of expensive activities, school was a respite for me. In the summer, I went home to stay in my mother's condo. She was hardly ever there because she took on so many overtime shifts to help defray my college expenses. I was planning to spend June taking an MCAT prep course, then work as a clerk in the hospital July and August. It would be harder work than studying, and I wasn't particularly looking forward to it.

Then one evening in May, a couple of weeks before the end of the year, I was at my desk, crick in my neck from poring over chemistry, and Gordon burst into my room without even knocking. He knew that when I was studying, I was studying, so it was unusual for him to stop by at that time. His presence was an intense distraction for me—it was as though my brain shut down completely and was replaced by the ac-tual fact of my body.

"Gordon?" I said.

"Student Travel Association," he said.

"What?" I was still deep in the Krebs cycle and didn't get what he was talking about. He was shifting back and forth from one foot to the other, eyes shining, hands hidden behind his back.

"An incredible deal. One ninety-nine. Round-trip."

"Gordon," I said. "I have no idea what you are talking about."

"I know," he said. "I know—that's the beauty of it." He was practi-cally dancing now. Fairly doing a jig. "My uncle Tommy sent me a check for five hundred dollars. Well, I'm gonna work all summer, so I figured it was fair game to spend it."

Gordon was grinning from ear to ear. Then from behind his back he whipped out two slim blue envelopes and waved them in the air in front of me.

"Paris!" he said, smiling. Smiling at me. Smiling at the whole world. He was constantly broke; his parents were dead in a plane crash; he would have had nowhere to stay if he hadn't gotten a job at a summer camp for July and August. And yet, he was smiling as if all the world had never had a thought but to smile back at him.

"The Left Bank, the Eiffel Tower . . ." He started to sing. *"I love Paris in ze springtime."* He grabbed my hand, attempting to pull me up out of my chair. *"I love Paris in ze fall . . ."*

"Gordon," I said.

"Yes?" he said, smiling at me, radiant.

"Gordon, this is ridiculous. You know that I can't. I have an MCAT prep course."

That didn't stop him at all. He just kept up with his hammy singing and his cajoling.

"Come on, Clara. This is a once-in-a-lifetime chance. I already bought the tickets. Take the MCAT course later. Skip the MCAT course for chrissakes. You are so smart I am absolutely sure you don't even need it. . . . *I love Paris in the winter when it drizzles . . ."*

I sat and watched him, and felt under my stubborn exterior how hard it was to keep sitting there. How much I wanted to melt into him, to go with him, to step inside his vision of the world, where bad things were just puffy little clouds passing across the sun.

"It's out of the question, Gordon."

"No, darlin', you know it isn't. Come with me, come with me. You know how bad you want to." By now he was touching me, nibbling around my neck, up under my hairline, stroking my thigh. He had reached over and closed the textbook that lay open in front of me. I was feeling that familiar sensation of vertigo: the room was spinning; my heart was pounding. I knew that feeling, and it never felt better until I let go.

I gripped the edge of my desk to steady myself, vowing not to let anything into my study time, but I couldn't hold out. A few seconds later we were sprawled against the narrow twin bed, my shirt shoved up, my pants shoved down, and we were tearing at each other like we had been separated for months instead of only hours.

Afterward we lay there, half on, half off the bed. He pulled up his jeans, but left them unbuttoned, so that I could still see the soft black hair at his groin. He picked up the two airplane tickets and waved them in the air again.

"Paris, Clara. Paris. The door is open. All you gotta do is walk through it."

*   *   *

I stayed home and took the MCAT course. I commuted every day from my mother's stuffy condo to an airless room over a convenience store, where I took practice test after practice test, until I could see Scantron sheets with multiple-choice bubbles even in my sleep.

I did very well on the MCATs and was eventually admitted to medical school. Gordon, he went without me, and came home and told me all about it, and how great it was, and how it would have been even better if I had been there.

Now it seems like the first little thing, the thing you should have seen, but missed, the tiny mole that is blacker than the others, the one lumpy spot in your breast.

I'm sure that in my place, Lydia would have gone with him. In fact the funny thing is, she did go to Paris that summer—term abroad or something like that. Maybe they sat next to each other in a Paris café or jostled each other for position while taking pictures on the Champs-Elysées. And how I wish they could have turned their heads, and seen each other, and known. Because I wish to God I could give them back some of the time beforehand, when Gordon could have been with Lydia if only he had known her, because obviously I couldn't give them back any of the future that they were supposed to have in front of them, the future that I had held so briefly in my hands before it slipped away.

The wind was rattling around the old barn like a dry cough. I tossed and turned in my bed, feeling the hot dusty air tickling the back of my throat. I had picked the path I was heading down twenty-three years ago at the age of fifteen. Now for the first time in all of that time, I was confronting indecision. Maybe Gordon was right, like he always told me, that saving the world isn't possible, no matter how hard you try, no matter how vigilant you are.

There was a frail baby, my namesake, who could neither breathe nor eat without the aid of machines. You could say that she was suffering, or that she had been given the gift of life, but either way whatever small flicker of being was left to her was there in part because of my actions. Didn't I owe as much to that one baby as to all of the others who had not yet been born? Safe passage, that had been my motto, to fall into the world into a rock-solid pair of hands.

But what if they didn't fall safely, then what?

Walter told me that I had been absolved by the hospital, but I did not yet feel absolution. I listened to the phlegmy rattle of the wind against the tile roof and the whipping of eucalyptus branches. I knew what Walter had told me—to just keep putting one foot ahead of the other—but what if he was wrong?

I closed my eyes and tried to imagine the sinewy presence of Gordon beside me, the perfectly formed second half that fit up against me like the missing piece in a jigsaw puzzle, the only pull I had ever felt that was stronger than the pull of gravity. But his presence wouldn't come, and I thought of Walter again, and remembered our office, with its row of exam rooms, every wall, every available space plastered with faces of babies in photographs—each one of whom had fallen into a well-trained, vigilant pair of hands. Each one had been caught, and had made safe landing.

Extension is basically the result of two forces: (1) uterine contractions exerting downward pressure and (2) the pelvic floor offering resistance.

—Oxorn-Foote

PART IV

EXTENSION

THIRTY

I smelled smoke. It woke me up. The loft room was hot. The window was open and the wind came through the window in fretful gasps. I rolled over and saw that Jazmyn's cot was empty. I sniffed. Sniffed again. It smelled like cigarette smoke. The wind seemed to be blowing harder than ever. I looked out into the courtyard and saw that one of the double Dutch doors had come unhitched and was banging. I guess that was what woke me up. I got up out of bed, kicked my feet halfway into my sneakers, and creaked down the dark stairway.

Through the wind, I could hear voices—a female voice, maybe Jazmyn, and a lower male voice that I didn't recognize. I couldn't quite tell where the voices were coming from. The wind was swirling around even inside the courtyard. The voices picked up and then died away again. I could feel the dust stinging my eyes. The Dutch door swung shut again with a loud bang. Eleanor kept the stable dark at night, except for a couple of floodlights at the arched stable door. I walked out to the gateway, so that I could see the illuminated parking lot.

There, parked in the gravel parking area, next to the Jeep and the battered stable Volvo, I saw Franny Baker's truck. Franny Baker? What was she doing here in the middle of the night? It didn't make any sense. My heart started to hammer again—

Unless one of the horses was hurt . . . maybe Eleanor had called Franny and woken Jazmyn to come help her.

But that made no sense. I was a light sleeper. She couldn't have woken Jazmyn without waking me. Besides, Eleanor would never allow cigarettes around the barn. The brush was as dry as tinder. . . . I looked across at the Villa de Vista. The house was dark. I could feel the hairs standing up on the back of my neck. Something wasn't right.

I walked over to refasten the stable door that had come unmoored, then couldn't help myself from crossing over to Benedetto's stall to check on him. All appeared well. The stall was fastened, the gate guard buckled across. At the sound of my footsteps he put his head out over the half door and whinnied, the pink insides of his nostrils glowing softly.

*   *   *

"No, I ain't! I ain't gonna."

I whirled around. This was unmistakably the voice of Jazmyn, and she sounded frightened. I tried to shine my flashlight into the empty corners of the courtyard, but the light was too weak to penetrate the penumbra.

Then I heard the sounds of thuds and jostling and the man's voice again—muffled. I couldn't hear what he was saying.

The voices were coming from the tack room, as was the smell of cigarette smoke. I walked across the courtyard. The tack room door was half ajar, but it was dark inside. I could see the bridles hung against the wall, the faint glow of the silver snaffles, but couldn't see anyone.

I was afraid to speak and give myself away, so I edged toward the door and peered into the shadows. I could see a man's broad back, with a white T-shirt. I could see the glowing ember of the cigarette that must've been in his mouth. Then I heard Jazmyn's voice clearly.

"Of course, Frankie, of course it's yours. Whose else would it be?" Her voice was soothing, but I could hear the underlying tremor of terror. I needed to act fast.

I appraised the man, whom I could barely see and whose back was to me. He didn't look too tall, maybe about my height, but even in the dim light, I could see that he was barrel-chested and looked powerful. I couldn't see Jazmyn at all—she was hidden in shadows—but I realized that she could likely see me at the doorway.

I held up my hand to make a signal, but still couldn't tell if she could see me or not. I wished I could see better—the way he was holding his arms suggested clenched fists, or . . . a weapon of some kind? I stood at the threshold of the doorway, uncertain. Should I use my advantage of surprise and step forward, but what if he was too much for me? Or should I go for Eleanor? Or for the cell phone that for once wasn't in my pocket?

"Yore mama told me you been fuckin' around. . . . Why did you leave me, baby?" I heard the frightening combination of crooning and menace in his voice.

No time to go anywhere. I stepped forward, with one hand yanked the string pull on the light, with the other grabbed a bridle from its rack on the wall.

Suddenly illuminated, the burly man swung around in surprise. Jazmyn was cowering against the wall in the corner. There was a flash of silver in the man's hand; I thought it might be a knife. I held on to the leather bridle, prepared to start swinging the heavy German snaffle bit if necessary.

"Step outside this tack room immediately," I said, somehow finding my authoritative doctor voice.

The man's stance was still aggressive, no sign of the knife. I saw his sunburned face, forehead creased in a frown, hands held up in front of him.

He took a step toward me. I fingered the leather in my hands. Time to start swinging?

"Leave the premises immediately." My voice sounded steady, not shot through with the fear that I felt.

He scowled, his black eyes flashing. "Says who?" He took another step toward me. One more step and I would have to start swinging or turn and run. I kept myself from glancing at the doorway, not wanting to project weakness.

"Out! Now!" I barked, pointing to the door.

He stepped toward me. I raised the bridle, ready to swing at his head. He held up his fists a little higher. Quaking inside, I held my ground. We stood like that in face-off. The moments dragged. Finally he lowered his fists just slightly.

"Whoa, there. Whoa, there, ma'am. Hold yer horses. Don't go all nuts on me now." His voice was slick with false subservience. "I'm just here having a little chitchat with my sweetheart." He dropped his fists to his sides, and took a step back. I just caught a glimpse of the silver blade he had pushed up his sleeve.

I lowered the bridle and pointed to the door again.

"You are trespassing. This is private property."

"Well, let me by then, sister. Let me by."

I stepped back and continued pointing. To my intense relief, he walked out the door into the courtyard.

Now what?

I gave Jazmyn a signal to stay where she was and followed him out into the courtyard. He walked out the front gate of the stable into the area that was lit by the floodlights, over next to the stable wall. I followed warily at a distance, watched his back for any sign that he was going to turn back. Out in the parking area, I saw a battered green Chevy Impala with the windows half rolled down. I hadn't noticed it before because of its dark color, and the fact that it was parked in the shadows. He got into the car, flipped the ignition, and made a rapid turn, then took off down the long driveway, spraying scattershot gravel behind him.

It wasn't until his taillights disappeared that I noticed that my knees were trembling. I walked back to the stable gate.

"Jaz," I said. "You can come out now. He's gone."

Jazmyn appeared a moment later.

"Shit, thanks, girl. You are pretty tough!"

"What was he doing here?"

"My low-down bitch of a mother—she told him I was here."

"How did your mother know?" Jazmyn looked really chagrined now, stared down at the gravel. I noticed that she was barefoot and still wearing the stained white T-shirt she usually wore to sleep in.

"She was getting all uppity with me. Telling me what a no-good loser I am, and so I told her. I told her I was up working at this big old house with a rich lady. . . . I didn't think she'd go and tell Frankie. I'm sure she's been fucking him in her own free time anyway."

"Jazmyn. Frankie's dangerous. You're not safe as long as he knows where you are."

"Well, don't I know that? I thought he was gonna cut the baby right out of me."

"We're going to have to get you into a shelter. Come on. I'm taking you to Eleanor. You're going to have to stay in the big house tonight. . . ."

"I'm not going into no shelter. Those places are nasty."

"You have to. Otherwise, he's gonna come grab you out of bed again and . . ." I stopped. How had he gotten her out of bed without me hearing anything?

"Jazmyn? Did you know he was coming?"

"Well, that SOB, he called me—he told me he knew where I was. He said he just wanted to talk. . . . I thought maybe if he came up here and saw where I was living, he would be impressed."

I looked at Jazmyn, belly round as a melon, bed-rumpled frizzy hair. She looked like an overgrown twelve-year-old, like she needed a mom to take care of her. I was intensely exasperated with her, but I tried to modulate it out of my tone.

"Jazmyn, Frankie could hurt you. You can't see him at all. You can't let him know where you are. If he gets in touch with you, you have to call the police. Eleanor told me you have a restraining order. Come on. I'm taking you up to the big house. We can call the police. You'll have to sleep there tonight."

And like the child that she was, she didn't protest at all, just followed me. Big belly, bare feet, blousy T-shirt, across the lit parking area, through the dark garden, and up onto the porch of the big house.

THIRTY-ONE

Eleanor came to the door wearing a blue dressing gown, looking every bit as awake as she usually did, though it was well past midnight.

I told her the facts quickly. Frankie, the threatening behavior, the knife.

"She'll sleep here tonight," Eleanor said, showing Jazmyn inside the house. I stood, waiting at the threshold, expecting something, a word of praise, perhaps.

"I'll call the police. Thank you for your help." Her words were curt. Dismissive. She shut the door. I turned and walked through the dark garden. I felt afraid now, in retrospect. Afraid that he might have hurt her, or might have hurt me. I thought back on other times when I had been in similar situations. There was a time when a fellow, recently out of jail, barged into an exam room demanding to see a patient's chart so he could see if she was "clean." I remembered how I had managed to fend him off too, despite the fact that I had been almost alone in the clinic and that no one would have heard if I had called for help.

Calm under fire. I always had been. I considered it one of my strengths.

As I walked back across the parking area, I remembered that I had seen Franny Baker's truck parked there earlier, and noticed that it was gone now. What had she been doing here anyway? I barely gave it a passing thought. Now after being so keyed up, I was bone tired and wanted to go back to sleep.

I trudged up the stairs to the loft room now empty, and lay down in the little cot. There was a momentary lull between gusts of hot wind, and I could hear the usual panoply of muffled barn sounds—stamping hooves and the old building shifting on its foundations. Then I heard a banging sound like a door slamming, and my heart started pounding.

What if Frankie came back? Jazmyn was probably safe in the big house, but what about me? I hadn't even thought of my own safety—usually abusers are interested only in their own domestic partners—but if he came back looking for her and found me instead . . . I stood up and crept over to the window. I heard the banging again. I could see that the tack room door wasn't shut all the way and it was banging in the wind.

I shoved my feet back into my sneakers, and tiptoed down the stairs again, hurrying across the stable courtyard to the corner stall. I unlatched the door and slipped inside, ducking under the rubber stall guard. Once inside the big horse's stall I could feel the reassuring horsey warmth radiating from Benedetto's neck. I crouched in the stall corner, my bottom resting in a soft pile of clean sawdust. My chin fell on my chest, and finally, after a few fits and starts, I could feel myself dropping into sleep.

THIRTY-TWO

Loud cracking sounds woke me up, and the smell of smoke so thick I could feel my eyes watering as I blinked them open in a panic. For a second I didn't realize where I was, but then I remembered. I was still crouched in the corner of the horse's stall. My legs were so stiff and leaden that at first I couldn't stand. Benedetto was pacing anxiously across the front of the stall.

Fire!

I pushed the stall door open, then latched it shut again, running across the courtyard to where the switch for the floodlights was. I flipped up the switch, and suddenly the courtyard was illuminated. I saw the horses putting their heads out over the half doors and blinking in the sudden light. All of them looked agitated—I could see the white rims encircling their eyes.

If I had thought the wind was blowing before, now it seemed relentless. It was hard to tell if the air was choked with smoke or dust. I looked around the courtyard, but saw nothing amiss, so I ran to the stable entrance and looked across toward the Villa de Vista.

I saw Eleanor just as she saw me. She was hurrying out of the garden in front of the villa, now fully dressed.

"Brush fire up on the Norton trail. It's not headed this way yet, but we're to be on alert. We're to hose down the adjacent areas and prepare the horses to evacuate if necessary."

I came around the bend of the stable and looked up through the darkness to the hills in the distance. Sure enough, up on the hillside, probably just below Jacaranda Canyon, I could see a jagged ring of orange traversing the hillside. Off in the distance, sirens were wailing.

"Is the fire department coming?" I asked.

"I've asked them to send a tanker, but they say it can't be spared. They're fighting from above, up around Jacaranda Canyon—now the fire is moving towards the houses up there."

"What should we do?"

"Help me hitch up the four-horse trailer. There are five horses in the barn—that will be two loads. We don't need to go yet, though. The wind is coming straight up from the ocean as usual, blowing the fire away from us. I very much doubt the winds will change. Let's wait and see how it goes."

Just as might have been expected, Eleanor was taking charge with calm effectiveness. In my years of doctoring I had realized that there were really two kinds of people—those who panicked in emergencies and those who didn't. It was clear which camp Eleanor fell into.

I looked up at the jagged line of fire again, could feel the wind whipping across my face, up from the ocean, driving the fire away from us, up the hill, up toward the million-dollar houses that lined the crest of the hill, about three miles away.

Eleanor was walking toward the pickup truck, and I went and stood next to the trailer hitch, getting ready to guide it into the ball and socket. Again I was impressed by this woman—pushing eighty and hitching a four-horse trailer in the middle of the night.

Just then, I saw Jazmyn emerge. Now she was dressed too, in jeans and the same white T-shirt she had been sleeping in.

"What do you want me to do? I'm ready to help," she said, and I could see Eleanor, like a proud mother, trying to push the corners of her mouth down to hide a smile.

After the trailer was hitched, we got the hoses and started spraying them around the periphery of the stable area. The water pressure was lousy, sometimes just a trickle, and the job seemed pretty hopeless, but so far the wind was holding in our favor. I couldn't really notice the smoke smell anymore—I guess I had gotten used to it. But my eyes were still stinging, and my body felt beat-up from fatigue, like I could fall asleep just standing there. I looked over at Jaz from time to time, anxiously, wondering if she was getting too tired, but most of the time I couldn't see her—she was around the other side of the barn.

Eleanor was on the phone on and off with the fire department getting updates. A couple of houses up the hill in Jacaranda Canyon had already burned, but so far the wind was holding steady and there was no movement down the hill toward us.

I think I was almost asleep standing there spraying the hose in the smoke-choked night, sleeping standing up, like a soldier. I know that I had no conscious thoughts and had completely lost track of time.

202 E L I Z A B E T H L E T T S

But then a spray of water directly into my face startled me wide-awake. Now the wind was whipping the water right back into its own path, and suddenly blowing cinders started gritting up my eyes. The wind had turned—I looked up the hill at the bright snake of fire, and could actually see it turning and folding back.

"Eleanor," I hollered. My voice was lost in the wind. I put down the hose and ran around to the front of the barn.

"The wind!"

"It's time to get the horses out now! The fire department says even with this wind, it will take several hours for the fire to get this far. Let's load up the first four." Jaz came around the front of the barn.

"Jazmyn, go get Seachild." Eleanor was referring to a gentle seal brown mare. "We'll load her first. She'll be a calming influence."

I unlatched the back of the trailer and put the ramp down.

Jazmyn led Seachild toward the empty trailer, and the mare stepped willingly up the ramp, her lead rope tossed over her shoulder. I went around the front to the hay window, reached in, grabbed her lead rope from over her neck, and tied it to the ring with a safety knot.

"Now Rideout," Eleanor commanded.

I went back to the barn and got out the bay mare, leading her out to the trailer. She too loaded easily, and stood quietly next to Seachild. We closed the gateway divider behind the two horses.

"Benedetto?" I said.

"Franklyn," she said. "We'll load the stallion last."

"But what about Blackmore?" Jazmyn asked, referring to Eleanor's usual mount.

"It's a four-horse trailer. We'll have to come back for him. Don't worry. We have plenty of time for two trips."

I felt a flicker of worry, wondered if we had waited too long to move the horses out. Thinking the wind wouldn't change might have been a mistake.

Jazmyn came up with Franklyn, but the horse was skittish and didn't want to load. He kept jumping off the ramp sideways and refusing to go in.

"Come on," Eleanor said. She and I closed in behind him, both swatting him hard on the haunches so that he couldn't move to either side. Feeling cornered, he clattered up the ramp and into the trailer. Now there was only one opening left.

I jogged into the barn and clipped the lead shank to Benedetto's halter. I could see that he was agitated. I had no idea if he trailered well. Some horses were difficult to load and others weren't.

The air was filled with noise, sirens wailing in the distance, wind, and an intense crackling sound that must have been the sound of the fire itself.

Benedetto jigged alongside me, head held high, obviously very strung up as I led him out to the lot where the trailer with the fourth, empty slot was waiting.

"We'll have to be clever about this," was Eleanor's matter-of-fact comment. "He doesn't trailer well. Usually I have Franny Baker give him a shot of something first."

Franny Baker, always there, but never when you needed her.

Knowing that horses respond best to resolute confidence, I stepped purposefully toward the trailer, tightening my grip on the lead shank and not shortening my stride at all. The remaining slot in the trailer yawned darkly, but I would walk right up the ramp, then duck out of the way, and in he would go, so that he could be whisked away to safety.

I strode quickly up the ramp, but Benedetto put only one hoof on the ramp before he jerked back sharply, rearing up, so that he almost jerked the lead rope out of my hand. I tightened my grasp on it, gave it a little jerk, and stepped forward again, but Benedetto just reared up higher, almost pulling me up off my feet and then backed up rapidly, dragging me along with him. I sank my heels into the gravel—no use. I was still getting dragged.

Eleanor swung around behind him, a black-and-white dressage whip in her hand, and stung him across the haunches. He moved forward again, but as soon as I started to bring him up the ramp, he reared again. I could feel that the thick white rope was burning my hands, but I held on tight.

I looked up at the hillside again and it was clear that the line of fire was much closer now—now instead of just the orange glow, you could almost see actual flames. It was still far away, probably farther than it looked because the big expanse of the Norton Hills was so empty.

I gave a sharp jerk on the rope, signaling I meant business, and approached the ramp again. This time Eleanor was square behind him with the whip, giving him the impression of being cornered. He stepped forward, then stopped on the ramp, but this time, he didn't rear, instead lifting his front foot and putting it down inside the trailer, where it made a hollow sound. I let the rope slip through my fingers just a little to give him room to slip inside. He took one step forward, then another. I let my fingers slide along the glossy crest of his neck, and along his shoulder. One more step. Two steps, and then I could shove from behind and swing the gate closed behind him.

Come on. One more step. I stood frozen next to him on the ramp, his head and forelegs inside the trailer, the rest of his body still on the ramp.

I kept my hand resting lightly on his barrel.

"Come on, boy, just one more step," I crooned soothingly. I was afraid to move, afraid that any sudden movement would startle him. I could see his ear cocked back, knew that he was listening to me.

"Come on, boy," I whispered.

Then Eleanor flicked the stinging whip onto his buttock, and Benedetto reared straight up, banging his poll hard on the metal edge of the trailer, and knocking me clear out of the way, so that I fell hard on my side off the ramp.

"Why did you use the whip? He was just about to go in."

"Why didn't you hold on?" Eleanor retorted. "If you hadn't let go, he'd be loaded."

Benedetto had stopped and stood, looking wary, his lead rope dangling. I stood up and brushed myself off. I saw Jazmyn looking at the horse, not sure if she should step forward or not.

I put out my hand, palm up, then stepped toward him. He was trumpeting his nose until you could see the pink interior, and his big brown eyes were ringed with white.

I looked at Eleanor to see if she was moving, but she wasn't, so I stepped forward and grabbed the lead shank, reaching up with my other hand to stroke his neck.

I was furious at Eleanor. She didn't click with this horse, always using the whip at just the wrong moment.

"Try again," she said.

"Unload the others and put him in first," I said.

We both looked up the hillside, where now the fire looked closer than ever.

Eleanor stood for a minute scanning the hills.

"It's twenty minutes round-trip to the barn. You're right. He'll load better if he's alone. Jazmyn. Load up Blackmore. I'll come back for Benedetto. You stay here and mind the horse." I thought of reminding her that she had fired me, but thought better of it.

"Send Jazmyn out with Maria and Julio," she said to me. Blackmore loaded easily, the lead rope tossed over his withers. Once the trailer was loaded and the back latched shut, Eleanor snapped her fingers for Oyster, and strode around to the front of the pickup and got in. Then, executing a perfect three-point turn, she drove off down the driveway, leaving me and Jazmyn, and the horse, alone in the dark night, the fire still far away, but creeping its way down the hill in a sinister snaking line.

THIRTY-THREE

"Oh, sweet Jesus. What a night!" Jazmyn said, blowing out so that she puffed up her sticky bangs. Then from the sheer understatement of that, we both started giggling, and then laughing outright, until I thought my sides would burst, and I would have sworn the horse was looking at us like we were crazy.

It did seem like the night had gone on forever, but I looked at my watch and saw that it was now three thirty a.m., only forty-five minutes from when the fire had first awakened me.

"Let's sit," I said, since it seemed like I should say something. We sat on two rocks. Benedetto, still on the lead shank, was lazily cropping at grass, all of his previous anxiety now gone.

"Jesus, my butt hurts," Jazmyn said, and this struck me as so funny that I started giggling again, and then she did too, but then it struck me that I was alone in a fire zone with a pregnant minor, and an Olympic-prospect horse, and then I thought of Julio and Maria, and as if by cue, they came out too, fully dressed, carrying a couple of cardboard boxes that looked like they contained photo albums and things they wanted to safegaurd. I noticed that the two pictures of the girl with the surfboard that I had noticed upstairs in the big house were balancing on top of the pile.

"Leaving?" I said.

"Yes. The phone has gone dead. It's not safe to stay when we don't know how close the fire is. You need to leave too," Julio said.

Just then, a big gust of wind blasted us in the face. The wind was full of cinders that were swirling madly in the path of light from the floodlights.

"I'm going to wait with the horse until Eleanor gets back. Jazmyn, you need to go."

"I'm staying with you," she said.

"No, Jazmyn you have to go. Think of the baby."

"I'm fine," she said. "Remember, she said that fire won't get here before two hours, and they're going to send some fire trucks down here anyway." She had her lip stuck out all stubborn looking.

"Go," I said. "You need to go."

"You can't load Benedetto unless there are three of us."

"Go," I said. "You are more important than the horse, and so is the baby."

But Jazmyn just jutted out her lip and settled herself on the rock. I didn't want her to stay, but I didn't think I could make her go either. In any case, the road was open and my rental car was still here. If worse came to worst, we could both get out in a hurry.

"I'll look after her," I said.

Maria and Julio took their boxes and put them in the trunk of their car, and then, after one more offer to Jazmyn, they too headed down the driveway toward the cliff road. Up on the hills we could hear the sound of choppers overhead. It was no longer clear if the fire was approaching or not. Maybe the fire would never get to us.

After that, the minutes seemed to drag. I looked down at my watch and each time I looked it was only a moment or two later. Jazmyn had been to Rolling Rock barn and she assured me it was just down the road. It wouldn't take long for Eleanor to get there and back. I wanted the horse and the girl out of there.

For a while nothing seemed to change. Hot wind. Sirens in the distance. The bright eerie snake of color on the hillside, and the smoke-choked air. There was no moon, no stars. The night was dark except for the floodlights over the barn, and the few lights illuminated in the big house. Benedetto was lipping grass peacefully at the end of his long cotton lead shank. Jazmyn had stretched out on the grass and was snoring gently, then shifting and groaning ocasionally. Time, it seemed, was standing still.

I must've slept because I awoke with a start in sudden darkness. I blinked my eyes, disoriented. Where was I? I couldn't see anything. The lights had gone out. The barn and the big house were clothed in darkness; the murky air seemed opaque. I couldn't make out the outline of the house, could just barely see the barn behind me. Benedetto had his head up, and was clearly anxious, pacing back and forth. His anxiety passed to me like an electric current. Suddenly I remembered. Jazmyn. Where was she? Her sleeping form had been right in front of me. Now I did not see her.

"Jaz?" I called out. "Jazmyn? Where are you?" The hot wind blew across my face, whipping hair into my eyes, which were stinging anyway from the smoke. I looked around but saw only a brownish blackness in all directions. Panic seized me.

"Jaz!"

"The lights went out." I saw a face emerge from the darkness, then a body. She was zipping up her fly. "I went to take a dump and the lights went out. Couldn't see a fucking thing. I ended up taking it right in one of the horse stalls. Isn't that gross?"

"I got worried."

"Yeah, me too. I was having the trots something wicked, and there I am all in a horse stall with no toilet paper or nothing. Not to go all gross on you."

I looked at the horse, the girl. It was time to make a decision.

Just then, I heard another sound approaching. It sounded staticky, like it was coming over a loud radio, or maybe a bullhorn.

ABATSAHEYA ABATSAHEYA, first tinny and distant, then getting louder and louder. But just as the string of sounds started sounding like it would separate into intelligible words, it started to fade again, growing more distant, until the sound was no longer audible.

I was afraid now. In the smoke-dense blackness, I could no longer judge whether the fire was getting closer or not. Jazmyn was just standing in front of me, not saying anything. It was so dark I couldn't see the expression on her face. I looked at the horse. He was calm, but clearly on the alert, not grazing peacefully like he had before.

"Jaz," I said. "We have to go. We can't wait any longer. It's not safe."

"You know, Clara, I don't feel that good," she said breathily, "I feel like I'm gonna . . ." She turned and started retching on the ground next to her.

"Clara, I really don't feel too good. I gotta take a dump again."

"Here," I said. "Take the flashlight. Here's some Kleenex." A new tension vibrated in me, but I tried not to put words to my feeling.

Jazmyn shuffled back into the stable courtyard. The thin beam of light only showed more clearly how yellow the air had become.

I ran my hand along Benedetto's withers, and he turned his head to my touch, blowing hot damp air onto my hand from his velvety nostril.

We couldn't wait for Eleanor any longer. We needed to get out immediately, now while there was still time. I needed to get Jazmyn out. There was only one way to do it. I would give her my keys and she would drive out—I would take the horse and go on foot. We needed to do it now, before it was too late.

A few moments later, Jazmyn came back, and I saw that she was hunched over a little and looked uncomfortable.

"We're leaving," I said.

"Clara, I don't feel too good."

"You're going to drive my car out. I'll take the horse."

"Clara . . ." Jazmyn's voice sounded pitiful, but I wasn't listening.

"Come on now. This is no time for . . ."

"Clara? This time when I wiped, there was a bunch of blood. Is that normal?"

If I was afraid before, that was the moment when the wind sucked out of me.

"Blood?" I said. "How much?"

"Well, not that much. Um, like a period, with a bunch of mucus mixed in."

"Does your belly hurt?"

"Nah, I mean I just feel kinda sick to my stomach, and my back hurts."

"The baby moving?"

"Yeah, he's kicking me right now."

"Jaz, how many weeks did you say you were?"

"The doctor told me thirty-four weeks. I'm due next month."

Doctor analysis kicked in, in spite of myself. In spite of everything else. Thirty-four weeks, backache, loose stool, bloody show—almost certainly labor, the baby was probably big enough to be born and do well. We needed to get her to the hospital.

"Anything else?"

"What do you mean?"

"I mean, did your doctor tell you anything else?"

"Well, no, I mean, well, yeah, kind of . . ."

"Kind of what?"

"Well, I mean she told me the baby was kinda sideways—"

"Kinda sideways?" I could hear my voice getting shrill. "Transverse?" I was yelling. "Did she say *transverse*?"

"Yeah, I think it was that, or something like that. She said kinda sideways. She said she thought the baby was gonna move into the birth canal, but if it didn't, she was gonna havta do a C-section." *Sweet Jesus.*

"Lie down," I commanded.

"What the fuck?"

"I said lie down. I need to check the baby's position. I mean it. Pronto."

Obediently, Jaz clambered to the ground and stretched out, flat on her back on the grass. Benedetto was watching the whole thing, and I had a momentary fear he might step on her, but somehow sensed that he wouldn't.

I kneeled down on my knees, pushed her T-shirt out of the way, and started to do Leopold's—a series of hand maneuvers that allow you to check the baby's position.

"Are you going kinky on me, girl?" Jazmyn piped up from the grass.

"I'm checking the baby's position."

"Yeah, and I'm the queen of England."

"Don't worry," I said. "I'm a doctor." It was out of my mouth before I had given it a thought.

There was a momentary silence from Jazmyn and then she said, "Oh, well, that explains a lot."

Quickly I cupped my hands around the belly to check the position of the baby, then repeated each move to recheck myself. I understood exactly what the problem was. The baby was not transverse—which means completely sideways, impossible to deliver vaginally—but she was slightly oblique; the head was down, but not engaged in the pelvis, and slightly off to the side. Usually with onset of labor the baby came down with its head down. Usually.

"I don't feel too good lying like this. I feel like I can't breathe."

"Roll over onto your side, then. You need to get up. I need to get you to a hospital." She reached out her hand, and I helped her up. Then she stood on her feet, a little wobbly, and moaned a little.

"Shit," she said. "I feel like crap warmed over."

I had my hands wrapped around the keys that were in my pocket, got ready to hold them out to her, then felt something freeze inside me. I knew I couldn't hand her the keys and ask her to drive out. She was in no condition to drive.

"Come on," I said, with all the strength I could muster. "Let's go. Get in the car."

"But, but we can't. We can't go now. We have to wait for Eleanor. *What about the horse?*"

"It's not safe to stay here a minute longer," I said, and as if to emphasize my words, a big gust of wind kicked up thick with smoke and cinders. I could swear that now, for the first time, I could hear the fire crackling and roaring in the distance.

"We have to go. Now!"

Benedetto took a step closer to me, brought his face up close to mine. I could feel his hot breath.

"But what about the horse?" Jazmyn was half sobbing now.

I looked at Benedetto, almost invisible in the darkness, ran my hand along the smooth hair on his neck, then down along the velour side of his muzzle.

"I'll throw the lead rope over his back. He'll have to find his way out on his own." I was strangling on my own words, but there was no other way.

I took the lead rope and tossed it over the horse's neck, reached forward, and pressed my mouth against the soft fur above his nostril. "Save yourself," I whispered, so softly that even Jazmyn couldn't have heard me.

Then I grasped her arm and walked firmly toward my parked car, which I couldn't even see, but which I knew was parked at the far end of the lot. Jaz was walking heavily, leaning on my arm. She stopped to retch a couple of times. Benedetto had hesitated for a moment, then reached down to crop some grass and let us walk away from him. He probably didn't even realize he wasn't tied, but I was praying fervently that he would be able to find his way out as the fire approached.

I pulled open the back door.

"Get in. Lay down on the backseat."

I slid into the front seat, shut the door, and slid the key into the ignition. I fired up the engine. Then when I turned on the headlights I looked around to see Benedetto, but couldn't see him. All I could see was the air illuminated by the beams of the headlights; it was thick with smoke and blowing bits of cinder. Hopefully the fire was now under control, and this smoke-choked air was just the aftermath.

I put my foot on the accelerator to head out.

Bump, bumpbump, bumpbump.

The car wouldn't move forward properly. It felt like I was rolling over something enormous. I put my foot on the brake.

Jazmyn sat up.

"What the fuck?"

My first thought, irrationally, was that somehow I had managed to run over Benedetto. My heart jumped around like a dog in a crate.

I put my foot on the gas again, ever so gently.

Bump. Bumpbump, bump.

I jumped out of the car, ran around to the front of the car. Nothing. The headlight beams illuminated only the empty driveway stretching down the hill.

Then I heard the same tinny staticky sound I had heard a few minutes earlier.

ABATSAHEYA ABATSAHEYA. I strained to listen. What was it? What was it? Then suddenly, the wind dropped and there was a moment of absolute stillness, across the fields, coming from the road down below, I heard the words crystal clear.

"EVACUATE THE AREA! EVACUATE THE AREA!"

Getting louder and more clear.

"EVACUATE THE AREA!"

"Jaz, gimme the flashlight," I said.

I needed to see what was under the car that was blocking us from moving forward.

I pointed the light in front of the car and then around the side.

When I saw it, I sucked in a big gulp of the smoke-singed air.

All four of my tires were flat.

"EVACUATE THE AREA! EVACUATE THE AREA!"

But thank God, they must be coming to get us. We were the only people left up here, and Eleanor knew we were here. The fire crews must have kept her out. She must have told them to come look for us here.

"EVACUATE THE AREA."

ABATSAHEYA.

With a shudder, I realized that the sound of the bullhorn was fading again; they had driven right past the long driveway and kept going. We were alone on this hillside. I looked back toward the barn. With a start, I saw the silhouette of burning Italian cypress trees in a line coming down the hill. There was no doubt. The fire was less than a quarter of a mile away.

THIRTY-FOUR

"Clara, Clara!" Jazmyn called out from the backseat of the car. "I'm all wet. I feel like I peed myself or something."

I opened the car door. Didn't even need a light to know. The car interior was filled with the distinctive sweetish odor of amniotic fluid.

"Are you feeling pressure? Do you feel like you want to push?"

"Nope. I just feel all gross and my back hurts a little."

Now was the time I had to do something fast. My mind was racing through the possibilities.

The cell phone! Why hadn't I even thought of that? It was upstairs in the loft room in the charger.

"Stay here," I commanded. "I'll be right back."

I ran through the stable courtyard and plunged my way blindly into the dark room. I felt my way across to my bunk and groped for the phone. I grabbed it; then as an afterthought, I pulled the clean sheet and blanket off my bed. I punched the familiar buttons on the cell phone and listened—nothing. Fumbling, I tried the buttons again. Nothing. Of course. The battery was dead. I had let it run low, then put it on the charger. The electricity was out. Gathering up the blankets, I ran back down and was startled to see Benedetto, standing right where we had left him. When he saw me he whinnied and took a step forward. I grabbed hold of his lead shank again and led him back to the car. I tossed the sheet and blanket into the front seat through the open window.

"Are you okay?"

"Yeah, I'm just all gross. I don't wanna lie here in this mess. I want to go get some dry clothes."

"Are you having any contractions?"

"No, but I keep getting this cramp in my stomach and then it goes away."

I knew that delivery might be imminent, or it might not be. I was afraid to do the internal exam in such unsterile conditions. *What do I do? Stay by her side and deliver the baby if it comes? And risk the three of us being trapped . . .*

Just then Benedetto leaned forward and nudged me with his nose, his hot breath tickling my ear.

There really wasn't any choice. I knew what I had to do. I turned back toward the stable headed for the tack room for the horse's bridle and saddle. Suddenly a blast of heat slammed into my face and I could see a huge burst of hot white light.

It looked like the stable rooftop was in flames. I spun and ran back. "Jaz, I'm going for help."

I took the cotton lead rope and tied the loose end to the horse's halter to make a type of reins.

I clambered up onto the car's fender, swaying already with such an intense sense of vertigo that I felt as if I were swimming sideways underwater. I looked back at the barn—I couldn't see it too well, but now, it didn't look like it was flaming anymore.

My hands and knees were shaking so much that I could barely stay balanced on the fender, and Benedetto was anxious and moving around. He didn't want to stand still.

"Clara? Clara?" Jazmyn's voice sounded childlike, afraid.

I stepped back off the car, relieved to be on solid ground.

"What should I do if the baby comes while you're gone?" I could see tears rolling down her cheeks. "What should I do?"

"I don't think it's going to, honey, but if it does, don't panic. Just wrap the baby in a blanket and hold it right up against your chest so it'll be warm. I'll be right back with an ambulance. I promise."

The horse looked ten feet tall. My knees were shaking so hard that I thought I might fall.

I led Benedetto into position and vaulted onto his bare back, off-kilter at first, but by instinct, I righted myself, my hands gathering up the thick white lead rope that would serve as reins. I wrapped my legs around his broad barrel and leaned forward, burying my hands deep into his mane, the wiry strands cutting into my fingers. Then squeezing my eyes shut, I closed my legs around him, first tentatively, then stronger, and urged him forward. Benedetto bolted at a fast gallop. Hooves clattering, we tore down the asphalt driveway, headed straight toward the road that ran along the cliff.

I was not in control. My fingers knotted into his mane—it was all I could do to hold on. He was at a full gallop, the flames behind him obviously making him panicky. The asphalt driveway was slick. I could feel his hooves losing purchase from time to time. My legs were gripping hard to his slippery sides; my crotch was banging hard on his withers with each bounding stride; my nose was almost pressed against his crest.

Almost immediately, the faint glow of the barricades came into view. Coming off the driveway, he needed to slow down or risk falling. We had to make a sharp turn to the left or right—if he didn't turn . . . the cliffs were directly in front of us.

I loosened one hand from the mane. One of his hooves slid. I was jolted off-balance; then holding tight to the mane, I righted myself. I sat down on his back and yanked on the rope. His pace didn't slacken at all. I was riding in a halter. I tugged on the rope as hard as I could. No response. He barreled straight ahead at top speed without slackening.

I could see the barricades in front of me, growing taller, sickly iridescent yellow against the night.

Slow down. Slow down. I sank my weight hard down on his back. I pulled hard on the rope.

Nothing. We were at the end of the driveway. The barricades loomed straight in front of us. One step, two, I would have to try to bail off. . . .

I threw my weight to the right and pulled hard on the rope. Abruptly he jagged to the right.

Like they were car wheels on ice, I felt his hooves going out from underneath him as the horse made a sharp right turn on the road. For a long moment, I hung in the balance as he skittered, about to go down, knowing it was too late now for me to get out from under him. His hooves rang on the slick pavement like a spoon caught in a Disposall.

I felt him going down—down—down—and me with him—a prolonged falling that seemed to go on and on . . .

But with his scrabbling, he clung to his equilibrium and managed to right himself, and somehow, I managed to cling on.

Then in front of me, people and barricades and blinking lights. There were police barricades stretched across the width of the road. Behind them were a lone cop car with its flashers on and a small crowd of people, their faces briefly illuminated yellow, and then hidden again in darkness. Benedetto had slowed, and this time when I pulled on the rope he came to a stop. I saw Eleanor step forward.

"What in heaven's name? Where's Jazmyn?"

I vaulted off, untied the loop from the halter, and tossed the rope to Eleanor.

"I need your help now!" I said to the officer. "There's a girl trapped up there who is about to have a baby."

The cop had the pink-eared look of a rookie.

"But, but I have to guard the crossing."

"Go!" Eleanor said. "I'll guard the barricade until then."

As we came up the driveway, now I could see burning trees clearly—the road was still passable, but it seemed like it wouldn't be for long. My eyes fretfully searched for the sight of the car, and soon I could see that it was still unscathed. We pulled up and I jumped out, the cop following close behind me. He shined the light into the backseat, making Jazmyn blink in the sudden bright light.

"Jaz," I said.

"Still here." Her voice was full of relief. "What took you so long?"

"Anything change?

"Um, Clara, I feel something sticking out, down there. I don't know what it is—is it like the baby or something?"

The cop was useless. He stood there looking frozen to the spot, but he did have an emergency delivery kit in his car. I washed my hands with antiseptic gel, put on gloves, cut away her pants.

There coiled between her legs was a twisted loop of purply white.

Damn it all to hell.

She had prolapsed her cord.

Of course, the head was oblique, not blocking the birth canal, allowing the cord to slip out first. Terrified of what I would find, I put my fingers on the cord—if it was pulsating, all was well. That meant the blood was flowing. If it was still, then the blood wasn't flowing, and most likely the baby was already dead.

I reached out my gloved hand, afraid, afraid, but I had to. I pressed my fingers gently against the gelatinous substance and held my breath.

Whoosh. Whoosh. Whoosh. Whoosh. The steady beating heart.

Ow, ow. Ow. Ow.

This was a strong contraction. I felt the gentle pulsing of the heart-beat grow fainter as the uterus bore down.

"Don't move, Jaz," I whispered. I slipped my hand up along the cord and spread the labia with my fingertips until I felt the firm surface of the baby's head, which was starting to come down the birth canal, trap-ping the cord alongside it. I knew the only hope. With firm but gentle pressure, I used my index and middle finger to apply pressure to the baby's head, to lift it up so that it would relieve the pressure on the cord. Gently, I pressed upward, and felt, reassuring as a ticking watch, the cord start pulsating against my wrist. It was working.

The cop hadn't said anything yet, but now in a panicky voice he said, "Hey, lady, what's going on in there? Did the baby come out?"

"Don't worry, I'm a doctor," I said. I could hear him sigh heavily with relief. "We need to get her into the squad car. Get the sheet from the front seat and lay it out on the seat. Jaz. Listen up. Your cord slipped out, and I think everything is okay, but I'm going to have to stay like this until we get to the hospital. You just do what I say, and everything will be okay." She was crying a little, more whimpering.

"Okay, okay, whatever, whatever, just make sure the baby is okay."

"It's okay, Jaz. You have my word." Still not moving, still slung out on the wet seat between her legs, my fingers inside her vagina, pushing on the baby's head, I craned my neck around to talk to the cop, whose name I still did not know.

"Okay, we're going to have to move her. Get in behind her and push her forward. You think you can carry her?"

"Yeah, sure, I can carry her." He sounded all bravado, relieved to be asked to do something he knew he could do.

"Okay, listen up. I've gotta keep my hand like this supporting the baby's head while you're moving her. You ready, Jaz?"

"Just don't hurt the baby, okay?"

"Don't worry. I won't. One, two, three . . ."

Somehow, we did it. The cop, whose name was Patrick, brought the car up as close as he could and he got in and we slid her along the back-seat, me taking care to keep a steady pressure on the baby's head. The amniotic fluid, greasy with chunks of buttery vernix, was soaking through my shirt as I slid along the backseat, holding my hand steady.

We inched across the short distance, two steps, three, and Patrick dragged her onto the waiting clean sheet, and I stumbled behind her into the car and curled my legs up into a fetal position so that he could shut the car door. Jazmyn was flat on her back with her knees bent and feet up and my two fingers, rock steady, were still holding up the world.

I didn't realize it then, but a burning ember had clung to my shirt as we crossed and then fallen onto my shoulder. I never felt any pain at all that I recall, just the gentle tick, tick, tick, rapid and steady, of the baby's heart.

THIRTY-FIVE

After the accident with Captain, everyone treated me as if I were a raw egg that might break and spill out my slippery guts all over everything. I could hear hushed conversations that people thought were out of earshot—*Should we ask her what happened? Should we ask her to talk about it? Let's just give her time.*

Of course, a police officer had come and asked me a few gentle questions about the accident, and I would recite the few details until the recital was so detached from the actual event that it was completely anesthetized of content. When I learned later about paresthesias, the loss of nerve sensations that diabetics sometimes get in their fingers and toes, it reminded me of that time—odd uncomfortable tingling sometimes, and sharp shooting pains at others, but most of the time, just numb.

It was a short story. Not too many details. I galloped down the trail at Norton Bend. I saw a white blur, then felt a thud.

Then we went over. Except that I was thrown from the horse and landed just a few feet below the cliff edge on a narrow rocky precipice, mouth full of dirt and blood from where I had bitten my tongue, and I held on and held on and I tried to tell myself that Captain had not been thrown over, but I knew that he had been because I could hear him squealing below me on the rocks.

I tried to tell everyone about how it happened.

There was a white blur and then a thud. But it seemed like no one was really listening then, like I was mouthing the words underwater.

"Yes, we know, dear. You were galloping. Maybe he spooked—maybe he stumbled."

No! I tried to tell everyone. There was a white blur. There was a thud. *What were they thinking? Horses don't just go up to the edge of the world and jump.*

The cop, I remember, seemed a little interested in the white blur. "What was it, exactly?"

I didn't know what it was.

I remember the officer told me that it couldn't have been a car. They were doing a sobriety checkpoint just down the road, just around the bend from there, just beyond the gatehouse, where the big road and the little road met. No cars had come around the curve that day. Not a single one.

My mother just sat on the edge of my bed and rubbed my arm absentmindedly, saying, "Don't worry about it, dear. What's done is done. We'll never know how it happened. Just let it go."

I had clung there, fingernails scraping against rocks and loose soil, wedged on a tiny ledge that I could feel crumbling right underneath me. I was clinging, clinging, holding on—not believing I could fall, not yet believing in the reality of falling, until my arms and hands and fingertips were shaking with exhaustion, until I could feel the loose dirt give way and my fingernails tearing on bare rocks.

Then down from heaven, I saw it. Lydia fingertips, Lydia's wrist. Lydia's bare arm.

Grab on. Grab on. I'll pull you up.

I don't know how I grabbed it, how I let go and grabbed without falling. I don't know how she pulled me up. I was almost as heavy as she was, and my ankle was twisted, so I couldn't really push.

But I scraped and dragged back over the edge, onto the road, and she said, *Stay there, Clara. Don't move. I'm going for help. I swear I'll be right back.*

Then I heard hoofbeats as she swung up on her white horse and galloped away. And then, a few minutes later, flashing lights and sirens and it wasn't just my story anymore.

THIRTY-SIX

Eleanor was my first visitor. I was lying in my thin hospital gown on the bed with the bed rails pulled up so that I, in my grogged-out state, wouldn't fall. My shoulder was hurting terribly now, so painful that I knew the morphine was wearing off. I winced at the memory of the night before. My T-shirt had been singed right onto the skin. The ER doc had had to cut it away with a scalpel.

"Well, Dr. Raymond." I heard her familiar raspy voice, but didn't roll over. "Well-done. Well-done."

I thought about turning to face her, but then I would also have to face all of the questions. No one had spoken to me about anything since I had gotten here. I didn't know how Jazmyn was, didn't know how the baby had fared. I feared the worst.

They had peeled me away from her in the ER, put me on a stretcher, and wheeled me away. I passed Jazmyn and her baby over, experiencing, perhaps for the first time in my own life, the intense relief of turning over an emergency into someone else's skilled hands. They had morphined me up in order to cut away the shirt fibers that were stuck to the wound. I had swum up periodically with a feeling of intense anxiety and then remembered—the preterm labor, the prolapsed cord, the careening ride in the back of a squad car.

"Guess what Jazmyn is planning to name the baby?"

I couldn't help it. I rolled over, feeling another stab of pain in my arm.

"How are they?" I asked.

"Jazmyn is the proud mother. Breast-feeding. The baby, five pounds even, she's going to name her . . ."

"Clara?"

"Not quite. Sierra Dakota—a little geographical for my taste, don't you think?"

"They're okay?"

"Fit as a fiddle."

"Benedetto."

"Perfectly content."

Then I remembered the flames blazing in the cypress trees.

"The house . . ."

"It's a miracle, Clara, isn't it? Neither the house nor the barn was touched."

"But the barn? I saw the barn go up in flames."

"The fire came right up behind it—the entire big haystack and shavings pile were entirely scorched. But it didn't go any farther. I guess the wind changed. Entirely unpredictable. But I feel blessed."

Then she stopped talking, and I just stared up at the ceiling, the mountain of things we now needed to talk about seeming too insurmountable, my head too heavy, my eyes too heavy to continue.

"So you know who I am," I was finally able to mutter.

"Indeed, and more importantly, I know *what* you are. I know what you are made of."

"I have some questions I need to ask you." I looked at her face while I said this, thought I saw her shoulders droop a little, definitely saw that she looked away from me and out the window.

"The first one is, why didn't you come back for us, Eleanor? Why did you leave us there?"

"Oh, Clara, that was inexcusable. I blame myself. By the time I got back, the barricades were up and the policeman wouldn't let me through. I had a fit—told him he had to let me through because two stable girls and a horse were still in there. He told me that a red-haired lady had told him that everyone was out . . ." I could see the look of puzzlement growing in her weathered face. "I should have made them double-check, though—I assumed Franny was . . ." She trailed off.

I closed my eyes, but then the room started to spin, so I opened them again.

"I want you to tell me what happened to my father."

"Of course," she said. "I've been waiting for you to ask. But you look exhausted, Dr. Raymond, so I really think that now is not the best time. I'm sure they won't keep you in for too much longer. Come up to the house. You deserve to have me tell you everything. I'll tell you whatever you want to know."

My head was throbbing; my eyes were heavy. I couldn't even open them to say good-bye as she walked out, but I let myself drift gently downward, like a leaf floating on a current.

Jazmyn was okay. The baby was okay. I slept.

One of the nurses brought me my cell phone in its charger and plugged it into the wall. I was half awake when she put it on the table, whispering, "Mrs. Norton thought you might need this." I stared at its sleek inanimate surface, then drifted back to sleep.

When I awoke again, and saw it lying there, my heart fluttered and I reached for it—somehow that phone had become the direct line to my heart.

I pushed the on button and punched buttons until I got to the call log.

Seven missed calls.

Three: Gordon.

Three: Walter.

One: my mother.

My shoulder still hurt, though I didn't care that much, and the pain medicine made me feel sick to my stomach whenever I sat up. So I put the phone back down and closed my eyes again, and slept, dreaming confusing dreams.

THIRTY-SEVEN

Well, how did it end? I remember how it ended, just as I remember how it started. Though the part in the middle is harder to remember sometimes.

So I'll start with the part in the middle. For a certain kind of person, bright, eclectic, with a high tolerance for living on almost no money, it is possible to stay in Boston for a very long time, if not forever, clinging to the odd fringes of academe, and occasionally doing something odd and clever, like working in an Indonesian tea shop serving *chai*.

Gordon is bright and clever, and he always seemed perfectly indifferent to money, in a way that I could never really understand. I was not indifferent to money. I had to carefully manage my financial aid, drawing up a budget and sticking to it. Gordon would get some grant check for something or other, and use up a hundred dollars taking me out for a fancy dinner that I didn't care about, while I spent the entire time worrying while I totted up the totals in my head.

So in the years after college, Gordon and I both lived around Boston. For a while he was doing geology, at Harvard, and I didn't see him too often. I was in med school at Tufts and studying all the time. Gordon had the key to my studio apartment, and sometimes I'd come home and there he'd be, lounging on my sofa reading a book, forking Thai noodles out of a cardboard box, or sipping on an Amstel dark.

He always had a complicated set of living arrangements—subletting from a graduate student doing fieldwork, house-sitting for a professor on sabbatical. "Dirt cheap," he would say, or "*He's* paying *me* to stay there." Sometimes there were short gaps when he was between places, and so he would dump his stuff in my living room, and we would shack up together for a while, squeezing into my single bed for two or three weeks at a time. Then, one summer, his Bug needed a new engine and his sublet fell through, and his stuff stayed in my living room so long that one morning I looked at him over coffee and said, "Gordon, why don't you just move in?" He grinned back and said, "I thought you would never ask." I don't know why his financial situation was always so dire, or I do know—it was a total lack of planning. But he came up with his half of the rent by hook or by crook, sometimes delivering piz-zas at the end of the month to make ends meet.

One day, I came home from the hospital and he was sitting in our worn brown easy chair, just staring out the window.

He watched me come in, dog-tired as usual, watched me throw down my coat and collapse on the sofa; I was so exhausted I could hear ringing in my ears. "I'm so sick of that goddamn hospital I could scream. I was a scut bunny all day. Triage. Eighteen straight hours of fucking triage!"

Gordon came over and stroked my hair and rubbed my shoulders. "You say you're sick of it, but you're not, really."

"I am sick of it. I swear, I am," but my voice lacked conviction.

"You're lucky, Clara."

"Oh, yeah, lucky me." I was in no mood to hear how lucky I was.

"You are lucky you know what you want."

He proceeded to drop out of geology and enroll in the Divinity School, to study comparative religious philosophy.

"I learned it from you, Clara," he said. "I learned how important it is to do what you love."

I was glad he found something that he liked. I was so busy that I was rarely home, but when I was there we would have sex and eat and he would tell me bits of information that seemed both useless and charming—what the prophet Muhammad ate for breakfast, where Thoreau had stolen his theories from, what the professor of ancient Sanskrit had said that day. Gordon spent most of his time reading—he had lots of free time, and he used to cook for us, vegetarian curry or sesame noodles.

"Keeping you fit to save the world," he used to say.

"You've got it made." That's what the other residents used to say, the ones who were dating other residents and whose meals together were most often stale pizza and watery coffee in the call room.

"I know," I always said. "I do."

That was the middle. Through four years of medical school and into my second year of residency, I worried about school and my patients and my grades and my performance in rounds, but I didn't think about what was going to happen with me and Gordon. I learned about home-ostasis in biology, and I was naïve enough to think that the concept ap-plied to human relationships too.

So, the end. By this time I'm a second-year resident in ob-gyn and I live inside the hospital so much that my home seems like a strange place, and I sleep so rarely in my own bed that the starchy sheets and rubber mattress in the call room at the hospital feel more like home. I'm often too tired for sex, or simply not there. We still fall on each other with the same eager voraciousness, but only sporadically, squeezed in, work permitting, when I'm both home and not over-exhausted.

Anyway, that day, I came home from the hospital as dead beat as I could possibly be, with a headache boring a hole between my eyes. I had to be back on at the hospital in only fourteen hours, and all I wanted to do at home was to stare at a blank wall and sleep and sleep and sleep. Ordinarily, Gordon would have been sweet about this. But this day, as it happened, was my birthday, and he had planned to take me out, for a surprise. He wanted to blow the 250-dollar Helen Choate Bell Prize for the best essay on American Transcendentalism that he had won just be-fore dropping out of the program, intending to reenroll in geology.

"I'm sorry, Gordon. I'm too tired. We'll have to do it another time." I had had a shitty-ass rotation at the hospital, delivering a stillborn baby that had died in utero a few days before. Sometimes the mom doesn't know right away. The baby slows down its kicks; then the kicks stop. She comes into the doctor's office. No heartbeat. The baby's dead. Depending on how long the baby has been dead, sometimes when the baby comes out, its bloated skin peels off in your hands, and you try to patch it back together, and make it look presentable, and wrap a blan-ket around the still, lifeless body really quick so the mom can hold the baby without realizing that the skin is falling off.

That's what happened this time. The mom was a teenager—the baby was full-term, a perfect little boy. Not my favorite thing in the world. Part of being in the birthday business, as we liked to say, but not my fa-vorite part. I wanted to sleep.

"Come on, Clara, it's your birthday. Sleep for a few hours and then I'll wake you up. I want to do something nice for you." He gave me the hangdog look. "Aren't you going to let me?"

I still had the feeling of peeling skin on my hands. I didn't feel like eating, thinking, talking, anything.

"Not today, Gordon. Can we do it another time? Just not today."

"Clara, this job is eating you up. You need to live a little. You need to get a little balance in the whole thing." This was getting to be a familiar subject between us—I was too tired; I was going to get burned out before I started; I was suffering from sleep deprivation that might end up impairing my judgment.

But Gordon just didn't understand. This was residency. This is what I signed on for. This was how I was going to learn absolutely everything there was to know about medicine so that I would be certain to be able to confront every emergency every time. This was just the price you had to pay.

"Look, Gordon, it's so nice of you, and everything. I just don't feel like it. Not today. I had kind of a shitty day."

He looked concerned, loving. "Do you want to talk about it?"

"No," I said, sounding more irritated than I meant to sound. "I just want to sleep. I already told you that."

"Okay," he said. "So sleep. We'll do it another time. It's just that . . ."

"What?"

I could see the little crease between his eyebrows, not there often enough to cause a permanent wrinkle. Gordon was sun in the garden. He avoided conflict whenever possible. I knew he didn't like whatever he was about to say. He paused, then said it anyway.

"Just that, it's hard for me to live like this."

He knew I would get mad if he said it. I did.

"You're not! You're not living like this. I'm in residency—you're just . . . You're just . . . well, I don't know what!"

I didn't think this would bother him, because that's the thing about Gordon. Not much bothered him. But this time he looked a little crestfallen. Lately, whenever I was home he wanted to talk to me about what he should do with his life; divinity wasn't what he thought it would be. He was wavering about whether he should go back to geology or maybe do something more practical, like study for a teaching degree. I hate to say that I was impatient about this, but I was. I knew what I wanted to do with my life—work—and if I was tired, I wanted to sleep.

"Come on, Clara, you know how much I admire you. You are so focused. You really know what you want." That soothed me enough—I would have just dropped it, but he kept going.

"I just want to know, though. Is it gonna get any better? This is gonna end and you're gonna take a normal job and you're gonna—I don't know—come up for air from time to time and go outside with me so I can remember what it's like to eat with you, or walk down the street with you. . . ." He was leaning back on the sofa, wearing an old ratty sweater I had knitted for him once over a dull Christmas vacation with my mother.

"I love you, Clara." That was Gordon—he said it easily, and often. "I just want us to be more—I don't know—more *fun*."

I ended up going to dinner with him. I had a splitting headache by then and felt like I couldn't keep my eyes focused on the menu. He ordered red wine, which just made my headache worse. I remember the whole thing just the way it was, the metallic taste of the wine, the throbbing behind my left eye, the hard edges of the chair against my thighs.

Gordon bantered on to fill in for my exhausted silence; he had a friend who could get him a job in Idaho for the summer to work as a river guide. He was hoping I could join him in July, maybe take a little time off. We could backpack together across the northwest, spend some time together, have some fun.

"I think you need to look at your priorities a little, Clara." I remember he was stroking his index finger lightly along my thigh under the table, and it was distracting me.

"My priorities are totally clear."

"I know your work is important, Clara, but something's got to give once in a while. For us, you know, for yourself."

I glanced at my watch. I had already used up six of the fourteen hours that I had set aside for sleep. I wanted to go home. I was exhausted. I didn't want to talk about it now.

The waitress came. *Dessert? Coffee?*

I was already grabbing my purse. I wanted to go home so bad I couldn't even pretend to be enjoying myself, even though I could see the hurt-but-trying-to-hide-it look on Gordon's face. We didn't take a walk. We didn't catch a movie. We went straight home and I fell into bed comatose until my alarm was ringing and I was dragging myself out of bed again to go back to work.

A few weeks after that, Gordon was getting ready to drive out to Idaho in his battered-up '78 VW, in which the windows only stayed up if you tied their handles with string. I knew that I'd miss him the moment he was gone, his warm body in the bed next to me, his silly banter that could get me laughing even on the hardest day. I'd been tossing and turning over it, missing out on the sleep I knew I needed, but I knew things were never going to change.

Gordon wanted more of me than I was willing to give. It didn't seem fair, because the only thing he ever asked me for was a little more time. But the truth was, I had one hundred percent of him, and he was sharing me with what I had discovered was my passion. Every day, time after time, in a routine that could never be a routine, I stretched out my hands and caught new lives as they tumbled into the world. That was as much as I needed, as much as I wanted.

I'd be lying if I said I didn't still want Gordon, with an intensity that was tinged with the fear of facing the world without him. Gordon, who had snapped me out of a trance of grief, who had saved me when I was falling. But if I put the two passions side by side and balanced it out, the scale still didn't tip in his favor. It wasn't until quite a while later, after I'd heard that he had met Lydia, that I realized the scale didn't tip in my favor either.

Gordon threw his backpack into the front trunk of his Beetle; I remember the early-morning sun was in his eyes, and he was squinting. I stuck out my hand and he handed my key back—for the first time in seven years.

"It's not going to work, Gordon."

"Think it over. I'll be back, Clara—I'm a homing pigeon."

I don't think he knew it was the end then. There were many teary phone calls, and meetings for coffee and even a couple of nights spent together after that. But I wrapped my fingers around the lone key clipped to a mountain climber's bungee ring, and I knew that it was over. I had made my choice.

THIRTY-EIGHT

My burn felt better. I did not need to be there. The nurses were bustling in and out, doing the dressing changes, taking my blood pressure, chitchatting in a way that was friendly but impersonal, leaving me alone to brood. I knew I would be discharged soon, and felt suddenly like an orphan. I thought of the times I had discharged young girls and their newborn babies to the Salvation Army homeless shelter—the baby strapped into a loaner car seat in the back of a taxicab, the young mom sometimes wearing the same baggy clothes she had been admitted in. So forlorn.

I was ashamed to feel maudlin tears spring to my eyes. Obviously I was not like them. I had a home. I had a job that I could have back if I wanted it. I had people who cared about me . . . *didn't I?*

I picked up my cell phone and looked at the call log again. The ringer was switched off. Sure enough—I scrolled through the call log—four calls from Walter, four from Gordon, two from my mother.

I am not alone. I am not alone. I am not alone.

I hesitated, almost dialed, then hesitated again, almost dialed a second time, then hesitated once more. . . .

Finally with a hasty abandon I dialed a number. Then I flopped my head back on the pillow and squinched my eyes shut, waiting for the tremor I knew I would feel.

"Hello?"

I kept my eyes squeezed shut, though I could feel tears forming behind them.

"Gordon, it's Clara," I said.

THIRTY-NINE

My next visitors were Julio and Maria—they came in, and I recognized the wary hesitant footsteps of those who approach the sick, and realized again with a start that I was the sick one.

Maria came in with a big plate, covered with tinfoil, the food under it so hot that beads of condensation had formed on top of the tinfoil. It wasn't until I smelled the delicious aroma of Maria's home cooking that I realized how hungry I was—they had brought me a couple of trays of hospital food, and I had pushed the rubbery stuff around with my fork, unable to eat it at all. Now, the beans and chorizo and warm homemade tortillas made me feel famished.

They had also brought my suitcase of borrowed clothes, everything freshly laundered and ironed, so that at least I had clothes to change into.

"Eleanor had the rental car cleaned, and she returned it to the agency for you," Julio said. "I will pick you up from the hospital when you are ready to leave. Eleanor said you will be coming back to the big house and staying with us for a day or two before you leave?" It was a question.

"I can come back to the big house, but then I want you to take me to the gatehouse. An old friend of mine is going to meet me there."

Next to come in was Jazmyn.

"Jayzuz, I practically had to pay them to let me out of there to come see you." She was dressed in the same hospital gown that I was wearing, except that it didn't seem to go all the way around her and in back it was flapping open so that I could see her mesh maternity underwear and the back of a maxi-pad.

She came over and tried to flop herself over on me to give me a big hug, but then drew back and thought better of it—suddenly realizing that I might be fragile.

"Well, can you believe it? They almost didn't have time to give me an epidural or nothing."

I couldn't help but start laughing. "Natural childbirth, huh?"

"Well, yeah, if careening around in a taxi with another lady's fingers up your butt and then getting an emergency C-section is what you call natural."

"How's the baby?"

"Sierra Dakota? She's beautiful. She's still in the special-care nursery—just for observation—they want to make sure she didn't get an infection."

"Do you know when they're going to let her out?"

"Same as me. In about three days."

"Do you have a place to go when you and the baby get out?" I asked, suddenly worried.

"Eleanor wants me to come back and stay with her for a couple of days, until I'm feeling better—then I'm gonna move into my new apartment."

"Does Frankie know what's going on?"

"My mom was here, but I wouldn't tell her where I was going."

"Jazmyn, you are not safe if he knows where you are, and neither is the baby. Don't tell your mom where you're going. Promise me. Do not tell her anything at all."

"Don't worry. I'm gonna protect my baby. I don't want to take any chances with her."

Then I felt tired again, like I had run out of things to say to her. I laid my head back and closed my eyes, but she started talking again.

"What's the chances of that? What's the chances of that whole thing happening anyway? There I am, having an emergency, and you turn out to be an OB doctor? It's gotta be a million to one, right? Everybody up there, every single person, told me that you saved my baby's life."

She stopped. I opened my eyes. I saw that she was crying.

"It's like you were put there for a reason or something. It's like you were there just when Sierra Dakota needed you. Like a guardian angel or something."

I could feel the beginnings of a headache starting to flicker behind one eye.

"It's just what I do . . . ," I said to her, not really hoping that she would understand. "I just do what I was trained to do. You don't even need to thank me. I'm glad I was able to help."

She jumped up. "I gotta go back to the baby. My boobs are starting to hurt. But jeez, Clara—I mean Dr. Raymond—you gotta let me say thank you." This time, she gave me a huge hug, and managed to catch me right on the sore part of my arm, and I tried not to wince, ended up wincing, but hung on to her for a moment nonetheless.

"You're welcome," I whispered, but not until she was already out the door and I knew that she hadn't really heard me.

I tried to imagine what a guardian angel was like. Did each person have her own, or were there not quite enough of them, flitting around the sky on a celestial beeper, a teeny bit tense from their eternal vigilance? Did a guardian angel ever miss a call? Or get overwhelmed? Or lack the exact combination of skills called for at the precise life-and-death moment? Did a guardian angel ever get there five minutes too late? Or not bring the right tools? Were all the souls that populated my mother's heaven the ones that the guardian angels had messed up on? And then did the angels grieve, and were they sorry?

Did they keep a running total? Good, good, good. Bad. Good, good. Bad. Did they strap on their wings and go back to work the next day anyway?

I woke up. It was discharge time, and the nurse, Polly, who seemed a little harried, like nurses always do, but nonetheless cheerful and thorough, was giving me my discharge instructions, and I was pulling on my clean clothes, and declining the offer of a wheelchair, and walking out completely startled into the same California sunshine and pleasant ocean breeze that I had left behind less than twenty-four hours before. I climbed into the seat of the Jeep beside Julio, my bandaged arm resting on the rolled-down window, my pilus erector muscles reacting to the cold, making the hair on my arms stand up, and the burn start to throb a little, as we pulled out of the parking lot and headed back, once again, toward the Norton Hills.

It couldn't have been a more perfect day. The Santa Ana wind had died away, and the air was fresh scrubbed and clean, smog and smoke and dust washed away completely. As we took the coast road, I could see Catalina Island off in the distance so clear that each mountain face seemed etched in a lithograph, a bit of ocean even visible beyond the isthmus connecting the two halves of the island. We passed the entrance to Ambler's Chapel and came around the bend to where the road got bumpy because of the slide area, and the barricades came into view—the barricades that had been pushed over were repaired now—and the orange-and-yellow columns stood upright like sentries across the cliff face.

As we came around the curve, I expected to feel the familiar skidding sensation of vertigo, felt nothing, just the ocean breeze on my face, and the scent of salt water in the air, but also now a strong scent of burned underbrush. I could also see the scorched hillsides—a large area had been blackened, although you could see how the fire had moved in unpredictable patterns, so that in some areas there were still patches of tawny dried grass surrounded by the silver-black ashes where the fire had passed.

Now you could actually see part of the Villa de Vista from the road—a number of the Italian cypresses that lined the driveway and surrounded the grounds had been scorched. The beautiful house and barn had been spared. I felt better to know that they were still there.

As we pulled up into the circular gravel driveway, the fire smell was very strong, but the garden was untouched—some of the sweet odor of roses in sunlight still came through.

Eleanor must have heard us drive up because she came out. We exchanged pleasantries—my burn, how well Jazmyn seemed to be doing—then she turned and ushered me into the big house.

Inside, it was cool and shadowy, and looked unchanged—there was no smoke smell inside. She took me into the living room and offered me a dark leather Morris chair to sit in. Then Maria walked in carrying thick white mugs steaming with Mexican coffee, which she set on the table in front of me. I noticed immediately that there was a manila folder on the table that was stamped PROPERTY OF THE NORTON COMMUNITY HOSPITAL.

With my good arm, I picked up the cup of coffee, and settled into my seat. I hoped I was ready.

When the head reaches the pelvic floor the shoulders enter the pelvis. Since the shoulders remain in the oblique diameter, the neck becomes twisted. Once the head is born and is free of the pelvis, the neck untwists and the head restitutes back 45° . . . to resume the normal relationship with the shoulders.

—Oxorn-Foote

PART V

RESTITUTION

I guess both of us thought it might be awkward, because Eleanor just started talking.

"It has been my experience that everyone comes to the Villa de Vista for something, and it wasn't clear to me, at first, for what reason you had come. Of course, I knew that you weren't a stable girl—the real girl showed up about ten minutes after you. Her name was Misty, not Clara—quite a contrast, in every sense of the word. But you seemed to be here for a reason, though I didn't know what the reason was, so I told her the position was taken, and I started to watch you. . . . I'm an old lady now, and it seemed a way to amuse myself."

I cradled the warm mug between my hands, and listened to her voice. She was clearly in no hurry to get where she was going with the story, but glancing at the yellowed folder on the coffee table between us, I wasn't either.

"Obviously, you were no ordinary stable girl—I thought perhaps you were on the run from a bad marriage or something. . . ."

"That's what Jazmyn thought too."

"Well, you see, it seemed like a reasonable guess. Are you married, Clara?"

"No," I said. A simple question that required just a one-word answer—not the million paragraphs that it would have taken to describe the actual state of my life.

"Of course, it wasn't long before I knew exactly who you were—that day, when you knocked your head? When I picked up your phone I saw that your name was stenciled on it. I guess I'm getting old because the name didn't ring a bell, but then Franny Baker saw you at that poor dear Lydia Robinson's funeral, and I told her the name, and then of course, we put two and two together. I didn't know you were a doctor—or exactly what you were doing here—so I watched."

My face reddened. And I had thought I was incognito as a stable girl! It already seemed impossible that I would have pretended such a thing. Why had I been so afraid to find out the truth about my father?

I remembered again, for an instant, vividly, that moment on the way home from my father's funeral—I had seen the look on my mother's face. Up until then, I had never guessed that anything was amiss—but when I saw her face I knew there was something so awful that she didn't want to tell me, something she had needed to clothe in the words "too technical." Now face-to-face with the folder on the table, I knew exactly why I hadn't wanted to ask Eleanor—because I already knew, at some level, what she was going to say.

"That reminds me, though, Clara. Before we discuss the other matters at hand, is there anyone else who knows you were here, or would have anything against you?"

"Knows I'm here? Or has something against me?"

"Well, yes, I mean, given what happened . . ."

"What happened?"

"Well, who would have slashed your tires? It makes absolutely no sense." It came back to me—the car, the four flat tires . . .

"The tires were . . . slashed?"

"I'm afraid so."

"On purpose?"

"Well, certainly, yes."

"Nobody knew I was here. Except you—well, and Jazmyn and Maria and Julio, and apparently Franny Baker—but nobody else."

Then I remembered what else I had seen that night—Franny Baker's truck, parked in the parking lot in the middle of the night.

"Is there some reason that Franny Baker was here in the middle of the night? The night of the fire? Her truck was parked here—I saw it, right before that no-good boyfriend of Jazmyn's showed up."

"Oh, Franny has permission to park in my lot whenever she wants."

"In the middle of the night?"

"Yes, exactly—she goes up into the hills at night. We used to have a terrible feral-cat problem here—this is the only open piece of land around here, so people come and dump their kittens and domestic cats. Some of them have gone to wild and have taken a huge toll on the native birds—so Franny captures the cats, then spays them and lets them go again. It's not uncommon for her to be prowling around these parts at night—in fact she called the night of the fire to let me know she'd be around—and I checked up with her when the fire started, to make sure she had gotten out safely. . . ."

"Franny Baker was prowling around the night of the fire, when my tires were slashed, and then she tells the police officer that I've gotten out safely when I'm stuck up here?"

"And . . . ?"

"You don't think that's strange?"

"Oh, for heaven's sake, don't for a moment think that Franny Baker had anything to do with it—I've known her for years. She's gruff, yes, but she is totally responsible."

"Still," I said. "It seems fishy to me. Why did she tell you that the barn was empty?"

"Well, I was as puzzled as you at first, so I checked into it. I just couldn't believe Franny would have told anyone that the barn was empty unless she was certain—she's just not like that. It turns out it was that rookie policeman. Would you believe it was his first night on the job? Apparently, he was so nervous that he got his story all mixed-up. He did talk to Franny at one point. She had come back to see if we needed help loading the horses. By then the road was barricaded, and the policeman told Franny no one else was up there."

"So how did the policeman get the idea that the barn was empty?"

"From a man in a beat-up car who came out just after Maria and Julio. He told the officer that he was one of my stable hands!"

"Frankie?" I said.

"I assume so. He must've still been prowling around there."

I shuddered, remembering how I had stood him down armed only with a bridle.

"He must have slashed the tires because he thought it was Jazmyn's car," Eleanor said, with a tone of finality that indicated that she was satisfied that enough had been said on the subject.

She leaned over slowly and picked up the manila folder that lay between us like a smoking gun. "All right," Eleanor said, her voice all business now. "Let's get on with it.

"You were a young girl when this happened, and I'm sure that everyone was trying to spare you. What precisely do you want to know?"

What did I want to know? What *did* I want to know anyway? At that moment I had a crushing feeling that I had no idea how I had arrived in this exact spot at this precise moment. The image of the cliffs came to me—but they were no longer the unfettered cliffs of my memory.

Now the cliffs had barricades in front of them, brightly painted in orange and yellow. What difference could any of this old stuff make anyway?

"My mother gave me the impression that my father did nothing wrong, yet he was hounded out of his practice, and the hospital, and not even a month later, he drove his car over a cliff in the middle of the night."

I stared at my hands, looked at their reassuring shape—hands I had always trusted, hands that I still trusted. Now my nails were clean and my cuticles neatly trimmed—a surgeon's hands. I was sure that I had the courage now to speak.

"But knowing what I know about medicine . . ." I paused. "It seems unlikely that he would have gotten that kind of treatment, unless . . ."

"Unless he had actually done something quite wrong?"

"Doctors make mistakes," I said. "It is not always possible to be . . ."

"Perfect?"

"Well, yes, I mean, it is usually enough to do the very best you can under the circumstances. Generally speaking, you are judged not only on any one individual action, but also on a general perception about the quality of care that you provide." I looked at her. She was listening, rather than passing judgment. "Not that I condone making mistakes or anything, it's just that, on aggregate, it is usually enough to do the best you possibly can the most possible amount of times."

"Clara, here are the facts. They are quite simple. Your father had a pattern of mistakes that had been documented over time—sloppy care, incomplete charts, failure to show up when he was supposed to. . . . I suppose he had been lucky. He had been reprimanded several times."

I nodded my head. Was this really a surprise?

"Finally, he just blew it completely. He was the anesthesiologist for a routine knee surgery—this was before arthroscopy, you know. . . . Well, he put the patient under, and then there was a call that the surgeon was scrubbing up and would be a few more minutes. I'm afraid your father chose that moment to leave the OR. The patient's heart stopped beating—they had to code him—and the nurses couldn't find him for seventeen minutes."

"Seventeen minutes?" I could feel the dull thudding of my heart inside my rib cage.

"They found him in the supply closet."

"The supply closet?"

"I'm sorry to say, Clara, his pants around his ankles, on top of a young nurse."

She paused a little to let that settle.

"We fired her too. If that is any comfort."

I tried to imagine my father's face, but instead all I could see was bare butt cheeks, like pale moons in the shadows of a supply closet. Then I did remember his face—and saw for the first time in a long time the way that face had looked up close, with bloodshot eyes.

"Is there anything else?" I asked.

"No," she said. "Only that I was as shocked as everyone to find out that he had lost all his money in cockamamy tax shelter schemes." She paused, lowered her voice a little. "And that I was terribly sorry about what happened to that beautiful horse of yours. I still remember you on that horse—everyone thought you would go so far."

"Thank you," I said.

"Not that it matters much now, but I tried to give your mother money to buy you another horse, but she refused it." Eleanor's voice was thicker now, almost as if with choked-back tears. "Said that was all behind you now and that she needed to take you somewhere that would be a better place to grow up."

"You tried to give my mother money?"

"Well, yes. I tried."

"But you didn't even know me."

"I suppose not," she said, now weary, and then suddenly preemptive—"Very well, then." She stood up. "I've told you everything I know. Sorry not to be able to paint a prettier picture. Julio tells me that you're leaving us. Why don't you run along down to the kitchen to tell Julio what time you need to get going."

"Eleanor? One more thing."

I saw her turn her head toward the window and look out at the tangled garden for a long moment, and then she turned back, as if in slow motion.

Her voice sounded oddly pinched now. The bright light from the window was unflattering, her white hair yellowish, her lips bluish gray. "What, Clara? What is it that you want?"

"Would it be all right if I go out to the barn to see the horses for a moment?"

"Oh," she said, looking weary, showing her age. "Oh, is that what you want? Well, then certainly, yes, go right ahead."

The scorched cypress trees jutted at crazy angles into the sky, harrowingly black against the cloudless gentle blue sky. As I got closer to the barn, I saw that there were smoke marks up the side of the barn— amazing that it hadn't burned, but then, with its stucco walls and red tiles, maybe it wasn't so flammable.

As I came round, through the gateway to the stable itself, I could hear the now familiar barn sounds, the thumping hooves, a few buzzing flies, companionable quiet sounds.

Then I heard a gentle whicker, and I stepped into the courtyard. I saw that Benedetto had pricked up his ears and was looking expectantly. My heart quickened with satisfaction.

I walked up to the stall, and tried not to, but couldn't help myself from checking the stall quickly—waterer full, hay net tied up snugly, stall guard latched up tight. I wondered who had been doing the stable work when I was gone, until a young girl, a bit thick through the middle, came around the side of the barn carrying a pitchfork.

"Hi," she called over. "You a new stable girl?"

"No." I shook my head. "No, I'm not. I'm . . ." Then I stopped, because I wasn't quite sure what I was anymore. "I'm just here visiting," I said.

"Well, watch out for that one," she said. "He's an Olympic prospect. The old lady goes all ballistic over him."

I opened my mouth to say something, then shut it again. "All right. I will."

But it was hard for me to walk away from the stall. I stood there stroking the side of Benedetto's neck, then pressing my cheek against his soft nose, feeling the bristling of the short clipped hair around his muzzle, holding out the flat of my hand for him to lip. I remembered the way it had felt to be astride him, galloping down the big driveway bareback, with nothing but a halter and lead rope to control him, and how somehow I had managed to stay on.

I glanced at my watch. It was time for me to go back to the big house. Julio would give me a ride to the gatehouse. Gordon had told me where the key was hidden. He was flying in later tonight. I waited to feel the thumping in my heart, but for once, this time, I didn't feel it.

Back at the house, in the warmth of the kitchen, Maria had made food for me, and though I thought I wasn't hungry, the smell of the chiles rellenos was so tempting that I felt my hunger quicken. She smiled as I walked in the door and came over to hug me; she was warm and scented like flour. I was surprised to find tears smarting in my eyes again from her simple act of kindness. As I settled on the long wooden bench, my shoulder started to throb. I had forgotten the pain for a little while. Obviously the painkiller was starting to wear off. I ate the hearty food gratefully.

"I'm so glad that the house and the barn were spared," I said.

"*Gracias a Dios*," Maria said, crossing herself.

I could see the look of true gratitude in her face, and I remembered that this was not just Eleanor's home but hers and Julio's as well. I remembered how she had carried out her belongings the night of the fire, not sure what she would find when she got back. "How long have you lived here?" I asked.

"Oh, very long," Maria said. "We have been here since 1954."

"Since 1954!" I said. "You have worked with Eleanor all this time?" She nodded.

"I'm amazed you could stand it," I blurted, then felt contrite for being so harsh.

"You know, Clara, she is a good woman. She took us in when we had nowhere to go, and gave us a place to live. She and her husband. She has always treated us like part of the family."

"Her husband," I said, remembering the story that Jazmyn had told. "Whatever happened to him, anyway? Is it true he went over the cliff?"

"Over the cliff? Oh, no. He died many years ago. Heart attack. It was very sudden."

"Is that her daughter, the one in the picture? The one who was holding the surfboard?"

Maria picked up a snowy dish towel and dried her hands with it. She puckered her eyebrows slightly. I thought she looked distressed, but wasn't sure why.

"Clara," Maria said. I liked the way she said my name *Clah-rah*—it made it sound so elegant. "I thought you and Eleanor were going to have a talk. She told me that she was going to . . ." She trailed off, looked out the window at the garden, then started scrubbing at imaginary marks on the spotless countertop. "Eleanor told me that she was going to tell you everything. Didn't she tell you about her daughter?"

"Why would she tell me about her daughter?" I got a horrible sinking feeling. I remembered the story of the supply room, the bare buttocks. Was it possible that . . . ?

"Oh," she said quietly, smoothing her apron, walking to the sink, wiping her hands on the red-and-white dish towel with a distracted look on her face.

"What is it? What is it about her daughter?" I had a terrible feeling of foreboding now, the sense that I really didn't want to know.

"Well," she said, "I suppose I can tell you. It's public knowledge. I don't see why it would hurt to tell. . . ."

"What is it?

"Her daughter—her name was Wendy—she died a long time ago."

"Died?"

"She poured gasoline over herself and set herself on fire, right out there. . . ."

Maria pointed out to where you could see the overgrown garden. "Right there, right in front of the three of us, me and Julio and Eleanor herself, and it was too quick for any of us to do anything. All we could do was watch."

There were tears streaming down Maria's cheeks now, and there were also tears running freely down mine.

"My father, my father—was it my father? Was she the one who my father was . . . ?"

Maria wiped her eyes with the corner of her clean apron and looked at me with an odd look of query on her face. "Why would it have anything to do with your father, Clah-rah? I don't understand."

"But I thought . . ."

The kitchen door pushed open and I saw Eleanor on the other side. Clearly she had been standing there listening. I saw that her brown cheeks too were wet with tears, and her face had an odd caved-in look that I had never seen there before.

"Maria, how could you . . . ?" she said, but her tone lacked its usual command—her voice quivered, sounded old.

Maria crossed herself again, looked at Eleanor, then back at me. "The Lord has already forgiven you," she said to Eleanor. "Why can't you forgive yourself?"

I was standing there, between the two of them, watching the looks pass between the two women, who clearly shared intimate secrets. I was riveted to the floor, like a deer caught in headlights, caught in the middle of some drama that I couldn't figure out.

"Go ahead," Maria said gently.

"I can't," Eleanor said, sounding as weak as a small child.

"Eleanor," Maria said, "it's the right thing to do, for both of you."

I saw Eleanor's hands shaking. "Clara, I owed you more of an explanation than I have given you. . . ."

I looked, uncomprehending, back and forth at the two women's faces.

"Oh, Clara, I'm just not sure where or how to begin."

I had stood up when she came in, but now I just sank back down in my chair. My shoulder was throbbing, and my head was fuzzy, no doubt from the painkiller, and the story that I thought I had finally gotten to the bottom of seemed to have no end.

"Well, remember I told you that girls who come to the Villa de Vista are always looking for something. At first, when you came, I didn't know what you were looking for, but as soon as I realized who you were, then I thought I did know."

"And you did know . . . ?" I said, but now it was a question, because obviously something was afoot. "That I wanted to know about my father?"

"No," Eleanor said quietly. She was leaning against the table now, tears rolling down her face so fast that she didn't even have time to wipe them away.

"I thought you were coming to confront me."

"Confront you?"

"For what I did." Now she was speaking so softly that her words were almost inaudible. "And for what my daughter did."

My mind was spinning; my shoulder was throbbing. I didn't understand what was going on here at all.

"The cliff," Eleanor said. "The day by the cliff."

Then her words seemed like they were all strung out, like they were coming at me from underwater, or echoing and bouncing off the walls of the kitchen, and inside my head.

"The day by the cliff. *Don't you remember what happened?*"

And like always, the same few images came back like a handful of coins scrounged from the bottom of a purse, a few pennies, a nickel, a dime—not much.

There was a white blur. There was a thud. I bit my tongue. I tasted blood. I hung on tight. I saw Lydia's arm, heard her voice. I could hear the sound of my horse in pain bellowing far below me on the rocks.

"I don't . . . I don't . . . I don't know," I said. Now I was crying, crying hard, and my head was filled with the sound, the terrible sound of waves crashing on rocks and a horse's faraway shrill death rattle.

There was a white blur. There was a thud.

Maria handed me a paper towel to wipe my eyes with. Eleanor squared her shoulders and looked like she was struggling to regain her composure.

For a moment, the three of us were silent, just the occasional sound of sniffing as each of us tried to dry up our tears.

When Eleanor finally started to speak, her voice was composed, but somehow muffled. She sat ramrod straight in the high-backed kitchen chair and she kept her eyes fixed out the window, on a patch of garden.

Then, steady and unwavering, she started to speak.

"I had a daughter. Just one daughter. Her name was Wendy. She was about ten years older than you. She was a beautiful girl, blond hair, green eyes. She wasn't interested in horses. You remember those days—all the kids were being hippies. . . . She had a surfboard, hung out at Rat Beach a lot. I didn't really like the people she associated with, but what can you do? Well, I thought that then."

I nodded my head.

"But you see, we just didn't know any better in those days. My husband had died a few years before, so I was trying to raise her alone. All the kids seemed like they were going a little crazy, and Wendy, she was a sweet girl, and I thought the whole thing was harmless, you know, just hairstyles, and music. . . . We didn't know any better. *I* didn't know any better. I should've known. But I didn't."

I remembered the picture of the girl I had seen, blond hair whipping in the wind, Hawaiian shirt, surfboard, just like any other California teenager from that era. What was there to know?

Eleanor continued. "But it was more than hairstyles, and music. Wendy got involved in using drugs. I think it was just marijuana at first, but then she started using harder stuff. She started acting different, but I thought it was just a phase."

"Sometimes it's hard to tell," I said.

"People know more about all that nowadays. In those days, we were oblivious. So I started yelling at her, telling her to stop, telling her not to see any of her friends, not to use drugs, but she just ignored me, started coming home"—I could hear the quaver start up in Eleanor's voice again—"with her hair all matted, like she had been sleeping in the street or something. And I used to beg her, *Wendy, please. You have a home—you have a beautiful home. You are Wendy Norton, heir to the Norton Hills—don't you understand? DON'T YOU UNDERSTAND?*"

Eleanor's eyes hadn't wavered from the spot outside the window in the garden, but I saw that Maria had reached over and rested her hand on Eleanor's forearm.

"Then she got pregnant," Eleanor said. "I knew she was pregnant. I heard her getting ill every morning, on the mornings when she was home, and I knew she had to stop that—*lifestyle*—because she was going to have a baby." Now Eleanor started sobbing outright again. "And she didn't even know who the father was."

Eleanor took her eyes away from the spot in the garden and looked straight at me. "You see, that is why I take in these poor girls in difficult situations, but I make them work, and help them get on their feet. But I don't help them too much. Because I can't continue helping them indefinitely, because really no one can."

She looked back out into the garden. It was getting later in the afternoon, and now the sun was slanting through the overgrown tangles of blooms, casting a lovely golden light on the garden.

"I am sorry, Clara, that I didn't know then what I know now. Nothing that I did helped in the long run anyway. It wasn't much more than a week after that that she . . . that she . . . well, that she did what Maria already told you about. She and the baby too, both of them completely wasted. Gone. So it turned out, despite all the love that a mother brings to her own daughter. It turned out"—she turned her gaze back to me again, and now it was completely steady—"it turned out that there was nothing I could do to save her."

I felt so sad, so sorry, when I heard this story, but still relieved that it didn't seem to have anything to do with my father's story. But then, why was she telling me?

"You can't save everyone," I said. My voice sounded listless.

Now Eleanor's voice was gentle. "What do you remember about your accident?"

"Nothing, nothing really. Just that, well, nothing. My horse went over the cliff—we were galloping. Maybe he spooked—maybe he stumbled. I never should have ridden down by the cliff alone anyway. I didn't have permission from my parents to do so."

"That's really it? That's all you remember?"

"Well, just that . . . and of course, I remember that Lydia found me. . . ."

"And . . . ?"

There was a white blur. There was a thud.

"And . . . and . . . I remember I kept telling everyone that I had seen something white . . . and felt like something had come along and . . ."

My voice was shaking now, reed thin, as though my ghost were talking. I breathed out the words in a spectral whisper. "*. . . pushed us . . . over the edge . . .*"

The words hung in the silent kitchen for a moment; then I cleared my throat and tried to regain my normal voice. "But I must have been imagining it, because there was no one else on the trail with me, and the police officer told me that no cars had come out of the bend that day."

"I was at the gatehouse, when it still belonged to me," Eleanor said, her voice now hardened into a decided monotone. "Before I started to hate the place so much that I gave it away. I was out on the terrace, sitting at a table, drinking a cup of tea. I thought I heard hoofbeats and so I looked up. I used to let riders all over my property in those days, before everything got so litigious, and I was just curious to see who was coming by. And of course I recognized you right away—that gorgeous flashy chestnut. You were the girl whose horse had jumped out of the ring at the trials the day before."

So she remembered that too.

"That's when it happened."

"The accident?" I was whispering, trembling. I suddenly realized that she had seen the accident, that she knew what had happened.

"Wendy's car came flying around that corner too fast, in a plume of dust—dust because she had skidded onto the shoulder."

There was a white blur. I was trembling so hard that the chair and table started to shake.

"And I saw . . . I saw"—she lowered her voice—"the impact. So sudden, like the horse itself was taking flight . . ."

Now we were looking at each other steady in the eyes.

"But the policeman told me no cars came around the bend that day. . . ." And then it dawned on me, what should have been obvious. The driveway, the driveway that led up to the Villa de Vista, came before the bend.

"But if you saw me, why didn't you come for me?"

"Because I never saw you land. I was out of there so fast, into my car, down the road, up the driveway, Wendy, Wendy, Wendy, my daughter, and the baby, and was she okay, and did anyone else see? Because she was my daughter, and I wanted to protect her." She fixed me with her eyes. "And I thought it was too late for you anyway, that you had gone down with the horse, that you must be already dead, that there was no hope." She put her head in her hands. "And then your friend Lydia came along, clattering up the driveway at full tilt calling out, *Has anyone seen Clara? Does anyone know where Clara is?*"

I was trembling so hard, I could hardly speak. "And what did you tell her?"

Now Eleanor was whispering more softly than the ocean breeze through a flower garden.

"I told her I hadn't seen you, but she could look . . . down around the bend, there where the trail gets narrow . . . in case there had been . . . an accident."

I could hear Lydia's voice the way it had been that day, so tentative, so worried, uncertain.

Clara? Clara?

Lydia!

I had called her name as loud as I possibly could, hoping against hope that she would hear me, and somehow through the din of the waves she did. I had never once, in the intervening years, dared to ask myself how she had figured out exactly where to look.

"I couldn't do anything for Wendy. I regret that I didn't call the police that day, Clara, but she was my daughter—maybe if you have children of your own someday, you might be able to understand. Not condone of course, because I was wrong. But maybe understand. I wish to God I hadn't been sitting on that terrace that day. It would have been better not to know."

This surprised me almost more than anything she had said.

"But then Lydia would never have found me."

Eleanor was silent for a long moment after I said that, like she was thinking it over. Then she wiped away her tears and almost smiled a little. "But of course you're right. I don't know why I never thought of it that way before. Thank you, Clara. There is no small measure of comfort in that."

There wasn't much more to say. I stood up now.

"I don't ask for your forgiveness, not even your understanding. But is there anything I could do that might help?"

"Actually, Eleanor, there is something I want."

"What is it? What can I do for you?"

I could hardly believe I was saying it.

"I want you to give me Benedetto."

FORTY-ONE

I n the end, I just walked away, right down the driveway, past the funny burned trees, then down along the road toward the gatehouse, being careful to stay on the trail, and off the road. The dog, Oyster, started to follow me, but when I said, "No," and pointed back to the barn he came no farther. My phone rang as I was walking. *Walter.*

"We got the clinic, Clara. We got it!" Walter sounded cheerful. Solid, just like his usual self.

"But I've been thinking about it, and I think we've been pushing the envelope too hard. Things were a lot different when I started the practice—yeah, it was solo practice, but I only did six or seven deliveries a month, and I made a living with that." Walter—it was so infinitely good to hear his steady, uncomplicated voice.

"So I've been thinking, Clara, and I hope it's okay with you. I think we should hire another doctor, and maybe get a nurse-midwife on board too. I think we can still do it—still provide the same quality of care, without spreading ourselves so thin. We're not at our best when we're tired all the time. . . . What do you think, Clara? What do you think?"

Suddenly I realized that I was already past the barricades, already past the cliff without the world spinning out of control, without me even noticing. There was the gatehouse, almost right in front of me—so striking with its high pink walls and almost impossibly breathtaking setting. My heart sank at the sight of it.

"Walter, listen, Walter. I'm sorry. It's not a good time. I need to call you back."

"Clara," he said. His tone got serious. "Every time I talk to you now, that's what you say. I need a partner. I want you to tell me before you hang up. When are you coming back?"

"Walter," I said. "I'm sorry. Really. I'll call you." I clicked off. *Damn it all to hell.*

I did notice that there was a light blinking on the phone in the gatehouse when I came in, but it wasn't my house, so I didn't think to listen to it. I got the key from under the planter, and thought about attaching it to my key ring, as Gordon had instructed me to do, but then I decided it would be better to put it back under the pot where I had found it.

It was gloomy in the house, with its dark rooms without windows, so I went down the hallway, and pushed open the salt-clouded French doors, out onto the flagstone terrace. There was a strong breeze coming off the ocean, and I was surprised to find that the flagstones, even up this high, were damp with ocean spray. The waves made a thundering sound as they crashed against the rocks below. It must have been high tide. I walked across the terrace and sat down on the granite bench facing west, straight out over the ocean. The view was so intensely beautiful that it almost hurt to look at it, a small inlet, a three-sided cove. You could see the cliff faces, the sheer drop-offs, and the way the waves formed tall white flumes as they crashed hard against the rocks.

I sat like that until my bottom was sore and I had had time to turn over each and every new piece of information in my mind like it was a case study and I was trying to arrive at a diagnosis.

I thought about my father—that wasn't news, really. I could imagine the infinite number of ways that my mother had tried to let me down gently. I remembered now what I had once known, but had managed to forget. My father's blood alcohol content had been elevated when they pulled his body out of the car that was mangled on the rocks.

I thought about Eleanor's daughter and the accident—surprisingly, not much changed there. After all was said and done, it was still just an accident, an unfortunate confluence of events, being in the wrong place at the wrong time for no apparent reason.

But I also realized something new as I sat there, staring out at the waves as they pummeled the rock-strewn shoreline. In front of me, plumes of water rose up as the waves hit the rocks, then hung in the air for the briefest moment, tossed toward heaven like angels taking flight.

I thought of my first obstetrics textbook, *Oxorn-Foote*, with its careful sketches of the mechanisms of birth. Stubbornly, persistently, I had failed to see what was so obvious. The female pelvis is not a chute, but a curved outlet, the coccyx sloping up gracefully like the arc of a wave.

Babies are not born falling at all. Labor pushes them down into the pelvis, but as birth nears, they round the curve of Carus and start an ascent. We are, all of us, born crowning: bregma, forehead, eyes, nose,

QUALITY OF CARE 255

mouth, chin, raising our faces toward daylight, ascending, even at the moment of birth, toward heaven.

Then, too tired to think anymore, I went upstairs and crawled into the bed that still smelled like Gordon and I lay there flat on my stomach and buried my head in the pillow and inhaled him. I picked up a stray one of his wiry hairs that I found in the bed and fingered it. Then I buried my face in the pillow that was filled with the scent of him and cried until the pillow itself was almost wet through. Then I turned over, and looked at my hands again, my strong familiar hands, my well-trained hands, trained, over so many years, to do my bidding.

Finally, I got up, and washed my face and put my shoes on. Then I called the airport.

Then I dialed Walter's phone number.

"Do you think you could get me at the airport? I'm coming home on the red-eye."

I gave him the flight number, and he said, "I'll be there."

The last thing I did was scribble a note.

Sorry. So sorry, Gordon. I love you. Good-bye.

Then I called a cab, and walked downstairs, past the insistent red blinking of the phone that was casting intermittent shadows on the dark wall.

I was bone tired and I slept a sound dreamless sleep all the way on the airplane home.

FORTY-TWO

If I had listened to the message that night, this is what I would have found out.

I would have found out that Gordon had called to tell me that he wasn't going to be able to meet me after all.

Clara was dead. Her poor little feeble heart had stopped. Thank God, the team from Children's Hospital had talked him into signing a Do Not Resuscitate order. They had taken her off the gavage feeding and ventilator. She had died peacefully, asleep, in his arms.

I was there for the memorial service. Gordon held it in the small chapel off the hospital, because he wanted all the NICU nurses he had grown so close to, and who had cared for the baby, to be able to attend.

It was a simple service. Gordon was not religious. I remember that the door to the chapel was open—it was a beautiful midsummer day, and I could see the flowers in the chapel garden through the open door. They were waving ever so gently in the breeze, like little souls aflutter. I sat very still, hands folded in my lap, and let myself cry, and cry and cry, and still somewhere, deep down, I could feel joy in the sight of the flowers, waving there, and my spirit reached out toward them, hoping in some inchoate and unarticulated way to connect the spirit of a baby that was never quite born to the bright colors of flowers in bloom.

Walter sat next to me, and when he saw the first tears start to brim in my eyes, he slipped his big hand around mine and squeezed it a little, and I leaned into him, feeling the unwavering steadiness of his strong shoulders.

I looked down at my feet. Then out at the sunlit flowers again.

On the way out the door, I saw how each of the nurses hugged Gordon in turn, and whispered encouraging things to him.

When it came to my turn, I hugged him, tight, tight as I could possibly hold him, and then released when if I had held on just one beat longer, it would have gotten, once again, completely impossible to let go. I whispered in his ear, *I'm sorry. I'm sorry. I'm so sorry, Gordon.* And when I pulled back from his embrace I looked into the gold flecks in his eyes, and saw, not peace—it was too soon for that—but some kind of understanding. And we both knew that it was over forever between us.

I walked out with Walter, and by the time we had hit the parking lot, we had already picked up the pace. Walter had a four o'clock scheduled C-section, and I had patients back at the office, waiting to see me. It was clinic day, and with the new clinic it was always busy and chaotic and never a moment to think.

External rotation of the head is really the outward manifestation of internal rotation of the shoulders.

—Oxorn-Foote

PART VI

EXTERNAL ROTATION

FORTY-THREE

There are trails out behind the stable that dip into cool glens along the banks of Pickering Creek. I take Benedetto out there whenever possible, let him stretch out his long neck while I let the reins out loose on the buckle. There is a hollow, resonant quality to the ground there, and his footsteps make a pleasant thumping sound when he walks.

I get out to the barn three, maybe four times a week, depending on how busy we are. I spend a long time grooming Benedetto, then ride until my muscles ache. When I'm done riding, I get off and carefully clean my tack, wiping the leather clean with the vegetable smell of Murphy oil soap.

Somehow, I have learned that when I'm with Benedetto, I'm completely away, living in each moment. When I'm cantering in the ring, I get absorbed in the one-two-three of his footfalls; when I'm out on the trail, I've gotten to know the birdsong, and the sounds of the water where it speeds up to rush over rocks.

Things are a lot better now that we've added staff; we talked Kim Rooney into leaving Uni-Group to join us, and we hired a midwife named Barbara, who is great with the teens. It has made all the difference in the world.

One of the unexpected pleasures is that now Walter and I are able to spend more time together—we go out to dinner, or sometimes catch a movie. The other morning, he came in to second for me on a C-section, and afterward, out in the hall near the nurses' station, he invited me to a Devils game, blushing and stammering over the two tickets, as though he were holding a ring in a box. The nurse Kathy, who never misses anything, managed to overhear, and she kept giving me little winks and meaningful smiles all afternoon. I tried to pretend I didn't notice until finally she caught my arm and coughed a couple of times and whispered in her husky whisper, "You know, hockey's like a religion with Walter—he doesn't invite *just anyone* to a Devils game." Then she winked again and said, "I'm sure happy to see two nice people like you spending more time together."

I know I turned beet red and stammered out something like, "He's my business partner," but Kathy just smiled and nodded like the cat who swallowed the canary. Nurses and that sixth sense. Somehow, they still always seem to know what's going on before I do, and this time, I felt a little dizzy with joy at the thought of it.

I have a German fellow named Fritz who gives me riding lessons on Sundays—three weekends a month, because the fourth weekend I'm on call. He has told me many times that my horse could compete at the highest levels, and why don't I find someone else to show him, because he would do well on the circuit? But I have no interest in that.

The women in the office know that they should keep calls to a minimum when I'm out at the horse barn, but let's face it—the phone still rings from time to time.

"Dr. Clara?"

"Yes?"

"It's Jaz."

"Hi, Jaz. What's up?"

"Sierra Dakota felt warm when I touched her and she has a temperature of 98.9. Should I take her to the doctor?"

"Is she eating okay?"

"Yeah."

"She's probably okay." But then worrywart that I am, I add, "But if you're not sure, you should call your pediatrician."

"Okay."

"Jaz, do you know the pediatrician's phone number?"

"Okay, yeah, I know her phone number. It's just, you know, I wanted to check with you first. Sorry to bother you, Dr. Clara."

"It's okay," I say. "You're not bothering me. You know you can call me anytime." I hang up the phone, and every time, I smile.

Eleanor tried to press charges against Frankie Mulligan—for trespassing, and tire slashing, and letting Benedetto out, but what with the fire that same night, started by a downed power line, the police didn't have enough to go on. They held him overnight, then let him go.

I talk to Jazmyn all the time, and warn her, "Don't let your guard down. Don't tell anyone where you are. Don't tell your mother where you are, because she might tell him."

I ask her, "Do you have the phone number for the crisis hotline? Do you have the number for the shelter?" *Just in case, just in case, just in case.*

Jazmyn's doing great, and so is the baby. She found a job in a day care center, and Sierra Dakota gets to come with her. She is able to support herself, and the last time we talked she told me she was planning to go back to night school and take some classes in early-childhood education. She puts the baby on the phone so that I can hear her make *babababa* sounds, and she tells me what she eats, and how many times she poops, and what percentile she's in on the height and weight chart.

But still I worry about her—out in California, with nobody there to look out for her—and I worry because I know that Frankie Mulligan is still out there somewhere, rattling around in the world, like an accident waiting to happen.

So I pray—little accidental prayers that are just small blossoms of my inherent hope for goodness.

Watch out for the little ones—watch out for the ones who are small and need assistance, and are defenseless. Please protect those who cannot protect themselves.

And me? I just get up every morning and put my shoes on, and try to do the very best I can that day, and every other single day that follows.

Elizabeth Letts, a practicing certified nurse-midwife, trained at Yale University School of Nursing. A former competitive equestrian rider, she also served as a Peace Corps volunteer in Morocco. *Quality of Care* is her first novel.

ELIZABETH LETTS

QUALITY of CARE

This Conversation Guide is intended to enrich the
individual reading experience, as well as encourage us
to explore these topics together—because books,
and life, are meant for sharing.

FICTION FOR THE WAY WE LIVE

A CONVERSATION WITH ELIZABETH LETTS

Q. *What inspired you to write* Quality of Care, *your debut novel?*

A. When you deliver babies for a living, people often say what a happy job it must be, and the truth is, it is very happy almost all the time, but when it is sad it is absolutely devastating. Since babies don't arrive during office hours, obstetricians are some of the most dedicated people in medicine. They give up nights and weekends and rarely get a full night's sleep—but even so, more than half of all obstetricians have been sued for malpractice at least once in their careers. So I became interested in the psychology of that person—what is it like, to care for people in the intimate moment of birth, to dedicate your life to helping people and doing good, all along knowing that if luck breaks against you and you do have a bad outcome, you may be accused of doing harm.

Q. *How do you balance your work life and your writing life?*

A. With difficulty! As a working mother with three school-aged children, I have to grab any spare moment and make the most of it. I work part-time, and fortunately, my schedule leaves me with some mornings free to write—my best time is when my kids are at school and the house is blissfully quiet and empty. But I also find that my work life enriches my writing life. I carry around an index card with me and am always on the lookout for bits of dialogue I might be able to steal.

Q. *Throughout the novel you describe the empathy and "sixth sense" that the nurses in Clara's hospital possess. Do you have real-life stories like these?*

A. Oh definitely. For example, a patient comes in and doesn't seem to be in labor, and so normally she would be sent home, but someone has a "feeling" that she'll go quick, so she ends up staying and delivering twenty minutes later. Or when you decide to check someone "just one more time" and that's when you realize that there is a problem.

But it would be a real disservice to nurses to imply that they operate on intuition alone. Calling it a "sixth sense" is only shorthand parlance for a real set of skills that they possess. That "feeling" is based on hours and hours of close observation. No one is closer to the patient than the nurses are, and they will very often pick up on early clues, long before any other member of the health care team has realized that anything is wrong. Nurses are highly trained in knowing how to use those clinical clues that fly under the radar.

Q. *Have you witnessed a fatal case like Lydia's before?*

A. Fortunately, I have never witnessed a case like Lydia's and I hope that I never will. In this country, maternal death is extremely rare, and most people can spend an entire career without ever seeing a single case—when it does occur, as in Lydia's case, it is highly traumatic for everyone involved.

Q. *What do you consider important themes or motifs in the book?*

A. Several of the characters face situations that are beyond their control—Clara's accident, Eleanor's struggles with her daughter, Gordon's tragic loss of his wife. When faced with the unpreventable and the inexplicable, what do you fall back on? That's why I feel that this book is primarily about Clara's spiritual journey. At the beginning of the book, she believes that if she tries hard enough she can guarantee a perfect outcome every time. That's not possible in medicine or in life.

I was also interested in the role of the caregiver—you see a variety of ways of caring in the book—the caring self-sacrifice of a nurse like Kathy with her smoker's habit and her arthritic knees. Clara's incredible sense of duty. Gordon's attempts to save his brain-damaged daughter. Eleanor's tough love. Lydia's belief that she was somehow fated to save Clara's life. All of them were showing their care in the best way they knew how. So the question that the book posits is where is the line between caring for the people you love, or for whom you feel responsible, but still letting go and accepting the fact that you do not control their destinies.

Q. *The California coastline that you describe is so beautiful and vivid. Is this a place close to your heart? Did you grow up there, like Clara?*

A. Yes, like Clara, I grew up in what was then a fairly underdeveloped enclave along the coast in southern California. We could keep horses at home—not in fancy stables like Eleanor has. Our corral was just a bare hillside with a fence around it. I used to collect horses down there: ponies and castoffs, any kind of horse I could get my hands on. When I got home from school, I would just get on my horse and take off and ride for miles and miles on the trails. I think that setting the book there was my way of revisiting a place that I love so much.

Q. *Clara is haunted by her childhood—the death of her horse, the saving grace of Lydia, her father's suicide. Did you know how you were going to resolve these issues for her when you began the book? Did the story change as you wrote it?*

A. I knew before I started the book that Clara was going to come full circle to a feeling of acceptance, and I knew that it would be a difficult journey for her. The character who surprised me the most in the story was Jazmyn. I had initially planned to have her come to a bad end, but she was such a tenacious and lovable character that I realized that she was going to hang on and find a way to turn her life around.

Q. *What is the most difficult aspect of writing for you? What is the most rewarding? Do you have any quirky habits that you indulge when you write?*

A. I think the most difficult aspect of writing for me is to stop writing—to get the characters and their stories out of my head and to come back to the present. I do a lot of thinking about the story at odd moments, when I'm washing dishes or driving the car pool. I get totally distracted, drive past my exit or something like that. Then my kids always yell, "Snap out of it, Mom."

The most rewarding part, by far, is in the telling itself, of setting out to tell a story and knowing that I got to the end.

As for as writing rituals . . . that sounds very glamorous, but I'm afraid I don't have the luxury. I write at a desk in my dining room right next to the kitchen. People traipse in and out all the time. Kids interrupt me. The phone rings, or I run to the store to pick a up a loaf of bread in the middle of a chapter. Virginia Woolf said that a woman writer needs "a room of one's own"—I mean, yes, it'd be nice, but a corner of the dining room will do in a pinch.

Q. *Is Clara a highly personal character? Which characters do you share traits with?*

A. No, Clara is really not like me at all. The only thing about Clara that I took from my own background is her history as a competitive three-day eventer. I actually did ride in the Olympic trials at the age of fifteen—the event that Clara never made it to. And like Clara, I gave up riding after my teens, though not for any traumatic reason. I just moved on to other things.

But besides that, I think I was interested in writing about a person like Clara because she is so unlike me. She is very single-minded, very driven, but she doesn't see herself, at the beginning of the story, as being particularly empathetic. She thinks that empathy is a special talent that nurses have. Believe me, I am the one who bursts into tears and hugs people in the delivery room—it's such a thrilling moment. I don't think Clara, especially at the beginning of the story, would have felt comfortable with that.

Q. What are you working on now?

A. Well, the great thing about working in women's health is that there is no shortage of interesting stories to tell. This time I'm writing about a nurse practitioner who works in a rural health clinic and is getting to the end of her rope. Her husband has job problems, her daughter has teenage problems, and the women who work with her are under constant pressure at work to care for the needy patients who stream through the doors. But when a crisis threatens to shut the clinic's doors, she and the overworked and underpaid medical assistants who work there band together to save the little clinic, overcoming what at first seem insurmountable odds.

QUESTIONS FOR DISCUSSION

1. Clara is drawn back to Gordon after his wife's death. Certainly, they have both changed over the years, but in what ways do they feel familiar to each other?

2. At the beginning of the book, Clara says, "I loved nurses. I often thought that they had been God-given all of the positive attributes that I lacked." Do you think that Clara lacked the ability to nurture or care at the beginning of the story? Discuss some of your own experiences with doctors and nurses. What are some of the qualities of an ideal doctor? Do you think Clara has those qualities?

3. After Lydia's death, Clara is advised by hospital risk management to stay away from Gordon. She feels that there is a conflict between her role as a part of the health care system and her role as Gordon's friend. Why does this conflict exist? Do you think Clara made the right decision to comfort Gordon about the baby? If you or a loved one were in a similar situation, how would you want your doctor to behave?

4. Why does Clara go to California? What does she hope to confront and accomplish during her trip? Have you ever gone back to a place that you haven't visited in a long time and about which you have strong memories? How does returning to her childhood home affect Clara? How does revisiting a place help to clarify your memories of what happened there?

5. How is Walter important to Clara and vice versa? How is this conveyed throughout the story?

6. At one point, Clara says her credo was "vigilance, eternal vigilance—it was the promise to try hard enough not to ever make a mistake." What do you think about this statement? Is it possible for a doctor, or for anyone, to be perfect? Have you ever had situations in your life where you were expected to be perfect and worried that you might not live up to it?

7. How do you feel about Eleanor's gruff and judgmental exterior? How has Clara's opinion of her changed by the end of the book? Has your opinion of Eleanor changed? Why?

8. How does the title apply to the story? How do characters throughout the story attempt to care for and protect each other? In what ways do they succeed and in what ways do they fail?

9. Why does Eleanor allow Clara to work for her under an assumed identity? In what ways are Eleanor and Clara alike?

10. What does the revelation about her father mean for Clara?

11. Describe the role of motherhood in *Quality of Care*. Compare and contrast the actions and attitudes of each mother and mother-to-be. What new revelations does Clara have about her own mother by the end of the novel?

12. Why does Clara ask Eleanor to give her Benedetto? What does the horse symbolize to her?

13. What has Clara proven to herself by the end of the book? Has she overcome the obstacles and fears that life has set in her path? What are those obstacles and fears?